# Summer of Love

## DANA'S STORY

A Novel By

Patricia McLaine

This book is a work of fiction. Names, characters, places and incidents are either the product of the author's imagination or are used fictitiously. Any resemblance to actual events or locales or persons, living or dead, is entirely coincidental.

For Carol, Ginny, Ginger, Maggie, Marilyn and Susan.

A few of the girls!

Purity
Is obscurity.

She without benefit of scruples
Her fun and money soon quadruples.

Ogden Nash

# Chapter 1

I still have many fond memories from the summer of 1967, the one known as the Summer of Love. I know for sure that I had more sex more times with more men that summer than in any other summer of my life. That was before I married my true love, of course. The Summer of Sex might be a better description of the scenarios that played out in my life during a wild and wonderful time when the world forever changed—and not just my world.

I remember dropping my friend Paula off at LAX on the morning after the Fourth of July. Our group had enjoyed a barbeque on the holiday on the beach next to her place in the Malibu Colony. That Wednesday, driving on the freeway toward Stromberg Pictures in Hollywood, I couldn't stop thinking about all the crazy and amazing things that had happened in just weeks. Every aspect of my life had fantastically and dramatically changed nearly overnight.

In the spring I had the female lead in a feature film shot on location near Fort Worth, Texas. *Down Amarillo Way* was my first Western, my role that of the typical hooker with a heart of gold. I got to wear these fabulous costumes that included sexy, lacey corsets from Frederick's of Hollywood and the elegant fashions of the 1850s. My character ran the local saloon and whorehouse under the mean but watchful gaze of a corrupt and ruthless sheriff. That bad man was played to the hilt by an actor with whom I'd enjoyed a madcap affair during my early twenties when he had a wife and two young children. Foolish on my part, granted, but he soon left that lovely lady to marry two other pretty women, one after the other, each one younger and more exquisite than the last. By adding four more cubs to his growing pride, Allen was happily begetting the pride of Leo the lion. Ruggedly handsome, he had an offbeat look and could curl his lip and snarl with the best of them. He also sat great on a horse, besides being an excellent shot with both a Colt revolver and Winchester rifle. The typical man's man, Allen could finesse a woman into the sack with just one long, lingering glance.

That spring Allen had wanted me to play with him again, but I'd passed. His present wife was a quasi-friend of mine, and by that time, married men were no longer worth my precious time or the exasperation that goes with being crazy about someone who is never there for you when you really need them, like on weekends, holidays, your birthday, or just when you happen to desperately need reassurance. Nevertheless, we had lots of fun making that picture in the Lone Star State. We laughed a lot, and the passion we'd shared in 1960 still remained among my most pleasurable memories, always serving me well in fantasyland in my single days when all else failed.

In that Western movie, my character captured the heart of the hero played by an aging favorite years older than my father. Bill drank way too much and often had bad breath for the love scenes. I finally convinced wardrobe to make him brush his teeth or use mouthwash before our takes, with breath spray my final defense.

A notable pincher and fanny patter, the old fart had no doubt bruised many a delicate behind in his day. I kept my distance whenever the cameras stopped rolling. That old geezer still thought he was the cat's meow with the ladies, but my pussy made fast tracks if he even looked at me for more than a minute. He was actually still appealing in an aging, decrepit sort of way, except that his recent plastic surgery had radically altered his former dynamite looks. Nothing about him had ever tempted me in the least. All I could say, when the picture finally wrapped, for the sake of the girls in wardrobe, makeup and me, was praise the Lord and what a character!

It was during the filming of that picture that I met the tall, blond and handsome drink of water, Beauregard Kandell, since most of the scenes in the film were shot on his ranch. The studio had apparently paid him well to include his huge herd of Black Angus steers and 30 Texas Longhorns. Some of his ranch hands became cowboys of the Old West and really seemed to enjoy being in the film. Beau's spread included the original ranch house used for indoor and outdoor scenes, along with a rushing creek and the scenic lake that bordered his property. Upon its brief release in 1968, the film was a forgettable miss at the box office and has yet to be seen on the

*Late Show*. In spite of appearing in that one inconsequential motion picture, I ended up playing a major role in the life of my best friend, Paula Marlow.

Paula was, and still is, an extremely talented artist, a fine painter. Famous now, as well she should be, but back in 1967 her work was just starting to get the attention it deserved. Nowadays, museums and galleries all over the country exhibit her creative genius. And the inspiration for some of her best and most memorable paintings came from people she met and events that transpired during the Summer of Love, a year that changed both our lives forever.

The first time Beau Kandell invited me to his brand new house alone, with dinner for just the two us, I was truly pleased. And yet, driving up to that massive, two-story house on a knoll overlooking a sparkling blue lake, I had more the impression of a Beverly Hills mansion than of any kind of ranch. In the massive entry I was greeted by a fine marble sculpture of a Greek-looking fellow, a spectacular male, nude without a fig leaf. Large and small oil paintings decorated the walls of nearly every room. I was impressed. But then, after being in Texas for a short period of time, I'd learned that those with the big bucks in that big state think really big all around. That is usually because of owning an oil well, or maybe several, or else a significant number of shares in an oil company. In Texas, nearly everything owned, or arranged by, the financially fixed was done on a scale that ranged from splendid to spectacular.

I wasn't exactly sure why, but from the very first moment that I met Beauregard Kandell, my friend Paula's essence continually intruded into my mind. On the other hand, the first time I entered Beau's spacious living room with its high-ceiling and sprawling white leather sectional before a massive stone fireplace, I started to 'get the picture'. For up on the wall to one side of that elegant sofa was one of my best friend's sensitive and exquisite paintings.

"Will Chablis be all right?" Beau inquired before he filled my glass.

I nodded and inquired, "Did you really design this magnificent house all by yourself?" as I made myself comfortable while taking in the many fine antiques and magnificent artifacts all around me.

"Architecture is a hobby of mine. And, as you may have already noticed, I'm something of a collector when it comes to art. I enjoy being surrounded by objects of great value and great beauty," and with that remark he toasted me with his wine while looking me over from head to toe with his pretty blue eyes.

"I see," I said, sipping wine from my glass, and intentionally glancing up at Paula's fine painting created in pastel shades in oil.

"I still have room for a lot more art in this house, but I just might have to paint a few of those pictures myself."

"So you're an artist as well?"

That was when he insisted on taking me on a grand tour of his lovely new home and brand new art studio. The chef in the kitchen was busy preparing our dinner assisted by two other cooks dressed in white. The kitchen was fantastic, as was the rest of his magnificent mansion, with the art studio Beau's pride and joy.

"All the windows and skylights are electrically-controlled to make the lighting just right, depending on the subject of the painting, of course. The studio and storeroom are temperature controlled, not only to preserve the paintings, but to put me in just the right mood to contact my muse." His smile was charming, though he did seem a touch amused with himself that time.

Paula had often mentioned her "muse," and yet, Beau had yet to discuss the large painting on his living room wall over the sofa. In my mind, that studio was the perfect place for one Paula Marlow to paint, with its wide view of the Texas terrain and Eagle Mountain Lake shimmering in the distance. With that thought, I actually got chills that ran from the top of my head down to my toes, which meant to me that I had hit upon the truth. Paula and Beau were absolutely perfect for each other.

That was when I gazed up at the painting and said, "Tell me about this painting."

"I bought that painting a while back at a little gallery on La Cienega Boulevard in Los Angeles. The first time I saw it, well, I just knew that I was looking directly into the soul of the artist. Kenneth, the fellow who owns the gallery where Paula Marlow's paintings are sold, told me all about her mysterious amber cat eyes and her luxurious, long copper hair. He said the artist is beautiful in every way a woman can be. It seems to me that Paula Marlow is an extremely fine artist with a fine soul to match her work."

"This may come as a surprise to you, but it just so happens that Paula Marlow is my closest and dearest friend. I can assure you that you can believe every word Kenneth had to say about her."

"That she has the body of a reincarnated Greek goddess?" Beau said, with an expression on his face that was priceless.

"Well, in my opinion, her body is more like that of a wood nymph," I said, realizing that Paula might well strangle me for that remark.

"Merciful heavens! Is there any way that you might be able to arrange for me to meet her?" he sounded almost pathetic. "Why, I'd be eternally grateful for the opportunity to meet Paula Marlow. Honest I would, both the woman and the artist."

Beauregard Kandell was ruggedly handsome. His sexy blue eyes were framed by a golden tan, his skin weathered to masculine perfection from too much Texas sun, with deep laugh lines around his pretty eyes and sensuous mouth. His blond hair ruffled slightly as we walked through a brisk breeze about to announce a Texas downpour. I thought Paula might really enjoy running her delicate fingers through those wavy locks. Why, there hadn't been a man worth mentioning in her life for the past year, with 30 hardly over the hill or anywhere near the summit. Beau was perfect, 36, in A-1 prime beefcake condition, a definite notch up from his entire herd of Black Angus steers.

"I'll be happy to introduce you to Paula the next time you come to L.A. How about brunch at my place in Beverly Hills? I could invite a few other artists and actors to put you both in a fun-filled atmosphere!"

From the look on his face, that trip was going to be "mighty soon," as they say down in Texas.

And I could hardly wait to tell Paula that I had had the incredible good fortune of finding her the man of her dreams!

It was her divorce from Dan Thurman, her second husband, a devious, scheming, alcoholic stockbroker, who inherited most of his money from his family in Michigan, that provided the funds for her beach house in the Malibu Colony. That house was an extremely wise investment considering how California property values have soared since 1964. The price: $55,000 for a house right on the beach in front of the Pacific Ocean!

Weekends with Paula in her cozy nest were always special for me. Sometimes we would sit on the sofa and gaze out at the sea with only the rumble of the surf and the tinkling of wind chimes to interrupt our reverie. I loved to take walks on the beach, swim in the ocean, or watch the sun slowly sink beneath the distant horizon in a brilliant wash of color.

Surfers rode those waves every month of the year, which amazed me in the winter. It was the perfect place for Paula to paint in her studio with its high-beamed ceiling and inspiring view of the sea. It was also a great place for our friends to gather to talk or just have fun. We could relax in the healing atmosphere of sand, sun, surf, and sea.

Back in 1961 when our friendship began, Paula Marlow was the most guileless woman I'd ever met. I felt privileged to be her friend. She was caring, intelligent, open and honest. I knew I could trust her with my life. She accepted me at face value, with her two great kids a definite plus: precocious Michele from her first marriage, nine going on 30, 10 that August. And there was impish, inquisitive Christopher whose bright amber eyes matched his mother's. Chris turned six that year before he entered first grade.

I could see from pictures of Michael Townsend that Michele's father was drop-dead gorgeous. Michele looked like a lot like him. Paula told me about the sexy, talented but crazy artist who hanged himself on a bad acid trip. It was only two months after Michael's suicide when Paula and I met in this bar on Hollywood Boulevard. I was out with actor friends after wrapping a bad B movie that never made it into the theaters. That night I consciously decided to get drunk and accidentally bumped into Paula in the ladies' room. But I don't really believe in accidents. Paula had forgotten her lipstick, so I loaned her one of mine. Neither of us was in very good shape on that night, emotionally, psychologically, or in any way. We got stinking drunk together until the bar closed and the owner made us leave.

At the time, Paula was boarding two-year-old Michele with friends during the week, so that she could work long hours as a commercial artist to cover expenses. Her divorce from Michael was not final at the time of his death and his creditors were starting to send her nasty notices. At the time, neither of us had a clue about where we were headed. We sat at the bar telling each other our sad tales of woe and crying over too many vodka gimlets that made us both sick puppies.

Paula spent the night at my place. Her car was repossessed, but she was in no shape to drive anyway, or to take public transportation. I lived three blocks from the bar in a one bedroom duplex. We passed out together on my double bed. The next morning we couldn't even remember how we had gotten there. That was when we became best friends forever.

We did our fair share of drinking in those days, playing games in Hollywood bars to pick up guys and bet on which lucky man was going to buy us our next drink. I was the sultry brunette, Paula the vivacious redhead, which made us more of a dynamic duo than Batman and Robin, except in gay bars. We seldom paid for our drinks. Even the bartenders took mercy on us, claiming they needed two sexy babes to help bring in the sharks.

In those days, my acting jobs were few and far between. Paula was living beyond her means trying to bring Michele up right without a father. Both her parents were dead. Paula was an only child, the same as me. Her options seemed non-existent.

Late one night after I almost signed on as a porn star, we got drunk together. Paula talked me out of signing that contract. That was when she started telling me about these books that could help us fulfill our fondest dreams: *The Magic of Believing* by Claude Bristol and *Key to Yourself* by Venice Bloodworth. We shared anything that hinted at helping us to get our heads together. After reading Harold Sherman's *How to Make ESP Work for You*, we did experiments in mental telepathy that scared the hell out of us. We became so psychic with each other that it was spooky!

After a few months, Paula had a job interview with quasi-agnostic, atheistic, skeptic Daniel Thurman. He drove a brand new black Ford Thunderbird and claimed to have certain investments, a Masters degree, and a penthouse apartment in the Wilshire District. At the time, Paula qualified to be Cinderella, but Daniel Thurman was no goddamn prince.

From what I learned during their two-year marriage, mostly from observation, was that Dan and his entire family did their best to make Paula's life miserable. Plainly, Dan disapproved of me. He was strictly conservative from old Michigan money, a class-conscious snob who never accepted any of Paula's artist friends, even though I was the one who told her how to get him to a full erection and orgasm, so he could engage in intercourse like a normal man. That was our little secret. I doubt that Dan ever knew that I was Paula's sex therapist.

Before his blissful moment of release, only high paid hookers had done the trick for Dan, plain and simple. The strangest part of it was that he was a good-looking man. But when Paula told me he had never been in love before, my advice was for her to dump him and find a man less neurotic. Thirty-nine seemed much too young for serious impotence, though he drank like a fish: beer, gin, scotch, wine or cognac for lunch and dinner. The alcohol probably anesthetized him. What kept him looking good may have been his hearty appetite and playing tennis four times a week at his exclusive club. But Dan Thurman had that ruddy glow, if you know what I mean, a sure sign of alcoholism.

After learning that his prior sex life had consisted of $50 hookers who performed expert blow jobs, I had serious doubts about their relationship. I thought it was unfortunate that some high school or college girl had never seriously toyed with his affections. He had pretty blue eyes and a nice smile. It seemed to me that many girls would have been happy to show him a good time, considering the size of his bankroll and his blueblood family: bloody multi-millionaires.

Nonetheless, coping with erectile dysfunction in a man at the tender age of 23 was hardly exciting for Paula Marlow. But then, she was never held captive late one night by an aging, married, lewd but famous film director, after refusing to give him a blow job. The pervert relieved himself by forcing me to watch him jack-off in the front seat of his Mercedes in an isolated parking lot God-knows-where in Culver City. That, of course, is another story, and hardly the typical casting couch. Needless to say, I didn't get the part. The fact that I made it home alive on that summer night was a plus in my mind, considering all his films had twisted plots with crazed serial killers or homicidal detectives.

Every time I went to Glendale to see Paula, Dan was unduly rude to me. That continued even after their marriage and Christopher's birth. By that time, my acting jobs were somewhat steady with decent roles, with my name frequently in the gossip columns of respectable newspapers. As I slept and clawed my way to the top, my roles got even bigger and better and I was able to avoid the perverts and the sadists. My rising star had to appeal to the dollar signs in Dan's blue eyes, which was probably the only reason that he even tolerated me. The others in our group had him pegged. Dan didn't want Paula to have any friends other than his, especially starving artists and penniless actors. His friends were members of the tennis club and the country club, with portfolios, and Dan was their stockbroker.

Fifteen years Paula's senior, Dan's premature white hair made him look 50 at 40. At 30, Paula was still carded. At 32, I looked younger too, and yet, my friend Paula never had to put her birthday on a bio passed out to casting directors and producers, along with her current black-and-white glossy to beg for work. An actress rarely thinks to lie about her age before 40, only when it's too late and the whole damn world knows the year you were born by looking you up on the internet. These days, actors do tend to lie about their age, in case you didn't happen to know that. And as the years go by, an actress sometimes find herself on the *Late Show, Turner Classic Movies,* or some cable show at two in the morning when she can't sleep. It is also difficult to ignore the shock on someone's face when you're recognized in public years after making a film. That person may be stuck in Movie-Time when you were a child, or back in 1960 when you were 25. Even actors don't stay young and gorgeous forever, except on film or tape. It can be upsetting when someone sees you out in public without your makeup and reacts in horror when you never made a horror flick.

Another thing, no woman enjoys being called "ma'am" whether she's an actress or not and may simply be unwilling to admit it. Actually, I wanted to hit that cute kid at the gas station the first time he called me "ma'am." He was maybe 16, with me approaching the dubious milestone of 30. That was the day I realized that I had reached a turning point in my life, something that becomes increasingly painful over the years considering all the vitamins, colonics, facials, massages, yoga classes, Pilates, aerobics, jogging, biking, lean and mean personal trainers, running, swimming, plastic surgery and other cosmetic procedures that cost me substantial time and an inordinate amount of money! In time, even an actress recognizes the law of gravity and that the world keeps on turning. But back in 1967, I still looked young and beautiful at the ripe age of 32. I still felt young and beautiful too, with my hormones in full throttle. I have the memories to prove it!

That Saturday in June of 1967, about an hour after getting home from the airport, I called my friend Paula. A dinner party was planned for that evening. Besides Scott and me, another couple was also invited: art connoisseur friends of mine I'd hoped might buy a painting or two from Paula, since I was the subject of quite a few of her paintings.

Her housekeeper, Maria, was an excellent cook. The dinner was sure to be tasty and the company stimulating, as a fire blazed in the great corner stone fireplace and the muted surf rumbled from beyond the deck. I enjoyed Paula's beach house as much I did my home in Beverly Hills. By that time, Paula and I were joined at the psyche as kindred souls. After all, according to a Hungarian gypsy who read our tarot cards on the pier in Santa Monica, we had spent many lifetimes together.

"You were dancing concubines in the same harem in ancient Mesopotamia," Ilona once said.

Over the years, our psychic connection became even stronger. We experienced remarkable mental telepathy and often showed up in each other's dreams. We read the same books and saw the same psychics in search of our distant pasts and futures. We took astrology classes together with Ilona. We read about Edgar Cayce, the *Sleeping Prophet*, the man who went into trance and spoke of people's past lives in ancient Egypt and Atlantis. Paula and I were sure we were friends in Atlantis. Ilona said that it was true.

Anyway, as it turned out on that day in June, Paula was sick in bed and sounded terrible. No dinner party. But I still wanted to see her and tell her all about Beau Kandell, the man who had fallen in love with her art dealer's description of her. It seemed to me that Ken Stone had a crush on Paula too.

The children were up at Lake Arrowhead for the weekend with Dan, which meant empty beds in Malibu. Necessities were thrown into my overnight bag and I was soon behind the wheel of my trusty Mercedes 450 SL heading down Sunset Boulevard for the Hollywood Hills.

While on location in Texas I had made up my mind to end my affair with Scott Wellington, Hollywood film director extraordinaire. Scott was the gorgeous, sexy, cinematic genius I had dated for the past two years. These days, Scott Wellington has Oscars, Golden Globes, People's Choice Awards and Emmys in every room of his palatial Palisades mansion. One Golden Globe, enshrined in glass above the urinal in the guest bathroom, is another story.

Between the sheets, Scott Wellington was an Academy Award performer in his amazing capacity to bring a woman to her peak time and again. That kind of action was not easy for me to dismiss with my hormones still fully in charge. And on that particular evening, Scott really surprised me.

"Will you marry me?" he shouted in my face.

"I don't love you!" I screamed back.

Now, wasn't it just like a man to ask me to marry him right after I'd decided to end it? Frankly, I could never really see how marriage to Scott was ever going to work. And, on the other hand, I couldn't be absolutely certain that it wouldn't. You see, I'm a Gemini. I can have trouble making up my mind.

The truth of the matter was, at the beginning of that summer, I didn't feel like settling down with just one man. That was the summer that I learned a whole lot about the true meaning of love. That was what actually happened during the wild and wonderful Summer of Love!

# Chapter 2

I can still remember the dinner that Maria served on my first night back in California that June: Roast beef with this really light gravy delicious on the new potatoes, fresh green beans with slivered almonds, a crisp salad of curly lettuce and ripe red tomatoes with vinaigrette dressing, and several glasses of a California Cabernet Sauvignon for a perfect meal. A fire crackled in the great stone fireplace and soft jazz played on the stereo, accompanied by the low rumble of the surf from out beyond the sliding glass doors.

After Maria left to take care of an ailing aunt, Paula and I sat on the marine blue sectional with snifters of cognac as a waxing moon rose higher over the dark blue sea. During dinner, I had given the women a full accounting of my adventures deep in the heart of Texas. Considering how Paula had sounded when I first called, there was marked improvement in her vocal tone and in her complexion.

Another log was added to the fire and decaf espresso poured, a special blend selected in Italy while I was working there earlier that year. It was only one of many items chosen for Paula's 30th birthday basket in March.

That February in Rome, I had to splash around in a fountain *La Dolce Vita*-style for a perfume commercial to be aired during warmer weather. I was wearing a fabulous silver sequined gown that the sponsor said I could keep. However, the gown was trashed by all the water. I was grateful to finish the shoot without getting pneumonia. An ounce of that divine perfume was also included in Paula's birthday basket: *Wild Affair* seemed an apt label, considering the gorgeous Italian cameraman, Salvatore, and our delightfully decadent days that followed. Salvatore was a handsome, skillful, sensual Sicilian in every way a woman could possibly imagine or require!

On that evening in Malibu, seated before a cozy fire, I thought of how Paula could dab that exquisite scent all over her nymph-like body to drive a certain tall Texan right out of his beautiful, fucking mind.

Experiencing the warmth of the fire on the outside and the glow of cognac on the inside, I observed the woman seated beside me. Paula looked delicate, but she was far stronger than most people might ever suspect. She was also ethical and honest to the core, besides being a creative genius. Her values were based on what we both considered as "universal spiritual principles." The two of us embraced almost everything that was part of the 1960s, except that neither of us ever experimented with dangerous drugs. And even though women's lib was all the rage, we still enjoyed having a man open our door or pick up the check. We both read *Sex and the Single Girl* by Helen Gurley Brown. And the moment "the pill" was legal, we were among the first to swallow those little suckers each and every pre-scribed morning. Our newfound sexual freedom was liberating. No more diaphragms, no more messy creams or jellies, no more silly rubbers to inter-rupt the flow in more ways than one. AIDS had yet to rear its ugly head and place our very lives in jeopardy. Think of how many might have perished if HIV had surfaced when the sexual revolution began?

Not long after Paula had young Christopher, her husband turned fully verbally abusive. Dan expected her to have another child while he destroyed everything she had ever felt for him. As he started to drink more and more, Paula went back on the pill. The alcohol not only made Dan impotent but mean. Perhaps the anger he directed at Paula was his unconscious rage toward his own demons. That was always my take.

After listening to her constant complaints and witnessing her intense frustration for more than a year, I gave Paula the name of a highly respected divorce attorney in Beverly Hills: Six-foot-three, Calvin was graying at the temples and had marvelous hazel eyes to go with the deep cleft in his deter-mined chin. More importantly, he had more than proven his worth with every woman he represented. My hope was he would do the same for Paula.

Apparently, Calvin didn't turn out to be nearly as good in the sack as he was in the courtroom. Or perhaps my friend was simply too desperate for a real romp in the hay after Mr. Impotent Abusive Alcoholic. Or else, the two of them just weren't meant for each other? Paula had a dream to that effect, which seemed a damn shame to me. Gorgeous Calvin was highly successful, and fortunately, he did serve his purpose. Paula was able to get on with her life.

That evening in Malibu, as Paul turned to me, the firelight reflected in her amber eyes as she said, "Okay, tell me all about the man you met in Texas ... Beauregard Kandell?"

In a moment of drama, I lit a cigarette and proceeded to blow smoke into the fire. Then, in my stage voice I said, "Beauregard Kandell, Beau for short, is a man among men. He is a big, tall, handsome man with a fantastic outlook on life. And, in my opinion, there isn't a petty bone in his beautiful body, all six-foot-three of him. Trust me, darling, you are going to adore this man!"

"I am going to adore this man? Why?"

"Well, you just are!"

"So far, you haven't told me a thing. Who is he? During dinner you only talked about making the picture on his ranch ... so?"

"His ranch is about 5,000 acres, which is apparently a small spread in the Lone Star State. He has a huge herd of Black Angus steers and 30 Texas Longhorns that make it just right for an old-fashioned Western movie. Most of the indoor scenes were shot in the original ranch house, which is small, quaint and charming. His land borders a lovely lake. Beau is also a photographer and plays semi-pro golf when he's not running his ranch or traveling around the world."

"How nice for him," Paula said in a tone of sarcasm.

"What I'm trying to telling you is ... Beau Kandell is a very sophisticated cowboy. He lives in a mansion that would fit right in here on Sunset Boulevard. His house is much larger and grander than mine. And he also rides Brahman bulls in rodeos!"

"No bull?"

"No bullshit! Riding bulls is dangerous, Paula. Bucking Brahman bulls! He has a whole wall of ribbons, pictures, and trophies he's won ... just for riding bulls!"

"How nice for him." Paula sipped her espresso and smirked.

"His back has been giving him trouble lately, probably because of the bulls! Beau is a genuine cowboy, Paula. Sometimes he checks out his herd on a horse, but mostly, he does that in his navy blue pickup truck. He has a red pickup too."

"Well, he'd have to have a red one if he has a blue one!" she said, giggling. "These days I guess all cowboys need a pickup truck or two." Paula inhaled the aroma of her Courvoisier and sipped. I introduced her to Courvoisier. It is still my favorite cognac.

I sat up straighter. She didn't seem to be getting my point. "Beau has integrity. He's an honorable man, sweet and highly considerate. He's good to his men who love and respect him. Not one of them said an unkind word to me about Beau Kandell during the entire time I was in Texas."

"Six-foot-three is tall. I'm only five-four. He's nearly a foot taller than I am," she said, turning toward the flickering flames of the fire.

"When he makes his next business trip to L.A., I'm throwing a party so you two can meet. I don't know what else to tell you, except that deep down inside I think Beauregard Kandell may be 'the one'!"

"May you both live happily ever after!"

"Beau is for you, Paula. Not me! When I first met him, your face filled my mind and I got chills. You know what that means! I had sensed the truth about your future!"

"My future?"

"I swear to God! I just know that you are going to take one look at that gorgeous drink of water and fall madly in love. He has enough money to make a good life for you and your children."

"I am doing just fine, thank you very much. Soon I may not even need Dan Thurman's alimony or child support, and that would suit me fine."

"That's great, Paula! But let's not be foolish about alimony ... or child support!"

"In fact, in October, Ken Stone is doing an exclusive show of just my work at his gallery. He says I'm ready! What do you think about that, Miss Movie Star?"

"I think that's fantastic! You are ready!" I took another drag on my cigarette. Her response to my description of Beau was not what I'd hoped for. "Did I tell you about his art studio with its special lighting and temperature control? In my humble opinion, that studio has your name written all over it!"

"Why?"

"You know I always save the best for last."

After narrowing her cat eyes to slits, Paula said, "You mean you have even more to tell me about the wonderful and handsome Beauregard Kandell who lives deep in the heart of Texas?"

"I do," I said, leaning back and looking directly into her amber eyes. "One evening he invited me to his house for dinner, just the two of us alone in this magnificent mansion with marble statues and priceless works of art, hardly my concept of a cattle ranch. There is a lot more money in beef than I ever imagined."

"Michele and Christopher do love their hamburgers."

"I want you to know that Beau was a perfect gentleman, soft spoken with his sexy Texas drawl. Why, honey drips from those sensuous lips." I wiggled my eyebrows and made her laugh.

"And?"

"He is highly intelligent and well bred, with a stable, dependable side, and yet, when he started talking about 'the painting,' without realizing I'd already seen it up on his living room wall, about how he'd purchased the painting in this gallery in Los Angeles and been attracted to 'the subtle vitality of the artist, her wonderful, sensitive style and exceptional concept in muted pastels.' It seems the painting spoke to him and helped him glimpse the soul of the artist who he thought was a special woman with talents to compliment his own, a woman he thought he might be able to love."

"Really?"

"And that woman is ... Paula Marlow!"

Momentarily, Paula studied me and finished off her cognac.

"Isn't that the most romantic story you've ever heard in your entire life?"

"Correct me if I'm wrong, but are you trying to tell me that Beau Kandell has fallen in love with one of my paintings?" Paula started to laugh. "Dana Scofield, not only are you an incurable romantic, but you have really lost it this time!"

"I find your lack of sensitivity troubling. I knew the painting was yours the moment I saw it. It's one of your larger paintings."

Four feet by six, the painting was from three years earlier and had brought a fair price: an impressionistic landscape in muted pastels with wildflowers, soft sunlight, and two naked lovers entwined under a tree, their discarded clothing crumpled amidst the tall grasses.

"It's your fate to meet him. I just know it! Why else would I have met him, if not to bring the two of you together?"

She said nothing, just watched me closely.

"I told Beau you're my dearest friend and that if he wants to love you, it's perfectly all right with me."

"You actually said that?"

"It was Kenneth who told him all about your copper red hair and your soulful amber eyes, your incredible, delicate beauty. But I was the one who said you have the body of a wood nymph."

"A wood nymph?" She sat up straight. "Ken said all those things about me, my art dealer?"

"He told Beau that you have the body of a 'reincarnated Greek goddess'!"

"Good Lord! Ken said that?"

"He used those exact words...soulful amber eyes, glistening copper hair, the body of a reincarnated Greek goddess."

Paula laughed.

"I hope you told him I'm actually English, Scot and German. You said he was conventional and dependable. No one of that description falls in love with a woman who paints two lovers copulating in a grassy field. He's probably a sex deviate!"

"He didn't lay a hand on me!"

"Maybe he just likes to watch."

We both laughed that time.

"Who posed for that painting, anyway?" I was still laughing.

Paula's surprising indifference toward the tall Texas rancher had me baffled. To my knowledge, no man of substance, or even one lacking in substance, had graced her life for over a year, and none with the potential of Beau Kandell. In my mind, the wedding was already planned with me as her Maid of Honor.

Then again, on the very next morning, while we were both enjoying breakfast out on the deck and watching the young surfers riding the waves, there was a loud knock at the front door.

Paula was busy trying to sketch the surfers and some sailboats, so I got the door.

And in walked gorgeous: Tall, dark and handsome, six feet tall, with the most tempting, lean, athletic young body. His bright chocolate brown eyes sparkled and the deep dimples on his face were adorable as he flashed his most captivating smile.

"I'm Jamie Remington," he said in a thick Southern accent in a mouth filled with the most magnificent straight white teeth. "Paula is expecting me," he added. He was carrying a rolled-up towel under one arm and a small bottle in his other hand.

Jamie could not have been more than 20 as he swaggered into the living room with the confidence typical of youth. And, in my opinion, he was the perfect male embodiment of testosterone with a heterosexual pref-erence. When he walked out onto the deck, from the way he looked at Paula and the way she looked back, love was in the air and sex was surging through those bloodstreams. Chemical lightning bolts fired to the point of making me uncomfortable. A mating dance was taking place right before my astonished green eyes.

Southern charm oozed from every pore of his beautiful, young body. Upon discovering who I was, and the reason I looked so familiar, with genuine southern gallantry Jamie gushed, "Why, I've seen *The Wind and The Rage* three times! You should have received the Academy Award for that performance and not just the nomination. I swear it!"

Those are words any actor craves and reveres. But, for me, the most interesting part of the equation was that Jamie Remington happened to be the nephew of none other than Dan Thurman, Paula's ex-husband. He was the eldest son of Dan's sister, June, the one we'd always called 'the bitch of Atlanta.' June had always treated Paula beyond badly. And, on that partic-ular Sunday, all those elements all mixed up together made for a prime soap opera plot that I could hardly wait to watch unfold before my very eyes.

No wonder it was called the Summer of Love!

Paula and Jamie were absolutely and positively smitten with each other.

And yet, in my opinion, it was high time for Paula to have some honest-to-goodness fun, even if Jamie were some sort of distant relative. My first cousins did it back in Indiana and ended up married. Paula had been celibate long enough, and Jamie seemed like an immediate solution to that particular problem, with no likelihood of erectile dysfunction day or night.

While Paula and Jamie were enthralled with each other, perhaps for-getting I was even there, I noticed four good-looking men traipsing in and out of the house next door. Paula's neighbors were off to the Mediterranean for the summer and had rented out their house to four bachelors in the process of moving in. Therefore, while Jamie went for a swim, Paula and I invoked the good neighbor policy. It was the least that we could do and the only way for me to check out the merchandise up close and personal.

Only two of the new hunks captured my full and undivided attention. The one with the vivid blue eyes and coal black hair was Dr. Eric Whitley, a biologist and biochemist with two PhDs, age 38. He had a fabulous tan and movie star, yummy, good looks. It was hard not to lose myself in those eyes. Eric made me feel as though he was looking right into my soul. And

I was fully prepared to open up to his even closer examination of my basic biological urges.

The other man of interest was Phillip Stacey, the dark-eyed, swarthy, muscular, Mr. Workout-type, age 36. As it turned out, Phil was part owner of an art gallery on Melrose and had heard of Paula's work. He also worked as a character actor in episodic television. Ironically, two years before he was cast in a small role in a mini-mystery on TV in which I'd had the lead. It was embarrassing to have forgotten the man who had supposedly raped me. I didn't remember his name, although his overall physique was vaguely familiar.

"I never have been good at remembering names," I lamely explained.

"I suppose my performance was less than memorable. Most of the rehearsal time was spent with your stand-in. Besides, why would you remember a guy who roughed you up and pinned you down in one show out of many?" he inquired, his smoldering brown eyes making me tingle in the most delightful manner in the most delightful places.

"I should think that would be a guy I'd definitely remember," I teased, batting my light green eyes at his dark brown eyes and that made him grin.

Another roommate was ivy-league Johnny Hargrove, 34, in the advertising business. Johnny had only recently moved to California from Connecticut. Five-eleven, medium build, he came across as arrogant and said he was dating a lady doctor in the Valley. Pediatrician.

Roomie number four was Brad Myerson, an attractive, blond college professor, 33, really buff with bulging biceps and bulging thighs. When we first met, Brad was carrying a typewriter in one hand and a 50-pound weight in the other. Quite impressive. He said he was writing a college textbook over the summer. Looks can be deceiving.

With all four men out on their deck, Paula told them about the art exhibit at Andy's house on the beach that afternoon. "You can't miss the sounds, the people, or the art. Just walk on down the beach. It's a great way to meet your new neighbors. The exhibits are every Sunday afternoon through Labor Day starting around two in the afternoon."

Three out of the four men showed up to sample Andy's wicked summer wine, poetry, the folk music, and all the tasty food. A considerable number attended the exhibit that day, more than I had ever seen there before. It was a fun day. Paula sold three paintings. That evening we danced to records until nearly midnight.

At different times during the afternoon I'd given my telephone number to Phil and to Eric. Phil invited me to his gallery and lunch. He was almost begging Paula to change galleries and ended up buying a small painting of hers that reminded him of his daughter. Recently, his ex-wife had moved to New York with his little girl and he really missed her. The painting he'd selected was of a much younger Michele, holding a pretty butterfly in both her hands.

All that afternoon and evening, Eric and Phil had hovered around me, asking me to dance, offering to get me more food or wine. The sharks were circling just like back on Hollywood Boulevard when Paula and I played our silly drinking games. Even though I had broken things off with Scott, something was holding me back. After all, he had asked me to marry him. Throughout that Sunday my previous night's encounter with Scott played in my mind, along with my extremely mixed emotions.

Eric, the biochemist, held more appeal for me more than the actor-art dealer, although Phil definitely had raw animal magnetism. In remembering the show, he had come across as a rapist. Now, he seemed gentle and hardly the violent type.

The young charmer from Atlanta rarely left Paula's side all that afternoon and evening, leaving little time for me to talk to her. Starting a love affair with Dan's nephew seemed like opening a big can of worms to me, although the attraction was obvious. Love had bloomed in June with summer not yet official. It seemed to me that a tall, blond and handsome Texas rancher had better hustle his bustle or he might lose the prize to a young, handsome and aspiring law student from Georgia. Jamie planned on a political career and was willing to serve his country in Vietnam. The young man was not lacking in courage or wealthy family connections. My curiosity was certainly piqued as to the outcome of future events in the life of my friend.

Watching them dance, Paula and Jamie seemed over the moon. The sexy vibes even made me think of calling Scott. Then I remembered the vibrator I'd purchased in a German sex shop while making a film in Berlin. That night the pink devil was coming out of its box to play in mine, with satisfaction guaranteed.

After all, sparkling blue eyes and smoldering brown eyes were hot on my trail, which made my prospects outstanding for that entire summer!

# Chapter 3

The sun was directly overhead as I entered my French country-style living room. Soon it would be time for me to shower and dress. I checked out the blush on my face, neck and bosom in the large beveled mirror over my marble fireplace. Sufficient for one day, I thought. At least my shoulders were more evenly tanned from exposing my back and top to the sun.

Not long after my first acting job in Europe, I started to wear just my bikini bottom at home, something that still shocked the average American. Considering the high brick wall around my back yard, all the leafy trees and tall cypresses, there was enough privacy for me to swim nude. That made me feel as I imagined a bird might feel flying through the sky. A robe or large towel was always near in case an unexpected visitor arrived.

I loved that house off Coldwater Canyon in the flats of Beverly Hills that was once the residence of legendary film star Errol Flynn. An older neighbor had told me all about the wild parties once held in my conservative-looking, white framed, two-story house with its white picket fence during what he called "the heyday of Hollywood motion picture making." Sex orgies, Hollywood-style, included many of the notables of the day. Some splashing about in the buff in my pool, while others apparently ran naked through the halls and up and down the stairs.

A two-way mirror in the ceiling of a downstairs guest room provided the voyeurs upstairs with ample viewing of the randy performances taking place below, compliments of the wild and abandoned movie stars of the day. An ingenious idea, I thought, upon purchasing the house, but the mirror was removed and the ceiling restored and that tidbit made the gossip columns.

A secret fantasy of mine was of being watched, naked and entwined with some exquisite male while lost in the throes of passion, my secret urge attributed to my tremendous need to perform. Making love in front of cameras and crews was par for the course for me by 1967, though not with complete abandonment, no holds barred, or for real. A few leading men shared my bed off camera during the making of a film, with such action rarely lasting beyond the final wrap party. The passions of the characters often spill from reel into real life, but performances off camera seldom fulfilled my great expectations. Actors are just men after all, with as many or more hang-ups as any other. And yet, hanky-panky with a director or cameraman, on occasion, did produce some of my better close-ups.

That house in Beverly Hills was not a mansion, but every room had a sense of style and grace provided by my special touch. Casual elegance, a touch formal by design, served my every want and need. I loved the French windows and doors. Light poured in through lacey curtains, those in the living room held back by blue velvet sashes. The high ceilings had ornate crown moldings and the doorways gracefully arched. At times, I could feel elegant just walking through them.

In my small, cozy library, one bookcase was filled with fine leather bound books, in addition to numerous newer releases. Other shelves and tables displayed my special treasures collected on various trips to Europe to make several foreign films. Because I was a successful actress, I had the privilege of meeting many of the celebrated and influential all around the world: kings, queens, lords and ladies, poets, writers, philosophers and politicians. It was an exciting time in my life.

The hardwood floors in my dining room were covered by a precious Persian carpet of blue, white, rose and gold, purchased in Paris during a madcap affair with a notorious, womanizing yet brilliant French film director.

The breakfast room was a favorite with its large windows that framed my magnificent rose garden. Until the dead of winter, roses of red, white, yellow, pink, fuchsia and peach bloomed outside the low windows not far from the swimming pool with its lion statuary and splashing fountain. My Japanese gardener was an absolute genius with the trees and shrubs. Hitoshi made sure there were assorted flowers for me to cut every month of the year.

My walls were covered with many fine paintings, large and small, several by Paula, in addition to those of Rembrandt and Whistler. I was glad to have my investments out in plain sight. Everything was thoroughly insured, with my housekeeper keeping a close watch on things as my constant protector.

Florence Becker, 57, was my live-in housekeeper and personal guardian angel for five years by then. Florence had a flawless sense of cleanliness and order besides being an excellent cook. For small dinner parties I preferred to cook. While traveling through Europe many gourmet chefs had honored me with a copy of my favorite recipes. With larger gatherings, Florence was extremely efficient dealing with the caterers and everything else, with the added plus that she mothered me.

My biological mother, Helen, was already married three times by 1967. After leaving Daddy and me, her maternal instincts seemed to vanish. That year Helen resided in Miami with her third husband, Arnold Henninger, a wealthy industrialist who seemed to enjoy catering to her expensive tastes. Her second husband was only slightly less wealthy, Horatio Parker of the Pittsburgh Parkers. Helen adored jewelry: diamonds, emeralds, sapphires, rubies, gold and platinum, expensive trinkets my father could rarely afford.

Helen and Arnold traveled extensively. On occasion, my mother sent me a postcard from some faraway place with a strange-sounding name. She rarely called and seldom visited. My relationship with her was more like that of a casual acquaintance, though she did say I should settle down with a rich husband and bear her some grandchildren to indulge with fancy gifts from Timbuktu or Kathmandu. After eight years of acting success on television and in feature films, she still wasn't pleased that her daughter was an actor, even after I was nominated for an Oscar and two Emmys! At least my father, George Scofield, was proud of me. George was my one and only parent.

Daddy forever resided in Indianapolis with his second and last wife Martha. He rarely left Indiana. In his opinion, he was doing fine with his small publishing business. He usually called me every week. He even suggested that I write my memoir, so he could publish it. At 32, I was hardly ready to write a memoir. I thought perhaps by the age of 40 I would have enough to say and fewer people to offend. Some of my revelations, or confessions, might ruffle a few feathers in Hollywood and Europe, and not only in the film business. It seemed to me that more time needed to pass before I could deal with all the intrigues of my past.

On my mahogany baby grand piano in the living room was an assortment of pictures in frames of various sizes and shapes: Family members and friends, fellow actors. Paula was framed in tortoise shell, Christopher and Michele in matching silver frames. There were also wedding pictures of Helen, smiling with each of her husband's. An Art Deco of silver and gold with lilies on the corners framed young Helen and young George, my parents, on their wedding day: June 6, 1931, in Indianapolis, Indiana. Helen wore an old-fashioned gown of white lace. George was in black tie and tails. Helen was small and petite, a beautiful brunette. At that time, I looked just like her in that picture, except for my father's green eyes.

Whenever Daddy came to town, which wasn't often, the pictures of Helen and each of her husband's on her various wedding days were hidden away, including the one with my father. The pictures were returned to their rightful place after Daddy left. It was a game I played with myself. Those pictures were there to keep me from marrying the wrong man. After all, Helen had left each husband for the next, each man less attractive but a great deal richer. I had no desire to repeat her pattern. In matters of the heart, I tended to be fickle. I was living the good life, except sometimes, Michele and Christopher, Paula's two children, made me think about having kids. And yet, at the start of that summer, the prospects of me marrying anyone seemed remote. My career was flourishing in those days.

Earlier that morning, my agent called about a role in a feature film. *In the Cool of the Night* was being shot locally at Stromberg Pictures in Hollywood. The role of Kathryn Martell was of a woman scorned by a womanizing heel, her revenge sweet by the end. Doing the picture meant staying home for the summer and spending weekends with my friends. The leading man was an actor I'd always wanted to work with, which made the deal even sweeter. In my genuine excitement, I called Paula.

"Are you still a virgin?" I inquired, lighting a cigarette.

"Whatever do you mean, dear?" Her laughter was self-conscious.

"After I got home last night, I used that pink vibrator from Germany. No man could do that for me. If Jamie doesn't pan out, I'll get you one for Christmas!"

"Sounds good to me," she said, laughing. "I'm glad you had a good time."

"Aren't you going to tell me anything? How convenient that Dan's car broke down at Lake Arrowhead, so he couldn't bring your kids home on Sunday. Another divine coincidence, perhaps?"

There was a long pause before she said, "Jamie is out on the beach building a sandcastle with my children," in the most dreamy tone. "I think I'm in love."

"No kidding!" My immediate thought: *Hurry up, Beau Kandell*, but what I said was, "He's beautiful, intelligent, virile, wild about you ... sexy?"

"All of that and more! I'm crazy about him, Dana. Or maybe I'm just plain crazy. It's so complicated with Dan as his uncle."

"So you had a wonderful night?"

"And a wonderful morning ... a wonderful everything."

"You deserve it, darling. I knew he was going to jump your delicate bones at your first sign of acceptance. That boy was on the prowl from the very first moment." It was easy enough for me to sense the depth of her feelings, but in my mind, Beau Kandell was still up front and center. "In a way, Jamie reminds me of Jeffrey Waters."

"Who was Jeffrey Waters?"

"My first true love in high school back in Indiana. I was 16. He was 17. He was the first boy I went all the way with and I was his first virgin. Jeffrey lost his cherry to a second cousin at a family reunion."

"Wow! A very friendly family reunion?"

"Sally was 18 and taught him everything she knew when he was only 14. Knowing Jeff, he was ready, willing and able. I was his first true love. I'd done some petting, but no orgasms until Jeffrey. He was a great beginning. It's probably his fault that I'm the way I am. To him, I shall be eternally grateful."

"Were you in love?"

"I thought so at the time. Jeff was the star quarterback of our football team, president of the student body, and he had this band that played for school dances. He played five musical instruments, no six, counting the one between his legs." I started to laugh.

"Dana Scofield, you're incorrigible!" Paula said, but she was laughing too. "Was he really that good?"

"Jeff was the best. I didn't know it then, being inexperienced, but I do now. He read every sex manual he could beg, borrow or steal, and there wasn't any part of his body that couldn't give me total and absolute pleasure."

"Is that right?"

"He went to great lengths to satisfy. The only other man that comes close, carnally speaking, is Scott, and his approach is much more practiced."

"You said Jeffrey read all the sex manuals. That sounds pretty practiced to me."

"He read the manuals. I was the practice. Other than Cousin Sally and what's-her-name, but those girls couldn't have picked a more willing partner. Jeff aimed to please and his aim was pleasing."

When she stopped laughing, Paula asked, "What did he look like?"

"He was tall with black as coal hair and Paul Newman drop dead blue eyes. He had the most fantastic body that made me cream in my jeans just by looking at him."

"Wow!"

"Not unlike Jamie's, I might add: young, strong, virile. Nineteen is a potent age with more than enough testosterone pumping through those beautiful veins. That Georgia peach is just ripe for the picking. Do enjoy!"

"I plan to," she said, sounding girlish. "What are you doing with yourself today?"

"I'm going to Phil's art gallery for lunch, and then later, I'm having dinner with Eric."

"Are you telling me that you have dates with two men who are roommates on the same day? Are you crazy? You could make my life very complicated. They are my new neighbors for the whole summer!"

"Don't get excited, dear. Harriet is going with me. I'm not having dinner with Eric until later, no ménage a trois, although that might be interesting with those two men. What can possibly happen in an art gallery in the middle of the day? It's the least that I can do after forgetting he once raped me ... on camera."

"He might like another chance ... off camera. I saw the way he was watching you."

"I have better chemistry with the bio-chemist. Besides being gorgeous, Eric is highly intelligent and I've never had a bio-chemist before."

"You're so bad!" Paula was laughing.

"So bad I'm good!"

"But can a simple bio-chemist afford to date a movie star?"

"We both know that free love is the most expensive kind!"

Our conversation ended. I found Paula narrow-minded about me dating roommates. She was a virgin at 20 when she married Michael, and I had yet to be married, besides being on the pill. In my mind, I had the freedom to explore my wildest dreams.

I went upstairs to shed my bikini bottoms and was about to turn on the shower when the telephone rang. Not wanting to get sunscreen on my new pink velvet chair, I wrapped myself in a towel before I said, "Hello!"

"Dana, I need to talk to you! You're being fully unreasonable!" Scott shouted, forcing me to hold the receiver away from my ear. He reminded me of the eight messages he'd left with my service. "Why haven't you returned any of my calls?" he said nearly hysterical.

I was about to hang up, but said, "We have nothing to discuss. I told you I'm not going to marry you. You waited too long to ask me." I felt calm, which surprised me. I was much more detached than with our other breakups.

"So don't marry me! Does that mean we can't see each other? I love you, Dana. I'll take you on your terms. Two and a half years is hardly a long time for a man to wait to make a full commitment. If you don't want to marry me, fine! At least see me! I miss you. We've been part of each other's lives far too long to throw it all away because of one little misunderstanding."

"It was not just one little misunderstanding. There are lots of reasons that we shouldn't be together. I want to see other men. I just don't feel the same about you, Scott, and you wouldn't want me to fake it."

"Go ahead and fake it," he moaned. "I miss your beautiful face, your fantastic breasts, your soft skin, your beautiful hair, your incredible wit, not to mention the depth of your passion. Go ahead and fake it, Dana, but you never faked those orgasms, my darling. Sex between us was fantastic. Those orgasms you had were earthshaking. You never faked those!"

"Only once or twice," I felt a sudden need to confess.

"DON'T TELL ME THAT! I fucking don't believe you! You're not that good an actress!"

"Well!" I indignantly shouted back, unable to blame him for insulting me, since no man really wants to know the truth. The male ego. I had no desire to castrate him. I was simply tired of his theatrics. Scott was a great lover, but I could never imagine him as my husband or the father of my unborn children.

"Orgasms aren't enough, Scott. You're a fantastic lover. I'll be happy to write you a recommendation to run in *The Hollywood Reporter* and *Variety* on the same day. But I don't have time to talk now. Stop calling me. I don't want to hurt your feelings. You need to leave me alone. Good-bye!" I said, slamming down the receiver and heading for the shower.

The telephone rang again.

I stared at the phone. Then, in something of a rage, I picked up the receiver and shouted, "I told you to stop calling me! Don't you understand I mean what I say?"

"I don't recall your having said that," a man drawled on the other end of the line, "In fact, the last time I saw you … you told me to give you a holler when I was coming to town. If you don't want to talk to me right now, Dana, it's perfectly all right. I'll call you some other time."

"Who is this?" I asked, suddenly feeling foolish.

"Beau Kandell," he said in his familiar drawl. "You may not remember me, but you made a movie down here in Texas a few weeks back and we had a right nice steak and lobster dinner one evening here at the house. You said you liked the lemon mousse my chef whipped up special for you. You'd told me that lemon mouse was your favorite."

"Oh, Beau!" I gushed. "I'm so sorry. I'd just gotten off the phone with a man who has been … harassing me. I thought you were him calling back and I'd just told him not to call me again."

"I'd be willing to bet he got the message," he said. "I'll be sure and tell the fellow not to bother you, if I ever meet him, that is. Is there something I can do to help you out? You just say the word and I'll do whatever I can."

"No, Beau, thanks, anyway. I think he got the message."

"I'd be willing to bet on that. You have a powerful way of making your wishes known for such a little lady. How tall are you, anyway, about five two?"

"Five two and a half," I said, since that half-inch had always been important to me.

"About a hundred pounds?"

"Something like that," I hedged, feeling the need to shed five pounds before once more facing the merciless lens of the camera. "When are you coming to town?"

"Friday or Saturday. I'm not exactly sure yet. A good friend of mine has a Lear jet and is flying out to L.A. Mark offered me a ride. You said to let you know when I'm coming to town, so I'm letting you know it will be Saturday, the latest."

"Then how about brunch at my place on Sunday to meet my friends?"

"Would one of those friends just happen to be Paula Marlow?"

"Absolutely! I told her all about you. She's looking forward to meeting you, Beau."

"Is that right? You and Ken Stone tell me she's beautiful. I already know how talented she is. I'm looking forward to meeting the little lady in person on Sunday."

"Noon in Beverly Hills. Call me for directions. We'll have a champagne brunch with lots of interesting artists. I'll invite Harlan Evans, the sculptor. Brilliant but eccentric."

"I've heard about his work. How about I send over a case of Dom Perignon special just for the occasion?"

"That isn't at all necessary," I said, quickly adding, "But it would be lovely, if you insist."

"I insist. I'll make sure it's delivered chilled. I'm looking forward to seeing you, Dana, and to meeting all your good friends, especially Paula Marlow."

After that, I sang in the shower. I had two dates with two gorgeous men on the same day, and I'd told Scott Wellington where to get off. Besides that, Beau Kandell was coming to town. I hoped just in the nick of time!

All my plans seemed to be falling into place on that day, including a beach party on Friday at the home of Paula's neighbors to celebrate the summer solstice. Those screenwriters always threw fabulous parties. On that day, the entire summer was starting to look promising to me, indeed.

# Chapter 4

The Grand Luna Gallery had a decent location on Melrose Avenue near the Design Center and featured the work of seven artists, mostly modern or abstract. Nothing came close to Paula's ethereal, impressionistic oil paintings. Her work would definitely class up the place. Harriet agreed. She also collected the paintings of Paula Marlow.

My socialite friend, Harriet Clybourne, wanted to check out the art with me that day. Harriet was always on the prowl for an artist to mentor, preferably one that was straight, young, handsome, male and also creative between the sheets, although most male artists she mentored were gay. But Harriet adored art and she also adored artists. Her altruistic heart was a good match for her unlimited resources. She was my richest female friend at the time with a great sense of humor. She also threw lavish parties attended by the elite, mostly in show business.

Harriet was more impressed with Phil's partner than with Phil. Keith Somers was a handsome, distinguished 50 and in great shape. He drove a red Ferrari that perfectly matched Harriet's. She had left her Ferrari in her Bel Air garage to keep her black Mercedes stretch limo company that day. My Mercedes 450 SL needed some exercise.

In those days, Harriet liked to do what she called "slumming." She was a woman accustomed to living on a truly grand scale, which she enjoyed doing solo since her significantly older ex was caught with his pants down and off with other women on more than one occasion. 'No fool like an old fool' is apparently not just a cliché. George Clybourne paid through the nose dearly in those days. But then, George was filthy rich, and Harriet enjoyed living "high off the hog" as we might say back in Indiana. She was a woman with class to spare. Every salesgirl on Rodeo Drive was on a first name basis with Harriet and she remembered each girl's first name. That meant excellent service and special treatment anytime she planned to shop.

For lunch, Phil took us to a little bistro where the food was just tolerable. No restaurant in that part of town was of any note in those days. We never let Phil know how cheap we thought he was. The tacky treatment did nothing to encourage a purchase by either of us. My advice to Paula was to stay with Ken Stone. Phil was unaware of what he had lost out on, since Harriet could have bought every painting in the gallery and the gallery itself.

Nevertheless, I accepted Phil's dinner invitation for Thursday. That was regardless of what my friend Paula thought about me dating roommates. His smoldering good looks and buff body made me wonder what he might be like without Harriet present, and I planned to find out.

First thing the next morning, I called Paula.

"So how was lunch with Phil?"

"Well below average. He's not a big spender."

"And dinner with Mr. Bright Blue Eyes?"

"Eric was the perfect gentleman. We went to Dino's on The Strip and enjoyed a good meal with fine wine, gazing into each other's eyes over the flickering flame of a candle. But he never really made a pass at me. He didn't even really kiss me. I don't know what that was all about."

"You are famous, dear. Perhaps he was afraid of being rejected."

"I hate it when my acting intimidates men I find attractive. I'm quite touchable, as you know! Eric is so gorgeous and intelligent he scares me. I could fall right into those eyes. Maybe I should have tried to seduce him." I lit a cigarette and blew smoke into the phone. "I suppose you were ravished again by the young stud from Atlanta!"

"Repeatedly," she said, sounding girlish. "Jamie is fantastic."

"I'm happy for you. Really I am. I just want my own playmate for my new pink love nest. My new bedspread is pink velvet and I have pink satin sheets. My new bidet is also pink. It keeps a girl kissing sweet, don't you know!"

Paula laughed. "How nice for you and him!"

"My new pink whirlpool tub is big enough for two. Knowing about you and Jamie and all your passion … maybe I should call Scott to get serviced."

"Wavering on Scott again?"

Suddenly, I felt a need to change the subject. "Did I tell you I got the part in a film playing opposite Kevin Matheson?"

"That means you'll be in town for the summer. Hooray!"

"I can stay up late and misbehave for two more weeks," I said, mentally tuning into shimmering blue eyes across from me at that dinner table. "Eric didn't even ask for another date. Do you think he didn't like me?"

"You may be the first actress he's dated. Even men in your business can have trouble dating an actress of international fame who has appeared in films with subtitles!"

"Phil doesn't have that problem. I'm having dinner with him on Thursday." Secretly, I wished it was going to be Eric again instead.

"Forget about Eric. You need to choose or there could be a murder in Malibu. Find someone else in the city. Please say you'll at least try?"

What I then said was, "What do you think of Paul McCartney admitting to dropping LSD on national television?"

"He did that?"

"If the Beatles admit to dropping acid, don't you think it's just a matter of time before the kids follow suit?"

"Maybe," Paula said. "Right now, I need to get back to my painting. I have to get ready for my show in October. What are you doing with yourself today?"

"Attending a cocktail party at Colossal Studios in Burbank where I hope to meet the handsome French actor, Louis Lamprais. He did a cameo in the film, singing and dancing. I've had an awful crush on him … forever."

"He is gorgeous. He was so sexy in that film we saw together. Yummy!"

"Women all over the world lust after Louis Lamprais! And he's such a good actor. He must be straight, or at least like women. He's been married a few times. But with the French, I guess you never know. Sex doesn't seem to be among their hang-ups."

"With all the sex in those films he appeared in, he must be a super stud!"

"I have yet to meet a Frenchman shy with women. And they did invent the best way to kiss. I just hope he knows who I am."

"You're as famous as he is."

"Hardly."

"Buy more batteries just in case," Paula said, giggling.

"My vibrator's name is Bob. You know, my Battery-Operated Boyfriend! A girl's got to do what a girl's got to do!"

"Do have fun! And give my regards to Louis!"

While I was swimming in the pool, my Yorkshire terrier, Frisky, started barking like crazy at the squirrels. I tried my best to ignore him, thinking about all the great sex that Paula was having with Jamie, and here I was dating a celibate biochemist. And yet, I couldn't help but wonder how Uncle Dan was going to handle finding out about the heat between his ex and his young nephew. Dan Thurman was a highly intelligent man and bound to figure things out sooner or later.

Floating on my back in the refreshing water, I honestly wished that I could be the fly on the wall when that shit hit the fan.

Poor, impotent Uncle Dan!

# Chapter 5

While standing under the warm shower, I started planning my menu for Sunday. I hadn't invited anyone yet and hadn't even mentioned the party to Florence or Paula. It had slipped my mind. Beau enjoyed the Hollywood crowd, so more actors seemed right, perhaps someone from the film in Texas other than groping Bill. Twelve guests were perfect for a Sunday brunch.

I thought of Eric or Phil. What about Louis Lamprais? The trades said he was in town for another film. The All-American Texas cowboy might enjoy meeting the Toast of Paris. In less than an hour, I planned to toast that gorgeous Frenchman with champagne on a soundstage in Burbank!

Without any warning, Jamie's image filled my mind. My sincere hope was that he had other plans for Sunday, but if Paula insisted, Jamie was invited. I was always a sucker for intrigue in other people's lives.

In my early days of acting, I'd learned how to expertly do my own hair and makeup. My long hair was now being blow-dried with a wisp of bang to one side, the rest reaching down past my shoulders. My new false eyelashes looked great with the brown and green eye shadow that matched my eyes and my dress. The liner and mascara of black-brown made my eyes look larger. Cherry red lipstick was my favorite.

My clingy halter dress was an emerald green and white-print mini, three inches above my knees. The plunging neckline revealed my breasts were genuine, since implants had not come into fashion yet. I was proud of my full, round breasts, appreciated by lovers both on screen and off.

Standing before my cheval glass, I slipped a karat diamond drop around my neck and added half-karat diamond studs to each ear. Daddy had given me the earrings for my 30th birthday. On that evening I was opting for understated elegance rather than the dangling diamonds Scott had recently given me for my 32nd birthday. No doubt expensive. If he insisted, the earrings would be returned. But Scott Wellington tended to be a gentleman, praise God.

In the kitchen, I told Florence, "We're having a champagne brunch on Sunday. Kindly make a list of all the things you know I love. We'll go over it in the morning. A case of champagne is arriving ... as a gift, no less."

"How nice!"

"Fresh squeezed orange juice for the mimosas for those silly enough to ruin the taste of Dom Perignon, vodka and tomato juice for my guests with a hangover. Lox, cream cheese, an assortment of quiches, fruit salad, brie. Think, Florence! Desserts with far too many calories. Beluga caviar. Everything will be done to perfection."

"I'll change my day off. Should I call Martin? Is Mrs. Clybourne invited?"

"Martin would be perfect. Naturally, Harriet is coming."

Behind the wheel of my trusty red Mercedes, I whizzed through Coldwater Canyon toward the San Fernando Valley and Colossal Studios.

Hundreds were milling around on the soundstage that was the nightclub set for *At the End of the Rainbow*. The large musical numbers were shot there. Actor extraordinaire, Louis Lamprais, was apparently a man of many talents.

Only that morning the trades had announced that Colossal had signed Lamprais on for the lead in a film based on a blockbuster bestselling novel by Garson Reeves: *View From The Mountain*. The historical saga told the story of the exploration and development of the West during the early 1800s. From the moment I finished Garson's epic novel, I wanted to be Victoria Rutherford, a role no doubt desired by most actresses in Hollywood. The physical attributes of Victoria were my attributes: small, petite, brunette, with a voluptuous figure. The film was going to be really big and could put me on Hollywood's A-list. To meet Louis Lamprais was my primary purpose for attending the party, especially after learning that he was already signed for the picture, although my lust for Louis was inflamed years before.

The famous, near famous, and wannabes were swarming like honeybees around the soundstage. Some waiters carried trays filled with glasses of champagne. There were long lines at three bars serving hard liquor and wine. On a round table, mountains of vegetable crudities were artfully displayed, along with creamy and tangy dips, and an assortment of fine cheeses and a variety of crackers. On another table was a tall cascade of cut fruit topped with a pineapple and orchids. The huge strawberries were delicious dipped in honeyed yogurt. On yet another table, there was a mountain of shrimp, cracked crab and lobster on ice, with artful tomato flowers with leaves made out of parsley.

Swedish meatballs simmered. Beluga caviar was served with sour cream. There was truffle, hare and chicken liver pate. Intermittently, waiters announced: "Rumaki. Quiche Lorraine. Oysters Rockefeller. Spareribs with plum sauce." The food was an epicurean's delight with the platters soon emptied: The caterer one of Hollywood's finest.

The producer of the motion picture extravaganza, Alvin Myerson, was a man the studio could bank on, with the lavish wrap party his special thank-you. Other than members of the press, receiving an outsider invitation was a coup d'état. Luckily, Alvin still had the hots for me. He produced my first major film, *Under the Rising Moon.* The movie made money at the box office and both of us stars.

While dipping a large shrimp into the red cocktail sauce, I looked up and saw Louis Lamprais in a tux across the crowded room. He was surrounded by a bevy of young beauties still in costume, no doubt the girls from the chorus.

In Europe, his films showcased his dramatic talent, all the roles emphasizing his immense appeal as a leading man. Upon catching sight of him in public, women on the continent were known to faint; screaming women tore at his clothes. Quite a few ladies wanted a piece of Louis Lamprais, along with a few of the men. During the past month, a French magazine had reported that a crazed male had tried to sexually assault him on a speeding train outside Paris. Apparently, the incident had left him shaken. In France, bodyguards now accompanied Louis Lamprais everywhere.

Five-foot-ten with a strong physique, his eyes were a dazzling hazel, his hair a wavy brown. His press release claimed that Louis was 35 when he was more likely 45. Apart from being drop dead handsome with his high cheekbones and angular jaw, he had the sex appeal of a Tyrone Power or Errol Flynn. Louis Lamprais was hot stuff at the box office! His name on a picture brought out the crowds. His public appearances brought out the fainting screamers. The studios loved it. The international press championed his talents, with his fame spreading far and wide. Louis had to love that!

Twice married and twice divorced, Louis was said to have fathered two children by his first wife, one by his second, Simone Perrot, an international model. Simone claimed to be devastated by the divorce, often appearing on TV talk shows to flaunt his infidelities that supposedly started the week of their wedding. Allegedly, Louis had fathered several illegitimate children in the past few years. His two-year-old daughter, Renee, was a stunner, having inherited the best from each parent. Because of Louis's international popularity, Simone had appeared on the covers of major fashion magazines and was cashing in on the fame of her famous ex. My guess was that Simone planned to enjoy a long run.

While selecting a fresh glass of champagne from a tray, I noticed Louis looking my way. However, at that exact moment, writer-producer Rosemary Caulfield walked up to me and started talking about a new film by an independent film company: American International Pictures: *The Trip*, starred Peter Fonda and Susan Strasberg, with a storyline of the psychedelic drug culture that was sweeping the nation. Tripping out on LSD was a frequent topic at Hollywood parties.

"Have you taken any trips?" Rosemary asked me.

"I don't do drugs, except for a little grass now and then." While attempting not to be rude to Rosemary, I was still trying to keep Louis in my line of vision as I said. "I was surprised when Harriet Glover had joints in a cigarette dish on her coffee table at a party I recently attended. This Senator was getting high right in her living room. No wonder our country is so fucked up with this Vietnam War. Frankly, I'm a touch afraid of psychedelics. Have you done any acid trips, Rosemary?"

"Three," she whispered, quickly scanning the room. "The first two were awesome, really hard to describe. It is an out-of-this-world experience."

"And the third?"

"A strange thing happened." She narrowed her eyes in an odd manner.

"Strange how?"

"This odd little oriental man suddenly appeared before me."

"Appeared?" I became fascinated. "And?"

"I guess I can trust you," she was whispering again, "You know what he said to me?"

I shook my head, still trying to eyeball Louis who was eyeballing me right back. The throngs still hovered around him. I hoped he knew who I was. From all the pawing and fawning, it seemed to me that he could write his own ticket in this town, perhaps indefinitely.

"Right before the little man appeared," Rosemary went on, "I'd seen all these fantastic colors, whirling lights, and I heard this incredibly beautiful music. I felt like I was flying through the universe with all these comets and whirling globes caressing me. The feeling was sensual, actually. And then, he showed up."

"Just showed up?"

"Yeah. This little oriental guy, small but fully formed. He was dressed in a florescent blue robe and he said, 'This is as far as you can go.'"

"He said that?"

"More or less, maybe telepathically. He claimed if I went any further with the acid, I'd get myself into serious trouble. Then, all at once, he was gone. Weird, huh? Really far out!" she said with a strange, faraway look in her eyes. "I haven't dropped acid since, because, you know, Dana, some-where deep down inside I just knew that little guy was right. I still smoke grass sometimes, like you, but no more acid. A friend of mine freaked out on LSD not long after that. I guess I'll never find out who he really was, will I?"

"You might," I felt the need to say, as a chill shot straight up my spine. "I don't know why I said that … just a feeling. I'd say that little guy did you a big favor."

"My friend, Louise, she's still in Camarillo State Hospital, the mental institution. She still sees all these strange people and has weird visions. She can't turn the stuff off. They've even given her electrical shock treatments. Some of these drugs make people real live crazy, Dana. It's scary. You're smart to abstain."

I snuck a quick peek and was surprised to see Louis edging my way without a studio executive near him. "I think you're right," I said to Rose-mary.

"Excuse me, Dana. But I see Richard Darvis across the room. He has an actor that's perfect for my new film. Nice talking to you," she said and she hurried on across the soundstage.

As I turned, Louis Lamprais was only feet away from me and carrying a plate on which he was placing oysters, shrimp and crab. With each item selected, he would pause and his beautiful eyes slowly moved down to my feet and back up the full length of my body to my stunned green eyes.

Suddenly feeling bold, I toasted him with my glass of champagne.

He nodded and flashed me a dazzling smile.

After finishing off that glass of champagne, I placed my empty on a tray held by a waiter, and before I could pick up another glass, Louis was right there beside me. Next, he handed me a fresh glass of champagne with the most beguiling smile on his handsome face.

"Allow me, mademoiselle!" he said in his sexy French accent while gazing into my eyes.

Unexpectedly feeling weak in my knees, I managed, "Merci beaucoup," toasting him before I sipped champagne, thinking two can play this game. Then warm and wonderful sensations wafted down to my toes and up into my brain. *Viva la France* was my thought!

"It is my pleasure," he said, toasting me with his fresh glass of champagne.

I had to admit that his approach was direct, but he still gave me butterflies as I recalled the tempestuous love scenes in *Farewell, My Love* and *Gabriella's Dance*. His face had served me well in acts of self-love. I was more than willing to try out those lips, on camera or off.

For a moment, our eyes locked. Then I intentionally lowered my eyes to reach for a large shrimp perched on the tall mountain of cracked ice so artfully arranged on the table.

"Allow me, ma cherie," he said, moving closer. He placed his glass on the table and removed a shrimp from his plate, holding the succulent shrimp up to my lips as his eyes moved from my eyes to my lips and back up to my eyes. "It would be my pleasure..." he started to say, as I opened my mouth and bit into the shrimp just short of his fingertips.

Still gazing into his gorgeous eyes, I chewed as delicately as possible before swallowing. Then, I seductively licked my lips and lowered my eyes, trying to ignore the slow trembling deep down inside me.

"I will be more than happy to feed you the rest," he said, "If you will allow me to feed you one small bite at a time." He paused and appeared to study me. "You know how beautiful you are. Thousands of men and women have sung your praises. You would make me a very happy man indeed if you allowed me to remind you of your beauty every day, shall we say, forever?"

What a great line, I thought, sipping champagne with my eyes glued on his.

Louis was exquisite. That was true in spite of the fact that part of me wanted to tell him he was full of shit, while the other part was willing to go along with his silly game.

After placing my glass on the table, I selected a large shrimp that I lightly dipped in the cocktail sauce before holding it up in front of his sensuous mouth. My gaze was steady as I positioned a napkin under the shrimp, since I didn't want to soil his pretty ruffled dress shirt.

Hesitating only briefly, Louis opened his mouth, with his eyes still on mine, as I stuffed the entire shrimp into his mouth. That surprised him. The look on his face made me laugh, as he tried to politely chew and swallow, but his eyes continued to smile.

"We could play great scenes together, ma cherie," he said, taking the napkin to wipe his mouth. "You are as beautiful a woman as you are an actress. I find you to be one of the most beautiful women in the world."

"Even now?" I teased, trying not to laugh, for our playful exchange was being observed by countless others as though we were perhaps doing a scene together in a film.

"Any day in the century."

"You are most gracious and most charming. Merci beaucoup."

He reached for my hand, bringing it up to his lips to kiss once, twice, three times, each kiss sending a chill up my spine that was impossible to ignore.

"You have captured my heart. Your emerald eyes have me hypnotized. Would you consider being my leading lady in my next motion picture, since you so perfectly fit the description of Victoria Rutherford? For me, you are Victoria."

"That sounds like a wonderful idea, but who does your producer or director have in mind for the role?"

"I see no problem in convincing my producer or director of my impartial wisdom in selecting you. My taste in women is impeccable, especially when it comes to fine actresses." Once again, he lifted my hand to his lips, and turning it over, he kissed my palm. "I have wanted to meet you for a very long time. Waiting for this moment has only increased my appetite for … emeralds." His eyes stopped at my cleavage before they moved on up to my eyes. "I have a distinct weakness for emeralds." Again, he kissed my palm, adding a touch of tongue that time.

Talk about temperatures rising!

Even with that ridiculous line coming out of his beautiful mouth, he had me all wrapped up in an instant. I rarely fell for actors. But I wanted this one, and that was in spite of all the gossip columnists rapidly taking notes on that soundstage at that very moment. We were sure to be news by morning, if not by the late edition.

"I am Louis Lamprais," he whispered, "Would you care to fuck?" A mischievous grin captured his wonderful face and champagne filled his sensuous mouth with his eyes still on mine.

"I'm Dana Scofield. Your place or mine?" I replied, noting the instant pleasure in his glorious eyes.

"Yours, of course."

I was aware that Louis wanted me to agree, although slapping his face was an option. Each of us had enough champagne that evening, and at that moment, we both apparently felt like being completely outrageous.

"I have always wanted to see how you Hollywood movie stars live. Perhaps you could show me … your etchings."

"Is that all you want to see, Louis?"

At once, his eyes scanned my body and he reached out to touch my hair. "I want to see it all… to touch it all… to taste it all. I have wanted to make love to you from the first moment I saw you on the screen. It is the truth, Dana Scofield, the 100 percent truth," he said, followed by a soft, sexy sigh.

"Shall we?" I said, taking his arm.

"May I at least take you to dinner? We have only had hors d'oeuvres!"

"You will do fine as a main course. Besides, I can cook."

"O la-la! You can cook too?"

"Oui, oui, mon cheri!"

Standing in the parking lot beside my car, Louis took me fully into his arms and could he kiss. The kiss was wet, long, deep and wonderful. By the time we arrived at my place in Beverly Hills, it was plain that he approved of my home.

More champagne, fresh strawberries, whipped cream, Brie and crackers were placed on a tray. My brand new pink love nest was finally about to be properly initiated.

Once we were locked inside my feminine bedroom, Louis kissed my neck and nibbled on my earlobes as he whispered, "I cannot believe that this is happening," and he held me close as we passionately kissed.

"That's my line," I said, hardly able to believe his words as my heart began to race.

"You are beautiful. But I am not telling you anything new, am I, ma cherie?"

He kissed me again and again and again. It was wonderful. Passionate. Wild.

"You too are beautiful and you know it, don't you, my dear, sweet, wonderful man?"

"We are two of the beautiful people, oui?" He twirled me around so we could see ourselves in my cheval glass, "Another Clark Gable and Vivien Leigh, perhaps? Our film will live forever. Our children and grandchildren will be proud of us. Together, we shall be magnificent!"

"Do you really think Colossal will cast me as Victoria?"

"I made the request before I even met you."

"You did?"

"Oui, ma cherie."

He kissed me again. And Louis Lamprais could really kiss!

"So you needn't fuck me to be my leading lady." Again, we kissed, with the kiss longer, wetter, deeper. "You must only fuck me if you want to fuck me and only suck me if you want to suck me. You understand?"

"Oh, oui!"

Louis kissed me again and again. He traced my lips with the tip of his tongue and brushed my lips with his, our breathing intermingling.

"I will not force you to make love unless you want me to force you … then I will force you." He kissed me with even greater passion, tongues blending, and then, he playfully paused. "Do you want me to make love to you, Dana Scofield?"

"Oui! Oui!" I squealed, running my hands over his magnificent shoulders. "I want you to make love to me, Louis Lamprais," and I ran my fingers through his silky hair and pulled his face closer to mine as I said, "and I want to make love to you."

His hands moved down over my backsides, perhaps to sense the warmth of my willing flesh under my clingy dress. Cupping my derriere, he pressed me into him hard to let me know that he was ready for love. Loosening his tie, he watched my fingers move to unbutton his shirt, which he swiftly peeled off and tossed aside.

I reached back to unzip my dress, and he stopped me. "Allow me," he said, unzipping my dress and swiftly pulling it off. There was further protest as I started to take off my bra.

"Patience, mi amour!" He stopped me again.

Wearing only his gold silk bikini, his body was even more exquisite than I remembered from his films, perfectly toned and perfectly tanned. Louis was a cameraman's dream.

"Allow me," Louis said, removing my bra, which he dropped to the floor. Then, he kissed my lips, my eyes, my cheeks, my chin, caressing one of my breasts as he moved me toward my turned down bed. After lifting me onto the bed, he bent down to kiss each of my breasts in turn, as his perfectly manicured hand slowly moved down my back in a long, lingering caress.

When I reached for the top of my panty hose, once again, Louis stopped me. Soon, one of my nipples was in his teasingly talented mouth as he sucked and licked until my nipple was hard and erect. The sweet pleasure was driving me wild as my deeper needs increased. Now, both my nipples were gently rubbed with his nose as his tongue moved across my chest, back and forth, as his fingers slipped into the top of my panty hose and swiftly pulled them down. My stockings and his bikini soon crumpled on the floor.

I partially sat up to pull him closer. His tongue explored mine with a passion that was building higher within each of us.

"Your skin is as I imagined," he whispered, "Like velvet woven by angels. You are so beautiful ... to touch you for me is heaven."

Again, his mouth savored my nipple, pleasing, titillating, one nipple, and then, the other. His head moved on down, his kisses covering my belly as he happily tasted of my flesh.

"Tell me what you want, my sweet. I want to please you ... to satisfy all your desires ... to fulfill your wildest dreams and fantasies."

"Whatever you want, Louis," I could hardly talk, my breathing uneven as I looked into his beautiful eyes. I was ready for just about anything.

"I want to taste you," he said, kissing my thighs, licking my flesh, as he gently pushed me back and spread my legs. He kissed the soft flesh of my belly and his wonderful mouth moved on down. "I want to drink from you... to drink deep..."

Opening his mouth, he fully tasted, which instantly sent a pleasurable shiver through my entire body. I felt his warm, wonderful mouth and tongue on me, licking and sucking, driving me wild, giving me pleasure greater than all my fantasies together. Louis appeared to relish the fullness of the lips between my legs as much as he did my mouth as he gently moved over the small hardness in perfect rhythm to increase my pleasure, as I began to writhe and moan on my bed.

The gratification was increasing by the second, intense pleasure streaming into my arms and down both my legs and up into my brain, filling my entire body with a throbbing, glorious bliss. His nimble fingers toyed with my nipples as he drank in my essence until I was forced to cry out, "Yes ... yes!" in response to his adept persuasion.

All my fantasies turned into reality on that night. I came again in minutes, crying out, "Oh, my god, Louis ... my god," as my entire body throbbed in pleasure that rushed down my legs and arms and up into my head again, pleasure so great I thought I might pass out. No one besides Jeffrey or Scott had been able to do that for me before. I fucking loved it.

Finally, feeling over-sensitized, I pleaded, "Stop! Please stop!" pushing his mouth away. It was just too much.

Slowly and gently, he stopped, gently running his hand up and down my thigh in a calming motion. Finally, Louis lay beside me, tracing his forefinger over my flushed flesh.

"May I kiss you?" he inquired.

"Where?"

"Anywhere you like."

We met halfway for a sweet, lingering kiss.

"Isn't it time to satisfy you?"

"The night is young." Again, he kissed me with greater passion. "I want it to be good for you."

"You're fantastic, Louis. I can't believe how fast you made me come."

Again, we kissed, that time longer.

"You would like more? Oui?"

"Oui, oh, oui!"

He started to move down the bed again but I stopped him. "How about a champagne break?"

"Oui?" His beautiful head was propped in his hand as he appeared to watch me closely.

"After champagne, strawberries and whipped cream, I might taste good to you again."

"You would taste good to me right now," he said, kissing my breast and moving his soft, full, seductive lips over my warm, flushed flesh. "I could well survive this very night just by eating you. You taste wonderful, ma cherie."

We kissed.

Soon, our arms and legs were again wrapped around each other. Our bodies pressed tighter together in sensual delight.

Finally, Louis popped the cork and poured champagne into two crystal glasses etched with doves in eager anticipation of a long night of love.

# Chapter 6

The rhythm and delights of sensual love continued into the wee hours, with only intermittent periods of sleep, before Louis was once more aroused and ardently inspired to awaken me to continue our long night of passion. We had discovered an equal in each other in terms of an appetite for sex and an enthusiasm for bedroom calisthenics. We adored sex. Relished sex. Thrived on sex. Each of us was uninhibited, inquisitive and experimental in our expressions of carnal knowledge. Each had his or her own brand of beauty, talent, intelligence and vanity. We were a perfect couple at that particular moment in my life.

I was staggered by the man's sheer stamina and genuine playfulness, mesmerized by his great need to satisfy a woman. It was something he accomplished with savoir-faire and French proficiency. Louis Lamprais was a rare find when it came to my search for a lover, a prize worthy of tying to my bedpost, even if he weren't into that sort of thing. It seemed I had found the gander with the golden cock, for Louis could wave his magic wand throughout the long night and into the morning hours. He was a better lover than Jeffrey or Scott, and that was saying something. Surprisingly, Scott had been replaced by a model with greater prowess and mastery. Poor Scott was no longer Great Scott. That summer produced many surprises.

Fortunately, I'd remembered to reverse the large red heart magnet on the refrigerator, my signal to Florence not to knock on or open my bedroom door until she was called. Over the years, we had worked out a system, with her my co-conspirator. She was tactful and considerate of my wants and needs. Not just any man spent the night in my bed, only prime candidates for eroticism, genuine love, or connubial bliss. On that morning, at least in my mind, Louis topped the list in all categories. I thought Florence might be pleased.

She was never really that sold on Scott and could be a gem in providing biased support. Florence had not yet met a man "good enough for her Dana."

I peeked at the clock.

10:30.

Louis was sleeping and my appetite for Eros thoroughly quenched. The thought of yet another encounter seemed pointless. I loved chocolate too, but too much once made me sick. After slipping out of bed, I made my way to the bathroom where my new bidet was a godsend throughout the long night.

The window over the whirlpool tub was of frosted glass, white butter-flies and roses filtered in the morning light. My new shower lined in pink marble had six showerheads that sprayed in different directions. I could choose one, two, or all. The twin sinks of pink marble were inlaid with roses and gold leaf. The cord on my dressing room phone reached to the tub. That line also rang in the kitchen. The phone beside the bed was the one on which to call Florence.

"Hello, Scofield residence," Florence answered in her professional tone after two rings.

"Florence," I whispered, "I have a gentleman in my room. It would be lovely if you could prepare us two cheese omelets, say with zucchini, tomato and basil, orange juice and English muffins ... and lots of strong coffee."

"Would you like your breakfast served in your room?"

"No, the breakfast room is fine. I'll call you back if he objects."

"When would you like breakfast?"

"In about an hour. It's Louis Lamprais," I whispered, "The French actor who starred in *Gabriella's Dance*. Do you remember him?"

"Oh, yes! My, he is incredibly handsome and debonair and such a fine actor! I'll be happy to make his breakfast. Would you like some fresh straw-berries too?"

Quickly glancing at the empty bowl, I briefly remembered how the strawberries were eaten. "No strawberries, raspberries perhaps? And how about that Columbian coffee that Paula gave me?"

Upon seeing Louis's eyes flutter open, I wondered how much he had heard. He reached out to me, palm upturned, fingers beckoning.

"We'll be down in about half an hour, Florence," I said, hanging up the telephone. Then I bent over and kissed his palm. "Would you like to shower alone or with me?"

"Silly question! Why would I shower alone when I can shower with the most beautiful woman in the world?"

"You are great for my ego."

"Only your ego?" He grabbed my hand and pulled me to him.

The kiss was tasty.

"Come on, handsome, time for a shower and shave." I lightly ran my fingertips over his stubble. "I have razors, electric or regular, shaving cream, and after shave from Rome, in addition to a brand new toothbrush just for you. There is also a robe that might fit you."

He scowled. "Louis will not wear a robe that has been worn by some other scoundrel who has been in your bed. I do not even want to see this ... robe!"

"Picky, picky. I'll get one especially for you!"

He toyed with the sash of my pink silk robe and quickly glanced around the room. "No pink, merci? I think you like pink very much, but pink is not for Louis."

"How about green to match the flecks in your eyes?"

The warm water felt good on my weary body as four showerheads streamed, and even though I hadn't thought I was up for it, I came one more time. We both did. Together. There was no end in sight of orgasmic delight, day or night, with Louis Lamprais. Finally, we made our way downstairs for breakfast.

Florence fussed over Louis like a mother hen, making sure he had everything that his little heart desired. Her attention seemed to both amuse and delight him. Many of the famous had graced my home, several celebrated the world over. Handsome actors only had to make the slightest suggestion and Florence was likely to sprint to the heart of Beverly Hills to fulfill a desire for a special type of food. Even after five years, Florence remained star struck.

Louis expressed his admiration for my home. He liked the view from my breakfast room of the swimming pool and the rose garden. Birds flocked to a feeder on the branch of a tree covered with lacy purple blossoms. The naughty blue jays chased off the smaller birds. We had another cup of coffee on the patio where I showed Louis how to hand-feed the blue jays that cleverly snatched crackers from his upraised hand.

Quickly glancing at his watch, Louis said, "A limo is picking me up at my hotel in an hour. I have wardrobe fittings at Marvel. The *Duke of Orleans* starts filming on Friday. Would it be possible for you to drop me off at the Beverly Hills Hotel?" He paused. "I don't want to show up at the studio in my tux."

It was a beautiful morning with the hotel only ten minutes away.

"I would like to see you again, but this evening I have a prior commitment," he said as I pulled my car up in front of the hotel lobby. "Tomorrow I'm invited to a party. Would you do me the honor of attending with me? It's black tie."

Nothing was going to keep me away from the beach party in Malibu that Friday. Phil and Eric were likely to be there. By that time, I had learned to hedge my bets with men, even though Louis was the most handsome, famous and highly sexed actor I'd ever had, and even though he wanted me as "his Victoria." Only time would tell if that dream came true.

"I'm so sorry, Louis, but I have other plans for tomorrow. How about dinner on Saturday evening?"

"Oui! May I take you to some fine restaurant...just the two of us alone together?"

"Oui! And, on Sunday I'm having a brunch in honor of a new friend, Beau Kandell. He's a Texas cowboy and wants to meet Paula, my artist friend, whose paintings you so admired. The other guests will be fellow actors and artists. You will stay over for brunch on Sunday, oui?"

"Oui! You say the man is ... a friend?"

"He owns one of Paula's paintings and is most eager to meet her. All my guests will be delighted to meet you as well. You'll make two guests of honor on Sunday, oui?"

"You flatter me, of course."

"However, on Saturday night I will need to get some rest or I'll have dark circles under my eyes on Sunday. And I just hate that, don't you?"

He leaned over and lightly kissed my lips.

"An early dinner and dessert in your room? I look forward to eating you again. You are delicious!" he whispered, closing the car door and blowing me a kiss before he entered the hotel.

Back home again, I made more telephone calls to extend invitations to my brunch. Phil and Eric were off the list. After discussing the menu with Florence, I called Paula.

Maria told me that Paula was out on the beach with Hannah and the children. Poor Hannah. Her husband, Harold, was killed in an automobile accident out on the highway two years before. Hannah was still trying to cope with the loss. Apparently, Harold was an excellent father to her children and a fabulous husband for her.

"How are you doing?" Paula breathlessly inquired.

"I got laid last night, again and again and again. It was absolutely marvelous."

"And the lucky man was?"

"Louis Lamprais, French actor extraordinaire, who just happens to be the most fabulous, stupendous, outrageous and sexiest piece of work I've ever had in my life, bar none."

"Better than Scott?"

"Pardon my French, but Louis can fuck circles around Scott standing on his head."

"That's an interesting position!" Paula said, laughing.

"You'll meet him on Sunday at a brunch in your honor!"

"My honor? What are you talking about?"

"You have to promise to be there ... PROMISE ME! Beau Kandell is who I'm talking about. He's coming to L.A. and I'm honoring him with your presence at a champagne brunch at noon sharp on Sunday. The man has class, Paula. He's sending me a case of Dom Perignon, chilled."

"He does have class."

"He's dying to meet you."

I lit cigarette. All night, Louis had objected to my smoking. But a cigarette after sex was essential, at least in my mind. That was the only thing about him that bothered me then, our breaks short-lived. I was amazed by how good I felt after so little sleep. Numerous injections of pure testosterone do great things for a girl, especially when injected with passion par excellence!

"Sunday?" Paula said, hesitating."Sure, why not? I am curious about the Texas tycoon you made sound so fantastic."

"Harlan Evans is coming. I know you love Harlan."

"Harlan is having an exhibit at the Corcoran Gallery in Washington, DC this fall. That is such an honor! He's becoming world famous and making a fortune in the process. It will be fun to see him. Who else is invited?"

"Harriet, of course. And Louis."

"My!"

"Irwin Thomas, the assistant director down in Texas, will be here. He and Beau hit it off riding the range on Beau's horses. Katie and Brad are coming. The rest aren't set yet. Not too many. With large groups I miss out on too much."

"How about Jamie?" Paula sounded tentative.

After a brief moment of silence, I said, "Do you really think it's a good idea, all things considered?"

After another pause, she said, "I don't even know if he's going to be in town this weekend. I'll find out tonight."

"Listen, if you want Jamie here, fine. You are my best friend. It's just that a tall, blond and handsome Texas cowboy will be awfully disappointed if you show up with a tall, dark and handsome Georgia peach."

"I don't know. It might be interesting!"

"Your game, darling. Play it anyway you like. You know how I love complications in other people's lives."

"So tell me all about your wild night of passion."

"He drank champagne from my vagina, ate strawberries from my navel and a few other sensitive spots, and licked whipped cream from my entire body. At times, I wondered what he liked best, the whipped cream or me? That tongue of his is so damn talented! Louis is one for the book, Paula. Are my memoirs ever going to be hot!"

# Chapter 7

The cool water felt refreshing against my bare flesh as I swam back and forth in the pool to get in a good workout. The sun was directly overhead, which made the water warm. During the hottest months, the heater was never turned on, but rarely before July. California June nights were chilly. The temperature tended to drop dramatically right after sunset. Whenever possible I swam in the morning. I never liked cold water for swimming, even back in Indiana.

Frisky was barking at the squirrels again. The squirrels had his number, chattering up in the tree as though telling him: 'Give it up, you idiot! You'll never catch me.' But Frisky barked anyway, running around in dog crazy circles. By the time I was out of the pool, the dog was really irritating me.

"Give it up, Frisky. You're being obnoxious," I hollered, pulling on a terry cloth robe before I entered the house.

The dog ran in after me. Wherever I went, Frisky was sure to follow. He was crazy about Florence and slept on her bed when she wasn't quick enough to shut him out at night. Frisky tended to scratch in the middle of the night, sometimes shaking the whole bed. But he also could be downright adorable.

Swimming had made me hungry. I sliced a peach and half a banana into a bowl, adding yogurt and wheat germ. Florence was cleaning upstairs. The telephone with the long extension cord reached the umbrella table. Shirley Ralston hadn't returned my call yet, so I called her again.

"Shirley, dahling," I said in my most affected Hollywood tone, trying to annoy her, "I do hope that you're planning on Sunday afternoon. My little soiree just won't be the same without you and Hal."

"You're full of shit, dear," she said, laughing.

I laughed with her.

"I love you, anyway, Dana. Whatever have you been doing with yourself, Miss Scofield? Hal and I miss you. You need to come out to the country and relax, take in some fresh air away from all the stagnant hot air trapped in Beverly Hills."

"The air can be pretty putrid around here. The fragrant farts of the filthy rich. Let's face it, Shirley, show business can be a stinking business."

"True."

"So how's life in the country?"

"It's great! Neither of us really regrets the move so far, except sometimes I miss my friends in the city. The people out here are definitely different, in some ways more genuine, in others ... a real pain in the ass."

"What do you expect all the way out in Calabasas? I hope the horses are worth it. From where I sit, you're all the way to hell and gone. Who shovels all that horseshit, anyway?"

"We hire someone, mostly. But you know Hal, he's full of shit himself. What's a little horseshit to keep him honest and real? Hal can use the exercise."

I loved Hal and Shirley Ralston. They were among some of the good people.

"Hal is writing a new screenplay... you know, sex and violence, the stuff that sells in Hollywood these days. People don't seem to be able to get enough of the stuff. I guess it's a statement of our times. The storyline is rah-rah America and anti-North Vietnam, anti-Russia and anti-China. We've got to keep our kids shipping out and putting their lives on the line over there in Vietnam, keep the propaganda patriotic, loud and clear, with a messianic message thrown in for good measure. I mean, don't we have to save the whole fucking world single-handedly, with John Wayne leading us through the jungles? I just heard on the radio that we've had heavy casualties in the Kontum Province. This war makes me sick, Dana. I cry nearly every time I read the damn newspapers. What the hell are we doing over there in the first place?"

There was a long pause as I had a sudden urge to change the subject. "May I count on you and Hal on Sunday? You'll be my token intellectual rebel rousers, God bless America crusaders, and Calabasas pacifists all wrapped into one. How about it?"

"Sure. Maybe someone will actually be interested in what I have to say. Out here we have the 'kill the gooks' mentality, along with the rah-rah patriots and the flower children over in Topanga, running around talking about peace and love stoned out of their fucking minds, or else chanting Hare Krishna and rattling tambourines. Me, I'm just a witness of the times."

There was another long pause before I said. "You're a dear, Shirley. I'm glad that you and Hal can make it on Sunday."

"Sure. Hal loves real Texas cowboys and I'm crazy about art. It seems like a good trade off for a Sunday in the city. It'll be nice to see you and Paula again."

"How is your painting coming along?"

"It isn't, mostly. Lately, I've been working on this collage, clipping pictures and advertisements from fashion magazines, along with news magazines and those newspaper pictures of the war: Dirty-faced, fighting and dying GIs of all colors, shapes and sizes, not to mention the displaced, terrorized Vietnamese civilians mixed in with all the gauche of Tiffany, Cartier, Chanel, and those disgusting ads for female crotch sprays and strawberry douches! It's my special wake-up call, or propaganda, depending on your point of view."

"I see." I was starting to feel uncomfortable.

"I've been thinking about doing another one with pictures of the starving kids in Africa and the street waifs in South America combined with lavish pictures of food from *Palatial Homes and Gardens*, *Five Star Eating* and *Architectural Wonders*. I've already started clipping with that one in mind."

"I'm glad that you're both coming to brunch on Sunday," was my immediate response. On occasion, Shirley's social conscience could bother me then. She always had a banner to wave about things she thought needed to be changed. "I'm sure you make people think about things they might not consider otherwise," I added, knowing I was in that group.

Shirley laughed.

"I guess I'm good at that, although Hal says that I should keep my big mouth shut. Lately, I'm seriously thinking of joining the protests against the war. Several actor and writer friends already have. I've attended a few meetings."

"With Hal writing a pro-war screenplay?"

"He's writing it and getting well paid for it, I might add. That doesn't mean he believes in the crap. It's a studio assignment." She paused. "We've had a few heated arguments lately. My husband doesn't like being called a 'studio whore'! The next script he's doing on spec is about the civil rights movement and all the changes going on down in Mississippi. I'll be surprised if he can sell that one. Aren't writers supposed to be the conscience of the people? It's been like that for centuries, but it seldom happens in Hollywood. In my opinion, the studio execs are a bunch of gutless wonders with money their god."

"Like you said, Shirley, sex and violence are the name of the game in Show Biz. I look forward to seeing you on Sunday."

I ended the conversation before she could trap me into one of her long philosophical diatribes. Shirley had opinions on things I didn't want to think about then, because most of them were downright depressing.

A young cousin of mine from Indiana was recently drafted and in army boot camp at Fort Hood "learning to go get the gooks," as he said. What bothered me the most was that my cousin had the mentality of a gook himself. Still, I didn't want him coming home in a pine box, because Aunt Helen and Uncle Harvey would never get over it. Colin was the only boy in a family of six and his daddy wanted him to take over the farm one day. Fat chance of that, I thought, although the army might teach Colin a few things, make a man out of him. I thought there was a fat chance of that, too. On that day, I didn't really want to think about Colin or Vietnam. Instead, I was thinking about what to wear for my dinner date with Phil. Shirley had definitely put a damper on my mood.

The hot shower felt great. Upon further reflection, I thought Shirley might like a picture of my new pink bathroom for one of her collages, probably the one with the starving children. That thought gave me chills. I planned to write checks to my favorite charities, those that helped starving children. It was the best I could do. I had no illusions about saving the world. But I could make some donations, maybe volunteer at Children's Hospital once a week, something that never happened in those times.

Talking to Shirley always made me think. Maybe it was good for me, but not too damn often. At that time, my conscience couldn't afford many friends like her. Those were things to think about much later, like in 20 years when I wasn't really having any fun anymore.

The blouse was peach silk, the skirt full, off-white linen. My toenails were peachy pink and my legs tan enough to forego pantyhose, one of the blessings of summer. Phil was taking me to the Matador in Santa Monica. I loved most kinds of food, and I was dressed for just about anywhere. The large gold hoop earrings went well with my gold chains. The heaviest chain was covered with solid gold charms collected over the years, mainly gifts for birthdays and Christmas. The tiny Ferris wheel was my first Christmas gift from Jeffrey Waters when I was 16. The wheel turned around and the itsy bitsy seats moved back and forth. I had never seen another one like it. It was my favorite charm.

On my first date with Jeff the summer after my sophomore year in high school, we went to the Indiana State Fair. The first time he kissed me was right on top of the Ferris wheel. There we were way up on the top, as another couple got on at the bottom, and he kisses me. I had kissed other guys, but not way up in the air. I was too nervous to really kiss him back. The seat started rocking back and forth. I was never crazy about heights. In those days, airplanes even made me nervous.

That kiss was nothing like those that followed. Kisses he planted all over my naked body from head to toe. That was a first I will never forget, and a memory that Jeffrey was happy to reinforce as often as I liked. We had shared tons of wonderful memories. Jeffrey was my first love. The guy I thought might be my only love back in high school, my first fantastic sexual experience. For that reason, every time I wore my charm necklace and saw that Ferris wheel, I remembered how much I loved him and the incredible sex we had for two years. During those years, I never looked at another guy. My guess was that he never looked at another girl. We were not only lovers but best friends. We never kept secrets from each other. There was trust, something I hadn't experienced with another man since.

And yet, during my senior year, I won these beauty contests: Miss Indianapolis. Miss Indiana. First Runner up in the Miss United States Pageant. That year I signed my first Hollywood film contract that included a small role in a poorly released detective film that starred actor David Jansen. I had six lines and was forced to wear these five-inch high heels that nearly crippled me, in addition to the tightest sweater and shortest skirt I've ever worn. Lucky me! I was cast as the brunette bimbo!

Not long after high school graduation my life totally changed. Jeffrey was already attending the University of Indiana in Indianapolis. He had chosen that school to be near me instead of going to Yale where he ended up in law school. By 1967, Jeffrey Waters had his own law practice in Indianapolis. Daddy told me he was doing nicely. For a long time I'd known about his marriage to Cindy Hanson, my close friend in high school. They were married two years after I left Indianapolis for my Hollywood film career.

Cindy and I were both Geminis born a week apart. The last I heard, they had two children, a boy and a girl. I sincerely hoped that they were happy. Mostly, I tried not to think about Jeffrey, because I'd never stopped wondering if I'd made a mistake by not marrying him. I was 18 when he proposed to me at my senior prom. That year I didn't want to marry anyone, even though I loved him madly. There were just too many things that I wanted to do before settling down, things I felt I could never do with a husband and children. That summer right after high school I left for Hollywood. Not long after that, I was sort of a movie star. I loved to act. Mostly, I loved my life. But every time Jeffrey Waters entered my mind he would tug at my heart.

Phil picked me up at seven sharp in his 1966 white Ford Mustang that matched Paula's. On the way to the restaurant, he kept apologizing about the car. I thought he may have been intimidated by my home and my red Mercedes. He chattered on nonstop during our first two drinks, even though I tried my best to reassure him.

"Paula's car is the same as yours, with the same white leather interior. I love her car. My Mercedes has a white leather interior, too. I just love white leather in cars, don't you?"

"But a Mercedes is a Mercedes."

"And a Mustang is a Mustang. Have another drink, Phil. You'll feel better."

He ordered another drink.

We both did.

Phil was acting so nervous that he was making me nervous. That bartender made great margaritas. The food was tasty. During dinner we talked show business. Halfway through, I agreed to have a third margarita. I didn't exactly feel drunk, but the tequila had definitely started to alter my perception. I ordered a fourth margarita, which was way over the top for me. And with each sip, Phil started to look better and better, not that he hadn't already looked pretty good. I just hadn't thought about having sex with him on that night until that moment.

Phillip Stacey was ruggedly handsome with raw animal magnetism and bulging biceps. He was attractive in a less refined way than perhaps Louis or Scott. His dark curly hair and soulful brown eyes made him look like a 'lovable heel.' On TV, he had played a gigolo more than once. He worked out religiously. The dark hair on his chest was visible through his partly open shirt where shiny gold chains helped to flaunt the merchandise.

Throughout dinner, it was plain that Phil had the hots for me. A woman just knows. His roommate, Eric, had not even asked me for another date and that pissed me off. I was really attracted to Eric. Earlier that evening, Phil had appeared intimidated, since by then I had appeared in 10 top box office motion pictures. Obviously, Phil was eager to make it as an actor. My guess was that he would be willing to forget about his art gallery if he could only be a 'star'.

After four margaritas, Phil began to act normal and as though maybe he was dating a normal woman with normal wants and needs. The tequila had significantly lowered my resistance, with sex suddenly foremost on my mind, especially considering the action of the past 24 hours. My libidinous urges were up front and center. Blame it on Louis Lamprais!

Suddenly, I remembered the rape scene with Phil as my attacker: how he had torn off my dress and pushed me down on the floor, pinning me with his powerful thighs, kneeling and forcefully spreading my legs. The recollection turned me on, kinky as it might sound, and even though my double did all the rehearsal. Initially, I hadn't even remembered his name, but on that night I remembered how he had tried to date my double. Helen was married to a grip much larger and stronger than Phil, a Neanderthal-type, so it was wise of Phil to back off.

All at once, Phil's husky shoulders and huge biceps captured my full attention, not to mention the size of his thighs. He reminded me of the lifeguards in those beach movies I tagged: *Bridget Goes Bananas.* Out of the blue, I was beginning to wonder what Phil would be like in bed. Did he measure up to his image? He seemed sensitive, besides having a great body. The more I consumed of that fourth margarita, the better Phil looked to me.

"What was it like when you raped me?" I inquired, gazing into his startled brown eyes.

Suddenly, the couple at the next table stopped talking and appeared shocked.

"On television," I said directly to them as a throwaway line.

Embarrassed, they turned away and stared at each other instead of at us.

My full attention was back on Phil, who had recovered nicely from my unforeseen question.

"It was hard work," he said, grinning. "There were 40 people on the set telling me what to do. It was my first rape." He then sipped from his fifth margarita, clearly feeling no pain, as his facial expression and body language registered intense interest in whatever else I might have to say.

"Your first?" I batted my big green eyes and new false eyelashes at him. "Have you raped anyone since?"

At that point, the couple across the aisle pretended not to listen, but I could see them hanging on our every word.

"Not lately," he said, swallowing with some difficulty.

At that point, the couple stopped talking. But they knew better than to turn and stare at us at our table.

"Off screen or on?" I inquired, providing our now rapt audience with something to really talk about after they got home. Blame it on the actress in my soul.

That was when Phil looked into my eyes and said, "I don't believe in forcing myself on a woman," in the most serious tone.

"Never?" I said, switching into my seductive screen siren mode as he was trying to figure out what was going on with me.

"Never," he said. "I've always felt that sex is a lot more fun with the full participation of both parties. Don't you agree?"

"I wasn't suggesting that you rape me," I said in feigned innocence, sipping my margarita and gazing into his eyes while peripherally noting the amazement on the faces of the now fully silent couple across the aisle.

"I just wondered what it might be like to be in bed with you ... to make love."

At that point, the woman dropped her fork. The man did nothing except stare straight ahead at his silent dinner companion.

In perfect control, with the stage presence of a true professional, I inquired, "What do you think, Phil?"

Still oblivious of our now captive audience across the aisle, Phil's eyes were fixed on mine as he said in a sexy tone, "I give free home demonstrations," and then he grinned, maybe to make sure I wasn't putting him on. "Anytime you're up for it ... I am."

"How about tonight?" I caressingly placed my hand on his as an added incentive.

He placed his hand on mine and said. "I'll pay the check and take you home for your free demonstration." Then he bent across the narrow table to softly kiss me. "You can change your mind, if you like. I won't hold you to it."

"I won't change my mind," I said and my tongue briefly mingled with his in a tangy taste of margarita. "Will you?"

"Not a chance."

Neither of us changed our minds.

Neither of us regretted it on that night.

It was the magic of margaritas.

Olé!

# Chapter 8

I had been looking forward to the summer solstice beach party all week. That Friday morning, Beau called for directions to my house. Everything seemed to be falling into place. And, regardless of his bulging muscles and swarthy good looks, Phil was fairly ordinary in bed. The all-American boy: Minimal foreplay, up, over, in and out, before a girl has really even gotten into it.

My role as the great seductress after too many margaritas was disclosed to Paula. What was I thinking? Phil was a nice enough guy, but I was not interested in a repeat performance. We were both very drunk and that much alcohol never produces great sex. I was so numb I faked an orgasm. It was the least that I could do. Louis was still Super Fuck.

That was the first time my friend called me a "slut puppy." Paula said I should start douching with Lysol. In the old days, women actually believed that stuff provided birth control, with most of those women called "Mommy." On the way to the beach, I stopped at a drugstore and bought some condoms, one box flavored. After all, we were celebrating the summer solstice: The return of the Sun. I planned on meeting a good-looking son of someone. Maybe I was a slut puppy?

Paula and Jamie had made considerable progress during the past week. They acted like two love struck teenagers. But then, Jamie was a teenager. He wouldn't even be 20 until August. I still had to wonder how Uncle Dan was dealing with his young and virile nephew getting it on with his ex-wife. During their marriage, Dan treated her more like a possession than his wife. The way he still acted around her made me think he hadn't begun to recover from the divorce, girlfriend or not.

It seemed strange that Dan was leaving Jamie at a beach with Paula and his prized Porsche and driving his station wagon up to Lake Arrowhead with the kids, his girlfriend, and her daughter, another college student Jamie's age. Later that day, I learned that Jamie was supposed to be taking some imaginary blonde to an imaginary beach party in Santa Monica. The soap opera plot of the life of my friend had taken a turn that had me eager for the very next installment. How good could Paula feel about Jamie lying to his uncle? Or even about him telling the truth? Dicey, no matter how he sliced it!

It was a fun beach party. All these great-looking guys started arriving, not all of them with dates and not all of them straight. Paula's neighbor, screenwriter Guy Hamilton, was known to play both sides in the game of love. But he always seemed more gay to me. Larry was straight enough. The striking black screenwriter was a really good friend to Paula and her kids.

That day, the men were wearing different types of swimwear, some with hairy chests, others bare-chested. Itsy bitsy bikinis flaunted the family jewels, making it hard to conceal the real deal. I was amazed by the number of yummy men. Before long, people were swimming, surfing, dancing, or sitting around with a margarita, sangria, or a beer. Everyone appeared to be having a really fun time.

Luckily, Eric arrived alone, and from the very first moment those blue eyes locked onto me, he was my constant companion, getting me drinks and waiting on me hand and foot. That made me feel good after not hearing from him. He liked my purple velour bikini with the gold peek-a-boo ring that better revealed my cleavage. Up until then, I was enjoying hungry glances from many other men on the patio or on the beach. My hair was up in twin ponytails, and fortunately, my new waterproof mascara and lipstick lived up to the advertisements.

Seated on a beach towel, I was sipping a margarita in the company of three interesting men, one of them, Eric. Paula's housekeeper, Maria, had cured my horrendous hangover with a cup of herb tea laced with Swedish Bitters! Nonetheless, I was pacing myself with the booze and grateful Phil was nowhere in sight. One of the other roommates, Johnny Hargrove, joined our group. The other man was Tom Levinson, a screenwriter working on a World War II drama for Colossal with Paul Newman or Steve McQueen as the possible male lead. The action was supposedly in the jungles of Africa with filming scheduled for the big island of Hawaii.

"How about a female colonel? I'd love to work in the jungles with Paul or Steve. Come on, Tom, use your imagination," I teased.

"There's a high class hooker the German commander flies in for his personal pleasure. Not a big role, but ..." Tom said, smiling, "You'd have to do a nude scene, of course."

At that point, all the men were smirking.

"Why do you screenwriters always have to be so sexist? How about a juicy script with a woman as the lead? Come on, Tom. Write me that one."

"You write that script."

"I just might. I could do a high class hooker, don't you think?"

All three men nodded and grinned.

"Isn't that something you've already done?" Johnny teased.

"Several times, darling. I always do classy hookers."

"You could play any part," Eric said. "You're a fantastic actress." His vivid blue eyes appeared to be glued to my cleavage. The margarita had obviously loosened him up. "You're so beautiful and talented, an excellent biological specimen of the female genus Homo-sapiens."

"I'm going to take that as a compliment, Dr. Whitley. Tell me ... are you more of a biologist or biochemist?"

"Today, I'm a biochemist. But you do great things for my chemistry and my biology!"

Suddenly, Johnny leapt to his feet. "Excuse me, but my lady has arrived. Catch you later," and he hurried across the patio toward a striking woman in green shorts and a white blouse with the most luxurious, long, red hair. She looked like a young Rita Hayworth.

"Johnny's lady is lovely," I said.

"Kathy is a pediatrician," Eric said. "Her practice is in Sherman Oaks. They've been dating for a year now. She's the real reason he moved to California. They met at the Club Med in Martinique, and the nicest part of it is, Kathy is as bright as she is beautiful. I think Johnny is ready to pop the question."

"Nice," Tom commented.

Johnny and Kathy were starting to dance.

"I like intelligent women," Tom said. "Does she have a single nurse or another female doctor in her office, a beautiful nursemaid might be nice to have around."

"I didn't know that you were a male chauvinist with a playboy mentality, Tom," I said to him.

"Afraid so, Dana. Heff happens to be a good friend."

"Naturally," I said, starting to get up.

At that moment, Eric leapt to his feet and extended his hand. "Allow me," he said, pulling me up to my feet. "Would you like to dance?"

"I'd love to," I replied.

Soon, Eric and I were on the dance floor, as Aretha Franklin sang out her recent recording of *RESPECT*. It was fun to dance to the rhythm of the beat.

After a short time, Larry announced, "It's body painting time!"

On a long table were numerous opened bottles of body paint of several different colors. Coffee cans held a large number of paint brushes. There were also cans of water, boxes of tissue, and an assortment of rags. In what seemed like only a few minutes, nearly everyone at the part was painting the exposed flesh of some other guest. I was painting a pink heart on Jamie's shoulder while Paula painted a red poinsettia on his chest. Eric painted a butterfly on my lower back right above my bikini bottoms, and my elegant butterfly with pink wings and gold and purple spots garnered lots of compliments. I had definitely brought out the biologist in Eric that time, and his effect on my biology and my chemistry was beginning to be outstanding.

The song playing over the stereo was *With A Little Help From My Friends* by Sergio Mendes and Brasil '66, as Eric and I did a slow, sexy rumba, while colorful, artsy designs began to appear on the bodies of nearly everyone attending the party. Soon, the bare flesh of those all around the patio and in the house was covered with wild and crazy designs in bright and vivid colors: Flowers and peace symbols showed up on arms, legs, chests, stomachs, backs, cheeks, and even a forehead. I had never before engaged in that kind of a fun activity at a beach party. The experience was psychedelic.

Snuggling together on the sand, Eric and I watched the bright orange ball of the sun slowly sink into a shimmering sea in a brilliance of red, orange, purple and gold as seagulls screeched above the waves. It was altogether romantic.

The Mexican food served on the buffet was truly tasty: tacos, chili rellenos, rice and beans, and the whole enchilada in several flavors prepared in several delicious styles: cheese, chicken and beef, most of it cooked by Paula's housekeeper, Maria. The magical brownies were made by friends who lived in Topanga Canyon and had grown their own stuff. I shared one with Eric that put us both in a remarkably mellow mood.

Later that evening, we climbed the stairs to the darkened, smoke-filled room where sandalwood incense intermingled with the identifiable aroma of high quality grass. Joints were being passed. Some guests sat on cushions near the wall with their eyes glazed. Others were sprawled on a paisley covered mattress in the middle of the room. Those with their backs to the wall vacantly stared into space, as Mary Jane took them on a magical journey to Never-Neverland.

Stan sat in the corner near the open window playing Dylan tunes on guitar. Another man accompanied him on harmonica, as Stan sang out, *Everybody Must Get Stoned* in his own stoned tone. Outside the window, the full moon rose higher than the smoky haze hanging near the ceiling.

Guy was wearing a flowing fuchsia and teal paisley guru gown and fuchsia turban, with purple peace symbols on each cheek and the Eye of Horus, an Egyptian hieroglyph, in black on his forehead. He was nowhere in this world as he made the Vulcan salute.

We sat on cushions on the floor with our backs to the wall, inhaling and exhaling, for an indefinite period of time. Then I realized I needed to use a bathroom. At that point, Stan was singing Dylan's, *The Times They Are A-Changing.*

As I stood, Eric did likewise. Then, we slowly made our way toward the door while trying not to step on anyone. Paula and Jamie were on the far side of the room, but I wasn't sure they had seen us. Then, much to my surprise, Phil walked through the door holding hands with a stacked blonde in hot pink hot pants and a hot pink strapless top. Fleetingly, I felt strange. After all, he had left my house at eight that morning after one last toss in the hay. I doubted Eric knew about that, but Phil did notice that Eric and I were holding hands.

Once we were out in the bright light of the hallway, I said, "I need to attend to my biology."

Eric smiled, with his blue eyes glazed, and I turned and headed down the hall. Eric was close behind me with the oddest look on his handsome face. He acted upset when I wouldn't let him into the bathroom with me.

"I'll just be a minute," I said, closing the door in his sad, stoned face.

Sitting there, it was a long, slow tinkle, something that could happen when I waited too long. In just minutes, there was a loud knock on the door. "Just a minute," I called out.

While washing my hands, there was another louder knock on the door.

"Let me in," Eric said in a stoned tone.

When I opened the door, I happened to glance down and Eric's biology was up and ready. "Do you need to use the bathroom?" I asked him, trying to pretend that I hadn't noticed.

"I need to talk to you!" he said in an urgent tone.

Before I knew it, Eric was in the bathroom and the door was closed behind him. Then he grabbed me and pulled me to him. "You're driving me crazy!" he said, ravishing my mouth with his open and eager mouth, as his tongue filled my mouth in a wild, animalistic kiss.

Instantly, Eric's passion spilled into me with some force, as his wild hands moved over my warm body in the most amazing manner. Up and down and around raced his hands, caressing my behind as I fiercely kissed him back. By then, I had completely surrendered and wrapped my arms around him. My mouth opened wider to more fully respond to his wonderful, uncontrollable, wild desires.

Eric was on fire.

And he really had me going. "You're going to mess up all my pretty little pictures," I teased, interrupting his fiery kiss. "Then what will I do?"

"I'll paint you more," he moaned, kissing me with even greater ardor as his wonderful hands moved over me in the most fantastic way, his hot biological hands, to which I willingly and joyfully responded. I was beginning to really enjoy the smooth warmness of his flesh as I explored his taut male muscles in eager anticipation of every conceivable pleasure that might be just ahead..

"I'll paint you everywhere," Eric groaned, "Paint you anything, anywhere you want." His fire was flaming higher and higher and higher.

We kissed again and again.

The heat was wonderful as his hands deftly moved inside my bikini bottoms to fondle my hot behind. I adored every sensation as his hands slid over my lower back and circled my hips in a motion that reminded me of needs I hadn't even been aware of until he brought the matter up.

And, believe me, his matter was up!

My hot little hands were inside his trunks, savoring his taut behind, moving up onto his strong back, as he held me even closer, his hot hands exploring the entire surface of my body. I was so turned on by his sudden and unexpected needs, his urgent desire for me, his sudden surge of passion made me feel like a wild animal as I pushed down his trunks with both my hands.

"Here, Eric? Do you want me here?"

"Yes! Here! NOW!"

Instantly sinking to the floor, we both quickly dispensed with our bathing suits. His fingers were soon exploring my wetness as I lay back on the cold bathroom tiles to spread my legs so he could kneel and fill me with up his wild self. In seconds, Eric was deep inside me, filling me up rather nicely, the two of us moving in wild and carefree abandonment, the pleasure increasing by the second. The grass may have helped Eric to sustain himself long enough for my passion to build to its own exquisite peak.

"I want you to come," Eric demanded, pumping his manhood in and out of me, "I want you to come. I want you to come... NOW!" he commanded in his male magnificence.

I moaned, "Oh, my god ... Eric ... Oh, my god ... my god...." and I fulfilled his great expectations.

The orgasm sent pulsations of pleasure up and down my legs and my arms, throughout my abdomen, and up into my head. It was fantastic. I knew Eric could feel my throbbing, which made him explode inside me. Soon, the two of us were crying out in glorious, animal gratification.

"My god! My god! My god," he cried out, with both of us soon fully spent on the bathroom floor. The tiles had heated up rather nicely by then from my hot, now fully flushed flesh.

For several minutes, we were just there in a sighing, panting heap of pulsating flesh until someone tried the bathroom doorknob.

"There's someone in here," I squeaked, trying not to giggle, muffling my silliness against Eric's bare shoulder that had a small purple heart painted on it that was still sort of recognizable.

Gratefully, the door stayed closed.

"Didn't you lock it?" I whispered.

Eric shook his head as a silly smile played on his flushed, handsome face.

Then someone knocked.

"Is everything all right in there?" the voice was Larry's.

"Everything is fine," I said, trying not to laugh, although the situation was beyond funny. "I just need a few more minutes, please," I managed, with no giggling that time.

"Sure," Larry sounded relieved. "She can use my bathroom," he said, and multiple footsteps retreated down the hall.

Eric rested his forehead against mine looking down at me for a long moment before he got to his feet. "That was terrific. I think you might have sobered me up."

"Sex can be a sobering experience."

We both laughed.

"Fun though," he responded.

After getting up, I could see that all the paint had smeared this way and that. Once artistic images were now smushed and smashed, making them nearly unrecognizable, especially in front.

"Do you think anyone is going to figure out what we've been doing?" Eric said, smirking.

We pulled on our swimsuits and looked at ourselves in the mirror.

Eric rearranged my ponytails and kissed my shoulder. "I hear they have a hot tub out on the balcony. Maybe we should soak off some of this under the light of that full moon out there." He kissed the side of my head.

"Good idea. Then you can rest a little before we do it again."

That was when he really kissed me.

"I think I'd like that," he said, and he kissed me again.

We each took a deep breath before carefully opening the bathroom door. As luck would have it, no one was out in the hall. We hurried off to find the hot tub before prying eyes could deduce the deducible. Sex was a sobering experience, but not that sobering.

We joined three others already in the hot tub. The five of us watched the moon rising higher over the deep blue Pacific as warm, bubbling water soothed our weary bodies. Ideas were shared on the changing times. We talked about the Beatles, Vietnam, peace, Civil rights, and the flower children. At one point, the other girl, stoned or simply bold, removed her bathing suit top. Mine stayed in place. After all, I was a film star and lived in a town where news traveled fast.

All in all, it was one hell of a Summer Solstice. And, solstice or not, it was one hell of a night!

# Chapter 9

The sex taking place in that house all night long was not to be believed: huffing and puffing, screaming and moaning, squeaky springs in four different bedrooms at the same time. The look on Phil's face, as he and Shelley, the blonde bombshell, joined Eric and me in the hot tub, and then again, on the sofa in their living room, was beyond priceless. Phil and I had enjoyed one last romp about seven that morning, and here I was with his scientist roommie on the very same day. And there he was with his blue-eyed babe for a sexual marathon in four bedrooms after a wild and crazy and utterly unforgettable beach party.

I don't remember ever having experienced that kind of night before. But I never had a sleepover with a man in a house with three other horny men and women there. Not ever. I never went to college, so I don't know what happened in those co-ed dorms. I've heard some pretty wild stories. However, it couldn't have been any wilder than what happened on the night of the Summer Solstice in 1967. You can trust me on that score!

Eric the biochemist-biologist was a real tiger. Great lover. Sweet and considerate. And a good cook. The only biochemist-biologist I'd ever had, so I'm not sure how others compare. Check it out in your playground. His mattress was not as good as my new super mattress, but he was snuggly all night and great with follow-through. He made me a tasty cheese and mushroom omelet for breakfast with whole wheat toast and orange marmalade. The coffee was excellent. For four bachelors, that kitchen was really stocked, but Phil had been married.

Once, with Eric out of the room, Phil said to me, "I'll cook you breakfast sometime when Eric is out of town." Like that was ever going to happen!

My suspicion: Phil was turned on by the idea of me doing his room-mate. Those dark, swarthy types can have a dark side. How many actors would agree to play a rapist? Apparently, after that mystery aired, some little old lady in a supermarket hit Phil over the head with her purse, screaming, "Police! Rapist!" Actors do need to be careful.

After Jamie left for Lake Arrowhead, I recounted the bizarre events of the previous night to Paula and we thought we both might wet our pants laughing. It was even funnier after the fact. All morning, the people in that house were giving each other funny looks, sheepish grins, even some of the men were blushing.

Since I had a date with Louis that evening, after my walk on the beach with Eric I headed for home. Sunday was brunch where artist extraordinaire would meet the King of the Cowboys. Before dealing with the sexual demands of one Louis Lamprais, I needed a nap.

"I want you at my place tomorrow by twelve o'clock sharp," I said to Paula as I walked out the door.

Barbara Darling also had dinner at Chasen's that evening. Our intimate tête-à-tête was sure to make her column for all to read by the early edition of the *Hollywood Tribune*, a tacky tabloid purchased only after I was seen out and about with someone worth mentioning. Scott and I often made Darling's column. I figured Louis rated prime copy.

* * *

Along with the other Sunday papers, Florence picked up the *Tribune*. I didn't want Louis to be bored waiting for the guests to arrive. I knew he adored seeing his name in print. Fame in America was what he craved, with me happy to confirm his international reputation as a womanizer. Everything I'd ever heard or read about the famous Frenchman was absolutely true, especially when it came to his boudoir antics. Maybe he was the best lover in the world, except for Warren Beatty. I had to think about it.

That night turned into another sexual marathon, for two. Only that morning, Eric was fairly demanding, or was I the demanding one? Regardless, Eric couldn't get enough of me. That was a revelation after him being Mr. Shy Nice Guy. Grass had done wonders for his libido, but no one could top Louis when it came to an innovative approach to getting it on. I suggested that he write a book. He said he'd already started his memoir. Did Louis plan to tell all? I certainly planned to do exactly that.

That night no food was eaten or licked from my body, only Courvoisier, which was welcomed as a disinfectant. I didn't really need that many orgasms. Nonetheless, Louis was diligent, with only one faked by me. I was pleasantly surprised to discover that there was a limit to my sexual excesses. Four days in a row staggered me when I stopped to think about it. Scott would never believe that I had found two contenders in just a week. My astrologer had said that the summer was going to be hot. Jeanne wasn't kidding.

On that morning, our shower together was quick. Enough was enough. I needed to watch over the buffet to see that everything was perfect.

By 10:00, the case of chilled Dom Perignon arrived, proving Beau Kandell was a prince of a cowboy.

Louis had only briefly pouted at being denied one more peak experience, and yet, he liked his new emerald green silk bathrobe. Standing before my cheval mirror, he was the picture of clean-shaven elegance, fully magnificent in his off-white silk suit, caramel silk shirt, and 24-karat gold chains from Florence, Italy. Louis created a 'look' and traveled with 10 suitcases. He could afford it, and so could the studios.

A continental breakfast was served at the skirted table in my bedroom: coffee, orange juice, flaky croissants and strawberry preserves. Much the same as a married couple, we read the Sunday papers together.

"This meal is only a taste, mon cherie. At brunch there will be many things to tantalize your palate."

"You tantalize my palate," he said, peering at me over the top of the front page of the *Los Angeles Times*.

My response was a sweet smile as I continued to read in the *Tribune*: *Where is Scott Wellington these days?* at the top of Barbara Darling's column: "For last night, Dana Scofield could be seen having dinner at Chasen's making goo-goo eyes over Veal Oscar with handsome, talented French actor extraordinaire, Louis Lamprais. Rumor has it that Lamprais will be her leading man in a major motion picture based upon the fantastic blockbuster bestseller by author Garson Reeves, *View From the Mountain*," I read aloud. Then I held the newspaper out to him and said, "We made Barbara Darling's column ... at the top."

His eyebrow went up and a glint filled his eyes as he scanned the column. "Oui! I am the one signed for the film, not you as yet, my pet." That time his smile looked really faked.

"I've no idea where Barbara got her information, since I have yet to be offered the part of Victoria. But you did ask for me, didn't you, my darling?"

"Oui." He picked up his coffee cup and guardedly inquired, "This Scott Wellington is ... your lover?"

"Was my lover." I looked at the print and avoided his eyes.

"He has a fine reputation as a film director."

"He is a fine film director," I said, scanning the Calendar section. "Scott is almost as talented as you are, Louis," I coyly added with my eyes glued to the newspaper.

"In all ways?"

"I don't really want to talk about it," I said, trying not to smile.

"I see." His eyes went back to reading. "Well, you had to learn somewhere. Now that you have met the master, you need look no further."

We laughed together like two co-conspirators in a wicked plot, with my thoughts kept strictly to myself.

Paula called.

"Exactly what do you want me to wear?" she sounded frustrated.

"Something ravishing, fully feminine, but not too seductive. Wear your hair down. You look lovely that way. No pants, a dress or skirt and blouse. Simple but elegant. And try not to be late."

"All of that?"

"How about your light blue lacy sundress?"

"It is clean."

"Or your white linen skirt with a silk blouse and jewelry, perhaps light green silk to compliment your eyes. Look elegant, dear. That's easy for you." I paused. "Louis is looking forward to meeting you."

He picked up his cup and toasted me, his eyes soon again reading.

"He loves your painting, the one in my room with the children playing on the beach. Who knows, he may need more art for his house in St. Tropes. He says the flat in Paris already has too many paintings and too many sculptures."

"I suppose you were ravished again?" Paula said. "However do you keep all their names straight with one man right after another in your bed?"

"You say, darling," I said, and noting the expression on Louis's face, I quickly added, "We made Barbara Darling's column. I'll save the paper for you. Opening line."

"I daresay Scott will be calling you again soon."

"Don't you mean again?" I took a deep breath, since the mention of his name still had a strange effect on me. "Kenny is coming to brunch. He promised to check out my hair. He's the sweetest man. I just love Kenny."

"How is his lover, Eduardo, the handsome older man with the gorgeous white hair? Eduardo is very handsome."

"They're off again, it seems. Off half the time, actually. Apparently, Eduardo is the jealous type, so possessive he makes Kenny crazy. Kenny can't help it that he's so handsome that other men are always hitting on him. He's seeing a younger man now, an actor on a new series still in the closet. Macho man and all that!" I lit a cigarette, choosing to ignore the disapproval on Louis's face.

"I'm wearing my new hot pink silk mini. No pink. Louis is wearing an off-white Italian silk suit that makes him look delectable." I winked at him.

"I gather that he is delectable?"

"Quite."

Together, we laughed.

Louis smirked.

"You just might have another patron who will take your art all the way to France. I'm taking Louis to Ken's gallery this week to see your work. See you soon, darling!"

# Chapter 10

The flowers in front of my white picket fence were a brilliant wash of color on that day: Iceland poppies. Charming. Lacy and feminine. They were among my favorite flowers as their delicate faces bobbed in the breeze. The birdbath, a housewarming gift from Paula, was filled with chickadees enjoying a late morning bath.

The moment I heard her footsteps and the chattering of scattering birds, I rushed to the front door and opened it before the musical doorbell could finish.

"Do come in, my dear."

"Miss Movie Star is done to perfection," Paula said, kissing my cheek.

Mr. Movie Star was leaning against the baby grand with a glass of champagne in his hand, his open shirt revealing his hairy chest and the gold chain with a large medallion of his birth sign: Aquarius. Louis flashed Paula his best smile.

"Paula Marlow … Louis Lamprais," I said, nodding to each of them in turn.

"It is my pleasure," Louis said, raising her hand to his lips to kiss. "Dana sings your praises, which are justified, of course. Your painting is magnificent. I am eager to see those at the gallery."

At that exact moment, Martin, the butler of the day, approached with a silver tray with one glass of champagne. Martin had also worked for Paula for large parties. Dignified and efficient, I'd always suspected that Florence had a crush on him. Martin was modestly attractive and quite charming.

"Thank you, Martin," Paula said, picking up the glass of champagne and turning to Louis. "You are as charming as you are talented. I've seen all your films, some more than once."

"You are too kind."

"Your friend, Beau Kandell, sent over a case of Dom Perignon, chilled as promised," I said to Paula.

"My friend? I have yet to meet the tall man from Texas."

Paula was wearing a royal blue silk blouse with her white linen skirt, gold jewelry and pearls. She looked like a natural redhead, since she had inherited her mother's redheaded complexion complete with freckles. Her copper hair fell to her shoulders, shiny and clean.

Lifting his glass, Louis toasted, "To beauty," and his eyes moved from Paula to me.

"I'll drink to that," Paula said, taking a sip. "Excellent!"

"More than sufficient for this day."

Large baskets and bowls of flowers were in every room, even the bathrooms. Classical music softly played. Mozart. Everything was arranged to create a pleasant ambiance for a social gathering with a few of my closest and most fascinating friends.

The musical doorbell rang. It was noon exactly.

"The gentleman is punctual," I said.

Martin answered the door.

"The name is Kandell," he said in his soft Texas drawl, "Beau Kandell. Miss Scofield is expecting me."

"Won't you come in, sir?" Martin said, stepping back and motioning toward the three of us in the living room. "Miss Scofield is expecting you."

Beau was standing directly under the crystal chandelier, all six-foot-three of him. Blond hair and blue eyes, the handsome drink of water from the Lone Star State was in A-1 prime condition. Judging from Paula's facial reaction, she agreed with me.

His intelligent blue eyes were framed by a golden tan, his jaw wide set and angular with a scant cleft in his strong chin. The deep laugh lines revealed his constant exposure to the Texas sun. Beau was rugged yet refined, neat yet tousled in his chamois pants and blue silk shirt, and on his feet, artfully tooled brown leather cowboy boots. He nodded to each of us in turn, zeroing in on the artist of the day with pleasure all over his face.

"Beau!" I gushed, rushing over. "I'm surprised you didn't wear your hat. Welcome to my humble abode!"

"My hat is in the car," he said, bending down to kiss my cheek as I pecked back. "You have a right pretty day for a party here in Southern California. And, that garden out front, why, Dana, it's mighty pretty.

Your home is quite lovely," he scanned the room with approval on his face.

"Beau dear, I want to introduce you to my closest and dearest friend, Paula Marlow, whose work you so admire, and to my fellow actor, Louis Lamprais, here from France to make some films." I turned to Louis and said, "Beauregard Kandell hails from Fort Worth, Texas. He's the gentleman who so generously provided us with the Dom Perignon champagne for our get-together today."

Louis shook hands with Beau. "Generous indeed! It is a pleasure to meet you, Beauregard. You have French blood, oui?"

"On my mother's side. But the pleasure is all mine, I can assure you. I've enjoyed your films, Mr. Lamprais. You're a mighty fine actor, first rate in my book!"

"Please call me, Louis, no formality, eh, Beau?" he said in his thick French accent.

"Louis," Beau repeated, before he turned directly to Paula. "I've heard all about your cat eyes. You have magnificent eyes, Paula Marlow."

Paula blushed.

Beau seemed to note the freckles on her nose, her slight over-bite, and her lips covered in salmon pink lipstick. Her long copper hair contrasted nicely with the royal blue silk blouse. Paula had put herself together nicely for that day, which was not wasted on Beau Kandell. Never before had I seen her act so shy with a man. She actually appeared flustered.

"I understand you own one of my paintings," she said.

"I now own three. I bought two more yesterday at the gallery. I love your work, your sensitivity, your rare talent with colors and textures. It seems to me that the soul of the artist ends up on the canvas. I'd say that you have a very deep and beautiful soul, Paula Marlow."

Louis and I instantly exchanged glances. Had Beau and Paula fallen in love right before our very eyes? For the next few moments, they appeared unaware that we were even there.

Then Martin walked up and extended his tray to Beau. "Mr. Kandell," he said, nodding at the single glass of champagne on the tray.

Beau picked up the glass and said, "Why, thank you. May I ask you your name?"

"Martin, sir. My name is Martin Brennan."

"Thank you, Martin. Thank you kindly."

And the musical doorbell again rang.

As Martin got the door, Florence suddenly appeared in her black and white serving attire, carrying a tray of fluted glasses filled with champagne.

"This is Florence," I said to Beau. "Florence, this is Mr. Beau Kandell from Texas."

"How do you do, Mr. Kandell. You're the gentleman who sent the case of champagne."

"That's right. You call me Beau and I'll call you Florence."

"Why, thank you, Beau," Florence said, and she curtsied without spilling a drop.

In walked Kenny Patrick in white silk slacks and a fuchsia silk shirt with multiple gold chains around his neck. Thick, curly, dark hair framed his handsome face and sparkling brown eyes. Part Italian and part Greek, Kenny was a toned five-foot-eight, his name a professional affectation. Immediately, he started to check out the men.

"Shall we toss for him, darling?" he whispered in my ear, kissing my cheek and quickly giving Louis the once-over. "He has definite possibilities."

"No chance, sweets," I whispered back, and then, I said aloud to the others, "This is Kenny Patrick, the finest hair dresser in Beverly Hills. Louis Lamprais, Beau Kandell, and, of course, you know Paula."

"How are you, lovely artist lady? You look tres elegant!" Kenny kissed her cheek.

"Why, thank you. You're your usual handsome self and haven't changed a bit. I love your shirt. Great color on you."

"I'm sorry I couldn't get here sooner. My mother kept me on the phone from Long Island for hours. Talk, talk, talk, the woman never shuts up. My ear hurts." He stepped back to look over my hair. "As usual, you did fine without me." Then he turned to the others and said, "If all my clients were as talented with their hair as Dana, I'd be out of business in no time. Look at her. Is that hair perfection or what?"

Harlan Evans sauntered in wearing an abstract print shirt of orange, yellow, red, green and blue with his white duck bellbottoms and brown leather sandals. Harlan loved to make a splash. His sculptures did the same. At that time, he was becoming an international sensation and he loved every minute of it.

"As you can see, I dressed formally just for you, dear," Harlan said, kissing my cheek. Then he extended his hand to Louis, "Harlan. Harlan Evans. Sculpture is my game. So very nice to meet you. You do look familiar."

"Louis Lamprais," he said, shaking his hand.

"You're an actor! French! Now I remember. Good job."

"I adore all your films," Kenny cooed. "I've seen every one of them at least twice. Fabulous! You're a very talented actor!" He was practically drooling.

"I'm from Fort Worth," Beau said. "Flew up to spend a few days here on business," he glanced at Paula, "I'm in town buying some art and making new friends. I've heard about your sculptures. I just might have room in my house for at least one of them."

"Great!" Harlan said, handing Beau his business card. "Check out my work at the gallery any old time."

Beau appeared to be having trouble keeping his eyes off Paula. She was obviously pleased with his attention. My instincts were right on. The chemistry was there, and yet, she also had chemistry with the young Georgia peach up in the mountains with her children and his uncle, her ex. With any luck, I hoped Jamie returned to Georgia real soon.

That was when Harriet Clybourne waltzed in wearing her Yves St. Laurent red linen suit with black trim and dripping in diamonds. In her mid-40s, Harriet was skillfully remodeled where nature had failed, her plastic surgeon one of Beverly Hill's finest. In her huge mansion were the paintings of Paula Marlow and the sculptures of Harlan Evans, besides other priceless paintings by masters of international fame.

Irwin Thomas was pleased to see Beau again, with the two men soon talking horses. In Texas, they had ridden Beau's horses. Irwin had a small spread in Malibu Canyon.

"You come on out any old time," Irwin said to Beau, "I have a guest house you're welcome to use and we can ride my horses through the canyon."

"I may take you up on that," Beau said before he turned to Paula. "Do you ride?"

"No. But I think horses are beautiful animals. I should paint one sometime."

"I have plenty of horses for you to paint, different breeds and colors, and I'm a fair riding instructor. How about I teach you how to ride a horse and let you paint one, and you teach me your technique with a brush. Does that sound like a fair trade to you?"

"Maybe," Paula cautiously replied.

The Texas cowboy was trying to rope her in. As luck would have it, Jamie just invited her on a trip to San Francisco. As long as I'd known her, Paula was always a one man woman. She seemed attracted to Beau. My hope was that Jamie would get lost in the woods.

Considering our strong psychic connection, it seemed that Paula was reading my mind. Immediately, I switched into overdrive, thinking how Jamie had law school and the military and wouldn't graduate from the university for another year. While Beau was a fully grown man with every asset Paula could ever desire or require.

Then I overheard Beau saying, "I hear you're a Pisces. That's why you're so sensitive and poetic with your painting. You're a true mystic."

I remembered that while working in Texas, he had asked me about her birthday. His interest in astrology seemed like the icing on that wedding cake.

"When is your birthday?" Paula responded.

"November 12th, Scorpio. My mother is into astrology and everything mystical. I had a great aunt in down New Orleans who was a spirit medium. She talked to dead folk, mainly relatives. We used to gather around this big old oak table in the dining room. It gave me the willies as a boy. Aunt Caitlin drew my horoscope in my baby book on the day I was born. I don't understand much about it, but I find it mighty interesting. Do you know anything about astrology?"

"I've had my chart done and have taken a few classes," Paula said, quickly glancing at me. We had both found the math far too complicated, so neither of us wanted to be astrologers.

"Is that right?" Beau looked mighty pleased.

"I know this amazing woman who casts horoscopes. She's a Hungarian-Russian gypsy who escaped the Nazis in World War II when Hitler invaded Hungary. She has a crystal ball she carried over the Alps in the dead of winter that has been in her family for centuries. Ilona still does astrology and reads tarot cards on the pier in Santa Monica."

"Is that right? Well, I'll bet she told you that you have a mighty fine future."

Once again, Paula and I exchanged glances. At the party on Friday, Ilona had done mini-tarot readings for each of us. I'd insisted that Paula ask one more question about Beau. The answer was the Tarot Ten of Cups. 'The man will make you very happy,' Ilona had said.

At that point, Shirley and Hal Ralston arrived. Hal had on his faded jeans and a tie-dye shirt. Shirley wore an aqua squaw dress and beaded moccasins. Another of her many causes: the Native American movement, besides being anti-war and in favor of women rights and the legalization of abortion. Some medical hack in the backstreets of Tijuana performed an illegal abortion on Shirley when she was 16 that left her unable to have children.

"That's a lovely squaw dress you're wearing," Beau said, "One of the nicest I've seen."

"Navajo. I picked it up in Arizona."

Katie Willard and Brad Sorensen were the last guests to arrive: Actor friends of mine. The three of us started out together, poor and struggling. But by 1967, Brad was playing an undercover vice squad officer on a successful TV series: *Justice and the Law*. His reputation as one of Hollywood's bachelors was untrue, however, since Brad and Katie were secretly married in my backyard. In those days, Katie portrayed a vixen on a soap opera, *The World Keeps Turning*. At that time, the networks preferred their stars to be 'single' to inflame the fans.

"The house looks great," Katie said, "and so do you. I love the dress and the shoes. Groovy!"

"Thanks all around. Have you met Louis?"

"I enjoy your work," Brad said. "I was impressed with your performance in *Once More, My Love*. Great film. You deserved the award. Maybe next time?"

"You are too kind."

"Brunch is served," Florence announced to the tinkle of a crystal bell.

On the dining room table was a stack of clear glass plates on which my guests now placed an assortment of the following: Brie, Beluga caviar, chicken liver pate, crab quiche, spinach quiche, lobster quiche, green salad, fresh fruit salad, sturgeon, cream cheese and bagels, along with giant strawberries with whipped cream or hot chocolate for dipping. On the side table were the mousses: lemon, raspberry and chocolate.

Everything looked and tasted delicious.

All my guests proceeded outside to the small tables and folding chairs set up near the pool to enjoy their food. The music became upbeat as Dean Martin softly crooned over the loudspeakers. Everyone seemed to be enjoying themselves on a divine June Sunday, with Florence and Martin repeatedly refilling the glasses with Dom Perignon, chilled, naturally.

Beau's passion for Paula's work seemed to both embarrass and please her.

"I have a Paula Marlow," Harlan said, "In my dining room."

"And my Harlan Evan's sculpture greets my guests near my entry," she responded.

"Don't you just love it? We exchanged our work years ago." Harlan turned to Beau. "My next show is in three weeks at the Keaton Gallery on Rodeo Drive. I hope you can fly out for my champagne reception. In fact, you're all invited! The caterer is superb. Maybe not as good as this, but tasty, I can assure you."

"I'll be there," I said.

"You know I'll be there," Harriet chimed in. "I have four of Harlan's fantastic sculptures that I absolutely adore. I also have four of Paula's paintings and I love every one of them."

"Just think, in a few weeks, you, too, can own an Evan's circa '67," Kenny said. "I'm sure you can find room in that place of yours for some of Harlan's sculptures. Dana says your Texas ranch house is quite magnificent and would fit right in here in Beverly Hills."

"He designed the house himself. Beau is a man of many talents," I added.

"Now, Dana...." Beau protested.

"He also has a fine herd of Black Angus steers and just enough Texas longhorns to make it perfect to shoot an old-fashioned Western movie," Irwin said. "Along with 20 horses and some ponies, isn't that right, Beau?"

"You're very observant, Irwin."

"He broke in his own horses," Irwin added. "Beau is a bona fide Texas cowboy."

"Easy does it, Irwin. Sounds like a tall Texas tale to me," Beau said, laughing.

"Were you born in Texas?" Katie inquired.

"No. In New Orleans. My mother is part French, part Irish and part English. My daddy was born in Houston of English, Welsh and Scottish stock. Daddy was in the oil business. However, when it came time for my mama to deliver, she preferred the comforts of the family home with her own mama and daddy around. So I was born in Louisiana, but reared in Texas. Texas is my home. It's where I was educated and have lived most of my life."

"I'd love to see a genuine Texas ranch," Katie said. "I haven't been anywhere in the middle of the country. Just out here California and back in New York to film my show."

"I've never been to Texas, either," Brad said.

"Well, you'all come on down. You'll have a fine time. In fact, you're all welcome to come on down to South Tarry's Bend. My ranch is named after a creek bed that can fill up all of a sudden during one of our notorious Texas thunderstorms. That creek bed on the south sometimes turns into a raging river. My land borders Eagle Mountain Lake, which is fair sized. And besides my little Cessna, I have a sailboat and speedboat. I can fly you around in my six-seater for an aerial view. The plane is just big enough to be downright useful."

"That creek bed was a raging river a month ago," I told the group. "I can't imagine it as a dry creek bed."

"Well, you needed a river in that motion picture you were making, so Mother Nature obliged you," Beau said, smiling.

"That's for sure," Irwin said.

I stood and addressed the group. "Would anyone like more champagne or more dessert?"

"How about some coffee?" Shirley said.

"I thought you only drank herb tea."

"Not with this repast. Today I sin. Tomorrow I drink herb tea."

Everyone laughed.

"Another sliver of that raspberry mousse with a cup of coffee would, as you say in America ... hit the spot?" Louis said, standing.

"I'll second that," Kenny said. "But I'm having a sliver of each of those fabulous mousses."

Harlan checked his watch. "I hate to be a party pooper, but I have another prior engagement. It's been grand, Dana. I had a great time. And, all of you, please do come to my show on July 16th, 3:00 p.m. at the Keaton Gallery on Rodeo. We'll drink champagne and eat caviar and you don't have to buy unless you fancy something. I hope to see you there, Beau ... Louis."

"You can count on it, Harlan," Beau said.

Harlan kissed my cheek and was soon out the door.

Slowly but surely, the house emptied.

It was nearly 4:00.

"I hate to let Andy down and not show up at the exhibit in Malibu," Paula said. "There are only a few of my smaller paintings left for him to sell."

"You mean to tell me that there's an art exhibit in Malibu today?" Beau sat up straight and turned to Paula with a look of downright expectancy on his handsome face.

"Yes. The exhibit mostly involves artists who live at the beach and in the canyons. We get together at the home of another artist every Sunday all summer. Andy Perugino is a painter and fine sculptor. His work is more old school, nothing like Harlan's modern pieces. Our exhibits are mainly an excuse to get together and party. But lately, lots of people have been showing up and buying. The word seems to have gotten out. We do have a group of rather talented artisans of different modes and styles."

"That sounds mighty interesting. Is there any chance that I might be able to attend this exhibit with you today?"

"That's a great idea!" I blurted out, jumping to my feet. "Beau would love it, Paula. Maybe he could even find something else to take home with him, such as one of Andy's wonderful sculptures, his alabaster lovers, perhaps? Beau has enough room in that house to include Andy's work for sure."

"This exhibit sounds interesting," Louis said. "Perhaps I could find something for my house in St. Tropes. Should we attend as well?" he enquired, turning to me.

After noting Paula's amusement, I instantly felt trapped. "I don't think so, Louis. How about staying here for a quiet dinner, just the two of us?"

Both Eric and Phil could well show up at the exhibit.

"Oui! Perhaps take a swim and relax?" Louis said.

"Oui!"

"We should get going if you're really serious about the exhibit," Paula said to Beau.

"Absolutely."

At that moment, I was beyond pleased.

"Such a pleasure," Louis said, shaking Beau's hand. "If you are ever in Paris or St. Tropes, you must be my guest."

"And if you're ever in Fort Worth, you'll be mine. I'd love to show you around my ranch with an aerial view of the entire State of Texas." Beau quickly turned and kissed my cheek. "It's been delightful, Dana. I don't know when I've enjoyed myself more. I'm truly honored that you put on this little shindig today so that I could meet your friends, especially this little lady," he nodded at Paula.

"It was nice of you to give me a perfect excuse to have a party. Thanks again for the case of champagne."

"You'll be seeing me again at Harlan's exhibit. It sounds like an excellent reason to fly back to California real soon."

"Have a cup of Andy's summer wine for me. It's wickedly delicious."

"I'll do that."

And they were out the door.

My clandestine plans seemed to be falling right into place. Beau Kandell was following Paula Marlow to the beaches of Malibu. And, if my intuition served me right, it was only the beginning of a beautiful love affair, with me as Maid of Honor at their wedding and godmother to at least one of their children.

Hallelujah and Amen!

# Chapter 11

We went to bed making love and we woke up making love. That was the way it always was with Louis Lamprais. He was insatiable. A monumental screwing machine. The man with the eternal hard-on. Hot and ready. Innovative and adept. Love in the pool. Love in the shower. Love on the floor. Love on the bed. Love in the chair. Love on the table. Love right side up. Love upside down, twisting this way. Twisting that. Love, love and MORE LOVE.

New records were being set between the sheets in Beverly Hills that summer. My suspicion: The ghost of Errol Flynn was haunting my house, mainly my bedroom, goading us on by whispering novel notions in Louis's ear. Perhaps his lusty, licentious cronies were ghostly directors of a porno flick for the Nether Regions where they were all likely spending their time. The probability grew more plausible as the patterns titillated and taunted, incited and excited, all throughout the long night.

The thought of an invisible audience only further inflamed Louis's colossal libido. There was little I could do to stop the man or slow him down. Louis craved me. Lusted after me. Hungered and thirsted after me. Maybe he was more insatiable than Warren Beatty, come to think of it. He only fell asleep after I insisted he swallow a sleeping pill. Then I sat on the bidet to savor the streams of warm water before listlessly falling into bed and blessing the Patron Saint of Seconal for granting me reprieve.

When the morning romp ended, after showering and dressing, Louis called the studio for a driver to pick him up. His wardrobe fitting was at 10:00. Our downstairs breakfast was a conventional repast of tasty leftovers and lots of coffee. We read the morning newspapers. The constant intimacy had reached a saturation point for me. I kept my face blank, not wanting to encourage him in the least. Nonetheless, Louis smiled, longing in his eyes. He was a rare phenomenon

At 9:30 a.m., Louis climbed into the back of a waiting limo. Only after the car turned the corner did I notice Scott's dark blue Mercedes parked on the other side of the street. Scott was staring at me from behind the wheel.

I froze.

After all the energy expended over the past two days, I was hardly up for a confrontation with Scott Wellington, especially after voracious, ravenous Louis. My primary thought was: Give me a break. I hurried toward my front door.

"Dana!" Scott called out, and I heard the car door slammed shut.

Before I could reach the front door, Scott was blocking my way. He had on tennis clothes and was holding out his arms with a determined look on his handsome face. He lunged for me, which forced me to take three quick steps back.

"Get out of the way!" I demanded. "How dare you!"

"Of course, I dare. I fucking love you, you silly slut!"

"How dare you call me a slut!" I screamed before I remembered my neighbors.

Suddenly, Florence was peering at us from behind a curtain and tapping on the windowpane with a 'should I rescue you' look on her face, as she mouthed, "Should I call the police?"

I firmly shook my head. That sort of publicity seemed totally unnecessary.

"What do you think you're doing with that two-bit French whore?" Scott shouted. "I deserve to know."

"Louis Lamprais is no two-bit French whore. He happens to be highly talented and one of the finest actors in the world. He's hot, Louis. HOT!" I glared at him, beside myself at that point.

"Is that right? How hot is he? Did he come all over you?"

"Don't be disgusting! Why should I excite you with all the fine details? Go direct your porn flicks and have your fucking actors do those scenes. You have no right to come here and spy on me. What the hell is the matter with you, Scott? You're 39-years old! Stop acting like a silly adolescent who's been jilted by the prom queen."

"You're no fucking prom queen!"

"I was." I felt the need to clarify that point.

"So what? What the hell does that have to do with your fucking Louis Lamprais and flaunting it in my face?"

"Oh, come, Scott! You come sneaking around my house on a Monday morning, to see who walks out my front door to climb into a waiting limo, and I'm flaunting it in your face! Don't be ridiculous!"

"I read Barbara Darling's column. You knew I would. That's why you had her write you up."

"I had no idea that Barbara Darling was going to be dining at Chasen's on Saturday evening. And I certainly didn't speak to her. You know I think the woman is a bitch."

"She is a bitch."

"At least we can agree on something." I folded my arms. "May I please go inside my house? I have important phone calls to make."

"You always have important calls to make, but none of them are to me. You had a brunch yesterday and you didn't invite me." He stared over my head into the street, avoiding my eyes and acting like a hurt child as tears filled his eyes.

"How do you know that I had a brunch yesterday?"

At first, he didn't answer. Then, he finally said, "I know, Dana. Trust me, I know."

"Don't tell me that you spied on me yesterday too? How sad for you, Scott. You need to stop doing this. You know you do."

Suddenly, I was feeling sorry for him and briefly remembered how crazed he had made me at times, some of the things I'd done that were equally as foolish. When I looked up, he was staring over my head. He was so damn striking, so tall and handsome. His dark hair contrasted nicely with his light blue eyes. He had already started to gray at the temples, which gave him a distinguished look. He was a good tennis player and he loved the game. Besides that, he was a fine film director with nominations and awards to prove it. He was brilliant. One of the most talented, intelligent, temperamental, and emotionally fucked up human beings I'd ever known, and for some strange reason, he still held sway in my heart. That was when I started to get the message.

"Did you spy on me yesterday?"

"I don't have to answer that." He was avoiding my eyes with a dejected look on his face.

"Your expression just gave me the answer."

He looked at me with his sad, probing eyes that suddenly made me feel as though I was standing between the devil and the deep blue sea.

"How is the picture going?"

"We haven't started shooting yet." Now, he looked at me. "I could use a cup of coffee. I've been sitting out here for two fucking hours. I'm hungry." His eyes pathetically searched mine.

"I think there's some coffee." Suddenly, I felt oddly resigned. Florence was still there behind the lace curtains, watching. "I could probably scare something up for you to eat. But that's it, Scott, I want that to be perfectly clear."

His expression registered relief. Then, he smiled and gallantly stepped aside, opening my front door with a flourish. He motioned me in, once more the consummate film director.

Scott greeted Florence in his usual high spirits, especially after she fixed him a plate of lobster quiche, fruit salad and croissants, which gave him an idea of exactly what he'd missed. Then, he started playing with Frisky, talking to the dog, something he always did. Frisky enjoyed the attention. I was trying my best to convince myself that his presence did not mean that Scott was back in my life.

His second helpings were not only of lobster but spinach quiche, more fruit salad and more coffee. Then he started to talk about a role he wanted me to play. The film was going to shoot in another month, perhaps August. *Speak Softly My Love* was written by a top Hollywood screenwriter.

"Jennifer is a woman of incredible beauty who haunts the man's dreams. He stalks her and gets her pregnant before he rejects her and his illegitimate daughter. You'd be fantastic in the role. It's tailor made for you."

"I see." I had to smile. "Who is the male lead?"

"Not set yet. We're thinking David Jansen."

"David has done much better since the film we did that was barely released."

"And you've done a whole lot better," he said, tenderly placing his hand on mine and fondly gazing into my eyes.

After withdrawing my hand, I stared at the roses outside instead of into eyes a different shade of blue than Eric's. It was not the first time Scott had dangled a leading role to keep me in his life. The same thing had happened four other times over the past two years. The other times his excuse was always that the studio executives wanted another actress, one blonder, younger, taller, leggier, perhaps one who had granted countless sexual favors? Scott always said it was not his fault that I never got the parts. He said he'd done everything in his power to change their minds. I always thought it was because Scott was such a wiener with the studio execs. It was surprising to find him a 'yes man' when he was a Leo. The Lion is supposedly the courageous King of the Beasts. But all male lions are apparently not the leader of the pride.

Scott insisted on sending me the script, without a word about me playing Victoria opposite Louis Lamprais. To have made that disclosure seemed pointless on that day. What if Louis was not being truthful? Then I could play Jennifer. Given the chance, it would be Victoria! My present plan was to satisfy Louis in every way possible to secure the part. By then, I was romantically attached to the highly sexed French performer.

"I still want to marry you," Scott said, his eyes suddenly turning all gooey.

I was quiet. When he tried to kiss me I turned away, but my stomach fluttered. And, after he finally left, I wondered if he really would send me the script. After pouring myself more coffee, I headed for the pool to smoke one cigarette after another. Finally, in sheer frustration, I stripped and dove in, swimming back and forth, back and forth, until the crazed feelings left.

After all, in just a week, I had slept with Louis, Phil and Eric. What could I possibly do with Scott Wellington back in my life? Floating on my back in the water I thought of all the madness in my life and all the gorgeous, sexy men. That was when I realized how tired I really was.

After sleeping for a few hours, intermittently thinking of Louis and Phil and Louis and Eric and Louis and Scott, I decided it might be wise for me to call Dr. Spencer and get my head shrunk back to normal size.

Instead, I called Paula the next morning. Talking to her always made a whole lot more sense to me and she didn't charge me $100 an hour for her advice or her ever loving friendship.

# Chapter 12

On that morning, Paula made me laugh. It was much the same as whenever I tried to make her laugh when she really needed it. Her friendship was a true blessing. Best friends forever. Two only children in need of love and friendship had found a soul mate in each other.

Jamie planned to take Paula sailing with friends of his out of San Francisco on a 150-foot yacht. It was the family of some kid he'd known in middle school back in Georgia. They planned to drive up Route 1 in her Mustang to the Big Sur and Monterey. My first thought: Poor Beau.

I was surprised to learn that Paula had enjoyed dinner with Beau the night before in Beverly Hills. He even invited her to bring her children to Texas at his expense. Praise God, the man wasn't wasting any time. My concern: Paula was really into Jamie. What was going to happen when his mother and his uncle tried to change his mind? Jamie would be 20 in August. He was young. June Remington was terrible to Paula when she was married to her brother. She could well fight her to the death over her eldest man-child. There were also the prospects that Paula might have to deal with her alcoholic ex over custody of the children. Things were not looking too peachy keen in the life of my friend at the beginning of that week.

My opinion: Paula should take both trips. She should go to San Francisco with Jamie and to Fort Worth with Beau. Both men seemed bonkers over her.

"Beau Kandell is in love with more than your paintings. He fell head over heels in love with you the moment he walked through my front door."

"But I love Jamie. That's the bottom line."

"And I love Scott, but what good is that going to do me?" I could not believe I had actually said that. "I guess I do need to get my head examined."

"Jamie keeps telling me how much he loves me," Paula said in a dreamy tone that tugged at my heart. Mostly, I wanted my friend to be happy. Still, I decided to give her a pep talk:

"In Texas, you'd feel like you were part of a first-rate John Wayne Western in a Beverly Hills mansion with every possible creature comfort available to you. He has an Olympic-sized pool, besides the lake and a motor boat for water skiing. He has tennis courts, horses, cows, goats, ducks, geese and chickens, and the kids could ride on his tractor. He even has his own eggs and milk just like back on your grandpa's farm in Kansas! Tell me your kids wouldn't go nuts over all that! You said you wanted to take them somewhere this summer. Beau is giving you your own suite, Paula. At least think about it!"

"He has two ponies for Michele and Christopher to ride."

"How can you turn all that down, with Dan taking the kids to Lake Arrowhead for the whole month of July, without bothering to even talk to you about it, I might add? That was pretty lowdown. In my opinion, the man is still a prime son-of-a-bitch!"

"That he is."

"You are nuts to even think about turning Beau down, especially since he's offering to pay for all airfares and you can bring along your kids for protection!"

"He is being highly generous."

"He's a prince, considering the future president of the world hasn't even started law school yet, and has yet to serve two years in the military in a highly dangerous war."

"Jamie has ROTC for two weeks in August."

"This goddamn war is killing off all our young blood. At least Beau spent four years in Korea and lived to tell his tales. That is a very good thing."

In spite of her reluctance, I kept pitching Beau Kandell like I was his goddamn press agent. But every time she talked about Jamie, it was plain to see that she was gone on the Georgia peach. At least Texas was not written off entirely. Saints be praised!

Only that morning, Beau had called again to thank me and said, "I'm not about to give up on Paula Marlow." My advice was for him to hang tough. I felt they belonged together. Regardless of Jamie, I never wavered on that position, although I said nothing to Beau on that score. How could I say anything? I was the captain of his team.

"What's this you told Beau about 'being involved with someone'? Are you out of your mind? Jamie doesn't even graduate from college until next year."

"Dana, I cannot be involved with several men at the same time like you can. My heart doesn't work that way. Frankly, my dear, I don't see how you can do it."

"It's not my heart that's involved. I can't help it if I'm on estrogen-overload. They say brunettes are more passionate. Did you know a woman with dark hairy arms is more passionate, like the Italians and the Greeks? I read that. I'm part Italian on my mother's side. That may have been her problem, actually. You redheads are only mildly passionate, especially you fake redheads."

We both laughed.

"You're biologically a redhead because of your mother," I added, "I'll give you that, but you used to be brunette. I'm glad you don't have a red-head's temper."

"The Irish women were well known for their passion," Paula said. "Men from all over Europe used to seek out Irish wives because of their sexuality and fiery natures."

"I guess you read that somewhere?"

"My Irish grandmother told me. Are you sure you don't just suffer from sexual obsessions?" she inquired, with both of us still laughing. "Have fun with Eric tonight, but what exactly do you plan to do about Scott?"

"Nothing. He called again to invite me to a party on Friday at Fontaine Studios. That's where he's planning to shoot *Speak Softly, My Love.* He wants me to be his Jennifer."

"Like all those other roles he promised you? Be careful, Dana. Scott Wellington doesn't always keep his promises."

"I'm calling Dr. Spencer the minute this conversation ends!"

Right after hanging up, Louis called. I agreed to have dinner with him on Thursday. Then Scott called again. I hedged. It sounded tempting. An hour later, two-dozen red roses arrived in a shiny gold box tied with a red ribbon. The card read: *I will always love you, Scott.* The roses were arranged in a crystal vase and placed on the dining room table.

Eric called for directions.

The last time I'd met him at Dino's on the Sunset Strip. This time he was picking me up for dinner at Scandia's. My plan was to wear my emerald green silk dress, low cut.

Phil called, "How about lunch tomorrow?"

"What kind of a roommate are you? I can't see both of you."

"Why not? I don't owe Eric a thing. I'm not committed to Shelley. Are you committed to Eric?" There was a long pause before he said, "I just met Eric when we moved into this house. He's hardly my best bud."

"I'm not committed to anyone, but I don't want to take things any further. Let's be friends, all right, Phil?"

"You went out with me first."

"What does that have to do with anything?"

There was another long pause.

"Your friend Harriet bought two paintings yesterday. I think she has the hots for Keith, and he seems to have the hots right back. She's a very attractive woman besides being very, very wealthy."

"Is that right?" Harriet had not said a thing.

"Let me know if you change your mind, beautiful. I'll take you to lunch, dinner, or anywhere else you want to go to do anything you might like to do. Keep that in mind."

And, in my mind, that was the end of that.

Three men seemed sufficient for one week. The next week there would be filming at Stromberg Pictures, my perfect excuse to decline any and all offers of carnal companionship. I would be getting up at dawn, which meant going to bed early and alone. Work would save my ass, as well as several other parts of my anatomy. A welcome relief when I really thought about it!

Wearing my bright yellow bikini, I sat by the pool sipping hot tea and studying my lines. Frisky was barking at the squirrels again, but I tuned him out. Eventually, the silly dog calmed down and curled up at my feet.

Scott called again.

"Thanks for the roses. They're beautiful."

"You're beautiful. How about Friday?"

My answer was a sigh.

"So you haven't made up your mind yet?"

That time the sigh was longer and louder. "We start filming Wednesday at the Stromberg on Melrose. You know, at the old studio."

"You didn't answer me, Dana. How about the party on Friday?"

"I don't know, Scott."

"I've already spoken with Harold Lawson, the producer, about you playing Jennifer, the old love who Terrence can't get out of his mind. The woman who drives him to distraction."

Sometimes Scott could be adorable. "I think I could play that part, don't you?"

His laugh was nervous before he turned quiet. "He thought with you as Jennifer ... the film might be a major hit."

"When does shooting start?" He was stroking my ego good, the handsome, sexy, devious devil.

"In about three weeks, but it isn't definite yet."

"I thought you said August. I won't be finished with this film in three weeks."

"We could shoot around you. How about early August? Most of the film will be shot here in town."

"You will have to talk to my agent."

"I'll call Tom when we hang up. I'll send you the script by messenger. Read it, Dana. You'll love the part."

The only time Scott had really come through for me was a small role in *Guns at Midnight*. My character died in the middle. My acting received slight mention in the *New York Times*. I had read in the trades only that morning about *Speak Softly, My Love*. Studio executives were starting to listen to Scott Wellington. Perhaps it was a good part? Perhaps we could combine our work and our relationship? Perhaps? Perhaps? Perhaps?

"I'll read the script. It sounded good in the trades."

"Don't they all?" He paused. "About Friday?" The hook was deliciously baited.

"I'll let you know after I read the script."

Deep down, I knew I'd go to the damn party with him. After all, Scott was a big part of my karma. Like my astrologer always said, there was glue between our charts. Honestly, with that remark, she made me wonder if Scott was my destiny. I just couldn't be absolutely certain.

"I love you and I miss you. I'll call you tomorrow," Scott said.

Only minutes later, the telephone rang again.

Lo and behold, Gloria Barnum was calling me from Casting at Colossal Studios.

"I just spoke with your agent. Tom Rawlings said it was all right to call you directly. I'm sending you the script for *View From the Mountain*. Louis Lamprais is making big noise that he wants you as 'his Victoria.' Keith Sutherland wants a screen test, which means wardrobe first. As I'm sure you already know, this is a period piece. 1800s. Fabulous costumes, Dana, and a great story. Grace Thomas is in charge of costumes. She's been nominated for an Oscar three times. Maybe this time she'll get to take the golden naked guy home. This is going to be a really big picture. You'll love the script, Dana, you'll just love it," Gloria finally stopped talking.

"When does filming start?" I was surprised she had called me herself. Gloria was a major casting director.

"In August. Locations are being scouted, as we speak. They want you to test next week, if you're interested, and I can't imagine that you wouldn't be. Let's get real! I'm sending you the script by messenger. Don't be alarmed by the size of it. There are lots of outdoor scenes to shoot in the Rockies, Colorado, Wyoming, with mega extras. Buffalo herds, horses and Indians." She paused. "Native Americans," she corrected herself. "You'll be doing lots of location work. This is a big picture, Dana. Colossal is sinking a whole bunch of bucks into this baby."

Gloria and I were party circuit friends. Half the actresses in Hollywood wanted to be Victoria. The rest probably wanted to be Sarah, the woman who dies. *View From The Mountain* was going to be a major motion picture.

"Thanks for the call, Gloria. I look forward to reading the script. I hope they haven't strayed too far from Garson's brilliant novel."

"You know Hollywood. Whatever the big boys think will pack them into the theaters is what ends up on the screen. The movie could never be as long as the book, of course. It's not going to be another *Gone With the Wind*."

Ironically, Scott's film and *View From The Mountain* started at the same time. Too bad, I thought. I knew almost nothing about the role of Jennifer, but all about Victoria Rutherford. I would start out young, grow to maturity, and then grow old during the final saga in the Old West. It was a chance to express the full range of my talents, an opportunity to make a name for myself perhaps around the world.

Keith Sutherland had seen my work. He was a talented film director. I'd wanted to work with him for some time. The chance had finally arrived, because Louis lusted after me, besides recognizing my talent. Louis was no fool. He had fallen for my screen image, the same as I had for his. Then, of course, there was the animal passion mixed with finesse that Louis thought might transfer to the big screen to the thrill of the thundering masses. He had put in his request before our first long night of passion. How sweet, I thought, considering the steamy love scenes in the book. Feigned passion. Passion in the dressing room more likely. Fortunately, the passion Louis Lamprais felt for me had also fanned the flames of the producer and director. Magnifique!

Perhaps I was hasty in putting Louis off until Thursday? Perhaps I was foolish to consider the party with Scott on Friday? Perhaps I was mad not to break my date with Eric on that very night? And yet, I had no intention of changing any of my plans. I wanted to see Eric. I wanted to see Scott. My jets were actually already starting to cool in terms of Louis, oddly enough. Both scripts would be read by me. Time would determine my destiny.

Back to studying my lines, I had trouble concentrating. Butterflies fluttered in my stomach because of the unexpected prospects for my career that now loomed before me. Because of all the men looming and zooming who appeared to hunger after the tangy taste of my flesh. Because of all the decisions zooming around in my head that had nearly overloaded my circuits. I decided to take a swim.

After all, I had a whole week to study my lines. The water felt cool, refreshing, as I swam back and forth, back and forth to release the nervous energy inside my chest and solar plexus. And yet, every time I reached the other end of the pool the anxiety hit me again. Finally, floating on my back, I saw only the clear blue California skies high above and all around me.

"More flowers, Dana!" Florence called out, holding a large arrangement of orchids and exotic-looking flowers in an exquisite vase. The blossoms stirred in the breeze.

"Read the card," I said, making my way into the shallows. Once out of the water, I wrapped myself in a large towel. The breeze gave me goose bumps.

Florence cleared her throat and read: "For the most beautiful woman in the world. My eternal love and adoration, Louis." Looking at me, she beamed. "This bouquet cost a great deal  more than two dozen red roses." She had that prissy look on her face, but the flowers were exquisite.

"On the piano, don't you think?"

"Perfect." Florence hesitated. "You wanted me to remind you to repaint your toe nails."

"Thank you."

Picking up the script of *In the Cool of the Night*, I entered the house, stopping briefly to admire the roses on my dining room table. Only three buds were open, delicate baby's breath and lacy ferns interlaced amongst the roses. Scott had always sent me two-dozen red roses to kiss and make up. Nothing had changed.

The doorbell rang.

Florence answered the door.

"Package for Miss Scofield from Mr. Wellington at Fontaine Pictures," the delivery man said.

Florence signed and handed the package to me.

"Another script will be arriving soon. I'll read this one now."

As I climbed the stairs, Scott's script came out of its manila envelope.

My life had become complicated but extremely exciting in just a week. Good scripts were coming my way. My house was filled with beautiful flowers from gorgeous, talented men, who found me irresistible. And I had a dinner date with a handsome biochemist onto something really big in genetic engineering. I couldn't help but wonder what another week might bring.

# Chapter 13

The screenwriter had done an excellent job on *Speak Softly, My Love.* The role of Jennifer was meaty and dramatic. I thought it might be fun to play a scorned female who drives a man insane. Still, that script paled next to the one based on Garson's brilliant novel, which I started to read as soon as the first script was finished. I had only read 20 pages before jumping into the shower to get ready for my dinner date with Eric.

My dress was emerald green silk, the diamonds from my 30th birthday: a karat drop around my neck from 'Mommy dearest' and my half-karat earrings from Daddy. Helen always gave me jewelry, from the time right after she abandoned my father and me. That was what she always wanted in return: Fine jewelry. My gifts were for her birthday, Christmas and Mother's Day. And that was that.

After her latest marriage to Arnold, I was hearing from her even less, only an occasional postcard. Arnie could afford to give her all the jewelry her little ole heart desired. All Helen had to do was drop a hint and wake up to find a bracelet, necklace, or earrings on her pillow or her breakfast tray. Mostly, Helen and Arnold Henninger cruised on luxury liners: the Mediterranean, Caribbean, Pacific, Atlantic, Indian Ocean and South China Sea. At last count, they had circled the globe 10 times, sometimes simply flying from one port to another to board yet another cruise ship to sail off into more multiple sunsets and sunrises. Helen was particularly fond of Asia because of the jewelry: Hong Kong, Singapore, Bangkok and Taipei. Those jewelers had to adore my mother.

Eric arrived early. Florence seemed to approve of the handsome bio-chemist with the startling blue eyes. My punctuality was reserved for the camera, otherwise, I was usually late. But for makeup or wardrobe, even at 4:00 a.m., I was prompt. My career was my priority. My love life could wait.

Eric had a brand new black Pontiac Grand Prix with red leather interior. The car suited him. He was the perfect gentleman, opening my car door and helping me with my chair at the restaurant. But dinner at Scandia was different from dinner at Dino's. Eric kept telling me how beautiful he thought I was, how talented I was, how sexy I was. Louis had said fairly much the same thing, but Eric sounded more sincere and was every bit as gorgeous. Women actually noticed him just as much as the international sensation, Louis Lamprais.

Back in my bedroom later that evening, a large pink candle flickered on the small round table. Pink was for love. The three red heart pillows on my bed were for passion. Small lamps were lit on either side of my bed, as Johnny Matthias crooned over the stereo, *The Twelfth of Never*.

Eric unzipped my dress and helped me out of it, which was a nice change of pace after the bathroom floor and our marathon after the beach party. My shoes were soon off, with me in only my teddy as I turned to find him fully naked. Six-foot-two, eyes of blue, with a remarkable brain too, the man was randy and ready. Camera or no camera, it was time for action!

"You're so beautiful," he said, gathering me into his arms for a long kiss. His kisses were warm and wonderful as his tongue mingled with mine and got my juices flowing. Deft hands moved over my willing flesh, which caused me to tingle almost everywhere. Knowing how much he wanted me only further fanned the flame inside me. His all-consuming passion actually had me trembling.

Soon, we were between the sheets, not satin, but top quality pink percale from the Home Shop at Saks. Mouths and tongues and hands and fingers and legs and feet and toes were soon having the very best of times. The breathing was hot and heavy, our bodies blending, touching, feeling, tasting, taking and giving on that night in June during the sexy Summer of Love.

Each of us was satisfied, several times, in fact, calling out in muffled animal ecstasy in the comfort of my soundproofed bedroom, compliments of Errol Flynn. That beautiful biological specimen of a male biologist was really something. He had even come up with a few tantalizing techniques unknown to Louis Lamprais. It seemed that Dr. Eric Whitley had spent considerable time in India, and in that exotic Asian land he had become fully acquainted with the contents of the Kama

Sutra. He promised me my very own copy by the end of the very next week. Delightful!

"The book has drawings with positions that provide pleasure to one, both, or several. We can use it as a sort of sensual manual," he said in his sexy baritone.

"Several?" That had gotten my attention.

"Men still have harems in various parts of the world."

"They do?" I said in feigned innocence, wondering if maybe I had my own harem while only playing with one lover at a time in either their bed or mine. I was convinced that both Louis and Jeffrey would love to have a colorful copy of the Kama Sutra. And frankly, I was surprised that Jeffrey even entered my mind on that night.

Eric had a flight to catch early the next morning. He left my bedroom at 2:00 a.m.

Right before falling asleep, I remembered I had to get up early to read scenes from *View From The Mountain* to prepare for my screen test with Louis Lamprais. For, with any luck at all, I was soon going to be the Victoria Rutherford of my dreams.

# Chapter 14

"We had dinner at Scandia's," I said to Paula on the telephone the next morning, "And each other for another dessert. Eric was yummy, but so was the crème brulee. Eric is the most brilliant scientist I've ever had." I briefly reflected. "Actually, Eric is the only scientist I've ever had. And he's going to give me my very own copy of the Kama Sutra with color prints."

"That sounds like fun. You must show me the book. I've heard about it, but I've never seen a copy."

We both giggled.

"Dan knows about Jamie and me," Paula suddenly sounded anxious. "This morning on the telephone, he said I'd have 'the chance to tell my toy boy good-bye when he brings the kids home.' I don't have the slightest idea what is really going on."

"So Mr. Impotent Alcoholic can't handle Young and Virile getting it on with his once-prized possession. Too damn bad! Let him stew in it, Paula. What did he ever give you but a whole lot of grief? Maybe his favorite hooker refused to give him a blow job. Tell him to have another drink and ignore the stupid son-of-a-bitch!" I was surprised by the level of my anger. But Dan had pissed me off from almost the beginning. He had never treated Paula right and probably never would.

Paula was worried about a possible custody suit over her children. I told her that I'd do everything in my power to make sure that never happened. Dan was a serious boozer, but he also had enough money to make her life miserable indefinitely. Damn him! Recently, Michele had confided in me that her father wanted them to live with him. Dan had adopted Michele shortly after he married Paula. According to Michele, Daddy Dan was also thinking of marrying his current girlfriend and also talking of buying a big house with a pool and tennis court in Toluca Lake. I never mentioned that to Paula. I didn't want to worry her without a genuine reason. It seemed there might be a reason for her to worry now.

"What have you done to demoralize your children?" I asked her, lighting a cigarette and blowing smoke into the receiver. "Has Jamie been in your bed with the kids there?"

"Of course not!"

"So you're sleeping with his nephew, big fucking deal! You can sleep with whoever you like. Jamie is of age. We're no longer living in the Dark Ages. This is 1967!"

"Jamie isn't 20 yet."

"But he is over 18. What can Dan do besides harass you? I wish he'd fuck off!" That was when I remembered a lawyer I'd met at the beach party. "If you need a good attorney, I met one at the beach party. Richard Randolph is a divorce attorney. He asked me for my number, but he hasn't called yet. All I need in my life is another man!"

"I'd say you have enough already," Paula said. "Which screenplay do you like best?"

"*View From The Mountain*. It's a fabulous part, although Jennifer isn't bad. I'd like to do both, but that isn't impossible. My agent wants the extravaganza, of course, more money and more prestige. I don't have the part yet. It seems to me that they should be able to cast me without a screen test, but quite a few actresses tested in costume for the part of Scarlet O'Hara in *Gone With the Wind*!"

"You'll be the perfect Victoria. I have this funny feeling that the part is already yours. How stiff is the competition?"

"Barbara Stuart is supposedly in the running."

"Similar types."

"Susan Strasberg."

"Small, petite and brunette. When do you test?"

"I need to talk to the director at Stromberg, maybe Wednesday. I wanted it to be Monday for the test at Colossal, the day before the Fourth. I have costume fittings for this film tomorrow, dinner with Louis tomorrow night, and I'm meeting him for lunch today. His role in *The Duke of Orleans* is nearly over. He sent me a gorgeous bouquet of tropical flowers. It's on the piano next to the wedding picture of Helen and Daddy, the one I always hide when Daddy visits with Martha."

"And red roses from Scott, I'll bet."

"On the dining room table. He knows how much I love red roses." I took a long drag on my cigarette. "Beau has called me twice since Sunday."

"He called me again this morning just before you called. He keeps inviting me to Texas."

"He says he's flying out for Harlan's show."

"Yes, I know. Did Beau say anything about me?"

I was pleased that my friend had asked that particular question. "He was charmed, enchanted and delighted with you, Miss Marlow, ready to whisk you off at your first sign of acceptance. With you saying you're already involved, he may want to check out the competition."

"It's like Beau wants me in Texas yesterday."

"You have nothing to lose by accepting his invitation. Isn't Jamie working at his uncle's law firm in Philadelphia, and didn't you say he has ROTC sometime soon? Before you know it, Jamie will be back at school again."

"Right now, I just need to know exactly what has happened between Jamie and Dan. From the tone of Dan's voice, it can't be good. With Jamie I have to take one step at a time. You must understand that, Dana."

"I do, my dear. But I still happen to be in Beau's corner. Playing hard to get only makes it that much more interesting for that cowboy. He's really keen to meet Michele and Christopher. He told me about the paintings he picked up at the exhibit, besides purchasing Andy's magnificent alabaster lovers. Beau Kandell is one lucky man!"

"From what you told me, he still has plenty of empty rooms in his 15,000 square foot house!"

"That's true. Were the paintings of the children from a few years back?"

"Yes. I did those years ago. And the sculpture is being shipped today. Beau took the small paintings with him on his private plane ride home. He said he has them on his bedroom dresser."

"He said he wouldn't mind having a ready-made family ... that he's 'hankering to settle down.'" That phrase made me giggle!

"Beau said that?" she sounded amazed.

"Would I lie to you, my dear?"

"Only embellish the truth to make it that much more interesting."

"You may be the only one who understands me besides Dr. Spencer, and he says I'm a 'chameleon.' Frankly, I've never cared much for reptiles."

"Well, you can be a dozen different people on the same day. You're a Gemini, after all. And yet, Michele is a Leo and acts a lot like you. My daughter says she wants to be an actress."

Suddenly, in the background I could hear Michele and Christopher calling out, "We're home!"

"My munchkins are home. I need to go."

"Good luck. Let me know when you're leaving for San Francisco."

"If I am," she sounded so anxious. "Catch you later."

I had the strangest sensation in my solar plexus as that conversation ended. Something was happening in my friend's life that I didn't understand. Something she may not have understood herself.

It was nearly one that afternoon when I met Louis at the Beverly Hills Hotel dressed to conquer in my salmon pink silk mini and gold jewelry, with my hair pulled back to one side with a comb. He was his usual handsome self in raw silk slacks and beige silk shirt, his collar opened enough to reveal his favorite gold chain on his suntanned chest. For his role as the Comte Jean de Toulouse, a fetching moustache and goatee were added in makeup. I had no doubts that he was portraying the French rapscallion with style and dash. Louis was also an amazing swordsman. Because of his pronounced French accent, Colossal had him scheduled for his first elocution lesson that afternoon.

Upon entering the Polo Lounge, I was sure that we gave the impression of the perfect Hollywood power couple. The hostess escorted us to a cozy booth not far from all the other beautiful people.

Immediately, Louis ordered a bottle of Dom Perignon.

"How elegant! Champagne for lunch!"

"Nothing but the best for you, ma cherie."

He had to be aware of all the other celebrities and power brokers having lunch there that day. Across the crowded room, 'James Bond' was no doubt in town to promote the latest sequel of his film: *You Only Live Twice*. Rona Barrett smiled and waved. I toasted her with my champagne. She toasted me with coffee. Her career was flourishing then. I hoped for a mention on her show. Her companion for lunch that day was novelist Harriet Glover. The whole town seemed to be talking about Louis Lamprais.

There were no empty tables in the restaurant that day. Business was brisk at the Polo Lounge in Beverly Hills, U.S.A.

Soon, we were enjoying cold lobster and Alaskan king crab, stuffed mushrooms, hearts of palm, and a Greek salad with feta cheese. Everything was done to perfection. Louis had outdoor scenes to shoot that evening with horses and carriages. All the exteriors were being filmed on the lot at Marvel.

"Will you be going anywhere to film on location?"

"Oui, ma cherie. Kindly forgive me, but I will not be able to do your screen test. Gregory will be in my costume for the scene. He is portraying Stephen Staley in the film. They told me only this morning that I must fly to New Orleans on Friday. I could be gone more than a week. You will forgive me, ma cherie? Merci?"

"But, of course. It's the price we actors pay for being at the beck and call of a studio. But I was under the impression that the main reason for the test was for us to be seen together on film!"

"Oui. It is not my fault. The right ship needed for the scenes is only available at this time. There was some problem with scheduling, which means someone made a very costly mistake."

"What about dinner tomorrow evening?"

"Only this morning we were invited to dine at the home of the director. Perfect, don't you think?"

"Keith Sutherland?"

"Oui. In the Pacific Palisades. Do you know where that is?"

"Of course. I'll pick you up at your hotel."

"Oui! Tonight we will be shooting late, and again tomorrow, at noon. Two scenes need to be reshot."

"That is most unfortunate. Delays are never fun."

"I hear that New Orleans is charming, a city with many fine restaurants. Oui?"

"Oui!"

"Perhaps you can join me there for a few days?"

"My film starts shooting tomorrow morning. Stromberg wanted me there today, but I begged off. I'll be working every day, the same as you, Louis. But I didn't want to miss out on our lunch today."

He kissed me. Many eyes were obviously observing our affectionate exchange.

"Makeup is early tomorrow," I said, sipping champagne during my last free weekday elegant lunch for no doubt some time to come.

Louis simply nodded.

"With both of us working, I hope we aren't too tired for dinner at Keith's. He's a fabulous director. Monday will be challenging. Stromberg is unhappy that I'm taking time off to test at Colossal. From now on, it looks as though it will be all work with little time for play."

"It is the price we pay for the glory of being actors," he said, checking his wristwatch. "Would you care to see my bungalow?" He softly kissed me.

"I would love to see your bungalow ... and your etchings." I kissed him back.

Presently, we were hurrying toward the bungalows. Once inside, our clothing was quickly removed with us soon between clean sheets to make mad, passionate love for hours. That day I learned that love in the afternoon with Louis Lamprais was as sweet as love in the morning and all night long—a French dessert with no calories!

Oui, oui, mon cherie. Tres magnifique!

# Chapter 15

After returning home in a relaxed state, I called Stromberg to confirm my makeup call for early the next morning. Playtime was over. It was time for work and a paycheck. But I had enjoyed my free weeks of frivolous fun and games in the sun.

Feeling curious as to how the stars and planets were affecting me, I called Jeanne, my astrologer in Hollywood. I wanted her to check out Louis' chart. Jeanne and I had a special rapport, with her always eager to accommodate my requests.

I had asked Eric for his birth data. He was unsure of his time of birth. He was born in Chicago on September 3rd, but I needed the degree of his moon and rising sign. The moon is important in relationships, since it deals with emotions. My moon in Pisces was supposedly why I enjoyed swimming, dancing, dreaming and acting. Jeffrey Waters was a Pisces. Jeanne said our charts were perfect for marriage with his Sun on my moon. She said we'd been married in another lifetime. Even though Jeffrey was married to Cindy, I'd always wondered if it was wise of me to decline his marriage proposal all those years ago.

Phil was a Taurus and built like a bull. I didn't know his exact birthday and wasn't really interested. Phil had called again, the same as Eric and Scott. All these glorious men were eager to jump my bones, and I couldn't have been more pleased.

"Retrograde Mercury," Jeanne said on the telephone. "Plans change. Messages get mixed up or missed. Everything can change at a moment's notice. Don't make any major plans now. It's not a good time to sign contracts or make serious commitments. It may be as simple as just not being able to carry through, despite the best of intentions. Mercury goes retrograde three times a year. Deciding on something now, you might change your mind after Mercury goes direct. It can be as simple as that."

"When did it start?" I groaned.

"Monday ... June 26th."

"Maybe that was the reason that the studio wanted me this week instead of next. Is that it?"

"And you could go in, and then, they might change their mind again. Be your flexible Gemini self, Dana. Take along a good book. You're ruled by Mercury, so it affects you more than it might some people."

"Are you serious? When I have to get up in the dark and drive to the studio that is not a pleasant thought. When is this bloody business over with?"

"July 20th. Wait a couple of days after that to sign papers. Sometimes you just have to take your chances. I wouldn't want you to miss out on anything important. Just stall signing contracts for a few weeks, if possible."

"On Monday I have a screen test for a film that could be the most important motion picture of my career. Damn Mercury! What's that going to do to me? Is it beyond awful?"

"If the screen test was scheduled before Mercury turned retrograde, it should be okay. There could be delays making the picture, though. It could start earlier or later, things like that."

"Like now. They wanted me here early."

"Starting your film before Mercury is direct, there will likely be changes or scenes done over, that sort of thing." I thought of Louis redoing his scenes. "Your scenes at Stromberg could be rewritten. Keep that in mind. An actor could even drop out or get sick."

"Great!"

"I'm giving you the worst case scenario."

"The film I'm testing for doesn't start shooting until August. We'll be on location in the Rockies and it could take six months. Does that mean Mercury might screw things up several times between now and then?"

"August is good. The next retrograde starts October 21st."

"I'll tell Paula. She's having an art exhibit in October, which shouldn't be on a retrograde Mercury, right?"

"Right. This is an important year for your career, Dana. I won't be surprised if this film isn't the beginning of something really big for you. I can also see politics in your future."

"Politics?" That surprised me. "Or just a politician?"

"Maybe both!"

When I tried to call Paula to let her know that Mercury was messing with our lives, I left a message with her service. Florence and I had an early dinner. Then I soaked in my warm bubbling whirlpool with candlelight flickering and went to bed early—alone.

\* \* \*

The next morning, I sat in my dressing room drinking coffee and smoking cigarettes for an hour before I called Paula. To escape the clutches of his evil uncle, Jamie had left for San Diego to visit friends, but not before being verbally thrashed by his Uncle Dan with regard to Paula. Jamie had told Dan that he loved her. Ballsy! Let's hear it for the boys from Atlanta! Behind that soft southern accent and dimpled smile he was a tough cookie. I hadn't been happy with his sneaking around and lying. I was pleased that the shit had finally hit the fan.

I told Paula about Retrograde Mercury then, and again, in October.

"The show is on the 7th and 8th, Saturday and Sunday," she said. "No sweat. But thanks for letting me know. How was lunch with Louis?"

"Nice. His bungalow is nearly as gorgeous as he is. He was on the set all night with indoor scenes today. Retrograde Mercury is working against that Aquarian. He's flying to New Orleans tomorrow morning. I don't see how we can possibly have dinner in the Palisades tonight, especially since I don't know when my scenes will be shot. Ten minutes ago the assistant director said I'd have to stay late. I wish they hadn't called me in early. This is beyond ridiculous!"

"Poor Miss Movie Star," Paula teased. "What is dinner in the Palisades all about?"

"Keith Sutherland, the director of *View From the Mountain*, invited us to dinner in his home. I was supposed to pick Louis up at his hotel, but I don't see how that's ever going to happen."

"Not from what you've been telling me. How can you go to the Palisades tonight and be at Stromberg at the crack of dawn with shooting late today?"

"I can't."

"And how can Louis? Isn't he already over forty?"

"Forty-five, but don't tell anybody!"

"Very well preserved. Of course, I'm calling *Variety* and Barbara Darling as soon as we hang up this phone," she teased.

"He works out a lot. His moon is in Leo and he has Gemini rising, a chart to be famous. According to Jeanne, Louis is an emotional mess, but she also said to have fun. There is a whole lot going on between our charts. She thinks he'll do great things for my career."

"It seems to me that he already has. But I'm glad that you're not in love with him. I don't want your heart broken by the suave, highly sexed Frenchman."

"Scott has left me more messages. He wants to know if I'll be his Jennifer."

"And?"

"I can't be Jennifer and Victoria. But I don't actually know if I am Victoria. Meanwhile, Scott wants me to go to the party with him on Friday."

At that point, Paula launched into a tirade on Dan Thurman, besides expressing her anxiety about leaving for San Francisco with Jamie. She was excited and nervous at the same time. Apparently, Jamie and Dan were at each other's throats. It didn't sound pretty.

"Jamie said that Dan has been waiting for me to make a false move so he can take away the kids."

"Naturally, since you've done such a great job raising them, the son-of-a-bitch! You won't lose them, Paula. I'll go to court and fight for you again. Michele and Christopher do not belong with an impotent, deceitful, alcoholic father!"

"I appreciate your support."

"Don't forget that I met a divorce lawyer at the party. He left me some messages. Perhaps it's unfair to say I'm not interested when everyone at that beach party was drunk, stoned, or both, and covered in body paint. I swear, this month I've had so much sex I didn't know I had in me, and have I ever had it in me!"

We both started laughing.

"Thanks for cheering me up, slut puppy. You also happen to be my funniest friend."

"I'm probably your most promiscuous friend, as well."

There was a light knock on my dressing room door.

The second assistant stuck his head in and said, "Ten minutes, Miss Scofield!"

I nodded and he closed the door.

"Miracles of miracles! I'm wanted on the set. I've only been here for five fucking hours."

"Break a leg. And call me tonight unless you have dinner in the Palisades. Sounds like Retrograde Mercury at Stromberg ... sorry you have to work late."

Immediately, I left for the sound stage, knowing that I had to cry in the scene. That wouldn't be too hard after my long morning of frustration. Ah, the glamorous life of an actress.

No dinner in the Palisades on that night. Damn Mercury running backwards. I stayed at Stromberg until nine o'clock. Louis and I said our fond good-byes on the telephone. He promised to call me from New Orleans. He was going to be gone for at least a week. So I had a reprieve from one Louis Lamprais. How lucky can one girl be?


After getting home late from the studio, the only call I made was to Scott. "I'll go to the party with you as your friend, but I can't promise you I'll be Jennifer. Okay?"

"Why?" he sounded disappointed, which made me feel good and bad at the same time. The time had come to fess up.

"On Monday, I'm being tested for Victoria Rutherford in *View From The Mountain.*"

"So I've heard," I heard him say with a sigh. "I've heard all about your French whore wanting you for his leading lady in his first real lead in a major American motion picture."

"Louis is not a whore. He's a fantastic actor. Look at his reputation!"

"I have ... in bed, off screen and on." I could swear I heard a smirk in his voice.

"I am not going to sanction that remark."

"Oh, come on, Dana. Is Louis really a good fuck? Tell me all about him, my dear, sweet, adorable Dana."

"You have no idea! None whatsoever!"

"Oh, come on. Let's have phone sex like we did when you were in Texas. Messy but fun!"

"Scott!" I paused. "What time is the party?"

"It starts at seven. Friends, huh?"

"I'll meet you at Fontaine. I'm not sure exactly when, but probably not seven."

"I'll see you when you get there. I'm looking forward to gazing upon your beautiful face and fantastic body once again. And we'll have to see about being ... friends."

After a quick shower, I put on a clean nightgown and thought of returning Richard Randolph's call. Dan was being a really big shit. But I was tired and about to turn off the light when the telephone rang.

"Hello," I said, against my better judgment.

"Hi, Dana. This is Richard Randolph. Do you remember me from the party down at the beach?"

"Yes, Richard, of course I do." Was the man telepathic?

"I left you a couple of messages. I read in the trades about you making a film at Stromberg with Kevin Matheson, *In the Cool of the Night*, right? I look forward to seeing the picture. I hear it's a good script."

"I just started working on it. I was about to turn out the light when the telephone rang. I can't stay on the phone long."

"Well, then, I'll cut to the chase. How about dinner on Saturday at the Luau? I love that restaurant, and we don't have time to make it to Honolulu and back if you're starring in a film. Some other time, perhaps?"

"Well, I'm not sure, Richard. I'm seeing several men right now, so it doesn't seem wise to start something with another man."

"I saw you with the biochemist at the party. Dr. Eric Whitley. He has quite the reputation in the world of science. I checked him out."

*Checked him out?* It took another moment before I said, "Eric is also a biologist."

"I know. Extensive research into genetic engineering at MIT. Huge grants. According to what I could glean, there's a whole lot of buzz going on about Dr. Eric Whitley, like Nobel prize, maybe."

*Nobel Prize? Mr. Kama Sutra?* "Is that right?" I said.

"There must be all kinds of men beating a path to your door. Why not add me to the list? You could probably use a good lawyer on your roster," he sounded utterly arrogant.

"I have a good lawyer and a good agent. But I was just telling my friend about meeting you. I don't know if you met Paula at the party, but she might need a good lawyer in the not too distant future. Her ex is giving her a hard time and might try to take custody of their two kids. We can't let that happen, can we, Richard?"

"Are you talking about your friend, Paula Marlow?"

"Right. Did you meet her at the party?"

"No. But wasn't Paula the attractive redhead hanging out with young Jamie Remington, Dan Thurman's nephew?"

Adrenalin shot straight into my brain. How did Richard know anything about Dan Thurman? How did he know Jamie was Dan's nephew? In stunned silence, I tried my best to remember to breathe.

"Doesn't Paula live next door to those screenwriters, Larry Renton and Guy Hamilton? The men who threw the wild beach party with the body paint, magical brownies, and funny cigarettes being smoked in the upstairs room they called the 'pot parlor'?"

With that, I lit a cigarette and took a very long drag. How in the hell did Richard know Paula's last name? Had Jamie said something? Why would he know who she was? Suddenly, I felt like I was standing on quicksand and sinking fast by opening my big, fat mouth!

"You met Jamie on Friday?" I cautiously ventured.

"Yes, at the buffet. His uncle is my stockbroker. Dan Thurman. It just so happens that I'm the new partner at the law offices of Sharman, Greene, and now Randolph. Last Tuesday I spoke with my partners about running into Jamie at the party. Dan is their stockbroker too. Harrison represented Dan in his divorce from your friend, Paula, who lives next door to the screenwriters with their kids, Michele and Christopher. Right? Chris is Dan's biological son and he adopted Michele from Paula's first marriage to some freaky drug addict who committed suicide stoned out of his mind on acid."

*Holy shit!*

"Right," I whispered, choking on some smoke and coughing, as I reached for a tissue with my heart pounding harder by the second. "Congratulations on joining the firm," I managed, "Those are some of the big boys in this town." I was surprised I wasn't hyperventilating.

"That they are," he said, sounding so fucking smug. "I'm one of those big boys now, too."

Instantly, I fell silent, stubbing out my cigarette.

"You say Paula Marlow needs a lawyer?" He paused. "Why is that?" he sounded more than a little curious at that point.

Suddenly, my lips were sealed. Too bad it hadn't happened sooner. Too bad I had even answered the goddamn telephone. Too bad I was about to have a major nervous breakdown.

"Paula would never use your firm. I'm sorry I brought the subject up." I was about to light another cigarette, but my hand was shaking so badly that the match was extinguished.

"Was Paula the pretty redhead snuggled up with Jamie in the pot parlor? They were sleeping together near the window. You were in that room, right? Maybe they passed out from all the booze and high quality grass." His laughter was derisive. "Maybe you'd already left that room by then with ... Dr. Whitley?"

"I don't know what you're talking about," I responded in feigned innocence. "So Dan Thurman is your stockbroker?" It was time for me to think fast.

"That's right. I hear they had a nasty divorce and you were a witness for Paula in the five day legal contest in court."

"I was."

"Was that Paula cuddled up with Jamie? The kid is 19. I hear she's 30, but she sure looks a lot younger. Jamie has another year of pre-law. Recently, he asked my partners about a job in our firm for the month of July."

"Is that right?"

"They met him at the country club with Dan for dinner one evening. Does Jamie want to stay in California because of Paula? That pretty lady at the party was all over the young guy, and he was all over her. Why not? She's beautiful and has a great body from what I could see. Isn't that right?"

I said nothing.

"Was that your friend Paula Marlow with young Jamie Remington?"

"I've no idea," I coolly responded, with my mind thrown into overdrive. It wasn't looking too good for Paula with how things were adding up. Not at all.

Richard chuckled low in his throat and said, "I see," in this gotcha tone, followed by silence. "How about dinner on Saturday, Dana? Then I might not say anything to my partners about seeing your friend Paula and young Jamie curled up together under a blanket in the pot parlor. What do you say? I'm a big fan of yours. Besides having plenty of talent, you are beautiful and highly intelligent, which is a great combination in a woman, in my humble opinion."

Pardon me, but had the hotshot divorce attorney from Sharman, Greene and Randolph just tried to blackmail me into going out with him? The creep was trying to coerce me because of my friendship with Paula. The stupid son-of-a-bitch!

What was I supposed to do to keep my best friend from being entangled in a nasty, expensive, heart wrenching custody battle over the two children she dearly loved? A lawsuit filed by one Daniel Thurman through the cunning, heartless, legal bastards at Sharman, Greene and Randolph? Goddamn it! What was I supposed to do? I'd kill myself before I'd do anything to hurt Paula, Michele or Christopher.

"How about eight o'clock?" I said through clenched teeth, which seemed like the only way to protect Paula from a ravenous pack of wolves intent on ripping out her heart and feeding her remains to the vultures.

After hanging up, I went directly downstairs and poured myself a snifter of Courvoisier. Two shots went down before I could sleep. The creep! I couldn't even remember what he looked like. And if he laid a hand on me, I planned to have his knees, maybe both of them broken, along with both arms in lots of different places.

I used to date a short, husky, yet brilliant science fiction writer, long since famous. Every other word out of his mouth was a vulgarity or some form of sarcasm. Harold was funny but also very short. He once talked about a guy who would do a job like that for about $500. Not murder someone exactly, just maim them, maybe permanently. Put them out of commission for months, or forever.

Notwithstanding, Harold had said that murder didn't cost much more. Jewish Mafia. Knowing that he even knew about such things made me nervous. I stopped seeing him. He was not a man I ever wanted to make angry, of course. Interesting in bed. And he did hang out with some of the most talented and interesting writers in film and television.

That night, the maiming of the arms and the legs sounded about right to take care of a certain unscrupulous, blackmailing lawyer by the name of Richard Randolph. And later, Daniel Thurman would get his. It was the least that I could do if anyone caused Paula serious emotional pain. I was willing to bet that I could still find Harold's telephone number in an old address book. If not, the Writers Guild could put me in touch with him through his agent.

Finally, I fell asleep, only to dream of menacing thugs and shattered knees.

# Chapter 16

The next morning, after finishing my first scene at the studio, I called Paula. My entire conversation with Richard Randolph, prime creep from the law offices of Sharman, Greene and Randolph, was recounted in minute detail. Pacing back and forth in my dressing room in a state of full and complete anxiety, I puffed on a cigarette as I talked to her. I would never forgive myself for fucking up Paula's life, even accidentally. I would slit my wrists or leap from the highest building.

"Do some deep breathing and count to ten," Paula said. "Consciousness creates, remember? Calm down, Dana." She was doing the deep breathing along with me, which made me wonder if she was pacing back and forth, too.

"The goddamn son-of-a-bitch is blackmailing me into going out with him," I nearly shouted, shoving my dressing room door shut with a bang and stubbing out one cigarette to light another. I took a long drag and sat on the sofa. A cloud of smoke filled my dressing trailer. The gray haze reminded me of my yoga class with Clara Spring, all that deep breathing. Why did I continue to smoke? Pure self-destruction? But that was not a day to quit.

"Richard never met Jamie before the party?" Paula said in a stunned tone.

"No. But Jamie met Harrison Greene and Leonard Sharman at the country club with Dan. Richard told them about the wild beach party, booze served to minors and smoking grass in the Malibu Colony."

"No one smoked grass in my house," she said with panic in her voice.

"Even Dan could see that the party was next door."

"But if the man already said all that, how is Richard blackmailing you? I don't understand."

"Richard saw Jamie with an attractive redhead and he didn't know if it was you. He saw Jamie, and maybe you, sleeping under a blanket in the pot parlor."

During the ensuing silence, I opened a diet cola and swallowed half the can before I said, "Jamie was looking into working at their law offices in July. Richard thought it might be so he could be near you. Did Jamie tell you about that?"

"No, I didn't know." Paula sighed. "I still don't see how Richard is blackmailing you. Isn't the cat already out of the bag?"

"If I go out with him, he says he won't tell his partners that he saw you sleeping together in the pot parlor."

"Did you say it was me?"

"Of course not! Are you crazy? I was in there. I gave my telephone number to Richard downstairs. At the time, I was stoned out of my mind on brownies, margaritas, and God knows what else! I didn't need psychedelics. I was already way out there!"

"Don't you even consider going out with him, Dana. Those lawyers are going to find out everything. Those hotshots have their own detectives. Since Harrison is Dan's lawyer, and Dan is everyone's stockbroker ... this can of worms will be opened for public viewing. Dan has been waiting for something like this to take me to court. I guess now he has the ammunition to destroy my life! Damn him!"

"Richard didn't see you smoking grass. He didn't see me or Jamie smoking, either. He went upstairs when the party was nearly over. He won't get me to testify. I was only in that room with you and Jamie for a few minutes." I swigged down more cola and started to pace again.

"I don't remember much about that room. I don't really remember seeing you in there."

"So you fell asleep with Jamie. So what? It was late. You'd been out in the sun all day. Maybe you went in there to hear the music. Stan was singing. And someone covered you up to keep you from getting cold. Probably Guy. Nobody saw you naked, kissing or fucking! All of us were half-naked in bathing suits!"

"Jamie and I were all over each other. How could Richard have missed that?"

"There were lots of people there, maybe 150. With all that body paint, who the hell knew who anyone was? We should have taken pictures." I stopped pacing. "So you're a redhead! You were a redhead with a yellow and black butterfly on your forehead, compliments of Eric the biologist, and purple Pisces symbols on your cheeks, compliments of Ilona, and a pink heart on your chin that I painted. We looked like a bunch of aborigines!"

"And you had a rose on your forehead!"

We both started to laugh.

"So you fell asleep with a gorgeous, young guy. Big fucking deal! People fall asleep next to each other on airplanes and trains and nobody makes anything out of it! Get real!"

"We passed out," she said, "and we didn't wake up until the next morning."

"Passing out ... that's sort of like falling asleep, isn't it?"

Again, we laughed, that time nervously.

"Passing out and falling asleep seems like the same thing to me!" I finished off the cola. "What I think is ... that if you go next door and talk to your neighbors, their mouths will stay closed. It was their pot party and their brownies, with all kinds of booze and underage kids drinking in their house, some younger than Jamie. No cops, praise the Lord. I'm sure Larry and Guy don't want some creep lawyer to give them trouble about illegal substances being provided to minors. They won't tell Richard or anyone else a goddamn thing. Finished ... end of story!"

"So Richard Randolph, creep lawyer, wants you to go out with him, or he'll tell Dan and his partners, and then, I'll be accused of corrupting the morals of a minor. Then, Dan might haul Jamie's ass into court to testify against me," her voice started to break, "That's just great!"

"I'll go out with him, but I won't sleep with him. I'm no whore! I may give it away, but this body is not for sale. According to Ilona, I did that in a past life and was strangled by my pimp for not turning over his share of the loot. I'm not sleeping with Richard Randolph!"

"And you're not going out with him, either! Going out with Richard is no guarantee he won't wreck my life, anyway. There is absolutely no sense in dragging your name through the mud."

"I'm having dinner with him on Saturday!"

"DANA!"

"Louis will be out of town. I'll see him. I haven't the slightest idea what he even looks like without body paint."

"You will NOT go out with him!" she shrieked. "I don't want you on my conscience. Richard Randolph is scum. He should be disbarred. He must be really desperate to go out with you with what he has to do to make it happen. How old is he, anyway?"

"Probably Dan's age ... in the middle of his midlife crisis."

"Are you sure he's even single?"

"Silly me. I never asked. I always think men who ask you out are single, men who go to parties without dates. I guess it's not always true, is it?"

I heard Paula release a very long, controlled sigh. "I'll probably get served next week. I hope it doesn't upset Jamie too much. I guess I'll have to tell him."

"Don't tell him now. You have a whole week together. Have wonderful orgasms and fun in the sun. Tell him after you've sailed the Pacific, or when there is really something to talk about like a custody suit. Right now, it's all speculation. Dan can't possibly have you in court next week. Look how long your divorce took!"

"Maybe I won't say anything. That sort of tension doesn't play well in bed."

There was a knock on my dressing room door. The second assistant stuck his head in and said, "Ten minutes, Stage Five, for your rehearsal with Mr. Matheson, Miss Scofield," and the door closed again.

"The spotlight beckons. I feel better now that you know. Last night I had two cognacs and took a sleeping pill. I'm glad I reached you before you left with Jamie."

"Me, too, I guess. Dan's girlfriend, Gerry, her father just died of a heart attack. Dan is picking up the kids sooner than planned. Are you going to the party with Scott?"

"As his friend. He knows about the screen test. I'm not accepting his part, even Scott Wellington knows how big the other film can be."

"Have fun. And tell Richard Randolph to go to hell, or I'll never speak to you again!" she said, "Tonight I'll be near Hearst Castle with Jamie Remington, consumer of dubious brownies, underage drinker, and great lover. I do love him, Dana."

"I know. And I love Scott, I think. Watch a sunset from a mountaintop for me. And call me the minute you get home!"

* * *

On the soundstage at Fontaine Studios that Friday evening, the principals of many films, either currently being made, or in the process of being edited, were there. That included actors, producers, directors and executives from several different studios gathered together in one place, many different facets of show business. The crowd was impressive even by Hollywood standards.

My scene hadn't finished shooting until six, which was when this talented makeup artist did my evening street makeup. Ginger was a doll and a true artist. I'd managed to discuss my screen test with the director and wondered why Stromberg was even shooting the day before a holiday. In my mind, the Fourth of July should always be a four day weekend and include Monday, something already practiced by many corporations.

So far, my picture was right on schedule in spite of Mercury being difficult. My character was a vixen played with sympathy, since in those days I still didn't want to be hated by my fans. At the rate things were moving along, my part in the film could be over by mid-July. That would mean a break between pictures and rest from a 16-hour workday. Ah, the glory of being an actor. If only the public knew the whole story!

There were many familiar faces on that soundstage at Fontaine, with several discussing Columbia's latest release: *Guess Who's Coming to Dinner,* which starred Katharine Houghton, Sidney Poitier, Spencer Tracy and Kathryn Hepburn. The story of interracial marriage was a first for a major studio. There was anxiety on the part of some executives, with more than a few saddened by the recent death of Spencer Tracy, a great actor and fine man. Tracy was going to be missed.

Finally, I caught sight of Scott on the opposite side of the room smoozing a studio exec. His face lit up the moment he saw me, and that made me feel good. The producer with him was involved with *Speak Softly, My Love.*

"So you finally decided to show up," he said, kissing my cheek and guiding me toward the bar. "Champagne, I presume?" He selected two glasses and handed me one, clicking my glass with his. "To us," he said, gazing into my eyes.

"I can't possibly be Jennifer. Have you let him know?" I nodded toward the producer.

Scott shook his head, his eyes glued to mine.

"It's only fair to let him know," I said, diverting my eyes from his intense gaze. I sipped my champagne, since looking into Scott's eyes had often made feel a need to please him. Maybe it was because of our horoscopes? I didn't want to feel a need to please anyone anymore. I wanted to be the one in charge.

"Wouldn't it be wiser on your part to wait until after the screen test? I can wait until Monday or for another week, for that matter. What if you aren't cast as Victoria? What if there's a last minute glitch and Louis can't have his way? It wouldn't be the first time with a famous actor."

His sudden interest in my career surprised me. Was this a brand new Scott Wellington standing before me? He was always more concerned with himself.

"Jennifer is not a great role, but it's good enough. The part would show off your talents to your advantage."

"Which talents?" I batted my false eyelashes at him. "You failed to mention the nude scenes." I sipped champagne not anywhere near as fine as Dom Perignon and stared into his amused eyes.

"I knew you'd read the script. What's the big deal? It's not like you've never done a nude scene before. How about those French films without Monsieur Lamprais? Or lucky Louis, as he's known in the trade!" He sipped champagne. "I'd say he's a damn lucky man all around."

Suddenly feeling self-conscious, I glanced away.

"You look great naked. The cameras just eat you up and spit you out magnificent up on the silver screen, with every man in the theater getting a hard-on at the sight of your ... beautiful face," he grinned, his eyes purposely moving down to my cleavage.

The low-cut purple silk dress fit me like a dream and complemented my dark hair, my green eyes and fair skin. I was wearing Scott's diamonds by design. He looked pleased to see me wearing the more conservative diamond drops from my birthday the previous year, a karat for each ear, the one around my neck on a fine gold chain. Scott's diamonds were always bigger than Daddy's, three karats altogether. And, at that moment, Scott looked like me might enjoy removing them, one by one, along with everything else I had on. Now, wasn't that just like him?

"I've missed you, really missed you," he murmured, softly kissing my temple. "You have no idea how much I've missed you, Dana. I've missed everything about you."

The hint of his breath on my sensitive ear instantly captured my full attention. The bastard. Moisture started to collect in all the appropriate places. He had to notice his effect on me from the glint in his eyes. It was the same heat that Scott had always generated in me from the first moment we met. Feeling mildly apprehensive, I tried to ignore the feelings welling up inside. Sipping champagne, I selected a canapé from the tray held out by a waiter. Salmon mousse. Even looking away from him, I could sense his breath on my eyes, on my forehead and my lips. Damn him.

"It's good for you to miss me," I managed, looking directly into his eyes.

"You're giving me a hard on," he said, moving closer.

"That has never been your problem, has it, darling? You'd make a wonderful porn star. Just the slightest suggestion and up it goes!"

"Don't be ridiculous! I don't walk around with a perpetual erection, except when I'm near you. But then, I might if I directed naked people fucking. That might be a turn on. What do you think? Are all porn directors simply voyeurs getting off on their work?"

I managed to keep a straight face, which wasn't easy. "This conversation is getting out of hand," I said in my mild attempt at anger.

That was when I noticed Barbara Darling across the crowded room. I was sure she had seen us together. Barbara had to know I'd seen her. I managed a slight wave, as Scott continued to hover with his heavy breathing. His actions had to be apparent to almost everyone in the room.

"I think we are about to be news," I said, adding a disgusted sigh.

"Of course," he said, looking utterly pleased and making a point to nod at Barbara. "That's what these shindigs are all about. Being in the news, getting publicity, getting your film projects talked about by anyone worth mentioning. Surely you have that one figured out. You've been in this business for some time now, baby girl."

"I'm not your baby girl!"

"Pity."

"Sexist!"

In selecting a mushroom cap from a tray extended my way, I was trying to cope with my mounting emotions from just standing so close to him. I sensed his body heat while noting his chiseled cheekbones, his perfect tan, and his sensuous mouth. The attraction was always overpowering. I was beginning to feel somewhat out of control.

"What's the matter, darling? Are you worried about your over-the-hill Frenchman reading our names romantically linked in the columns?" Scott popped a mushroom cap into his mouth and picked up another before nodding the waiter on with directorial aplomb.

Sipping champagne seemed my only line of defense.

"Are you worried that the news might rob you of the role of Victoria? Which I'd say is impossible at this late date, since Lamprais seems to have so damn much clout in this town at the present time. I know for a fact, through my studio connections, that Lamprais will accept no one but you in the role. The execs at Colossal have basically come to an agreement, if you must know the truth. Most impressive, I say. I don't see how you can miss, my darling woman, so please don't fret about losing your plum role. The part is already as good as announced in the trades."

He was looking across the room above my head, his expression suddenly sobering, as I weighed in on his astonishing disclosure.

"The man seems to be quite taken with you," he said, looking down at me. "I can understand how just about any man could be completely and totally taken with you."

"I see."

"The studio execs insisted on the test as a formality. It's something of a power play, my dearest, darling, adorable Dana. What is it that worries you? Losing Louis or losing Victoria? Are you afraid Lamprais might change his mind if he learned about us being together? Surely, there is no commitment!"

"Whatever do you mean, great Scott?" I said in a mild attempt at humor, confounded by the fact that he seemed to know me so well. Great Scott was always used in bed, since he satisfied me thoroughly each and every time. Scott could not be fooled, something appreciated by most women, since so many men seemed clueless when it came to satisfying a woman.

"Let me be great Scott tonight," he whispered, quickly glancing at his wristwatch.

I sensed his breath on my lips right before he kissed me. It happened before I could raise my glass in self defense. "Must you kiss me in public?" I flared, quickly stepping back. "Must you create a spectacle in front of all these people? Whatever is the matter with you?" I stepped farther back and finished my champagne.

"I'm sorry. I've wanted to kiss you since you walked onto this soundstage. You look beautiful, as always." Plainly irritated, he glanced away.

Inside, I was starting to tremble.

"Let's get out of here. I'll take you to Musso and Franks and we'll have some real food. I could use a good martini."

Admittedly, I was hungry.

Soon, we were seated in a cozy booth ordering vodka martinis with extra olives, steaks medium rare, baked potatoes with sour cream and chives, and Caesar salads. Immediately, Scott launched into a rant on his film about to be released, a suspense thriller the studio titled *Uncertain Danger*.

Occasionally, Scott's hand found its way to my thigh. Old habits are hard to break. Each time, I simply removed his hand and he grinned.

"Funny, it doesn't look like polyester."

"It's silk, Scott. My dress is made of silk."

He cut another bite of steak and glanced across the room as he chewed.

For a short time, Scott kept his hand to himself. After a second martini, I stopped objecting. The magnetism was getting stronger by the minute, especially after he kissed me and sent electrical charges from my head down to my tingling toes and everywhere else in between.

Shortly after dinner, my Mercedes followed his Mercedes up into the Hollywood Hills to his bachelor pad with its king-sized bed and wide view of the sparkling lights of the City of Los Angeles.

We made love for hours, as we had so many times before, moving in perfect harmony to each other's wants and needs. In the background, the music of the 1940s played: Frank Sinatra. Ella Fitzgerald. Tony Bennett. All songs of love, as a pleasant accompaniment to the sensuous touching and feeling, as the kissing and lovemaking went on and on.

Finally, we slept soundly in each other's arms. Old habits are hard to break, in spite of the very best of intentions.

# Chapter 17

Being the typical bachelor, there was no food in Scott's kitchen that Saturday, not an egg nor an ounce of fresh coffee. We drove to Schwab's in his Mercedes, a Hollywood hangout where he often had breakfast. It was where the notables of day had breakfast or lunch in those days.

"I miss Florence's cooking," he said, pouring catsup onto his scrambled eggs.

"Really? I guess you can take the boy out of the Midwest, but you can't take the Midwest out of the boy." An uncle had taught me to eat catsup on my eggs back in Indiana, something I rarely did anymore. "Is that what you really missed the most, Scott?"

His response was a sheepish grin and he kissed the air. "We made up for lost time last night and this morning, don't you agree? I enjoyed your stellar performance, Miss Scofield."

My response was a soft kick in his shins under the table while draining the coffee from my cup, which a waitress instantly replenished. "Thank you," I said to her, as she smiled and moved on, and I spread grape jelly on my toast. "You've given me quite an appetite, dear man."

"I've heard that orgasms burn up like 500 calories," he whispered. "No wonder you're hungry. Eat everything and anything to your heart's content. I'll be more than happy to help you burn up more calories in any manner or position you fancy." He grinned and nodded at someone at the counter, and the man nodded back. Then his full attention returned to me.

"How about this evening? Harold Sparrow is having one of his infamous parties where we can hobnob with the rich, the famous, the wannabes, and the utterly decadent. Just your sort of bash, I'd say!"

"However did you finagle an invitation to his party?"

"I met him on the lot at Colossal back in April. I told you while you were working in Texas. He writes wonderful trash, don't you think? His characters translate to film and Hollywood brilliantly, especially now that everything is bursting wide open: sex, money, power! Whatever else is there?" He gently touched my hand. "You will go to the party with me, won't you? Pretty please with sugar and cream on it, my beautiful, fascinating, darling woman? Tell me you will, Dana, please say that it's true?" he was all smiles and displaying his usual, irresistible charm.

"I do have a prior commitment," I hedged, instantly weakening. After all, did I really want to miss a Harold Sparrow party to have dinner with a blackmailing scumbag when I might not be able to protect Paula, anyway? The legal bloodhounds were sniffing at her door and about to snarl at her in the courtroom.

"Please!" he said.

"I suppose I could change my plans. Dressy?"

"To the nines." Scott looked pleased. "I may wear my tux. It's optional."

"Please do wear your tux. You look gorgeous in your tux." I glanced at my wristwatch. "I really do need to go, Scott. I have lines to study and errands to run."

"Of course, you do."

Back at his house, with its glorious view on a rare smog-free California day, Scott said, "I'll pick you up at 7:30, love. I know I can count on you to dazzle. You always do, my dear, darling, exceptionally sexy Dana."

Our kiss was long, wet and deep and made my toes tingle.

Behind the wheel of my classic 450 SL, I zipped down Sunset Boulevard, leaving the Hollywood Hills behind to enter the plusher Hills of Beverly. The sun was shining and all seemed right in my world.

As I entered the house, Florence was seated in the breakfast room reading the morning newspapers. I had slammed the door a touch too hard and she scowled at me.

"Good morning, Florence."

"Good afternoon," she responded, peering over her reading glasses at my crumpled dress and the unsightly run in my black pantyhose. "Did you have a pleasant evening?" she said in her haughty tone.

"Lovely!" I said, thinking there was no way that my housekeeper was going to spoil my good mood. "I had breakfast at Schwab's, but I'd like some green tea with honey. I plan to sit by the pool and study my lines. I could also use a morning swim."

"It's afternoon," she said in her haughty tone again. Sometimes Florence acted like a mother hen with me her errant daughter. That wasn't the way things actually were, but that had never stopped her.

"I suppose it is afternoon. Did anything exciting happen while I was gone?"

The newspaper was put aside and she picked up a notepad and held it out to me with a blank expression. "Daniel Thurman wants you to call him at your first opportunity. He said it's urgent for him to talk to you."

"Urgent?" Instant panic gripped me. "Is it about the children? When did he call?" My heart started to race. "Has something happened to Christopher or Michele? For heaven's sake, Florence, why is it urgent? Did you even bother to ask?"

"He called about 15 minutes ago," she said. "I don't think it's the children. But he did say something about a death." The blood suddenly drained from her face and she forced the notepad into my hand. "You should call him now, Dana. It seems he's having trouble locating Paula. Do you happen to know where she is?"

"Oh, my God! I'll call him from upstairs," I said, running for the stairs and my room.

Rapidly, I undressed and pulled on my red bikini, all the while staring at the telephone number on the notepad. Then, I began to pace back and forth, wondering how much to say to Dan about Paula or Jamie, if anything. He probably didn't know about their trip to San Francisco. Paula hadn't told the children, and I didn't really know where they were at that moment, perhaps somewhere between Malibu and Hearst Castle, or even at the castle? I had no idea where they planned to stay. Paula had said something about the Big Sur and an inn where Hannah and Harold had stayed on their honeymoon. I wondered if I had Hannah's telephone number.

I remembered Paula and Jamie were supposed to be in San Francisco by Sunday to sail on some yacht. My knowledge of their whereabouts was vague at best. Paula wasn't sure how long they might be gone, perhaps a week, maybe longer. With the children in the mountains for July, it seemed like a good time for her to have some fun. I remembered her saying that the father of Dan's girlfriend had died. Could that be the death? Who in heaven's name had died?

At that moment, Retrograde Mercury seemed to be changing every-one's plans. Paula was a Pisces. Dan a Cancer. And Jamie Leo. No Gemini. The whole world was being turned upside down by Mercury. My plans had certainly changed overnight. Here I was with Scott, which was not really my plan.

Finally, I stopped pacing and picked up the telephone. My heart was still pounding in my chest. Slowly, I dialed Dan's number, taking several deep breaths as the telephone rang and rang and rang. I was ready to hang up when someone finally answered.

"Hello?" a man said.

"Dan Thurman?"

"That's me."

"This is Dana Scofield. My housekeeper said you needed to talk to me. Something about a death," my voice caught with the word *death*. "Michele and Christopher are all right, aren't they?" I whispered, my eyes instantly filling with tears. "Is there something wrong with the children?" I was barely able to ask the question.

"No. The children are fine, Dana," Dan said, "It's my mother," his voice caught and he started to softly sob.

"Your mother," I said, sinking into a chair. "I'm so sorry." I took another very deep breath, my hands still shaking as tears rolled down my face.

"Mother had a massive stroke early this morning. There was no warn-ing. My cousin Tully came by the house when she didn't answer the telephone. They usually had coffee together every morning..." he broke off, softly sobbing again, "I'm sorry, Dana."

Poor Dan. He was a mama's boy, after all. Something I had always sus-pected.

"I'm very sorry about the loss of your mother," I said, briefly wondering if I would feel any grief over Helen. The thought of her death might not even sadden me, and that thought made me even sadder at that moment.

"I've been trying to reach Paula," he said in a calmer voice, "But she isn't answering the telephone. I've only been able to reach her service. Does Maria work on Saturdays?"

""Maria has the week off. Paula gave her a vacation."

"So Paula might be working and not answering the telephone? Taking a walk, perhaps? The kids thought Maria was on vacation, but they weren't absolutely certain."

Determined not to volunteer any relevant information, I said, "Does this mean you're leaving for Michigan right away?"

"Yes, right away," he said. "I thought of leaving the children here with Paula, but I'd really like them with me. Christopher is pretty young for a funeral, but Michele wants to say good-bye to her grandmother," his voice started to break again. "We're booked on a three o'clock flight through Chicago. We won't get there until sometime tomorrow morning. We have to take a commuter flight up the peninsula."

"I see."

"I don't have time to make a trip to Malibu. Michele says her mother sometimes takes long walks. I've already left three messages."

"I'll tell Paula. I'm doing a film at Stromberg right now, so I haven't seen her this week." We had talked on the telephone, but the rest of it was true. "I wasn't here earlier. My schedule is rather demanding right now."

There was a long pause.

"I've also been trying to find my nephew, Jamie. You met him, right?" There was a definite edge to his voice with that question.

"Yes. I've met Jamie."

"He left telephone numbers in San Diego and San Francisco that I've passed on to his mother, my sister, June. She's the one who called me early this morning to let me know about mother," his voice broke again. "I immediately drove home with the kids. There wasn't time to go to Malibu for dresses for Michele. I keep a couple of dresses here. Paula didn't include any dresses with the clothes she sent to Lake Arrowhead. No nice slacks for Chris. No dress shirts."

"You were taking the children to the mountains for a month, Dan. Why would Paula pack dressy clothes? Does Michele wear dresses other than sun dresses in the mountains?"

"You're right, of course. I wasn't thinking. Death isn't something we can plan for, is it?" he said in a flat tone. I could hear him blow his nose.

"I guess not. I'll tell Paula when I see her." I desperately wanted the conversation to end. It was 1:30 and Dan had a plane to catch. "You must be ready to leave for the airport. I'm glad I caught you first."

"My neighbor is driving us to the airport in just minutes."

I somehow knew that Dan's mind was filled with questions about Paula and Jamie. Separately. Together. Jamie had told his uncle that he loved her. Dan had to know they had spent plenty of time together lately. In my heart of hearts, it seemed to me that Richard Randolph had already spilled his entire can of beans, even though he tired to blackmail me to keep his big mouth shut. Not only was he a scumbag, but a goddamn liar to boot.

A date was going to be broken. Better yet, I would stand up the son-of-a-bitch and leave him standing at my front door. Scott was picking me up at 7:30. Florence was leaving for Palm Springs before that. I thought maybe I should call Harold and hire those thugs to break both of Richard Randolph's arms and legs.

"Best of luck in Michigan," I said. "I'm sorry for your loss."

"I've tried to reach Jamie in San Diego, but no one answered the phone. There wasn't even an answering machine. Don't you find that odd?"

"Not everyone has an answering machine, Dan. And, it is Saturday. People go out on Saturday, even I have errands to run."

"I'm sorry, Dana. Please don't let me keep you any longer. Thanks for calling. Tell Paula I'll be in touch tomorrow. This is not the sort of family reunion I'm crazy about. The woman in my life is in Ohio burying her father today. He was the same age as my mother."

"I'm really sorry, Dan," I said, eager for the conversation to end. "They say deaths come in numbers." I was breathing easier, knowing the children were fine. "I suppose you'll be in Michigan for some time to tend to your mother's affairs."

"Probably. Tell Paula that the kids need to talk to her, especially Michele."

"Give them my love. Tell them I'm sorry about their grandmother. I know they both loved the family reunions with your mother in Michigan. Lately, Michele has been worried about her. You could say that your daughter had a psychic premonition."

"I see." He paused. "I'll give my children your best."

The conversation ended.

For several minutes, I just stood there doing deep breathing and wondering what I should do next. Minimal effort was made to locate Hannah's telephone number. She wasn't listed. Since I didn't know where Paula and Jamie were, there was nothing else for me to do. I picked up my script and headed downstairs to the pool. Frisky was barking at the squirrels again, running around dog nuts.

It seemed to me that it was business as usual in Beverly Hills, USA. Where Paula and Jamie were concerned, I had acted my part in the unfolding drama of their lives by keeping as many secrets as possible. Hopefully, the cat would stay in the bag for yet another day.

# Chapter 18

The Sparrows' party was over the top. The huge mansion decorated in Beverly Hills gauche, expensive everything, large and grand, not my taste but impressive. Perhaps the house was done up like a mansion of one of his wealthy character's in one of his bestselling novels and films. Many of the guests seemed gauche as well, over the top when it came to attire, name, fame or notoriety.

The affluent arrived in multi-colored chauffeured limos, mostly black or white. Two pink. One lime green. Another fluorescent purple. Rolls Royce's. Mercedes. Cadillac's. Lincoln Town Cars. Flashy sports cars. All with flashy show biz personalities inside. Attendants parked the cars. The starlets were out in large numbers, sparkling throughout the rooms: Young. Pretty. Voluptuous. Svelte. Mostly blonde. A few redheads. Few actors were under contract to the studios anymore, the way it was the first three years of my acting career. Sadly, times had changed for the young and the talented in Tinseltown.

Bars were set up everywhere: The permanent bar in a nicely crafted den, another bar in the three bedroom guesthouse, another beside the pool, and one on the far side of the sprawling patio with all the flowers and trees. All the bars were well stocked with handsome bartenders and the best booze available to intoxicate the bright-eyed and the beautiful, even the ugly. Waiters and waitresses served drinks and hors d'oeuvres: Mushrooms stuffed with crab. Rumaki. Salmon mousse. Shrimp. Oysters on the half shell. An amazing assortment of bite-size edibles were constantly at my fingertips. All of them tasty. That party was catered on a scale I'd never seen before in a private home. Trashy novels do sell well, hear tell!

The double tennis courts were tented and transformed into The Cotton Club with red and black lettering above the entry. Inside the quasi-nightclub, Les Brown and his Band of Renown played the dance music of the '40s and '50s, the settings of most Sparrow novels. The guests danced or watched or simply listened. Scott was an excellent dancer. We danced under the revolving mirrored ball that reflected a prism of multi-colored light. It was magical and romantic. The party was something non-actors might think of as 'like being in a movie.' Most show biz outsiders are ignorant of the amount of work that goes into creating the grand illusion up on a wide screen in a darkened theater, or even on a TV screen.

Multiple starlight crystal chandeliers were suspended from the newly constructed ceiling of the dimly lit 'nightclub.' All the round tables were covered with white linen with silver and linen napkins, fine crystal wine and champagne glasses, not the usual party ware. The extravagance was par excellence. Quite wonderful and grand.

It was fun to dance to the old tunes so important in my youth. No records that evening. Sequined ladies sang in strapless gowns, alternately black and white in complexion. Professional dancers entertained. Male singers in tuxes crooned ala Mathis or Sinatra. Occasionally, the real deal grabbed the mike and sang for his supper, perhaps as a thank you to his generous host and hostess. Mr. and Mrs. Sparrow constantly made the rounds, chatting with and charming their delighted and well entertained guests.

Professional dancers performed singly, or in couples, and finally, in chorus. All wore fabulous costumes that reflected 30 years of motion picture musical history. One entertainer, a voluptuous transvestite Carmen Miranda, delighted everyone, with several encores. When the band took a break, a three piece combo played in front of the bandstand, so everyone could continue to dance. The presentations were unreal! That party was 'like being in a movie!'

Around the tented walls of the nightclub were tables with chefs dressed in white serving the finest cuisine from the finest restaurants in the city. Everything was delicious. Japanese. Chinese. Indian. Italian. Hungarian. French. Greek. Spanish. Mexican. The desserts were gorgeous and to die for. Flambé this. Flambé that. There was everything you could imagine and then some. All my epicurean desires were fulfilled as waiters constantly refilled our glasses with champagne and the finest wines. The party was beyond amazing!

When the union musicians stopped playing at two on Sunday morning, Les Brown and a few of his musicians joined the party. The hangers-on, including Scott and me, adjourned to the living room to dance and drink. Candlelight flickered in the flamboyantly furnished room that displayed museum-sized oil paintings. One black musician played the baby grand, another was on bass, while a cute white guy played clarinet. A lounge singer in purple sequins sang until the wee hours, as we danced and drank champagne until we were ready to fall asleep standing up.

We got back to my place around 4:30 a.m.

Scott approved of my new pink love nest, his first sleepover since my return from Texas. We only made love once as the sun rose higher over the treetops. Between all the champagne and strong coffee, I tossed and turned, fully unable to turn off my mind, with Scott sleeping soundly beside me. I remembered how easily Louis had fallen asleep after making love once, only to reawaken in an hour or two to start over again.

Suddenly, I was wide awake. My brain would not turn off, as the men in my life with the most voracious sexual appetites were mentally compared one with the other. In the past week, I had slept with two highly sexed males besides Scott. Phil was not even in the league. Eric was good at pleasing. The three men possessed innate lovemaking skills.

With Florence in Palm Springs with her friends for a few days, the house was ours that Sunday. For several days, it would just be Frisky and me. It would be fun to fend for myself. And yet, while still trying to fall asleep, my thoughts suddenly turned to Paula and Jamie. It seemed a shame that their trip was going to be cut short by the death of Margaret Thurman. The woman was in her seventies. Three score and ten was all the Good Book promised, according to my daddy. After that, we are living on borrowed time, Daddy said. My father was a Methodist.

In those days, I wasn't sure what I was. Maybe a Universalist. And yet, that Sunday it seemed to me that the Bitch of Atlanta was going to find her son, but hopefully, not before the ship sailed. Paula said they planned to watch the fireworks on the Fourth on a yacht on San Francisco Bay. That seemed highly unlikely to me, as I finally fell sound asleep.

\* \* \*

We slept until noon and had a quickie before Scott climbed into the bubbling whirlpool with me. We languished with our espressos, orange juice, flaky croissants and strawberry preserves. Our continental breakfast was tasty amidst soothing bubbles, as sunlight streamed through the skylight and the frosted windowpane.

Then, we made love again. His body was so familiar to me after two years. Each of us had been with others during our not infrequent tiffs, like me with the handsome Italian cameraman in Rome, but I never asked Scott about other women. What I didn't know couldn't hurt me, could it?

That afternoon in the breakfast room we enjoyed mushroom omelets and green salads with cherry tomatoes before taking our naked swim. Then, we made love all afternoon.

"I'm limp, Scott. Please!" I pleaded on my bed.

He covered my body with tiny, wet, warm kisses, moving on down to plant kisses in every spot imaginable.

"How many times can I come in one day?"

"You keep score?" he murmured, working me over with his talented tongue.

He licked and aroused me with as much finesse as Louis, which suddenly had me confused. How could I not compare the different men who had so recently occupied my bed? Each man had felt good to me when he was there, although Scott probably knew me better than the others. Was I really in love with Scott? Or was it lust? We had leapt into bed on the very first night, both of us definitely in heat. Was it love or was it just raging hormones?

Before long, I was crying out again, "Oh, my god ... my god!" and shuddering from head to toe in a divine orgasm. "Four," I said, making him stop. "How about some sleep? I'm still pretty tired."

Scott slid up beside me. "We can sleep ... for a while."

Before long, he was inside me again, filling me up with his heat, plunging in and out, hitting me just right. It was Insatiable Sunday. Our bodies a perfect fit. I liked the way he smelled and the way he tasted. Was it love or lust circling through my body and my brain, as the energy coursed through me in wonderful waves of pleasure one more time?

"Five!" I cried out as he exploded inside me.

"Dana ... my darling!" Scott cried out, but what else could the dear man do?

Again, Scott slept.

Once again, I found myself comparing Scott with Louis, and strangely enough, with Jeffrey Waters. The man who all of them needed to thank for awakening me to my true needs as a female. Otherwise, I might have remained a virgin much longer, but probably not too long. Until Scott, no other man had again fulfilled my great expectations. There were not even orgasms with some men who thought of themselves as great lovers. Many men seemed to suffer from delusions of grandeur when it came to their ability to make love to a woman. I had learned that early on.

Once more, I was thinking of Paula and Jamie. Were they still together? Had they escaped the clutches of the wicked witch of the east? Was there any real hope for Paula and Beau?

Fortunately, Stromberg Pictures didn't need me that Monday. Retrograde Mercury was on my side for my afternoon screen test at Colossal. When it was still dark on that Sunday morning, I'd discovered Richard Randolph's business card tucked into my front door with *Too bad for your friend* written on the back. Scumbag! Creep! Asshole!

And much later on that same night, I finally fell into a very deep sleep lying next to the sexy, snoring, cinematic genius of the day.

# Chapter 19

"I didn't really expect to find you at home," I said to Paula on the phone early that Monday morning. "I thought I might be leaving a message with your answering service."

Her immediate response: an audible yawn.

"Frankly, I'm not really all that surprised. What time did you get home?"

"Around midnight. Do you know what happened? Margaret died of a stroke."

"Dan called me trying to find you. I figured the bloodhounds would sniff you out soon enough. Sorry, dear!" I paused. "So Jamie is back in Michigan for the funeral?"

"His flight left at four and I started driving. I stopped for gas in San Lucas and didn't stop again until Buellton for Andersen's split pea soup. It hit the spot."

"I buy it in the store in cans."

"After a hot shower to release some tension, I fell into bed." Again, she yawned. "Are you at the studio?"

"Mercury Retrograde," I said. "At least I'll be rested for the screen test this afternoon, which I pray to God happens. I'm sorry I woke you up so early."

7:30.

Scott had just left.

"I need to get up, anyway. I need to paint. I have lots to do before October."

We talked about Margaret's death on Retrograde Mercury without a clue as to what it meant, except that things had changed for both of us in just days.

"I'm still achy from the drive. It took me eight hours."

"When Dan called, I really didn't know where you were. But I figured they would find you." I sipped my now tepid coffee. Fortunately, I still had hours to goof off before makeup, costume and the test.

"No one would have found out if she hadn't died. Leave it to Margaret Thurman to die to spite me."

"Dan wanted the kids with him, Paula. He thought Chris might be a little young, but Michele wanted to go. I hope you and Jamie at least had a couple of great days."

"Inspiring days in beautiful places," her tone revealed the depth of her feelings. "Enlightening, loving, sensual days I wouldn't have missed for the whole world," her voice caught. "Jamie asked me to marry him after he graduates."

Stunned, I stubbed out my cigarette. That Georgia peach was full of surprises. "What did you say?" I was almost afraid to ask.

"I never answered him. It happened during the throes of passion and we fell asleep. There wasn't time for him to ask me again. But our time together was cosmic." She paused. "We thought we had more time, Dana. I'll have to see what I say if he asks me again, since everything has changed."

"What do you mean?"

"Jamie is there and I'm here, with miles of relatives between us, with my son his first cousin, Dan his uncle, and then, there's June, another kink in the family chain. There's the difference in our ages, our life experiences, with me divorced twice, a child with each husband, and one of those exes just happens to be his Uncle Dan."

"It is complicated."

"Michele is as much younger than Jamie as I am older. She's right in the middle. The girl Dan adopted and loves. The girl who was worried that her grandmother might die." She paused. "We were planning to see the old mining towns in Nevada and stop in Carmel, maybe take another tour of Hearst Castle. It is huge and quite impressive. Those people knew how to live."

"I'm so sorry, Paula."

Her bout with self-pity continued, something we women can do with each other. Bitch and moan. Paula was being dramatic. The difference in their ages really bothered her. That was a much bigger deal in '67 than it is now. Older men have always married women decades younger: Another aspect of the double standard that persists without comment. Her two children were the bigger issue, along with the fact that Jamie was Christopher's first cousin, which didn't seem to bother Jamie.

"Crimony, Paula, please stop!" I could feel her pain. "Driving home alone gave you way too much time to think. Give things time. It'll blow over."

"How can Margaret's death blow over? She was everyone's grandmother. All of this is so damn convoluted that I don't see how it can ever work out with Jamie, unless Dan and June die, too. And even then, they'd probably just haunt us."

We both laughed.

"Better in spirit than in body?"

"I'm not some innocent adolescent. I'm 30. I've been married twice and have two kids. I know a few things."

"God knows that's true!" I lit another cigarette. "By the way, no Richard Randolph. I never went out with the prime creep."

"Good. He was a lost cause. Before I left on Friday, Dan said I'd be hearing from his lawyers."

"Goddamn him. I'll be in your corner, Paula. Just play the continuance game and drag things into infinity. Then, both kids will grow up and you'll no longer have to deal with the son-of-a-bitch."

"I'll have to deal with Dan until one of us dies. With any luck, I'll be served today. That seems a fitting gift for his ex on his birthday and the day of his mother's funeral! He'll never forget this birthday!"

"Forty-five?"

"Forty-five. And he has my children and the man I love, along with his entire goddamn family, in Michigan." Paula started to cry. "Why not send out a process server on a sunny California Monday? How perfect can one life be?"

"I'm really sorry, Paula. It is a bit much, isn't it?"

"How is Louis?" she said between her sobs, and I heard her blowing her nose.

"Louis is still in New Orleans. He's left messages." I finished off the coffee. "I didn't answer the phone, because I was with Scott all weekend."

"Surprise! Surprise!"

"We went to a Harold Sparrow party ... really over the top, swell and all that jazz. I met the fabulous, the filthy rich, and the exceedingly famous. We danced until four in the morning and spent Sunday in bed."

"You are beyond amazing."

"Florence is still in Palm Springs. So no one was here when Richard arrived. Scott and I had the run the house yesterday, which was nice. He started to put on Louis' new silk robe and that turned into a major argument. But he cooled his jets. He wore the terry cloth robe I got him last year. We only had to deal with Frisky and the chattering squirrels."

"So Scott knows that Louis has a silk robe? You are wonder woman!" Paula paused. "And Louis knows about the terry cloth bathrobe, right?"

"Of course. He refused to wear it."

"You are way beyond amazing!"

"Good sex always calms Scott down." Suddenly, a strange sensation wafted through me, which reminded me of my mental gymnastics over lust and love ... about Scott ... about Louis ... about Eric. Maybe I was only in lust with Scott Wellington, with any of them, for that matter. Or was I really in love with Scott? I just couldn't be sure.

"Beau left another message."

"And you're calling him back, right? He's such a nice guy, Paula."

"My life is much too complicated at the moment. I'm not about to fly to Texas. I don't want to jeopardize my position with my children in any way."

"How can Texas do that? Beau Kandell is single and mature, besides being perfect for you. You are divorced. Beau could marry you tomorrow, not when he graduates from college." I paused and cringed. "I'm sorry. That was a cheap shot."

"It was no shot. Jamie won't be 20 until next month. But I do love him."

"My instincts about Michele and Christopher have always been right, haven't they? I say you are not losing your children. End of subject."

"I certainly hope you're right," she said. "I need to get something to eat, and I need to paint. Break a leg with your screen test. And let me know how it goes, okay?"

"I will," I said, hoping and praying that my instincts about her kids were right. I would never forgive myself if I was in anyway responsible for Paula losing those children.

I made it to Colossal in plenty of time for makeup and wardrobe. My late breakfast had provided me with enough energy to act with a cool, calm and clear head. My lines were memorized for the benefit of Keith Sutherland and the other head honchos at Colossal. In the silence of my dressing room, I did some deep breathing exercises and clearly visualized myself as the Victoria Rutherford of the 1800s, the strong, passionate heroine of the wonderful story.

Then, I was called to the set.

"Action!" Keith called out.

Swishing around in the voluminous skirts with graceful aplomb, I confronted the swaggering hero who had just killed a man in a duel because the lawless cowboy had the nerve to insult me. The act was foolish on the part of his opponent, since Pierre Pomeroy always got his man. The rugged frontiersman would be played to perfection by one Louis Lamprais.

The wine red period costume on Gregory was stunning, an elegant plume dangled from his broad-brimmed hat. The actor was a handsome devil. Acting with two handsome male actors with charm and dash was going to make my work on location enjoyable.

After the test, Greg bought me a drink at the restaurant across the street. Twenty-six, tall, dark and handsome, he made a pass. Nonetheless, I was not prepared to add him to my growing list of admirers. After all, it was the beginning of July. What advantage was there for me to be outright greedy that early during the sensational Summer of Love?

# Chapter 20

The next morning there was an early telephone call from Eric, "You will come on down to the beach, won't you, to play in the sun and swim in the sea? We'll take a long walk. I've been in a grueling laboratory all week. I need fresh salt air and to swim in the sea with beautiful you," he made it sound inviting.

"Well, it is the Fourth of July!"

Scott had called the evening before and tried to pin me down. And yet, we had already done that for three days. I told him I had previous plans. Louis was stuck in New Orleans. And, with the recent turn of events in the life of my friend, I felt the need to be there for her.

"How about it?"

"Why not! I'd love to spend the day at the beach. It's going to be hot and sticky here in town, and Guy and Larry always do fun fireworks. Buy some fireworks so we can add our share and don't forget the sparklers. I'll bring along some fresh fruit. I'm sure the men will invite us to their barbecue."

After that, my agent called me with the incredible news.

In moments, I was on the telephone with Paula.

"I GOT THE PART!" I nearly screamed into the telephone. "I'm going to be Victoria! Paula. I'm going to be Victoria Rutherford!"

"Did you ever doubt it for a minute? You will be fantastic," she said in a strangely flat tone.

"We'll start filming in Colorado, only one location of several. Maybe you can visit and bring along your sketch pad." I was beyond excited.

"That sounds like fun, maybe after my show in October. Fall in Colorado sounds lovely. The autumn colors must be gorgeous."

"Paula, you cannot imagine what this film is going to do for my career!"

"Your screen test must have gone well," Paula said in an odd tone.

"The salary is great. I'm so glad Tom didn't wait until tomorrow to call. He called me today. Wasn't it sweet of him to call on a national holiday?"

Frisky started to bark at the squirrels, but I didn't care. Frisky was going to Malibu. Maybe he could chase seagulls instead of squirrels and prance in the surf.

"I'm bringing Frisky. With the top down, he loves to bite at the wind. I'll bring along some dog food."

"Frisky is welcome. Have you told Scott?"

"No. But Louis called right after Tom. He said, 'I told them you were magnifique.' Louis will be here for the weekend and he wants Saturday for us."

"Scott should be overjoyed."

"Scott is going to have to learn to share. I may not be in love with Scott, after all, Paula. I may just be in lust, the same as with Louis. Imagine, me in lust with Louis Lamprais, my brand new leading man!"

"Good girl! All that without your therapist! You are making progress."

"Well, Louis and I will be spending lots of time together on this film. It could take months. Greg is a peach, too, by the way. A 26-year-old stunner!"

"Oh, my god! Not another one!"

"Scott refused to cast another actress until I heard about the screen test. Sweet, huh? I guess I need to let him know. What are you up to this afternoon?"

"I don't know. It's the Fourth, isn't it?" By that time, her tone was downright gloomy. "Larry and Guy will be doing their thing, barbeque, fireworks on the beach. You should come on down."

"Earlier this morning, I had a call from a certain biochemist and accepted his invitation. I don't remember if I mentioned Frisky. Eric will simply have to cope."

"I still have the doggy bed and cage." Paula paused. "How do you keep them all straight, Miss Slut Puppy? You are one remarkable woman!"

"Just say 'darling' during crucial moments. You know what I mean?"

We both laughed.

"Daddy called this morning from Indianapolis."

"How is George?"

"My stepmother is having a bladder lift. Daddy is concerned. But the doctor says it's routine. But surgery is surgery. Martha is 55, young for such a procedure."

"The joys of feminine aging. I can wait, can't you?"

"Daddy also gave me some disturbing news about Cindy Waters, Jeff's wife. The guy who was my first love back in Indiana."

"What sort of news?"

"It seems that Cindy is fighting a losing battle with ovarian cancer. She's my age, Paula, 32!"

"That's awful. Didn't you say they have two children?"

"A boy and a girl. The boy must be eleven. Poor Jeff. My father has kept in touch with him over the years. Jeff practices law in Indianapolis. When we were young, he always talked politics, the same as Jamie. He was student-body president and had plenty of charisma. I can see him as a congressman or senator one day."

"Tall with black hair and blue eyes, right?"

"A dream walking. He's probably aged nicely. I always thought he might."

"How long has it been since you've seen him?"

"Five years ago at my grandmother's funeral. It was sweet of him to be there. He always liked my grandmother. Cindy was there, too. I thought she acted a little uncomfortable. At least that was my psychic sense. They didn't bring the kids."

"Are you still attracted to him?"

"You're probably the only one I'd ever admit it to, but yes. My guess was that I still hold an attraction for him, too, from the way he stared at me."

"Cindy must have been thrilled to pieces."

"She may not have noticed. It can't be easy for him with her so sick. Cindy and I used to be close. Cheerleaders. People always said we looked like sisters. It was weird. We were born a week apart, Gemini look-alikes."

"That was why he married her. You were in Hollywood being a movie star and Cindy was your stand-in with Jeffrey Waters."

Out of the blue, I had chills from head to toe. "I never thought of it that way. I've always wondered if I did the right thing by not marrying him. I did love him. He was handsome, smart, ambitious and great in bed. He spoiled me rotten. That kind of man is a rare find, although I've found a few since. Lucky me!"

We both laughed.

"You could still end up as Mrs. Jeffrey Waters," Paula said in a wistful tone.

Again, I got the chills. "Paula, she's not dead yet. Don't be morbid." More chills ran up and down my arms and legs. "You're giving me the chills and weirding me out. Stop it!"

Years ago, Ilona the gypsy had said that chills meant something was true.

"When are you coming down to the beach?" she was sounding stressed again.

"Noon. Stromberg changed everything again. I shoot tomorrow afternoon, of all things. You must have empty beds with Maria and the kids gone."

"I have enough room for Eric too, unless you want to be with all the other male animals, huffing and puffing. That house will be filled with women and sex tonight, the same as after the party."

"Don't be vulgar, darling, but you're probably right."

That made us both laugh.

"I accept your invitation to spend the night, complete with your doggie bed."

"My home is your home, you know that."

"Any word from Jamie?"

There was a long pause before Paula said, "It seems there's a pregnant girl in Philadelphia who insists that Jamie marry her."

"WHAT?" I shrieked. "You're kidding, right? Tell me that you're kidding!"

"Afraid not. Some college girl named Stephanie claims she's pregnant and the child is Jamie's. She expects him to marry her to make things right."

"OH MY GOD!" I shrieked, and Frisky immediately started barking. No wonder Paula was down in the dumps. So the Georgia peach had turned downright rotten! Damn him!

"My instincts were right about being served yesterday."

"On his birthday ... the day of his mother's funeral?"

"Right."

"The bastard! Bastards run in that family, Paula. Good grief!"

"This clean-cut, cute, young guy in his 20s served me. I'm sure he was part of the plan. He couldn't have been much older than Jamie, maybe 21."

"Your life is beginning to sound like a bad B movie. You need me today. I promise not to spend all my time with Eric."

"It would be really nice if we could talk."

"I'll see you as soon as I can get there. Meanwhile, do some deep breathing. Take a walk and go see Andy. He's always good for fatherly advice. So far, my dear, this has not been your month."

"That's an understatement. Hurry on down. You always cheer me up."

Clothes were thrown into my overnight bag. Frisky loved the car with the top down. He wasn't really big enough to stick his head out the window, but he would bite at the air in pure dog heaven. It was the Fourth of July, and I was going to be Victoria Rutherford! All seemed right in my world on that day!

The drive down Sunset involved less traffic than anticipated, especially since it was a national holiday with the sun shining over the blue Pacific. Frisky pranced like a puppy, lapping at the wind, no doubt dog food for his soul. I'll never understand why dogs do that. Maybe he was extracting microorganisms from the air? I planned to ask Eric. Surely a biologist would know that much about dogs.

The sliding glass door on the deck was unlocked. My things were placed in Maria's room with the double bed. The kids had smaller beds which were quite unsuitable for six-foot-two, eyes of blue. The maid's room was also on the other side of the house where low animal groans were unlikely to disturb Paula. I didn't want to drive her up the wall after learning about Jamie and his pregnant girlfriend, or after dishonest Dan and bitchy June entered the mix. The young stud was clearly no virgin and learning about birth control the hard way, the same as a great many of his elders. Perhaps a shotgun wedding was being planned?

Poor Jamie.

Poor Paula.

What could I say to her to make her feel better? In my opinion, it was way past time for Paula Marlow to accept an invitation from a tall, blue eyed, Texas cowboy, especially since the Georgia peach had gotten himself into such a lowdown, rotten jam.

Secretly, I sympathized with Jamie.

Right after I left Indianapolis for Hollywood at the age of 18, and after Jeffrey Waters, 20, finished his second year at the university, he got Cindy Hanson pregnant. It was devastating news for me. I'd always thought he might wait until I'd fulfilled a few of my Hollywood dreams. Foolish on my part! Jeff was pressured by both families into doing the right thing. At least that was what I heard from that old gang of mine.

At first, I was puzzled. Jeff was always careful with me. I had a hard time imagining him being careless with Cindy. And yet, frankly, I wouldn't have been surprised if carelessness wasn't part of her plan. Or maybe Jeffrey was 'sticking it to me' and letting me know how much I'd screwed up by not accepting that half-karat antique diamond ring on the night of my senior prom.

Back then, I had worlds to conquer, places to go, men to meet, things I'd never bothered to tell him. Plus, there was no way that I wanted to spend my entire life in Indianapolis. Maybe that was the saddest part. Since, at that time, I hadn't seen much of the world. And besides, Cindy always had a thing for Jeff during the time that we were screwing our brains out in high school. I was stupid enough to tell her all about how great he was in bed. That must have whetted more than her appetite. She would stare at him with a love struck expression after I told her about him going down on me and giving me these incredible orgasms. All Cindy may have needed was for Jeff to make the slightest move and she would have been putty in his hands. I had a feeling that she called him minutes after I left town, and that was what happened, according to that old gang of mine.

In the 1950s, I wasn't the only girl in high school to enjoy wild and crazy sex, although some wanted to be virgins on their wedding night. Girls like Paula. She never went all the way until she was married. According to her, they had done everything but commit the final act. Sex was great for Paula in her first marriage, except when Michael was drunk or got stoned. She sometimes used sex to sober him up. Then, sadly, Michael killed himself under the influence of LSD not long after she left him.

Some of the guys in high school would get a girl drunk to take advantage of her. That was never necessary for Jeff. All he had to do was touch me and our clothes were soon off to better improve upon the action. One high school girlfriend was raped at a college fraternity party. Gang banged. The last I heard, Alice was happy with a woman. That kind of action can ruin a woman in every possible way. Drunken men can be ruthlessly criminal in terms of sex.

After spending six months in California, in my last letter to Jeff I advised him to see other girls. I was dating other men: actors, cameramen, advertising executives and an agent. But he kept on writing and asking me to marry him until he got Cindy pregnant. By that time, he must have thought I was some kind of Hollywood slut prostrating myself on casting couches. I sort of was, until one producer at Stromberg finally cast me in a decent role. Then, I told him to zip his fly when he said I owed him another blow job. By then, I had proven myself to be a genuine actress. Sex was no longer necessary to secure a job, which didn't really happen that often, only a few times with men who were attractive.

It was the belly dancing that finally landed me the role in that low budget Arabian Nights picture made in Death Valley. I thought it was going to be the death of me before I could get away from the scorpions, shiny black spiders as big as my hand, Gila monsters, and rattlesnakes in that Godforsaken hellhole. It was not a fun location.

Then, I met Paula and changed my ways. I no longer paid for anything with my body, which was something I had done in past lives in terms of woman's oldest profession.

By 1967, my acting career was in high gear. Gorgeous, talented men wanted me. And, I was about to become Victoria Rutherford on the big screen.

# Chapter 21

Ipicked up Paula's wide-brimmed straw hat that tied under my chin and headed next door to Eric's place. My outfit was very Fourth of July: red shorts, red, white and blue flag spaghetti strap top, and white leather sandals. My hair was down. The hat kept my hair out of my face walking into the ocean breeze.

"Hello, beautiful," Eric said, kissing me lightly when he noticed my bright red lipstick.

Soon, we were walking, hand in hand, over the sand. I could see Paula coming toward us farther down the beach and sensed she had seen Andy, the local prophet of our times. Andy could help us to get our heads on straight. He reminded me of some old-fashioned priest from Greece or some other ancient civilization. He was entirely metaphysical. During my considerable travels, I'd visited cathedrals, Hindu temples, Buddhist temples, synagogues and Celtic stone circles, all magical, with that ancient sense of the sacred.

I called out, "Hello, Paula!" but the rumbling surf drowned me out.

Paula didn't look up until she noticed Frisky running through the foam. I gave her my sandals to take back to the house. The water was up to my calves on that beautiful, sunny, summer day.

"Larry has invited us to the barbeque. We'll watch the fireworks together."

"That will be fun. I'll make a salad," she said.

"I'm bringing baked beans," Eric said in his cut off jeans and open red shirt.

"We're taking a walk," I said, "I'll be over to see you in a bit."

"Sounds good. I've come to a decision." There was an edge in her voice that matched her expression. My curiosity was piqued.

Eric started to tug on me. "We're taking a walk, remember?" he sounded bossy, which rubbed me the wrong way.

"See you," I said, walking through the foam with the male chauvinist pig biochemist as Paula started toward her house.

Many people were gathering on the beach. Some sat under umbrellas, others on towels or blankets. There were plenty of coolers and baskets in sight. The sun was directly overhead. Children and adults were enjoying the surf and the sea.

The cool water felt soothing on my feet and ankles. I doubted Scott had the nerve to show up uninvited. Our renewed intimacy had brought out his possessive side again, something that could happen after a split. But things had changed. I no longer belonged to Scott Wellington, even though the sex was still as great as ever. My feelings for him were no longer nearly as deep or as strong.

Onetime, Andy had explained that souls recapitulated patterns every time they reincarnate. Individuals nearly always repeated the patterns and relationships from the past in a summation of everything ever experienced. That sounded strange to me at first. As the soul evolves, he said, lessons are learned with less time spent on the useless and the meaningless. Patterns become more easily recognized as our awareness expands and grows.

As a past life husband, double Virgo made Eric highly critical and analytical, which was good for the scientist, but not working out with my Leo rising. Jeanne had said that I was important to his destiny and perhaps dazzled by a brilliant man with a lousy chart for marriage. That was good to know. According to Andy, resistance was the first step toward embrace, unless you become enlightened. Tell a man to beat it and he tends to be more persistent. Fully ignore him, and sooner or later, he takes the hint.

"Paula seems troubled," Eric said, as we were walking back along the water.

"She is," I said, with no intentions of telling him anything about her custody battle or a pregnant girl in Philly. Or about a witchy ex-sister-in-law brewing up bad magic in the east. Or an alcoholic ex with a weak backhand who was also an apt son-of-a-bitch. All of it together seemed like enough to trouble anyone.

"I suppose she can use some comfort," he said. "I need to check on the slow cooker with the beans."

Standing at the bottom of the stairs, Eric kissed me long and deep, my lipstick no longer a deterrent. "Take as much time as you like," he said, as though I needed his permission. With him six years my senior, Eric was having trouble with my independence. That summer I was not even close to being a submissive female.

"Thanks, darling," I cooed, going along with his silly game.

On the way to the refrigerator to get a cold drink, I heard Paula talking on the telephone:

"You want me to fly to Texas tomorrow?" she said, and suddenly, I was all ears. "Oh, you did!" she sounded buoyant. "You'll never guess who just walked in," she said, holding out the receiver to me. "Beau Kandell," she said, smiling.

"Why, Beau Kandell?" I said. "It's Dana here. How are you on this beautiful Independence Day? It's gorgeous here at the beach in Southern California."

"Is that a fact? I wish I were there with you two lovely young ladies, but I'm afraid the party would be over before I could get anywhere near Malibu," he said in his Texas twang.

"We'll miss you. We're having a barbeque. It won't be anything like the one you threw for our cast and crew on your ranch. No Texas chili or square dancing."

"Is that right? Well, that's a dang shame. You dance a mighty fine square."

"I hear you bought Andy's alabaster lovers, you lucky devil! Where are you going to put them in that big house?"

"I thought I might let Paula help me decide that when she arrives tomorrow. My guess is in the living room or entry. I'll see what she thinks," he sounded like a happy man.

"Is that a fact?" I said, turning to Paula. "You say she's flying to Texas tomorrow?"

She shrugged. But she looked a lot better than earlier.

"I can drop her off at the airport tomorrow. What time is her flight?"

"Once she gives me the go ahead, I'll call the airline and reserve a first class ticket in her name. Then, I'll call back with the flight number and time of departure, if that's all right?"

Extending the telephone receiver to Paula, I said, "Here, dear. You don't want to keep the man waiting. What time do you plan to leave for Texas tomorrow?"

Paula tried to suppress a grin and released a long sigh as she took back the telephone. "What time were you thinking?" she inquired.

A pregnant girl in Philly had just pushed Paula Marlow into the outstretched and eager arms of a handsome Texas cowboy!

Bingo for Beau! I thought.

Hallelujah and Amen!

# Chapter 22

Paula had not yet unpacked from her trip up the coast. There were still clean, unworn clothes in her suitcase. More jeans were added, a denim western shirt, sundresses, and the saddest-looking cowboy boots I'd ever seen. But those boots were good enough to ride a horse.

Her flight was nonstop to Dallas-Fort Worth. Paula had never flown in first class before. She was excited. And I was more than happy to take her to the airport. My angels had been listening. Plans kept changing because of Retrograde Mercury, and life in general, but some things were working out fine, in my opinion.

At 7:30, we left Malibu after a light breakfast. Paula was too nervous to eat. Everything was happening so fast she didn't have time to think. Her canvas bag of art supplies was her carry-on, although I thought Beau would have everything she might need or want in his art studio. That was the perfect place for Paula to paint.

"You're going to have a wonderful time. I don't need to be at the studio until noon, so we have time to spare. I'll stay until you board."

"I really appreciate this, Dana. Without you, I wouldn't even know Beau or be invited to Texas." Her nervousness was making me nervous.

"Stop being nervous! You'll be fine."

She sighed and said, "I guess," staring out the car window at the houses whizzing by, with an occasional glimpse of the wide blue sea.

The skies were hazy and overcast, with the traffic light all the way to the airport. In my opinion, everything was perfect in spite of her trepidation.

"You'll have a good time. Beauregard Kandell is a southern gentleman after the First Order of the Old South of Texas." She smiled at that remark.

"And his house is as gorgeous as he is, elegant and grand. You may have trouble taking it all in on just one visit."

"Dana…"

"It seems to me that 5,000 acres aren't that many in Texas. Some ranches have hundreds of thousands of acres. But you are going to love the art studio. It is groovy!"

"Groovy?" She smiled.

"Magnificently groovy and twice as big as yours."

"He said he has newly primed canvases waiting."

"You see! You are going to love it. You may not even want to come home."

Both eyebrows went up with that comment.

"This trip is just what the doctor ordered with everything going on in your life. You can use a vacation, one without your children, without Dan and without Jamie's shenanigans. My friend, you are going to have a wonderful time—deep in the heart of Texas."

With her boarding pass in hand, we sat near the gate drinking another cup of coffee. Paula still appeared nervous.

"It's not that I don't have feelings for Jamie. I do love him," she said, tears spilling from her eyes. "It's best to let him go. I told him that. There's just too much baggage that goes with me. He has his whole life ahead of him." She paused. "What bothers me the most is that he refuses to take any responsibility for the baby! Some other guy is marrying Stephanie, and the Remingtons are giving them a $10,000 wedding gift for Stephanie to keep her mouth shut. Dana, that's just not right."

"It sheds significant light on Jamie's character! I'll bet that was June's idea. That's the kind of bitch she is. What if this really is her grandchild?"

Paula searched her purse for tissue and dabbed at her eyes.

"Paula, once we love someone, it never ends. Didn't Andy say love is forever? We just keep meeting the same people over and over and loving them again and again lifetime after lifetime."

"Something like that!" she said and she was crying.

"Didn't you feel something when you first met Beau? It seemed to me that you two were taken with each other. Louis and I both noticed."

"I am attracted to him. That was true even before this mess. I've never understood you, Dana, how you can be attracted to so many men at the same time. And here I am attracted to two men at once. Is that wrong?" She sounded serious.

"My dear, you are asking the slut puppy of the Western world that question. I hope you understand that." I grinned.

Paula started to laugh and I laughed with her.

"You are going to have a great time in Texas. Try not to think about Dan, about lawyers, or Jamie, even though that might not be a simple task. Telling Jamie about Beau was the wisest thing you've done this month. Forget about your kids for a week and just have fun. You deserve it, Paula. Honest!"

Her flight was announced.

Paula smiled as she boarded early with first class. The first class ticket bought at the last minute must have cost Beau a small fortune. The man did have class. He also had a white stallion he sometimes rode into a Texas sunset.

After leaving the airport, I headed for Stromberg Pictures. The scene set for the afternoon was one where I would get knocked around by a lousy heel and be left with a bleeding heart.

At least for the moment, Paula was out of harm's way.

I thought I was too—until later that very same day.

# Chapter 23

The man was separated, not single, and not even close to being divorced, as his lawful wife, Lulu Mae Randolph, parked her flashy gold '66 Eldorado Cadillac convertible across the street from my house that July evening.

"Dana Scofield!" the Amazon shouted in a loud nasally twang as I was starting up my front sidewalk.

My first impression was that an over-zealous fan had found out where I lived. As I turned to pleasantly greet the woman, there was such an antagonistic look on her contorted face that I instantly feared for my life. I was ready to run for the porch when the fairly attractive, over-bleached blonde with these enormous knockers blocked my path.

It had been a long day, especially after getting up early to drive Paula to the airport. I was tired. I wanted to eat something rather than deal with an angry woman, five-ten minimum, towering over me and glaring with her bloodshot blue eyes. There was the distinctive scent of gin on her breath as she thrust her flushed face closer to mine.

"Leave my husband alone!" she shrieked, spraying spittle all over my face as I took note of her perfectly capped teeth. *Good dentist*, I thought. Though I hoped she didn't plan to hit me with her upraised fist. Her breath was becoming more obnoxious by the second. The alcohol had done nothing to alleviate her anxiety over whoever her husband was screwing. And what he had to do with me, I had no idea. I was sorry that Florence was in Palm Springs and unable to help me out in the difficult situation.

"Who is your husband?" I inquired. "I'll be happy to leave him alone." I took a step back and tried to stand taller, visualizing myself as a giant while knowing that my five-two, small boned frame, 105 pounds, was no match for the lady wrestler who had to weigh at least 200 pounds.

"Richard Randolph!" she shouted, imparting yet more spittle in my direction. "Don't you pretend you don't know me! I'm his wife! That's who! Lulu Mae Randolph! You leave Richard alone, you bitch! You stay away from my man!" Her wild eyes looked even more bloodshot as she pulled back her fist in apparent readiness to strike. "He's my husband and I want him to stay that way, even though he's living in the Wilshire District where he sees you all the time. You bitch! I love Richard. You can't have him! You hear me! You can't have him!" she shouted loud enough to disturb every neighbor up and down my street.

"I don't want him," I said, stepping back again, my eyes steadily on her fist. After all, I had close-ups in the morning. "I didn't know Richard was married," I said, wondering why I'd even said that. "He never told me he was married. Besides, I've never been out with him!"

"Liar!" she shrieked, tears streaming down her flushed face, "Big fat liar, Dana Scofield. You've been screwing my husband for years. He told me, so don't you dare deny it!"

"I beg your pardon?" I stepped back yet again, thinking about running for my car to get away from her. I needed to alert the police to a possible assault! I'd started to perspire and my stomach growled. I hadn't eaten for hours to have a flat stomach for my scene.

"Richard told me all about you, you husband stealing bitch. How great it is when you go down on him. How nice it is to fuck your little ass!"

I was appalled.

"I've never fucked Richard, and he's never fucked me!" I said, about to turn and run, but the Amazon grabbed my wrist and held fast.

At that point, Florence opened the front door and said in a loud voice, "I have called the police!"

Lulu Mae turned her crazed eyes on Florence and yanked me toward her, which nearly made me topple over. "Good!" she raged. "Let the whole fucking world know what a son-of-a-bitch my husband is. If he doesn't take me back, I'll ruin him. What about our children? He never sees them anymore." Now sobbing, she turned to me. "It's all your fault. He told me how great the sex is with you. I've been having trouble since my hysterectomy," her sobbing increased and her body began to shake. "I've tried to get my hormones right!" she said, now shaking all over.

I pitied the poor woman, considering what a bastard her husband was. Richard had not only tried to blackmail me, he had lied to his wife about us having some imaginary love affair. It was absurd.

"I've never had sex with your husband," I said, finding the strength to wrench free of her. "Regardless of what Richard told you, he's lying! I've never slept with him. I'd swear to that on a stack of Bibles."

The patrol car pulled up in front of my house and two police officers got out and started up the brick sidewalk.

Lulu Mae glanced from me to Florence, and then, at the policemen with the most pathetic look on her face. My guess was no one likes the idea of being arrested.

"Is there a problem here?" the older policeman inquired, obviously trying to assess the situation.

His younger partner looked from Lulu Mae to me, perhaps trying to figure things out. "Are you bothering Miss Scofield, ma'am?" he inquired, turning to me with the nicest smile on his handsome, young face.

A few months back, I'd autographed pictures at the police station with other actors to raise money for charity. I recognized the handsome officer in his crisp blue uniform. He was supposedly a big fan, praise the Lord.

"Officer Johnson?" His smile widened as I mentioned his name.

"Yes, Miss Scofield," he said before he turned to the intruder, "And your name, please, ma'am?"

"Lulu Mae Randolph," she said through clenched teeth, wiping away her tears with the back of her hand as she continued to glare at me.

Clearly, Lulu Mae was not convinced of my innocence. I opened my purse and removed some tissues that I handed to the delusional woman. "Here! You need to blow your nose." A runny nose was not attractive on anyone, especially a grown woman.

She took the tissues and filled them both. Big girl. Big nose.

"What seems to be the problem?" Officer Johnson inquired, while the other officer observed the exchange.

All eyes were now on Lulu Mae, who was still blowing her nose. I was extremely thankful that Florence was home. I now gave the woman every tissue in my purse.

"Mrs. Randolph is under the impression that I'm having an affair with her husband."

"Are you?" the older officer instantly inquired, staring me in the eyes.

"No, sir. I only met Mr. Randolph at a beach party two weeks ago. I've never been out with him. I agreed to dinner last Saturday, but then changed my mind and never saw him. I was with another gentleman on Saturday evening at a Harold Sparrow party."

Both policemen looked impressed.

"Quite some party!"

"She's lying," Lulu Mae said. "She spent the entire weekend with Richard. He told me," she said, crying again as she mournfully shook her head. "She's lying," she said, looking at Officer Johnson with the sweetest smile imaginable.

"Richard is lying to you. I spent the weekend with a film director by the name of Scott Wellington. He is single, a man with whom I've been romantically linked for two years. I never saw your husband. Richard is lying to you at my expense."

"Richard has been in love with you ever since we saw *The Wind and The Rage*. He talks about you all the time. He's been having an affair with you for two years." She hesitated. "He did say he met you at a beach party."

"That party was on June 23, 1967, at the home of friends of mine in the Malibu Colony."

A curious expression captured her face. "He said Malibu."

"Richard is a liar. Frankly, I don't see how a man can be so cruel to a wife who has borne him children. You should have dumped him the minute he started this imaginary affair with me. People get crushes on actors. What Richard has done to you is mean and unflattering to both of us. I don't date married men. And I don't understand why you even want him. The man is a mean liar. I'm sorry he hurt you. You both have hurt me. I may have to sue your husband for slander."

Lulu Mae stopped crying and studied me. I planned to call Paula in Texas as soon as the ordeal was over. She needed to know about a lying, scheming lawyer who was worse than either of us had even suspected. Richard should be disbarred.

"On the telephone, your housekeeper, Florence Becker, said that Mrs. Randolph was assaulting you on your property," the older policemen said. "Is that correct, Miss Scofield?" He turned to Lulu Mae with a reproachful look on his face as I began to seriously search my soul.

The woman looked pathetic, her nose still running and me out of tissue. Tears streamed down her somewhat attractive face streaked with black mascara. I was unsure of what to say to the knights in blue armor. A scorned woman had lost it and taken her misguided revenge out on me. It was true that Lulu Mae assaulted me, bruised my wrist, and accused me of false deeds with her lying, blackmailing husband. The situation had me beyond grateful that I had never gone out with the scumbag or she might have killed me. Richard Randolph was one of the worst psychopaths I had the bad karma to meet.

On the other hand, Lulu Mae Randolph's accusations might end up being helpful in a court of law with respect to a certain friend of mine faced with a child custody suit instigated by the Law Offices of Sharman, Greene and Randolph; a suit that would never be tried if I had my way.

Turning to Lulu Mae, I said, "I'll have Scott Wellington call you to confirm we spent the weekend together, if you'll give me your telephone number. I won't give you his address or telephone number. Is that understood?"

She stared at me with her bloodshot eyes and instantly stopped crying. A semblance of sanity swept over her tear-stained face. Then she sighed, frowned, and nodded.

The officers seemed to be losing interest in the situation. No more fireworks. No hysteria. No arrest.

"I never was alone with Richard. I met him recently and spoke to him briefly. I gave him my telephone number without finding out if he was married. In the future, I plan to ask a man that question before I give out my telephone number. I don't want to cause any woman grief. And I don't understand how you even got my address."

"I hired a private detective."

"A detective? When?"

"On Monday. It was Sunday when Richard said he'd spent the weekend with you. I decided to confront you myself and put an end to the affair."

"There was never a beginning. I'm sure Richard will be thrilled with what you've done, since he's been lying to you for so long." I studied her. "You never filed for separation?"

Slowly, she shook her head. "Maybe I will," she said, her expression softening.

"Maybe you should."

"Maybe you should," Officer Johnson said, and he turned to me and inquired, "Do you want to file a complaint against Mrs. Randolph and press charges?"

"Not if she promises, in front of you two officers, to stay away from me. I've had nothing to do with her husband. I'll have Scott call her, if she likes." I turned to her. "You will stay away from me, won't you? I mean you no harm and want no harm from you. Promise me you'll stay away. Otherwise, you'll force me to take legal actions and get a restraining order against you."

Biting her lip, a reluctant Lulu Mae nodded. "I'll stay away. I'm sorry, Miss Scofield. I believed him. I never thought Richard would lie to me about anything this serious."

"I'm sorry he hurt you. He needs to get his head examined. Get him some therapy."

"He says I'm the crazy one."

"How about we escort you off Miss Scofield's property and make sure that you leave? We'll follow you," Officer Johnson said to the pathetic woman.

Solemnly, Lulu Mae nodded and turned to go.

The officers tipped their hats and followed her to her car, watching her get in behind the wheel before returning to their patrol car. They watched her drive away and followed her to the corner.

Florence and I stood there, watching, until both cars were out of sight.

"I thought you were going to be in Palm Springs for a few days," I said to Florence.

"It was too hot in the desert. I decided to come home."

"I'm glad that you did."

After the unanticipated, unscripted dramatic scene, I soaked in my whirlpool for an hour. Florence fixed us chicken with mushrooms for supper. Down in Fort Worth, Texas, Beau Kandell and Paula Marlow were attending a party in Dallas that evening.

All I could say was, after discovering that Paula and Beau were having a nice time on her first full day in Texas: Thank you, God, for protecting me on this day!

# Chapter 24

That Friday, things were fairly demanding at the studio, making the time zoom by. Even though Scott and Eric had called to invite me out for dinner, I'd passed. After Lulu Mae, I needed a break from men for one night. It was time to watch some mindless TV or read a good book. Florence and I had dinner alone. That evening was peaceful and relaxing.

Paula called.

"My suite has a soaking tub and lovely view of the lake. The balcony has natural wicker furniture with soft cushions. This ranch is everything you said it would be and more."

No hanky-panky for Beau Kandell. Poor man. But the handsome cowboy was taking her all over by horse, jeep, truck, car, boat and plane. He'd impressed her with the dazzle of Dallas and the old Western charm of Fort Worth with its museums and art galleries.

"I've already used his studio to paint my horse. Shelley's mane matches mine."

The ponies, the deer, and the rest were ready and waiting for Michele and Christopher, with the return trip set for the first two weeks of August. Beau insisted on paying for all the first class airfares. Wow! Those kids were going to love his ranch, and how could they not love him? There didn't seem to be an unlovable bone in Beau Kandell's tall and beautiful body.

My secret plan for Paula's future seemed more likely on that day. I could almost see her marching down the aisle. Let's see. What color would my gown be? I couldn't decide.

Paula was highly amused when I recounted the saga of Lulu Mae Randolph. Surely, Richard Randolph was not representing Dan in his custody battle, though that would make things almost perfect.

By Saturday, Louis was back at the Beverly Hills Hotel. He had enjoyed the Big Easy in spite of working day and night. That evening we went to Don the Beachcombers in Hollywood for dinner, a restaurant he had heard about from several of the actors.

The Cantonese faire was tasty, including the assorted appetizers and exotic rum drinks. I chose a Mai Tai to sip while observing all the tikis, fishnets, ukuleles, dugout canoes, and artificial tropical fish that created a South Seas atmosphere. The restaurants were all the rage at the time, with most originating in Honolulu. I had yet to see Hawaii then.

"After the picture ends, perhaps we can take a trip to the Hawaiian Islands for some rest and relaxation," Louis said, with the usual longing in his eyes. "We'll be in the snow in Colorado during the winter, and I've never seen the South Pacific. We could spend a month and do all the islands."

"A month?" I tried not to sound alarmed, while seriously doubting I could take a whole month of Louis. "We'll see," I added, wondering how each of us might feel by the end of making the picture, especially with Scott back in my life.

Then, of course, there was Eric. But Louis's libido topped the rest. Truthfully, my recent encounter with Lulu Mae had brought about some serious thinking with regard to men. Then, I just happened to glance across the crowded restaurant, and who should I see but Scott Wellington helping a shapely blonde with her chair at a table across the room. It was not Lulu Mae, but a tall, leggy, young starlet-type. I was uncertain if Scott had seen me with Louis. The young stunner had to be in her early 20s, and she had very large breasts. Could she be the actress that Scott was going to use for Jennifer? She seemed too young. Big boobs were presenting me with major challenges that week.

After he ordered us another round of drinks, Louis's eyes followed mine to where Scott was seated with the blonde bimbo.

"Someone you know?" Louis enquired, checking out the pretty blonde, while not even noticing the two-timing, brunette, film director.

"Vaguely," I said, trying to ignore the  intense jealousy inside me. Damn him! I thought. How dare Scott make me feel like this! Who the hell was she? I'd never seen her before in my life!

"That's Miss Sweden from the Miss International Pageant," Louis casually remarked. Was he a minder reader? "She was first runner up in 1965."

"1965?" I repeated, gulping down my drink. "I'm surprised you know beauty contestants from two years ago. I suppose you even know her name?"

"Bridget."

"Bridget?"

"When I stop noticing beautiful women, I will either be blind or quite dead."

At that point, Louis was toasting Big Boobs Bridget with the long blonde hair with his fresh Mai Tai.

I was trying my best to control the rage building up in my brain and my solar plexus, thinking I might be able to use one of my chopsticks to stab either Scott, or the young beauty from Sweden. But it probably wouldn't work. No real point on a chopstick.

Louis was sure to escape my wrath, since he had the good sense to conceal his escapades. He probably got laid in New Orleans, since hookers were numbered among some of his closest friends. After all, we had no commitment!

All at once, I heard a familiar male voice right next to me saying, "Hello Dana."

When I looked up, Scott was standing there. How he had managed to sneak up on me was beyond my comprehension in my increasing state of anxiety. At that moment, I had absolutely nothing to say to him.

"Are you going to introduce me to your friend?" Scott inquired, staring into my startled face with a smirk on his.

He had tried to get me to go out with him for the past two days. Even after glancing over at the ditsy blonde with the over-developed mammary glands, nothing came out of my mouth.

Louis stood and extended his hand. "Louis Lamprais," he said.

Scott shook his hand. "Naturally, I know who you are. I've seen all your films, even those with subtitles."

Louis smiled and nodded. "I see."

Scott turned to me with expectancy in his big blue eyes. "Scott Wellington," I managed, taking in a deep breath and picking up my drink to swallow some rum.

Louis's eyes lit up. "Ah, oui, the film director. It is a true pleasure to meet you, Mr. Wellington. Your companion this evening, I think, is Bridget Knudsen, Miss Sweden of 1965?"

In unison, the three of us suddenly turned toward Miss Sweden of 1965, whose face instantly registered recognition. She brightly nodded at

Louis and smiled at Scott before turning back to the waiter placing food on the table.

"You know each other?" a now stunned Scott said to Louis, quickly glancing from Louis to Bridget and back to Louis, which pleased me no end.

The plot was thickening.

"Oui," Louis said, nodding, as a mischievous expression captured his eyes and his handsome face.

Miss Sweden of 1965 smiled and nodded in a sexy manner at Mr. International Film Star of 1967, as Louis turned to me with a sheepish grin and a wicked glint in his hazel eyes.

"Bridget models all over the world," Louis said. "It seems she is currently embarking on a film career here in Hollywood. Good for her, I say." He paused. "She's a very talented young woman. Will Bridget be appearing in the role in your film that Dana declined? She seems rather young for the part, but perhaps not with Hollywood makeup? Oui?"

Instantly, Scott appeared flustered. Was it because Louis had knowledge of his offer to me? "I'm not sure," he said. "Your ex-wife is a model, right?" He was trying to recover from Louis's unexpected disclosures.

"Oui. Bridget was friends with my former wife," Louis said in a tone of some hesitation, with obviously no intentions of saying anything further.

At that moment, it seemed to me that Louis Lamprais had slept with at least two of Scott Wellington's women. And Scott, no doubt, had slept with both of us, as well. Amusement drained from his eyes, as Louis appeared to size up Scott, with Scott sizing him up right back. Surely, Scott had not missed the fact that Louis looked older in person than he did on the screen. Louis had his own personal cinematographer. After all, he was an international film star.

I never expected fidelity from my new French lover, but I had expected some level of allegiance from Scott Wellington, the man who had repeatedly asked me to marry him that year. How foolish of me, I suddenly realized, sitting beside artificial fish and silent ukuleles. How foolish of me, indeed!

Back in my pink boudoir that evening, things turned seriously sensuous, as usual, and yet, in the back of mind, I couldn't help but compare one man with the other in terms of look, feel, taste, touch, smell, size, vocal quality, muscle tone, skin texture, furriness, smoothness, stroke and technique. Louis to Scott. Scott to Louis. Eric to Louis. Eric to Scott. Louis to

Jeffrey. Jeffrey to Louis. Talk about kaleidoscopic flashbacks! Back and forth my mind raced, interrupting the flow of my concentration and the enjoyment of the matter at hand, or mouth, or leg, or finger, or toe. Whichever part of my naked anatomy was included in securing ultimate, or fleeting, pleasure throughout the long night.

In all honesty, the lovemaking was much less pleasurable, less stimulating, and shall we say, less satisfying than the carnal act might have been had not the two most talented, handsome and amorous men in my life presented themselves before me in tandem in a dimly lit exotic restaurant on that very evening. Damn them! After all, I was no longer in Mesopotamia or Babylon, although Beverly Hills may have been close in terms of the power-hungry, devious, and decadent societies of the distant past.

Nonetheless, my role as temptress and seductress was acted out with my usual savoir faire, and, I was grateful that Scott had not said a word about our self-indulgent weekend together. I had noted what I surmised might be hurt mixed with guilt in his big blue eyes before he returned to Miss Sweden of 1965. There were no doubt plenty of pretty girls named Bridget in Sweden. Had she perhaps lost the title because of being overly endowed, the poor, sweet, young, former beauty contestant?

The roses from Scott that arrived on Wednesday were pink. Two dozen. The blooms sweetly scented my bedroom. The note: *I hope these tickle you pink. I'll love you forever, Scott*, tucked away in a drawer. Notwithstanding, Louis had stared at the roses as he artfully removed my dress. Louis had a thing about undressing a woman. Scott never cared how the clothes came off, as long as they did. The two men were quite different in many other more subtle ways, with both of them fairly self-involved, perhaps the same as I was at the time?

There was a message from Daddy on my service. Martha was fine. I would return my father's call on the following day.

# Chapter 25

Florence left on vacation again; this time to Phoenix to see friends in another hot desert. For breakfast, I fixed mushroom and spinach omelets with cheddar cheese, which we enjoyed at the umbrella table near the pool.

"I am unable to spend the day with you, ma cherie. Tomorrow I have an early meeting and need to call my children. Maurice misses his Papa. I tried to call him from New Orleans, but it was difficult with all the work. We will speak this evening, his time in France."

"You may call him from here, if you like." It was the first time Louis had spoken of his children. "How old are your children?"

"Maurice is 20, a student at the Sorbonne in Paris, studying to be an architect. He is not interested in acting like his Papa." He poured more coffee. "He is close to his mother, my first wife, Alicia. My daughter, Frances, studies in Switzerland. She is 18 and as beautiful as her mother." Suddenly, he seemed pensive.

"Does Maurice look like you?"

"Oui. He reminds me of myself as a young man, but is taller and stronger, an athlete, fond of tennis and skiing, especially snow skiing." He paused. "And Renee, she is exquisite like her Mama. She plans to be a model. A decision already made at the age of two."

"So you have three children?"

"More. I am very fond of children."

"I see."

"You take the pill, oui?"

"I told you I do." I was seeing a different side of Louis that day.

"Perhaps we can have a child together," he said in a casual tone, glancing at me with only the slightest longing as he added, "in time."

"But we hardly know each other," I said, avoiding his eyes, thinking, *a child without being married?* Perhaps I was more old-fashioned than I realized.

Louis glanced at his watch and stood. "I must leave you in your beautiful garden. On Wednesday, I fly to Paris. My father is ill. I also need to take care of business before we start the film." He bent down and kissed me. "I shall miss you," he said, turning to gaze at the rose garden. "It seems you are very fond of roses." Suddenly, his expression sobered.

"My favorite flowers," I said, wondering if what he meant was the pink roses in my bedroom.

"You will drive me to my hotel, oui?"

"Oui."

Strange as it seemed, I was feeling oddly reluctant toward Louis as unusual sensations washed through me from out of nowhere.

Back home again, I felt the need to talk to my dad. The telephone rang so many times that I was about to hang up when he answered.

"Hello, George Scofield here," my father said in his usual manner.

"Hello, Daddy. How is Martha? Is she comfortable?"

"I'm bringing her home from the hospital tomorrow. The roses you sent to her are beautiful, Dana. You know how much Martha loves yellow roses. I'll be bringing home some of the flowers today. It seems as though everyone and their brother sent flowers. She said it looks like a funeral home in there." He chuckled. "Martha doesn't care much for one of the nurses. The old bag should retire. She's old, ugly as sin and grumpy as hell!"

"Martha doesn't care much for hospitals, as I recall. But who does? All old nurses are probably grumpy, Daddy. They've had to take care of sick, difficult people. How would you like to deal with bedpans, sponge baths and enemas all day?"

He grunted. "Hard to get any sleep in a hospital. Damn nurses and orderlies keep waking her up, giving her pills or some other damn thing. Martha wants to come home. She took a shower yesterday."

"That's good."

"What I actually called you about is ... Cindy Waters. She's in hospice now."

"Hospice?" I was stunned.

"Cindy is dying, Dana. The ovarian cancer spread all over before the doctors could find the problem. They thought it was irritable bowel or some other damn thing. The cancer is in her lungs now, her bones, even in her brain."

"Good God! She's only 32, a week younger than me. That's terrible," I started to pace and reached for my cigarettes.

"I went to see her last Monday. Jeff called to tell me about hospice. I took her some flowers. Terence is 12 now, Angela is 10. It's hard on those kids, and they're beautiful children." He paused. "A month ago, Jeff went over my will with me. After Martha dies, you get almost everything, including the house. After all, you paid for all the improvements. You've probably invested more in this place than I did."

"Whatever you say, Daddy. Just stick around for a long time, okay?" I lit a cigarette as a deep sadness filled me up. "I love you, Daddy. I'd rather have you around than your house." I was really bowled over about Cindy in hospice. "Is that the kind of law Jeffrey practices ... estate law?"

"He does a little bit of everything. He was planning to run for Congress before Cindy got sick. He'd like to be a senator or on the Supreme Court. You know him, he's always been ambitious with his eyes set on Washington. He'd probably like to be president, for all I know." He chuckled low in his throat.

"I remember."

In the old days, Jeff and I had many talks about him going to Washington. It was another way that Jamie reminded me of him. Politics. President of the World. Besides the gorgeous faces and bodies, the two men were strangely similar. Jeff was 19 the summer I left Indiana, the same age as Jamie was that summer.

"Cindy asked about you," Daddy said, "How you're doing. She can still think straight sometimes, even though it's harder for her with the tumors in her brain. She told me she used to be jealous of you back in high school."

"She did?" I had suspected as much, mostly regarding Jeff.

"She never misses one of your movies and neither does Jeff. But then, I've known that for a long time. He and I run into each other at the Chamber of Commerce meetings sometimes, and when I do things with the Boy Scouts. Terry is a Scout, damn good one. I'll bet he makes Eagle Scout like his dad."

"Nice," I said, and suddenly, the word sounded inane to me. Pitiful even. My father had never condoned small talk. He was a man of substance.

He even refused to talk about the weather. When I wanted to goad him, I'd asked him about the weather. Then, Daddy would laugh. Asking him about the weather could break the ice.

"Yeah. Terry is a good kid. He's smart. Angie is pretty as a picture. She reminds me of you when you were a little girl," he said. "Cindy is trying to make peace with everyone before she goes. She'd really like to see you, Dana. She knows she doesn't have much time left."

"Not much time left?" Suddenly, I was appalled. This immense sadness enveloped me and tears filled my eyes. My cigarette was extinguished as I thought of Cindy Waters wanting to see me again before she died.

I remembered running into the two of them at a Christmas party in my mid-twenties when I'd started to make enough money to fly home for the holidays. By then, my mother was married to Arnie, husband number three, and living in Florida. I wasn't crazy about spending Christmas in another place with sandy beaches and palm trees. More often than not, Mother Nature accommodated us with a white Christmas in Indiana. It was fun to be in the snow for a week or two, then I'd return to La La Land, as my friends in the Midwest called Los Angeles.

The first time I ran into Mr. and Mrs. Jeffrey Waters, they were already married and had two kids. Angela was a beautiful baby. Jeff acted strange around me, somewhat self-conscious. After all, I'd rejected him when he'd sworn me his undying love. I might have acted strange around a man who had rejected me, though none ever had. I was spoiled. I did all the rejecting. There were never that many men I wanted around me for long. None, in fact, besides Jeffrey Waters.

"Jeff would like to see you, too," Daddy said. "Frankly, I don't think he's ever gotten over you, Dana. He's followed your career every step of the way."

"Oh, come on, Daddy. I was 18 when he asked me to marry him. That was 14 years ago, two kids and a marriage ago."

*He married your stand-in when he married Cindy* ran through my head, Paula's remark.

"True love is true love. When a man loves a woman, almost any woman, he always loves her." Daddy paused. "I'll always love your mother, although I love her a lot less these days, since she's such a mess, in my humble opinion. I love Martha with every beat of my heart. It is possible for a man to love more than one woman in his life. Look at all the men you've already had in your life, not that you actually loved them all. I read in a movie magazine about you dating some Frenchie, some film star from France, Louis Lamprais," he mispronounced his name.

In Daddy's mind, all Frenchmen were Frenchies. He'd served in the army in World War II during the allied invasion of Normandy. He had helped to free France from the Nazi occupation.

"What magazine?" I found it hard to believe that Louis and I were already "a couple" in some Hollywood gossip magazine. It had only been weeks. That had to irritate Scott no end.

"*Hollywood Today*. It says you're making a film together. Is that true?"

"Yes, Daddy. I only found out days ago. It's going to be a really big film. I'll be Victoria Rutherford in *View From the Mountain* based on Garson Reeves' blockbuster novel. Have you read the book?"

"Of course, I've read it," he was plainly irritated. "You used to call and tell me when you were doing a film." He sighed in disgust. "Now, I have to read about it in the goddamn movie magazines."

"I'm sorry, Daddy. I'm shooting at Stromberg Pictures this week. You know about me being *In the Cool of the Night*, don't you?"

"Yeah. You told me about that one. I'm really happy that your career is doing so well, Dana, but just maybe you should come home to cheer up Martha and me and see Cindy in hospice. Maybe take your old friend some roses. That would be mighty decent of you, daughter. After all, you've known her since elementary school. She would really like to see you, Dana. She keeps telling me that over and over and over again."

"She does?" At that point, I had to do some deep breathing and sighed so loud I was sure that Daddy had heard me. I could not shake off the heaviness creeping over me. Cindy Hanson Waters was dying and wanted to see me.

"You should think about coming home, Dana. You really should."

"I finish shooting this week. I'll let you know, okay? Maybe I can come home for a few days. But I have wardrobe fittings for the next picture. Costumes from the 1800s. I'm really looking forward to playing Victoria, Daddy. We'll be shooting in Colorado and California, maybe Nevada. Perhaps you and Martha can visit me on location. Would you like that?"

"Maybe," he said. "Right now, I need to get to the hospital. I hope to see you, Dana, I hope to see you real soon."

For the rest of the day I was miserable. I kept thinking about Cindy in hospice, a place people go to die. Repeated laps in the pool did nothing to dispel the dark cloud hanging over me.

When Eric invited me out to dinner, I accepted, feeling the need to be with someone to help me stop thinking about Cindy and Jeffrey Waters and children about to lose their mother.

I had the benefit of my mother's love until my teen years. Helen had lost it in mid-life. When I was a sophomore in high school she won a contest to go to a fancy Florida spa where she met wealthy Walter the widower. Soon, Helen ran off with her rich catch, 15 years her senior, leaving my father and me with our broken hearts. I looked a lot like my mother, who was still beautiful at age 54. After her recent plastic surgery, we looked about the same age. That was unnerving for me, especially in 1967.

During dinner, I'd tried to pay attention to Eric as he talked about genetic engineering, without a clue about what he was really saying. He was returning to MIT the next day. Being out with him had accomplished nothing for me. Cindy still preyed on my mind.

When Eric brought me home early, I lied about having my period. I needed time alone to think about going home to say good-bye to a dying friend, married to a man I had once loved madly, when I was very young and nowhere near as foolish.

# Chapter 26

"Eric is in Boston. Louis is in Paris. And Scott is in Albuquerque scouting locations. So even though I'm dreading it, it seems like a good time for me to go home. I haven't been home for a while. What do you think, Paula?" I asked her, driving her home from the airport that Thursday.

We stopped at the Chart House at the beach for dinner and watched the end of a magnificent sunset: Pink, orange, and lavender. Mother Nature showing off in her glorious summer colors.

"A trip home sounds about right to me, regardless of Cindy. I'm sure your father and Martha will be delighted to see you. How is George these days, anyway?"

"I have a great father. What can I say? George is fine, and Martha is recovering nicely."

I ordered a dirty martini and was grateful the picture had wrapped. I would have already left for Indiana if Paula hadn't asked me to pick her up. Plus, I really felt the need to talk to her about all the things whirling around in my head. For days, I had trouble falling asleep.

"So Cindy is dying," Paula said in winsome tone, sympathy in her amber eyes. "How sad. It is scary to think of someone our age dying from cancer. I know it happens. It just never happened to anyone we've known before, right? It makes you really stop and think."

"It sure does," I said, cutting into my filet mignon the perfect shade of pink. My baked potato was covered with sour cream, butter and chives. I thought it was the perfect dinner at that time. "So how did things go with Beau? All that you've talked about is the ranch and how well you got along with his ranch hands. I'm sure you were a big hit. Isn't his chef the greatest?"

"Fabulous. Too many rich desserts, though. Howard does a crème brulee to die for."

"To die for?" I flatly repeated.

"Poor choice of words. Sorry." Paula looked pensive. "I'm better at riding a horse, but I'm hardly Annie Oakley. Shelly and I got along just fine."

"Shelly?"

"My horse. Beau says she's mine. She's a beautiful horse. I painted her portrait that isn't finished yet. There wasn't that much time to paint. We had a really good time and did lots of fun things. He showed me both towns and all around the country. He flew me around in his Cessna and took me shopping several times. He's a very generous man. I now own a new pair of fancy tooled cowboy boots, so I fit right in."

"And you have to go back to finish the painting of your horse, right?"

Paula grinned, sipping from her glass of Cabernet Sauvignon. "Beau is paying for all the airfares when I go back! Will my kids ever be impressed or what? Besides the horses, ponies, deer and gigantic swimming pool, the boat and the plane and everything else, my kids may never want to leave Texas."

"But ... has Beau Kandell won you over?"

Paula hesitated, glancing toward the distant horizon still awash with color as the sun sank closer to the sea. "He's a wonderful man. Good to me, gracious and charming."

"Sexy?"

After casting me one of her looks, she said, "I'd imagine," and looked at her plate to cut another bite of steak.

"Still no sex?" I shook my head. "Poor Beau."

"Kisses ... and holding."

"Kisses are good. Holding is good. But there are other aspects of boy meets girl that are much more satisfying and interesting. Trust me."

"I can't jump from one man to another like you do. I wish I could be more like you, Dana. Honest!"

"Oh, I wouldn't go as far as all that." Fleetingly, I reflected on my recent encounters in Eric's bed. Louis's bed. Scott's bed. And my bed. "You don't want to turn into a regular slut puppy!"

"You probably have more fun."

"Maybe." I laughed.

We ordered two more glasses of red wine.

The waiter smiled as he left our booth, which made me wonder if he'd overheard our conversation. He was cute and young and had been watching me closely.

"I'll bet he's an aspiring actor or has the hots for you," Paula whispered. "Just think, you could add another hot, young body to the group! He is handsome."

We were both giggling when the fresh glasses of wine were served.

"Ladies," the young waiter inquired, "Is there anything else at all that you'd like right now?"

Glancing up, my initial thoughts were: *You'd do nicely on my pink satin sheets*, but, in a moment of amazing restraint, I said, "Tell me, are you an actor?"

"I've done some modeling, but no acting yet," he replied.

"How old are you?"

"Twenty-one," he said, and his smile revealed two deep dimples.

"Sounds about right," I said, feeling Paula's gentle kick under the table as she grinned. "This is my friend, Paula Marlow. She's a very fine artist. I'm Dana Scofield."

His smile broadened. "I know who you are. I've seen all your movies, some of them more than once. And my father is madly in love with you, which ticks off my mother no end." He grinned, shaking his head. "He talks about you way too much to suit my mother."

"Your father?"

"Yeah. Dad is 40. I was born when he was only 20, pretty young to be a father, in my opinion. I don't want kids any time soon. I don't even plan to get married before I'm 30."

"Wise decision. Would you mind bringing us the dessert menu?"

"Right away," he said and rushed off.

"His father is in love with me," I muttered. "How about that?" I added, picking up my wine glass as I turned to Paula. "Why didn't you stay in Texas longer? You were only there eight days. That's not enough time with that cowboy."

"I have an art exhibit in October, remember? Lots of painting for me to do, especially since I'm taking the kids to his ranch for two weeks. I warned Beau that I'll be painting some of the time. I did some painting while I was there, which seemed to make him happy." She paused. "And don't forget about Dan Thurman and our impending courtroom drama. I can hardly wait to play that scene!"

"Two weeks aren't enough time for yours kids in Texas, either. There are amusement parks, the zoo, museums, the lake and the pool, ponies to ride, and great Mexican food."

"It will have to do," her tone sounded final. "When I called my service there were messages from Jamie, Dan, my lawyer, and Ken asking for more paintings. Most of the work I've already done for the show is still in my storeroom. I told him I'd make his trip to Malibu, with his van, worthwhile, complete with lunch with an ocean view."

"I suppose you do have to paint."

The young waiter returned. We ordered chocolate mousse and decaf Cappuccinos.

"That waiter sure is cute," I said with him out of earshot.

"Not as cute as Jamie," Paula said. "It will be painful for me to talk to him. I'm surprised he's still calling after telling him about a man in Texas with a ranch."

"He loves you. Why should he just give up? You're not married to anyone, although my plan is to be your Maid of Honor, regardless of who ends up as your groom."

There was a strange look on her face as she briefly glanced away. "Beau is a really nice guy, and that is all I am going to say now." She paused. "There's much to love about the man. We could talk and talk for hours on end. That part was amazing."

"You mean you had real honest-to-goodness conversations like two grown-ups?"

The look on her face was priceless.

"I'd say that's a step in the right direction."

"I still have feelings for Jamie, which I don't seem to be able to ignore just yet."

The waiter was soon back with, "Is there anything else I can get for you, ma'am?"

"More cream, perhaps," Paula said, softly repeating, "Ma'am?" after he was gone. "If Jamie had ever called me 'ma'am,' I'd have slapped his face."

"They say 'ma'am' a lot down in Texas. Those Texans can be awfully polite."

"Some of Beau's ranch hands did call me ma'am, come to think of it. But somehow, it sounds different in Malibu."

"Everything is different in Malibu. Nearly everything is different in the State of California."

# Chapter 27

On Friday, I had costume fittings at Colossal. On Saturday morning, my flight to Indianapolis was early. Instead of reading on the plane, I slept. Other than that, my mind was filled with Cindy Waters. How was I going to handle seeing her in hospice? It was something I had to do and not just because my daddy said so.

There was a time, which seemed very long ago by then, when Cindy Hanson and I were the very best of friends. We were in Campfire Girls together in fifth grade. Her mother was always active in school affairs, with mine conspicuous by her absence. I never liked to camp. Perhaps I got that from my mother. Unless a hotel was at least four stars, Helen refused to stay.

My mother nearly broke the bank with Daddy before she found a man who could cater to her extravagant taste. No simple woman, Helen. I hoped our karma didn't force us to be together in another life, especially with her as my mother. For that reason, I tried to be as pleasant as possible whenever she sought me out, which wasn't often. A postcard had recently arrived from Madagascar. They were circling the globe again, with seldom a word to be heard. There was no place for me to write back, since they were somewhere else before the mail arrived. Wealthy vagabonds, Helen and Arnie.

Daddy was waiting for me at the gate. He was in good shape for a man of 60. He walked regularly and played tennis. He quit smoking at the age of 50 and tended to lecture me about giving up the 'coffin nails.' His older brother, my Uncle Seymour, had died from lung cancer at the age of 55. That made Daddy quit. None of the men in my life smoked then. Daddy wouldn't allow me to smoke in his car. He would rant at me if I even took my cigarettes out of my purse.

"You have to smoke outside. No smoking in the house or the car. Martha doesn't smoke. We both quit. If you must, then smoke on the porch. It's summer, after all."

With tremendous reluctance, the cigarettes went back into my purse. I had only smoked one in first class. I was already prepared for the lecture.

"It's a beautiful day in Indianapolis," I remarked.

"It's summer! It should be beautiful," Daddy grumbled with his eyes straight ahead. "Damn traffic."

Of course, the traffic was nothing compared to Los Angeles. Daddy had yet to discover the true meaning of 'traffic'. And yet, we were soon driving down my old tree-lined street passing houses with massive green lawns. I always loved our street, which now seemed more like living out in the country. When I was a kid, our house was one of the nicest on the block. Since then, some of the neighbors had added on or remodeled. Our house was no longer the largest or the most impressive. Some houses were even torn down and replaced, or the property divided with another house built in front or behind. Every house on the block was once on at least two acres of land.

My successful acting career had provided the tennis court and the swimming pool on their three acres. Martha liked to swim. Daddy enjoyed playing tennis on his own court. I also provided the monthly gardener and pool service in those days. But Daddy liked to ride around on his John Deer tractor mower like a gentleman farmer. No lawn service for him. Daddy had a small publishing firm that released around six books a year. At the time, two editors were helping him with the two books scheduled for fall release.

After my father placed my suitcase in my old bedroom, which was still pink, we went to the master suite where Martha was lying on her chintz chaise reading a book. She was fully dressed and got up to greet me.

"Dana, my dear, how wonderful to have you here, even if only for a few days," Martha said, hugging me and planting a kiss on my cheek. Her hair was a pretty shade of gray, thick and curly, her eyes a soft blue with thick lashes. Martha was pretty and plump, but Daddy never objected. She was a sweet and caring woman.

"Don't strain yourself, Martha. You're just getting over surgery." I kissed her cheek.

"I won't strain myself. George has me pampered something awful."

"You need to rest," Daddy said, kissing her forehead. "The doctor doesn't want you to do too much yet. So you take it easy, you hear me?"

"I hear you, George."

Vases of beautiful flowers were all around the room, with more bouquets in the living room and dining room. My yellow roses were on a skirted table near the bedroom window. Sunlight poured into the rooms on that side of the house. On the other side there was a huge maple tree that shaded my room from the afternoon sun. My parents' room was always filled with sunlight. Even my mother liked that room, which was small compared to her Miami mansion on the beach with its room-sized closet filled with expensive clothes she seldom wore. Helen was a shop-a-holic.

"You look thin," Martha said, sitting down. "Do you eat enough?"

"You always ask me that, Martha. I eat everything and anything. But it is necessary to stay slender when I'm working, since the cameras add at least ten pounds."

"I always forget that part. I won't be able to cook much while you're here. Mrs. Bennett is helping out some. Later this evening, she's bringing over a meatloaf for dinner."

"I'm a better cook than Mrs. Bennett," I said to my father. "You know I can cook."

"She cooks fine," he said to Martha. "I can fix some wicked-good scrambled eggs for breakfast, and I haven't burned the bacon yet. I make damn good coffee. Stop your fussing, Martha. We'll do just fine. I just hope you'll be up to going to that new Chinese restaurant we've been meaning to try out," he said, turning to me, "The Peking Red Chicken! They might be communists. Who the hell knows? And who gives a damn, anyway?"

I laughed. "As long as they make good Chinese, I don't care."

Martha and I laughed. My father was unlikely to ever change.

"Who cares if they're communists, George?" Martha said.

We all laughed again, together.

"I'm going to take you for a ride and show you what's been going on here in Indianapolis," Daddy said. "Lots of changes since you were here two years ago. Later, I'll bake some of those potatoes to go with Clara's meatloaf, and you can fix us a salad. Clara's meatloaf is usually pretty good." He quickly glanced at Martha. "Not as good as Martha's, of course," he added, grinning.

Martha smiled. "George is pulling my leg again. He likes Clara Bennett's meatloaf a whole lot better than he does mine." There was love in her eyes for my father, something that always made me feel good about seeing the two of them together.

"Let's not get into that," my father grunted, heading for the hall. "She's a homely woman and grossly overweight. That's why she can cook. And that's the end of that."

Daddy drove me all over town in his 1959 Cadillac Coupe De Ville. Compared to my 450 SL, his car seemed like a tank. Daddy was right. Many new homes and businesses were springing up all over town. New office buildings too. Daddy was a fan of the Indianapolis 500, the yearly car races. He never missed them. In 1967, A.J. Foyt won for the third time.

"That was some race," Daddy said. "I won a hundred bucks."

"Are you still gambling?"

"Only on the Indy. And mostly, I win."

"Mostly?"

That was when Daddy changed the subject and started to tell me about the books he was publishing: One book was about the Hoosier soldiers and their families in the Civil War. The other was a novel about the Gold Rush days in the Old West. Daddy loved history. Every year there was some kind of historical book published.

"*Gold!* would make a damn good movie," he said, casting me a sideways glance. "Lots of drama. Miners fighting over claims, fighting Indians, hangings and shootings. You can be the saloon girl, Nellie Mae."

"How about Lulu Mae?" I sarcastically replied.

"You can change the name, if you like that one better."

"Just thinking out loud, Daddy."

"How about a cup of coffee? We can stop at Denny's. They have excellent apple pie. Barbara still works there, as a matter of fact."

Barbara was a friend of mine in high school. I found it depressing that she still waited on tables after all these years. She had always talked about becoming a writer.

"Have you done anything with your writing?" I asked Barbara as she took our orders.

"I'm working on a screenplay and taking a class at the university." She hesitated. "Your father said I should give it to you when it's finished."

"Sure. What's the story line?"

"It's a love story. You would be great as the lead, of course. I'll get your address from your daddy and send it to you in a few months. Will that be all right?"

"Sure," I said, turning to my father after she left, "I hope she can write."

"Me, too," he whispered. "Her husband left her and the two kids last year, ran off with some floozy from Chicago. He never sends her any money. She had to move back home with her mom. Her dad died last year. Helmet was 62," Daddy said, thoughtfully shaking his head. "I've lost too many friends lately. That's the trouble with getting old, your friends start dying on you. It's a goddamn shame."

"Even at 32, Daddy."

"Sure is. Damn shame about Cindy. If they had caught it earlier, maybe they could have saved her. Her parents are really upset, I can tell you that much for damn sure."

"I'm upset too, even though I haven't seen her for a long time."

The apple pie tasted good with the vanilla ice cream. With all the current upsets and tragedies in my life I ate every bite of sugar and drank two cups of coffee, hoping I'd be able to sleep that night.

"I'll take you to see her tomorrow. I told Jeff you were coming. He seemed mighty pleased."

"Did he?" I said, suddenly feeling sad and nervous.

"I know Cindy is looking forward to seeing you, Dana. It seemed important to her somehow before … she leaves us and all."

# Chapter 28

Breakfast was hard to swallow on that morning. There was a lump in my throat and a tangible shroud hanging over me: A palpable strangeness. I called my favorite florist to order yellow roses for Cindy, remembering Martha's reaction to all the flowers after her surgery. I wondered if Jeff would be there, secretly hoping he wouldn't be. Seeing Cindy alone might be easier for me.

"Don't wear dark colors," Martha said with me still in my bathrobe. "Wear something cheerful, no black or navy blue. You're not attending her funeral. Don't make her even think about it. Nobody likes to lose a child." Martha stared past me and said, "Margaret and Fred haven't been doing so well lately. Sometimes I see them at church. No one knows what to say them anymore. What do you say after you've said you're sorry?"

Martha had lost a son in an automobile accident when he was 16. She knew about losing a child. Her daughter, Rebecca, was married and lived in Columbus with her two grandchildren. I'd always liked Rebecca and Ted. Their two kids were adorable.

"It's just awful," Martha muttered. "Really awful."

"How about yellow?" I forced a smile.

"Yellow is good. You've always looked good in yellow ... to go with your roses."

I tried to finish my bacon and eggs to fortify myself, along with two cups of coffee. Bright yellow Capri pants and my yellow and white flowered blouse went with my brown sandals. All bright and cheerful, I hoped. My hair was up in twin ponytails. The Indiana summer was its usual muggy consistency. I tended to sweat in Indiana. Even movie stars sweat.

Central air was added to the house two years earlier, praise the Lord. It was pleasant inside, but by 10:00 a.m. it was a sultry 88 outside, with high humidity. The newspaper reported the Midwest was going to swelter with a projected high of 100 to include the Mid-Atlantic States. I loved the California weather: Warm, breezy days. Nights that cooled the house, except for the terrible summer smog. Those weekends, I'd drive to Paula's at the beach to escape the yucky, brown air in town.

My father and I didn't talk much on the way to hospice. I was trying to think of what to say to a dying friend and feeling pretty much at a loss.

While parking the car, Daddy said, "She's lost a lot of weight. It was hard to even recognize her the last time I saw her. I just wanted to warn you."

A slight shudder went through me. "That means she can eat anything she wants, I guess," I said, half-smiling at my silly attempt at humor.

He nodded. "Maybe we should have brought her a hot fudge sundae. You girls used to love those hot fudge sundaes at Heckle and Jeckle's when you were kids."

"Maybe we'll bring her one if she wants one," I said, hoping deep down that Jeffrey wasn't there. All at once, I wondered what I was doing there myself. Whatever had possessed me to make such a trip between films?

The doctor was in the room with her, so we waited out in the hall. Cindy had a corner room with a view of peace roses in bloom outside her window. The roses reminded me of my garden with every imaginable color, including peace roses. So beautiful.

Feeling uneasy, I finally entered Cindy's private room.

"You look just like you did when we were girls," Cindy said the moment she saw me, all smiles, with an IV dripping into her left arm. "Ponytails. I used to wear them, too, remember? People said we looked like sisters, especially in high school." She had on a honey blonde wig of artificial hair. Other than that, she looked like she had only recently been released from Auschwitz.

"You're a blonde now," I said, trying to make light. Her hair was always as dark as mine.

"Finally! I have four wigs. Some days, I'm a redhead. You know, Las Vegas hooker red. On others days, I'm a sultry brunette, the usual. Carol Hughes got me a synthetic purple wig. The kids really like that one ... mom on Halloween or some weird character from *Star Trek*." She forced a smile and looked at the two dozen yellow roses on a nearby table: My trademark with all my friends, living and dying.

For all my effort to remain cool, calm and collected, tears spilled from my eyes.

"I love the roses. Yellow roses were always your favorite and your trademark." She saw my tears. "Sit here, Dana, please," she said, patting the bed. "It'll be fine. A hug would be nice." Tears streamed down both our faces and she was watching me closely.

With care, I sat on her bed, reaching out to hug her. She felt so fragile, as though she might break if I hugged her too hard. Then, we stared into each other's eyes as though neither of us knew what to say next. I was certainly at a loss.

"Thanks for coming," Cindy said, reaching for the tissues on her bed stand, wiping her nose and handing me a tissue. "Thanks for making the long trip. I know how busy you are with your career. I read all about you in the movie magazines. About your films, the parties you attend, the handsome men you date like that French actor, Louis Lamprais. Wow, Dana! You're a really big star just like you always wanted to be. It seems to me that all your dreams came true. I knew they would after you were the Miss United States runner up. If anyone was going to make it in Hollywood and the movies, it would be Dana Scofield."

"I'll just step outside," Daddy said, "and leave you two girls alone to talk. Jerome's wife is down the hall. I'll pay her a visit."

I had forgotten Daddy was even there.

"Thanks for bringing Dana, Mr. Scofield. It means a whole lot to me."

Daddy nodded and gently closed the door behind him.

"You just missed Jeff," Cindy said. "He brought the kids by earlier this morning. Mom and Daddy are taking them to the river for a swim and picnic. They're growing up so fast, Dana. It's amazing how fast kids grow up."

"How old are they now?" I asked, blowing my nose and thinking of how brave she was. I was amazed by how well she was holding up, under the circumstances. The cancer was in her brain, but she seemed fairly lucid. At least, she knew who I was. I wasn't sure what to expect.

"Terence just turned 12. He's a big boy, tall like his daddy. His voice hasn't started to change yet, and no whiskers, but that will come soon enough. Angela turned 10 in April, already double digits. She's the feisty one, strong willed and stubborn. Terry will be a teenager in another year."

Suddenly, her expression looked strained and she took my hand, wincing slightly, as though she were in pain.

I watched and waited, as Cindy struggled with her thoughts and her feelings.

"You will help me out, won't you, Dana? Help Jeff take care of the children? Help him raise them?" Her eyes appeared to frantically search mine. "They're great kids, really. Not much trouble at all." With that, she turned away before she looked at me again. "Please promise me that you'll help him out, Dana. Please promise?" and she squeezed my hand with desperation on her face.

I was beyond shocked, unsure of what Cindy was really asking me to do: To help Jeffrey raise their two children? Good grief! How did I qualify for that job? Was it something that Jeff wanted? I hadn't seen him in years and hadn't talked to him in what seemed like forever. I could hardly believe what Cindy was asking me to do. I didn't know what to say to her for a very long moment.

"Is this something that Jeffrey wants?" I finally asked. "Something that you've talked over with him ... for me to help him raise your children?"

"Not exactly," she whispered. "But I'm sure he'd agree with me." She hesitated, looking down before she looked up at me again. "He's always loved you, Dana. You must know that. He's never stopped loving you, not really." She paused, tears coursing down her face as she looked at me again. "He'll need taking care of, too, of course. It may not be easy for him at first. I've spoiled him by taking care of everything so that he could have his space and do his thing. I've tried to keep out of his way as much as I could."

Feeling stunned and at a loss, I finally said, "I think this is something you need to talk over with your husband. Jeff and I haven't seen each other for years." I paused, my mind suddenly started to race. "I'm sure your parents and his parents will help out with the children."

"I know how busy you are with your career and all, so you couldn't be here all the time. But you will help, won't you? Tell me you will at least try, Dana. Please?"

"Okay, Cindy, I promise I'll try," I said, unsure of exactly what I meant by those words.

The look on her face was one of relief after I said that. It was as though I'd lifted a heavy load off her fragile shoulders. I wasn't sure of how I could help out with the children, or with Jeff. I lived in California. The Waters resided in Indianapolis. Perhaps I could help out financially, invite the children to California and take them to Disneyland and Universal Studios to see how movies are made. Maybe contribute to a college fund or set up some trusts. My mind raced from one thought to another in an incoherent hodgepodge of ideas.

Cindy was still holding my hand, when suddenly she looked at me with a startled expression on her face and asked, "Who are you?" instantly releasing my hand with a frightened look on her face as she laid back against the pillows and stared at the ceiling. "Do I know you?" she asked, and, all at once, she was gasping for air.

I was entirely confused. I watched her, not knowing what to do. The woman lying in that bed had just extracted a serious promise from me to help out with her husband and children after she was gone, and now, without warning, she didn't even know who I was. Did that mean I was off the hook? Or was a promise really a promise?

At once, a nurse rushed into the room. Cindy was staring at the ceiling and completely out of it, seemingly unaware I was even there.

"I'm sorry," the nurse said. "This happens from time to time. Mr. Waters is in the reception area waiting for you."

Those words caused a catch in my solar plexus that I tried to ignore. I pulled myself together, wiping away my tears and blowing my nose, as I searched my mind for what everything meant.

"Will she be all right?" I asked the nurse, shaken by the unexpected turn of events.

The nurse responded with a blank expression and said, "That depends on what you mean by all right. She's here, and then, she's not. Sometimes she knows everyone. Other times, no one. The malignancy is eating away at her brain. The faster she leaves, the better it might be for Cindy."

Stunned, I stood there, staring at the woman who no longer seemed to know who I was. She had known me just long enough to extract an important promise, which was amazing when I really thought about it. Strange karma. I had made a promise to a dying friend to help to raise her children. Children I didn't even know and could barely remember. Strange karma, indeed.

After taking a deep breath, I entered the hall and slowly walked toward the reception area. Jeffrey was talking to a woman and bending over some papers. He had on a light tan suit with the collar of his white shirt unbuttoned, his tie loose. He looked taller than I remembered, but he was every bit as handsome: High cheekbones, tan, with a cleft in his strong chin, his blue eyes sparkled as he turned to me. Instantly, keen pleasure registered on his face. Pleasure I had seen almost anytime he looked at me those many years ago.

He smiled as I approached him, butterflies fluttering in my stomach. It was nearly noon, and for some silly reason, I was very hungry. My stomach loudly growled.

"Lunch?" Jeff inquired with a grin. "May I take you out to lunch?"

I hesitated, glancing around before I said, "My father ...."

"I told George I'd bring you home." He stood taller. "Cindy's folks took the kids to the river for a picnic, and my lunch date canceled. I think that's what you used to call 'destiny'."

"Destiny," I repeated, looking up into his clear blue eyes.

And we soon left in his blue Ford station wagon.

It was the Peking Red Rooster, not Chicken. Daddy had the name wrong. It was the same restaurant where my family planned to dine that evening, one of the few new restaurants in Indianapolis then, although I'd heard the El Paso was good for Mexican. And there was Denny's, the Holiday Inn and McDonald's. Thankfully, I only had a few more days in Indiana. I was spoiled by all the great restaurants in California.

"Your Dad still drives his Caddie," Jeffrey said after we were seated at a table.

"I've offered to buy him a new one. But he won't part with Matilda. He's crazy about that car. He's even thought of being buried in it."

We both laughed.

"Your dad is great. I'm very fond of George."

"He's a wonderful father."

"You look wonderful," he said after the waitress took our order. "You've always looked wonderful, and you've always been beautiful."

I could feel myself blushing. In self-defense, I sipped my Chinese tea. I wasn't sure of what to say to him next. I was still somewhat shaken by my encounter with Cindy and her suddenly blanking out on me.

"You're as handsome as ever. No gray hair. Those kids mustn't be too hard on you."

"Not too bad." He appeared to study me. "No wrinkles. Thirty two, right, the same as Cindy?"

"I'm a week older."

"Thanks for coming, Dana," he said, turning serious. "It means a lot to Cindy that you came all this way." He was plainly struggling. "She wanted to see you, for some reason of her own, I presume. I guess the two of you were pretty close at one time."

The waitress served our appetizers.

"And thanks for the roses. She loves yellow roses." He picked up an egg roll. "Both of your favorites, as I recall."

He wasn't undressing me with his eyes the way he did so long ago. After all, he was nearly middle-aged, 33. Before we knew it, we would both be 40. That was a scary thought to me then!

"I've seen all your films ... Most of them twice at least."

"Twice? No wonder they did so well at the box office."

He laughed in a way I fondly remembered. And, all at once, I found myself thinking, *you can't go back, Dana, that doesn't work. You're a grown woman and you can't go back!* But those old feeling were invading my entire body and mind.

"So what's it like being a movie star? Being famous? Being rich?"

"Not so rich. But the salary on my next film puts me in a brand new bracket. The fact is, I can still go to the supermarket without being asked for my autograph."

At that moment, the Chinese waitress approached our table with a pen and piece of paper in her hand. "Would you mind, please, Miss, to give me your autograph? You are Dana Scofield, right? Famous actress? You were born right here in Indianapolis, right? I read that in a movie magazine. Please!" Her eyes pleaded as she extended the pen and paper to me.

Perfect timing, I thought, to impress my old boyfriend.

"Of course," I said, writing my autograph on the piece of paper. Something that hadn't happened to me in a restaurant in some time. Perhaps I needed to return to Indianapolis more often.

"Thank you so very much, Miss Scofield," she said, smiling and nodding. "Sorry to bother you. I bring you your lemon chicken and steamed rice right away."

Jeff smiled. "You see. You're even recognized in the Peking Red Rooster in Indianapolis. How about that?"

"How about that?" I repeated, biting into an egg roll while noticing other people in the restaurant looking our way trying to figure out who the hell I was. "So tell me about your children. I hope to meet them." I had no plan to bring up my promise to Cindy, which seemed too sad to even talk about over Chinese food. I didn't want to cry while I was eating.

"Terry is in the Boy Scouts. The fathers and sons are going camping and sailing in August on Lake Michigan. We're looking forward to it. He's a really smart kid, in the gifted program and wants to be a lawyer like his dad. However, he is also very good at science. Angela is my angel and looks a lot like Cindy. Right now, she wants to be a ballerina. At 10, she's pretty good at ballet. She also plays violin, not too bad, sometimes," he grimaced slightly, pulling his wallet out of his pocket. "The kids would love to meet you." He held out two school pictures. "They both have trouble believing that their parents went to school with a genuine movie star. Terry thinks it's ... groovy!"

"He looks a lot like you," I said of Terry. Both were beautiful children. "And Angela looks like a ballerina ... and like Cindy. How nice ... one for each," I said, handing the pictures back to him, with me still bowled over by the prospect of helping him to care for them, in addition to taking care of the good-looking guy seated across the table. "When may I meet them?"

"Do you like pizza?"

"Sure."

"How about tomorrow? We'll all take you out for pizza. I'm still learning how to cook, and we don't care much for the pre-frozen kind. Pizza?"

"Pizza it shall be."

# Chapter 29

Terry looked a lot like a much younger Jeff with his big blue eyes and his tousled dark hair. Jeffrey and I hadn't met until high school. His family lived in a slightly ritzier part of town. Terry was very animated and open, so I learned a lot about him in around five minutes, like about his entire life.

On the other hand, Angela was pretty and shy with freckles on her upturned nose. Her eyes were hazel with lots of green in them, her straight dark hair long with bangs. She looked very ballerina to me and reminded me of myself at 10. That thought gave me chills that ran up and down my spine at least twice.

"Do you like being an actress?" Angela inquired.

"Very much. I love to act."

"You won a beauty contest," Terry said. "Dad told me. You were Miss Indiana in the Miss United States Pageant."

"But I didn't win the pageant."

"You were first runner up," he said, quickly glancing at his father. "That's right, isn't it, Dad?"

"Right," Jeff said, suddenly appearing ill at ease.

"Then, you went to Hollywood and became a famous actress," Terry said, taking a bite of pizza. As he chewed he smiled at me with his blue eyes sparkling.

Angela was carefully picking the mushrooms off her pizza and casting a wary glance my way. "I don't really like mushrooms. I hope you don't mind."

"I don't mind. I do like them. But I don't care much for broccoli."

"Me neither," she said, making a face. "But Daddy likes broccoli."

Jeff nodded. "I'm not wild about broccoli, but I eat it. It's good for you, Angie." He poured more red wine from the carafe into our glasses. "It's good for your toes. Broccoli will help you to make faster pirouettes and help you get up on your toes faster." He wrinkled his nose and winked at his daughter.

Angie grinned. "You know that isn't true, Daddy."

"You're old enough to try out for a major ballet company," I said to her. "Have you thought of auditioning?"

Abruptly, Jeff cast me a stern glance and said, "Not just yet, thank you. There is plenty of time for her to do that sort of thing. She's only 10."

"Daddy can be provincial," Angela said in a tone that instantly reminded me of Michele.

"I have another friend your age you remind me of, except Michele won't be 10 until August. She wants to be an actress, but her parents won't let her, especially her father. He wants her to wait until she's older. She thinks he's provincial too."

"Do you have lots of friends my age?" she inquired.

"Only Michele. Her mother is my best friend."

"What's her mother's name?"

"Paula Marlow. Her mother is an artist. Paula and her two children live in Malibu on the beach right on the Pacific Ocean. I see them often. Her son, Christopher, will be six in September. He's a great kid too."

"Is she divorced?" Terry inquired.

"Yes, she's divorced."

"Lots of people in California get divorced, right, Dad?"

Jeff hesitated. "Perhaps more out there than in some states, but I'm not really sure. Actors don't seem to have a great track record when it comes to marriage." He didn't look at me with that remark.

"Paula is an artist, not an actor. Paula's first husband, Michele's father, died," I said in defense of my friend. "Paula is a very fine painter. She's having an exhibit at an important gallery this fall. I'm the subject in some of her paintings. She's a really a very exceptional artist."

"Really?" Angela brightened. "Well, you're very pretty and you are famous. You should be in at least some of her paintings."

"Sometimes divorce is necessary," I said, perhaps in stronger tones than intended.

Immediately, everyone at the table was silent. Mentally, I chastised myself and had another bite of pizza. It was good pizza, and I wasn't sure of what to say next.

"You visited my mother," Angela said. "You sent her yellow roses."

"Yes."

"Yellow roses are her favorite."

"Mine, too," I said, swallowing with difficulty.

"Mom and Dad have seen all your movies," Terry said, fighting back his tears. "We've seen several, but not the R rated ones you made in Europe. Dad wouldn't take me to the French films. Mom wouldn't let him. You did nude scenes, right?" A sheepish grin filled his handsome, young face and he narrowed his eyes in scrutiny.

I could feel myself blushing and instantly noticed the amusement in Jeff's eyes.

"You have to be 17 to see those films," Jeff said, helping himself to more pizza.

"Would you like more pizza?" Terry asked with the silly grin on his face.

"No, thanks. I've already had enough. I'm making a film where I have to wear these corsets from the 1800s. No pizza for me in Colorado, that's for sure!"

"That sounds like fun," Angela said. "Maybe we can come to California and see you act."

Out of the corner of my eye, I noted alarm on the face of her father.

"Mom used to talk about that," Terry said. "She was sorry she hadn't stayed in touch. We went to Disneyland when I was seven and Angie was five."

"1962," Jeff said. "I checked with your dad. You were in Europe making a film, in Italy, I think he said."

"I was in Rome in 1962 making *A Little Affair*, hardly a picture for children."

"I guess I can't see that one until I'm 17, either," Terry said, taking another bite, chewing and grinning, as his dancing eyes observed me.

Briefly, Jeff and I made eye contact before I self-consciously looked away. There was this strong magnetic pull every time I looked at him. The same pull that was there the first time I set eyes on him. I became aware of him in high school right before I turned 16. Jeff was 17. Strange, I thought, being attracted to him in 1967 with the same intensity.

"You're not too old to go to Disneyland again, are you?" I asked the children.

Instantly, both kids shook their heads and expectantly turned to their father.

"No," Terry blurted out. "Maybe this time we can visit you."

"Do you have room for us to stay with you?" Angie inquired.

Instantly, Jeff said, "Angela, it isn't nice to invite yourself to someone else's home."

"I'm sorry," she said. "I didn't mean to be rude. We don't have to stay with you."

"Of course, I have enough room for all of you. I have two guest rooms besides the housekeeper's room when she isn't there. And there's plenty of room in the backyard near the pool to pitch a tent."

"You have a swimming pool?" Terry inquired as his blue eyes widened.

"It's 40 feet ... a nice size."

"We might get a pool sometime. Do you live in one of those Beverly Hills mansions on Sunset Boulevard?"

"No. I live in a house not much bigger than my parent's home here on a quiet street in the flats of Beverly Hills."

"And your friend, Paula, lives at the beach?" Angela said.

"That's right ... in Malibu."

"Maybe we could visit her, and I could meet Michele."

"Yes. You'd like Michele. I'm sure you two would like each other. In some ways, you seem very much alike. Michele takes ballet lessons, too."

"Really?"

"And we could go body surfing in the Pacific Ocean," Terry said. "That would be groovy!"

"Hey, wait a minute!" Jeff said with his hands up in protest.

He was watching our friendly exchange, watching me very closely, his eyes filled with countless questions. He was probably unsure of what to make of plans being made with his children right in front of him.

"You can come, too," I said to Jeff. "You like Disneyland, don't you? Ferris wheels and roller coasters? But you'll never get me on the roller coaster," I said to the children.

"Oh, come on," Terry said. "You're not too chicken to ride on a roller coaster, are you? You can sit with me. I'll hold your hand and protect you." He grinned.

Jeff looked askance at his son. "A chip off the old block," he said, ruffling his hair. "You can sit with your sister and hold her hand and protect her."

"Yuck!" Terry said in disgust.

"I don't want him to hold my hand!" Angie said. "I don't like roller coasters, either," she added. "We'll stay on the ground and watch, okay? They can ride together."

"I'm with you," I said, hugging her. She felt delicate and about the same size as Michele. I was sure that the two girls could be fast friends.

Jeffrey was watching me with a level of distrust in his eyes, glancing at his children with uncertainty. At that moment, Cindy was in hospice with cancer eating away and an IV in her arm, unaware of anyone else too much of the time. While Cindy was wasting away, here we were eating pizza and planning a trip to Disneyland. Suddenly, sadness enveloped me.

"We won't be able to come right away," Angela explained, "Probably not this summer."

Expressions sobered all around the table.

Terry stared at his plate. "Mom isn't well enough to make the trip."

"No, she isn't," I said, exchanging somber glances with Jeffrey.

"Maybe when she gets better," Angela said, turning to her father with a hopeful look on her adorable, young face. "She might still get better, Daddy. Really."

"Maybe," he said, "But only maybe, Angie."

Turning back to me, Angela said, "When my mother gets well, we can all come to California and visit you. Then, we can all go to Disneyland together."

I made one more trip to hospice to see Cindy before I left. At first, she didn't recognize me. I was in her room for half an hour, mostly making small talk with Daddy and the nurse. Then, right before I was about to leave, Cindy came around and opened her eyes.

"You'll keep your promise, won't you, Dana?" she said in a soft voice, her eyes glazed and out of focus. For a brief moment, she seemed to know exactly who I was.

Right after I said, "Yes, Cindy. I'll keep my promise," she was off again somewhere in the twilight zone completely out of touch. It was bizarre!

From what I heard soon after that, Jeffrey was at her side several times a day. He brought the children to see her often. But it was starting to wear on them. Every week, he took his children out for pizza and Chinese food. Both grandmothers helped with the cooking. His mother made spaghetti sauce with several portions frozen. All kids seemed to love spaghetti.

The last time I saw Jeff at hospice, he looked haggard and drained.

"I can't thank you enough for coming, Dana. It's like she's slipping away more each day. I feel so helpless." Tears spilled from his eyes. In embarrassment, he turned away.

"It's all right, Jeff," I said, tearing up myself. "I'm really sorry." I hesitated. "Please bring the kids to California. There is really plenty of room for all of you in my house, and there is plenty to do. I can get you on television filming sets, maybe *Lost in Space* and *Batman*. I have friends on the Fox lot. Right now, they're filming *Planet of the Apes*. The kids might get a kick out of seeing human apes walking around. I'm not sure when the film wraps. But there is always something going on, and I have lots of connections at the studios."

"I'm sure that you do. Thanks for the invitation." He glanced down the hall toward Cindy's room, apprehension on his face as he reached into his pocket. "Here's my business card. The house number and home address are written on the back. The kids really enjoyed spending time with you. I think you have two new fans forever." He looked as though he was in desperate need of sleep.

"I'd like to think I have two new friends forever."

His eyes searched mine for the longest moment. "You're leaving in the morning?"

"Right. I have wardrobe fittings. In two weeks, I'll be in Colorado shooting outdoor scenes near Aspen. This will be my only real summer break."

He frowned and hesitated. "I wish we could have spent more time together under more pleasant circumstances, but..."

"I understand," I said. "You're a wonderful man with two wonderful children. I'm sorry this terrible thing has happened to Cindy. It seems unfair. And frankly, it's scary to think that something like this can happen to someone my age." Tears rolled down my cheek. "Your children are losing a wonderful mother. I'm sure of it."

Suddenly, Jeff reached out and pulled me into his arms, holding on tight. The feeling was not sexual. It was simply as though he needed someone to hold onto, perhaps a woman, for fear he might never hold a healthy woman in his arms again.

Then, just as suddenly, he let go and stepped away, just as a nurse urgently called out to him, "Mr. Waters, could you please come in here now?"

Jeff turned and hurried down the long hallway, and I hurried out the front door in serious need of a breath of fresh air. I needed to be somewhere where people weren't dying. I was crying, searching my purse for tissue, as my father walked over and put his arms around me.

I dissolved into tears and cried like a baby, my head against my father's strong shoulder.

"There, there," my father said, as he had when I was a child, patting my back. "It's a good thing you came, Dana. … that you met the children. It was the decent thing for you to do."

"Decent?" I said, blowing my nose and searching my father's green eyes. "I don't even know if it was a decent thing for me to leave him to begin with. I don't know that for sure anymore, Daddy. I really don't."

He opened the car door for me and gently closed it after me. Martha had fixed her famous pot roast and Daddy didn't want us to be late for supper.

"You did the right thing," he repeated.

And we went home to eat pot roast, potatoes, carrots, celery, string beans and homemade biscuits, along with homemade chocolate ice cream.

Later that evening, there was a thunderstorm with great bolts of lightning flashing across the night sky. Fireflies darted around, blinking on and off in the backyard. We watched the fireflies from where we were on the screened porch, as we drank iced tea and reminisced about the past.

Fairy lights. That was what I always called them. That was what fireflies always looked like to me. Fairy lights. And that is what I still call them until this very day.

# Chapter 30

There were no glitches on the flight back to LAX. Indiana receded behind me, as the settlement in the West known as Los Angeles twinkled in magical patterns beneath the huge jet lowering in the evening sky. During the flight back, my thoughts were often of Cindy, Jeffrey, Terry and Angela. Together. Separately. Fond thoughts for everyone left in Indiana.

Paula picked me up at the airport. We planned to have dinner in the city. I wasn't sure what had happened to all the men in my life while I was away. And, at that moment, I didn't care. Jeffrey's face constantly intruded into my thoughts. His smile and the terrible tragedy he was facing without any choice. I thought about two great kids about to lose their mother and of a promise made to a dying friend never mentioned to her husband or her children.

"So how are George and Martha?" Paula inquired. "I always think of them as our first couple ... the Washington's!"

"I told Daddy that. It still makes him laugh."

"And?"

"George and Martha are fine. Martha is healing. Daddy is dealing with the Civil War and the Gold Rush. The books will be out in September and October. You can expect two more historical books signed by the publisher and the authors for Christmas."

"A good historical book to read on a California winter's night before a crackling fire sounds perfect to me."

I freshened up at home and changed into a dress before we drove to Lawry's Prime Rib on La Cienega. My celebrity status immediately secured us an excellent booth.

Martini in hand, I inquired, "So how was Harlan's opening? Sorry to have missed it, but this trip was absolutely necessary."

"It was fun. Beau bought two more sculptures. He's still buying lots of art, but you know that house is the size of a small hotel. By the way, his money isn't just from cattle, but from the oil wells his daddy left him. John Kandell, Kandy to his men, had a substantial number of oil wells that still enable Beau and his mother to live nicely without doing another single thing."

"Every other person in Texas seemed to have an oil well. There is a whole lot of money in Texas, Paula. But I guess they have poverty, as well."

The prime rib was medium rare, with Yorkshire pudding, baked potatoes with sour cream and chives, and we shared a Caesar salad without the anchovies. I loved the horseradish sauce with my prime rib. I was happy to be in a posh restaurant with fine cuisine, although that pizza wasn't half-bad. A full-bodied Cabernet rounded out our meal. We split a bottle.

"So how is Cindy?" Paula somberly inquired.

"Beyond bad."

"I'm sorry to hear that."

"Her days are numbered, to quote a miserably apt phrase."

"How about Jeffrey?"

"What about him?" I even sounded defensive to myself in noting the look on Paula's face. "Jeffrey is wonderful. What can I say? He's a devoted father and devoted husband. He sees Cindy several times a day. Jeffrey Waters is one amazing human being."

"Is he working on sainthood?" she quipped, with her smiling eyes watching me closely.

"Perhaps. Both the kids are angels. Angela is 10. I told her all about Michele. She's studying ballet. Maybe the girls can be friends."

"That might be nice."

That was when I told her about the promise Cindy had extracted from me, not once but twice, to help with her kids and Jeff, with no mention of her death.

"Really? Miss Movie Star is going to be a fairy godmother?"

"I resent that. Just because I'm an actress doesn't mean I never want children."

"Well, at least those two are half-raised. You can be a mother without being pregnant. Pregnancy is not much fun, actually."

"I'd still like to have a child. I'm not too old yet."

"You are not."

"Louis suggested we have a child someday."

"Good grief! The man has children all over the world. Why should you add to his lineage? Like ... this is your half-sister and your half-brother and your half-sister and your half-brother .... Why would you even think about it?"

"I'm not."

"I can't envision Scott as a father. He's much too grand to play that role."

"Eric is starting to get possessive. He spoke of commitment when we were having dinner the last time, about us not seeing other people."

"So he's getting serious on you after how many dates?"

"The sex is great, but ..."

"Not that great?"

"It isn't the sex. You have to consider more than sex when it comes to marriage. You had great sex with Jamie, but look at all the complications!"

"I talked to him again," Paula said, looking serious. "He's trying to hold on, Dana, which surprises me. He asked if I'd slept with Beau. He seemed concerned."

"Did you tell him?"

"It relieved his mind when I said no. He's been trying to talk his Uncle Dan out of taking me to court. Dan isn't listening to his young nephew, of course."

"Good for Jamie. Ballsy kid. I like him."

"He wants to transfer to UCLA so we can spend time together."

"Wow! The Georgia Peach is bucking mom and dad and his Uncle Dan!"

"There's no way his parents will pay, of course. He doesn't get money from a trust fund until he's 21, and he has to be 25 for the bigger chunk of change. That family's purse strings control the kids. I'm glad I never had to cope with inheritance. That wasn't my karma."

"So how do you feel about Beau now?"

Paula narrowed her eyes in a pensive manner.

"You did spend a whole week with him in Texas, and more time when he came here for Harlan's show. So?"

Paula picked up her wine and smiled before she said, "I like him."

"A lot?"

She grinned. "I like Beau a lot."

"Still no sex?"

She shook her head and smiled.

"That's a damn shame. He's obviously a very patient man."

"There is plenty of time for sex, Dana. Beau is not rushing me. Like you said, Beauregard Kandell is a perfect southern gentleman after the Order of the Old South of Texas."

"Apparently, so is Jeffrey Waters. And he was born in Indiana!"

Home again, I couldn't stop thinking about sad Cindy. My father still visited her once a week. Sweet, I thought. Jeff had to appreciate that. Mostly, Daddy just sat with her and read from the local newspaper, as though she could understand. Daddy was still working on the books, but that didn't stop him from visiting my dying childhood friend in hospice.

Jeff had started to give Daddy messages:

"Tell her, thanks. Tell her, hello. Tell her, the kids send their love." Nothing personal. No phone calls. Nothing about his feelings. After all, his wife was dying. They had been married for 13 years. Jeff was being friendly, I told myself. Just being a normal, compassionate human being grateful for any kindness during an extremely stressful time.

That Friday, I accepted Paula's invitation to the beach. I enjoyed Maria's cooking and her unique humor. Once again, Florence was off vacationing somewhere. Lately, she was acting mysterious. I was starting to wonder if she had met a man. Over the years, Florence was always way too wrapped up in me and my life. It was about time she had a life of her own.

That Saturday evening, Paula and I went to the Moonlight Sonata restaurant at the beach for a leisurely dinner and some good jazz. Paula talked me into staying longer. On those days, long walks were taken on the beach. Alone. Or the two of us together. The blue Pacific was washing away my anxieties. Paula told me about a ritual that Andy had given to her. Twelve waves were to wash over my feet and ankles and return to the sea. With each receding wave, another sorrow was released and washed away. It seemed to me I could have used 20 waves. But I felt better after thinking things through. With one wave, I released Helen for abandoning me. That was a tough one. Twelve waves had washed away 12 sorrows freely taken on by the Great Mother, the Sea of Life.

Paula was beginning to really miss her kids. She talked to them on the telephone often and managed to avoid surly Dan. The kids were having a good time in the mountains. Michele was writing in her diary daily and sketching animals, mainly squirrels. Dan's girlfriend, Gerry, had joined them. She was doing the cooking and cleaning, but the kids supposedly helped.

"We're going to Texas with Mother," Michele said on the telephone, "On an airplane. Mother is taking us to see her new boyfriend's ranch for two whole weeks. We're going to ride on ponies. I've never been to a ranch before,' she whispered, then added, "It's probably not as boring as just being up here for so long. I miss the beach."

"I see." So Beau was 'her mother's new boyfriend.' "I've been to the ranch. You're going to just love it. Beau has a huge swimming pool, big lake and several boats."

"And an airplane. We're going to have a really good time." Michele paused. "Christopher wants to talk to you, Dana."

"Hello, Dana," Chris said. "I wish I was at the beach with you to go body surfing."

"I'll bet you're having lots of fun in the mountains."

"It's okay. We'll be home on Sunday. The day before July ends."

"Your mother will be happy to have you home again."

"May I please talk to her?"

"Sure." I handed the telephone receiver to Paula. "Your son would like to speak with you."

I went back to studying my lines, surprised by the number of scenes I was in. By then, I was really looking forward to working again. Paula usually painted, but she helped me with my lines in the evening.

That Tuesday, Paula surprised me by inviting Eric and Phil for dinner. The two men had become chummy, which surprised me.

"Both of them? Are you nuts?"

"We are all grownups here. Besides, Phil keeps bugging me about his gallery. I'm having lunch with him on Friday to see the place."

"Stay on La Cienega, my dear, and watch out. He's sure to make a move on you."

"I thought you were the one who made the move. Anyway, he's not my type."

Dinner was tasty and interesting.

"Would you like me to spend the night?" Eric inquired, when we were out in the swing on the deck under a nearly moonless sky. He began to nibble on my earlobe.

"Not tonight. I have things to think about. I'm craving alone time, Eric."

"Fair enough. I'll be in Boston for another week."

"That has to be great for your career. I'll soon be in Aspen. It looks like this picture might take several months on location." I was aware that Eric cared for me a lot more than I did for him. "You need to be open to dating other women."

"I am," he said, looking at me with hurt in his eyes.

"When do you move back into the city?"

"Labor Day. Phil and I are taking a two bedroom apartment together in Westwood."

That was a big surprise. Changing patterns all around. Eric had another month at the beach, which I considered with a sense of relief. Soon I could visit Paula without the bachelors next door. When I was finally alone with her, she poured us each a snifter of cognac.

"How is Louis?" she inquired, settling onto the sofa. "Any word?"

"There was a blurb in Barbara Darling's column about Louis Lamprais and Sophia Basso being seen out together in Rome. That gorgeous, well-endowed Tuscany temptress with volumes of hair. Rumor has it that her six-year old daughter, Angelica, was sired by none other than Louis!"

"The man does get around!"

"Indeed."

"You don't seem to be upset about it," Paula said.

"He's a fantastic lover, an excellent actor, and I'm exceedingly grateful to be his leading lady. Other than that, I've no plans to spend the rest of my life with Louis Lamprais. It's been fun, but nothing more than an erotic romp in the hay, though an exceedingly fine one."

"An erotic romp in the hay! Wow! I'm using that as a theme for a painting."

"It was an affair, a caper ... a dance."

"What sort of dance?"

"Any sort you can possibly imagine. His skills are beyond incredible. Why should I deprive other women in this world of his wondrous bedroom talents?"

"How about Scott? Will you see him again soon?"

"Scott made Marty Mantrell's column. Recently, Scott was seen in New York out and about with Miss Sweden of 1965. You know, Bridget of Don the Beachcombers? In addition to her, he was seen with Sandy Perlman, the up and coming actress with a Tony to her credit. She's apparently going to be Jennifer in *Speak Softly, My Love*."

"It seems to me that the two men in your life can't handle knowing about the other, is that it? It may not suit their sexual fantasies or male egos."

"What about you?" I inquired, sipping my Courvoisier.

"We go to court in November. That's all I know now for sure."

"It looks like Jamie didn't change Uncle Dan's mind."

"I guess not."

"And Jamie is still trying to get you back?'""

"He called again, but I wasn't encouraging."

"Jamie is sweet, Paula. But it seems to me that he is only going to end up making things that much more interesting for one Beau Kandell."

"Jamie knows I haven't slept with Beau yet. But he also knows I'm taking Michele and Christopher to Texas for two weeks. My two munchkins will have their own suite with separate bedrooms and a whirlpool bathtub."

"Well, Jamie has to realize that you're at least thinking about sleeping with Beau. I mean you are seeing him again and you like him enough to take your children to his ranch deep in the heart of Fort Worth?"

Her gaze turned quizzical right before she grinned. "Beau is quite handsome, isn't he? Ethical, intelligent ... so masterful." Her smile warmed.

"Tall, blond and handsome with pretty blue eyes, sort of like Paul Newman's, don't you think?"

"Sort of. But Beau is much blonder than Paul, and he has more hair. He's taller, too. Paul is not tall."

"Beau is almost a foot taller than me."

"That shouldn't stop you ... from anything."

We both giggled.

"Jamie wants to come back to California and see me again."

"And?"

"I said I'd think about it." Paula sat forward to glance out at the rumbling surf with a distant look on her face. The fact was that she was leaving for Texas with her children in days.

"Like they say ... it's not over until it's over."

"Right," she said.

"Beau is tempting?"

Paula smiled. "At this point, my dear friend, you will just have to wait and see."

# Chapter 31

The telephone seldom rang that week except for calls from my agent and the costume department at Colossal. I made two trips to Burbank for fittings. Neither Phil nor Eric nor Louis nor Scott had even left a message. Strangely enough, I was relieved and feeling the need to distance myself from all of them. I didn't care who anyone was dating or with what woman any man was sleeping. I was thrilled to have the time to prepare for what could well become the role of a lifetime.

I reread Garson's glorious novel. The author and I planned lunch so I could gain greater insight into Victoria and the history of the Old West in the 1800s. Gold. Silver mines. The Mother Load. Garson lived in Connecticut but would be in Colorado for filming. He was pleased with the screenplay written by Carl Warner, a brilliant screenwriter. A great many authors ended up disappointed by what finally made it to the big screen. My hope was that Garson would not be disappointed, especially with my performance.

The next weekend I was back in the Malibu to escape from the oppressive heat and mucky brown air in the city. I missed Paula's kids and would be in Colorado by the time they returned from Texas, with little time to spend with her and her children that fall. I planned to fly back in October for her exhibit.

We had a surprise telephone call early on Saturday. Dan was bringing the kids home a day earlier than planned. Our plans changed. Michele and Christopher arrived in time for lunch with us on the deck: tuna salad sandwiches, potato chips and iced tea. After lunch, we headed for the water with towels. It was a beautiful summer day.

"May we come and see you on location?" Michele inquired. "I've never been to Colorado."

"Maybe. But I can't promise." I was unsure about bringing children to the set.

"You're going to Texas," Paula said to Michele, "And you've never been to Texas before. When we get back, you'll be in school, and Dana will be making a film. You'll see Colorado some other time. Maybe we'll go to Yellowstone Park next summer. How about that?"

"That would be good!" Chris chimed in. "I want to go to Texas and ride horses, maybe rustle up some cattle." His grin looked silly.

"You won't be rustling any of Beau's cattle. That is not in the plan," Paula said.

We all laughed.

"You've seen too many Western movies," she said to her son.

"You'll have fun, Chris. You'll love all the animals!"

"Beau has his own deer," Christopher said.

"Beau has two ponies. One for each of us," Michele said, with Chris nodding. "He sounded nice on the telephone."

"He is nice."

Christopher jumped up and challenged his sister, "Race you!" and the two of them made a mad dash for the surf.

"Are you coming?" Michele yelled back.

"In a while," Paula called out.

We watched the children body surfing to shore time and again.

"Those two are happy to be home."

"No happier than I am to have them here. I guess they haven't grown that much."

"In a month? I guess not."

"Larry is upset that we won't be here when his two kids arrive from Chicago. By the way, they've invited us over for a barbeque."

"That should be fun."

"My life has certainly changed because of you."

"My pleasure, Miss Marlow. We girls from the Midwest have to stick together."

"Beau's ranch is the perfect place for my kids. I can hardly believe that Chris is starting first grade with Michele in fifth grade in weeks."

"It seems like only yesterday that Chris was a baby and she was just starting school. Look at them. Your two great kids are growing up fast. You're leaving on Thursday, right?"

"Maria is washing, ironing and packing. At least they'll have a few days of ocean breeze before that Texas heat. You worked there in the spring when the weather was cool. Gratefully, Beau has the pool, the lake, and air conditioning. Otherwise, we might vaporize."

"That bad?"

"He's going to fly us to San Antonio to see the Alamo, and we may visit Galveston. His plane holds six, so it's perfect."

"That man is definitely marriage and father material. I'm willing to bet your kids will adore him."

Paula glanced away. "Would that make Dan Thurman happy?"

"Probably not. Who cares? Dan is not going to get your kids. Trust me!"

"My lawyer sent him a letter to inform him of my plans. Tactical. I'm not beholden to tell him anything if I'm only taking them out of state for two weeks. I only need permission if it's going to be longer."

"He had them for a month," I said in a tone of irritation, as sunscreen was vigorously applied to my middle. "Would you mind?"

Paula did my back. Under those clear blue skies I could feel the sun starting to burn my skin. "At least he's leaving Jamie alone," she said, rubbing lotion on my shoulders and lower back. "Jamie has ROTC in the Carolinas for two weeks. The way this war is going, Jamie is sure to end up in Vietnam as soon he graduates from the university."

"Weren't you supposed to marry him then?" I asked in a tone of sarcasm.

Paula simply gave me a look. "He asked me again," she said, glancing toward her children.

I blanched. "And?"

"I told him it's not an option at the moment."

"At the moment? You are taking your kids to Texas!"

"That's right," Paula bristled, "But I do still have feelings for Jamie."

"You still love him?"

"That's what I said."

"And he keeps calling," I said in singsong.

"And he keeps calling," she repeated, "Except lately, his mother has been giving him a really hard time about talking to me."

"No shit? Considering how thrilled she was to have you for a sister-in-law, the thought of you as her daughter-in-law has to send her right into orbit without a rocket." I laughed out loud. "She's probably sticking pins into her Paula doll."

The look on her face was of startled amusement.

We both laughed.

Paula tried to scowl, but she couldn't. "That might be interesting. Perhaps I should find myself a June doll."

"Now, that might be interesting."

"Are you coming in the water?" Christopher ran up, soaking wet, and shook drops on me like he was some silly dog.

We both got up.

"Come on, Victoria," Paula chided. "Time for a swim!"

And we ran into the water after Christopher and body surfed for the rest of the day.


Barbequed chicken and fish, potato salad, green salad, green beans and corn on the cob dripping in butter. Simple but delicious faire. Flaky biscuits, compliments of Maria, baked Louisiana style with hot peppers flakes and black olive bits. Paula brought along two bottles of white wine. We ate dinner on the patio next door, as the sun slowly sank toward the sea.

"It's a good thing you didn't ask me to clean these fish," Maria said. "I cleaned enough fish down in Rosarito Beach to last me a lifetime. Lordy me! From now on, Carlos can clean the fish."

"I don't like to clean fish, either." Chris made a face. "Did you catch lots of fish?"

"A fair amount. Except, I didn't need to be quiet like you said, Chris, because the ocean is really noisy and we fished in the sea."

"I've never fished in the sea."

"That Carlos, he kept screaming at those fish, 'Come here, come on and grab this here bait, you suckers, so we can cook you up for supper or breakfast.'" She grinned. "I praised him, of course. So he'd be the one to catch the fish. I didn't like baiting the hooks, and that's the truth!"

"But you had a good time, didn't you?" I inquired.

"A fine time!" Maria winked at me. "That Carlos is one mighty fine man. Uh-huh!"

"He's good-looking, that Carlos," Guy said, rolling his dark eyes.

"That's right." Maria said, casting a suspicious glance his way. "And you'll be leaving him alone, you hear me. Or else, you'll have to deal with one angry Cajun woman, and I just might have to cast an evil spell on you, Mr. Guy Hamilton."

Guy quickly glanced at the children, who were watching him closely, confusion on their young faces. "I hear you," he said, grinning, "I won't be bothering him, Maria. Don't you worry now." He grinned at Paula and winked at me.

"You'd best not," she said and bit into a juicy leg of chicken.

"Why would you put a spell on him?" Christopher inquired, scowling.

"He knows what I'm talking about," Maria said, making a face at Guy and casting a playful evil eye his way.

Larry grinned and shook his head. All the adults were aware of Guy's bi-sexuality.

"You'd better behave or she will put a hex on you," Michele said to Guy. "Maria knows all about voodoo."

Everyone at the table looked from Michele to Maria to Guy, and back to Maria, who had a serious look on her face as she had another bite of chicken.

"Is that right?" Larry inquired. "I know some folks I'd like to cause some serious harm, maybe stick pins in," he said to Maria. "Maybe we can work something out between us, just you and me," and he wiggled his eyebrows in a playful manner.

Maria laughed. "Got you going, doesn't she?" she nodded at Michele who grinned. "Don't you go telling folks all my secrets, you hear, Miss Michele," and she hugged her. Then she said to Guy, "It seems to me that what you really need is some kind of love potion!"

"That's not a bad idea. Can you mix up something with those herbs of yours?"

"Maybe."

"Looks like you've been mixing up lots of love potions for these ladies with all the men hanging around here!" Larry said, grinning.

"These beautiful women don't need any love potions. But you," she said to Guy, "You could use some help, considering how ugly you are," and she threw back her head and laughed.

Everyone laughed.

"Don't you worry, Maria. Carlos isn't my type."

The children were ignorant of the innuendos. Maria simply rolled her eyes and laughed.

"How was it in the mountains?" Larry asked the children.

Immediately, the two children launched into numerous tales about what had happened up at Lake Arrowhead ... about life with father in the wilds of the California mountains.

"It was more fun the week our friends came," Christopher said.

"A month is too long to be in the mountains," Michele said. "I missed the ocean and all my friends here at the beach."

"We missed you, too," Larry said. "But you two are becoming world travelers just like your mother here, going off to Texas. How about writing me a postcard, Michele?"

"Okay," she said. "I'll send one to you, too," she said to me."I'll send all of you postcards from Texas."

# Chapter 32

Sunday was the usual art exhibit down the beach at Andy's complete with hippie fanfare. A bohemian-looking crowd gathered as the latest folk music blasted over the loud speakers. People were there in even larger numbers than usual, some browsing, others buying or talking about the latest casualties in Vietnam. Many were becoming opposed to the war. Most were wearing bathing suits. The kids wanted to go in the water, but we objected. Paula and I were wearing shorts, T-shirts and floppy hats. My sunglasses were my vain attempt at incognito, but no one asked for my autograph. My fame only valued by a Chinese waitress at the Peking Red Rooster in Indianapolis.

While sipping a glass of Andy's wicked summer wine, I came upon a painting of a young ballerina stretching at the bar, her reflection artfully reproduced in the mirror. Instantly, I thought of Angela, wondering how long it might be before I saw her again. I picked up the painting and studied it. Then, I started searching for something for Terry who was into scouting and baseball.

I found an old-fashioned baseball player up to bat about 15 inches tall cleverly sculpted out of papier-mâché and mounted on wood. The player had a comical expression, the bat poised to make contact with an imaginary ball. It was perfect for Terry. How could I give something to Angela without getting something for Terry? My promise to Cindy was free of favoritism, though I was definitely drawn to the young ballerina.

"That's nice," Michele said, seeing me with the painting, "And it isn't even me." She started to search for another. "Do they have any more? Who painted it?"

"Kathryn Courier. I haven't seen her here today, have you?"

Michele scanned the crowd. "No. She doesn't seem to be here."

"Your mother can paint you as a ballerina. My guess is ... you only need to ask."

"I know." She studied the painting. "But sometimes I'm going to have to buy a painting that isn't me or wasn't painted by my mother, if I'm really going to be an art collector." She was watching me closely. "Are you buying that for Angela?"

"I think so. Do you like it?"

"I do. You must really like her. I thought you only saw her once when you had pizza with her and her brother."

"I saw her twice. But the second time was brief. She had just seen her mother at hospice and was crying."

Michele looked at the papier-mâché baseball player. "And that's for her brother, Terry?"

"He likes baseball." I thought of sending the gifts to the children for Christmas, seriously doubting that Cindy would last that long. It was disconcerting to have her here one moment and gone the next. That had to fully upset her children. "Angela and Terry's mother is dying," I said to Michele.

"She is?" She reacted in alarm. "From some terrible disease?"

"From cancer. There's no hope of saving her."

"Really? Does that mean you're going to be their mother?"

Stunned, I was speechless and just stared at Michele. "Not necessarily," I finally said, trying my best to recover, as my mind filled with Jeffrey and his hug that had left me trembling.

"You'd probably be a good mother. I've always thought so."

Paula had overheard her remark and turned to me with, "Is there something you'd like to tell me, dear?"

"I'm not pregnant, if that's what you mean."

That was when Paula noticed the painting and the sculpture. "I'm sure they'll like them."

"Don't you think Dana will be a good mother?" Michele inquired.

"Absolutely," Paula said, winking at me, as Andy walked up.

"Hello, hello," Andy said, kissing Paula's cheek. "I've just sold the last two paintings I have of yours. Do you have anything else we can sell next weekend?"

"I'm sorry, Andy. But I've promised Kenneth everything unless he doesn't want something I've already painted."

"That will be a cold day in hell. Your star is rising, beautiful one. Your tall friend from Texas called to tell me how exquisite my lovers look in his huge entry. I gather he made the right choice in positioning my sculpture with your approval?"

"It's a perfect place for them. He bought two sculptures from Harlan and still has plenty of room. The children and I are leaving for Texas on Thursday. Larry is taking us to the airport in his station wagon, since all our luggage would never fit in Dana's trunk."

"So you're going to Texas!" Andy said to Michele, "To be a cowgirl, no doubt. That is quite marvelous, Michele."

"He has horses and cattle, his own goats and chickens. I'll send you a postcard."

"You will?" Andy grinned. "I've never received a postcard from Texas before."

"Being first is always nice," Michele said and her expression changed. "My friend just got here. See you later, alligator," and off she ran.

"May I help you with those?" Andy noticed the items in my hands.

"Gifts for my new friends. My checkbook is at Paula's. I'll have to pay you later."

"Your check will be fine when you collect them. I'll do some pricing and put them inside, so no one else grabs them." He turned to Paula and said, "I have $800 for you. Soon, you'll be self-sufficient with your art priced beyond these Sunday exhibits. I'll be there in October to sing your praises. Kenneth is a very lucky art dealer to have your talent. Lucky, indeed."

Soon, Andy was helping others. Apparently, many sales were made that day. More people were showing up every weekend. News of the Sunday exhibits had spread far and wide.

"Daddy Andy," I said to Paula, with my selections safely in a cupboard.

"He's amazing! Those were small paintings to bring in $800. Andy has saved the day for me more than once. These exhibits have helped me out over the past two years ... given me cash for more of everything."

"I'm sure my dad and Martha would like Andy. Helen probably wouldn't. She has turned into a strange bird indeed, according to my father. I fear it's true."

"I'm glad I've never met her. Poor you. George is such a good man."

"You're sure to meet Helen one day. She'll show up and want to purchase a painting or come to my premiere for *View From the Mountain* with all the razzle dazzle and red carpet. Helen and Arnie are presently sailing through the Panama Canal. Daddy and Martha may visit me on location."

"I may do a weekend, but not before my October exhibit."

"I wouldn't dream of getting in the way of the beautiful, mad, mystic artist of Malibu about to make a name for herself all over the universe!"

"All over the universe?"

"Well, at least all over the world."

# Chapter 33

Fortunately, none of the men in my life showed up at the exhibit that Sunday, not one of Paula's handsome neighbors, including a certain biochemist. Paula and I had dinner with the children and the others artists. Then, we went home early to watch TV.

There was a meeting of the entire cast at Colossal set for Monday afternoon. I heard Louis was back in town and planned to be there. He'd left no messages on my service, however. Paula was up at the crack of dawn, painting. The children and I had to drag her out of her studio to get her to eat some breakfast.

"You can't survive on just coffee. You'll destroy your body and your brain."

"I already have Maria on my case … now you?" she protested. "How many keepers does one artist need?"

"You've got me, too," Christopher chirped, eating his cereal with sliced banana as fast as he could chew and swallow.

"Hey, not so fast!" Paula said. "You don't want indigestion."

"I have to see my friends," he said, finishing off his cereal. "I'm going to be gone again and I won't get to see them for a long time." He got up and wiped his mouth on a napkin. "See you later."

"Hey!" I called out to the boy bounding for the stairs, "How about a kiss and a hug? You won't see me for a while." I opened both arms and knew I had a pleading look on my face.

Christopher gave me a look, added a boyish shrug, and ran back and kissed my puckered lips and he kind of sort of hugged me. "Okay?" he said before making a mad dash for the stairs.

"Hey! You have a birthday coming up. You'd better start thinking about what you want for your sixth birthday. Okay, Chris?"

He stopped on the stairs. "Probably something from *Star Trek*," he said and ran on down the beach without another backward glance.

"Don't forget to stop at Andy's to leave a check and pick up your purchases," Paula said.

"I know that Angela and Terry are going to like what you got them," Michele added.

"I won't forget. You'll be having your birthday in Texas. Any special plans?"

"Beau is taking us to a Mexican restaurant with a band that will sing to me."

"Mariachis!"

"Thanks again for the beautiful dress and sweater and skirt. I always like what you give me, Dana. You're very generous and you have excellent taste."

"You're very welcome." I finished my coffee. "As much as I hate to leave you lovely folks, I need to go home and change. I'm really excited about making this film."

"You should be excited," Paula said, smiling.

"I have this feeling deep down inside that Angela and I are going to be very good friends ... maybe as good as you and my mother," Michele said.

"You'll be very lucky if that happens," Paula said.

"May I be excused?" Michele asked as she stood.

"All finished?"

"I started while you were still painting. I need to see Sally, okay?"

"Okay. You may be excused."

Michele came over and kissed my cheek. "I'll send you a postcard to let you know how we're doing. You can always call. I know Mother called you while she was in Texas."

"Give my best to Beau. Tell him hello from Dana."

"I will. It seems he has enough room in that house for you to come too."

"Maybe sometime," I said. "You never know."

"I know he likes Mother a whole lot. She's needed a man in her life for a while now."

Paula and I looked at each other in amazement.

"Is that right?" Paula said.

"Beau must like you a lot," Michele said to her mother. "Why else would he invite you to bring your children? He probably wants to marry you and he just wants to check us out first to make sure he likes us."

Speechless, Paula simply stared at her daughter.

Michele turned to me. "I guess it's your fault. You introduced them, right?"

"Guilty as charged. And, in my opinion, they are perfect for each other!"

"Dana!" Paula said. "That is quite enough!"

"I'll let you know what I think, okay?" Michele said, backing toward the stairs. "Good luck with your movie," she said. "Break a leg!" and soon she was running down the beach.

"Did I ever tell you that you have a big, fat mouth?" Paula said, buttering another slice of toast.

"I think maybe, once or twice."

"I'm not going to lecture you, but you said way too much to her."

"Nothing she couldn't figure out on her own. She knew how keen I was to introduce you to Beau. She knows you spent a week with him while they were at Lake Arrowhead. And you are taking them to his ranch for two weeks."

Glancing away, Paula thoughtfully chewed. "Did I tell you that Hannah met someone?"

"Really? How did they meet?"

"At the supermarket, of all places. He sells insurance and lost his wife to cancer around the same time that Harold died in the accident. His kids are older. One is in college. Hannah is all bleary-eyed over ... Steve, I think. He invited her to Mexico for a week without the kids. Puerto Vallarta."

"I hope she goes and falls madly in love!"

"She's thinking about it. He's 10 years older, but she already thinks he's wonderful."

"How nice. Hannah deserves someone. But those three kids of hers can be a handful."

"Two kids are a handful. I think any man is pretty courageous to take on another man's children, even for two weeks."

"I can't wait to hear all about your trip. The two of you did spend an entire week alone. Well, not exactly alone considering his housekeeper, chef and 20 hands. We'll see how the tall cowboy does with Michele and Christopher. If all goes well, maybe you should marry him and just stay in Texas.

Maria and I can pack everything up. I'll visit, of course. At least you'll have lots of guest rooms."

"You're such a schemer! How about Thanksgiving in Texas with all of us together riding the range?"

"Look at you ... planning ahead."

"Beau already brought the subject up." Paula laughed. "But which man would you bring? Louis? Scott? Eric? Or maybe Jeffrey?"

"I can't think that far ahead." I said, remembering Jeff's endearing smile at the pizza parlor. "Besides, Cindy may still be here. And even if she isn't, I've no idea how Jeff and I would even get together. Our lives are so radically different, Paula. And we both have changed a lot."

"You grew up. Any word on Cindy lately?"

"I need to call Daddy and find out."

"Call Jeff and ask him," she said with a sly smile on her face.

"I think not. You haven't seen his pain, Paula. It's not easy for him at all."

"Would you have any respect for him if he acted any other way? If he were cavalier and uncaring, you'd hate him. Admit it."

"You're probably right. I guess what a man does to one woman he'll do to another—the leopard's spots and all that. They say a tiger's skin is even striped."

"A shrink once said that an unfaithful man is an unfaithful man. Whenever he gets an itch, he's likely going to scratch it."

"Remember what Ilona said: We attract what we deserve. It's universal law." I drained my coffee cup and checked my watch. "It's time for me to do some house cleaning in my life, but for now, I need to get into town."

"You're okay, Dana. After all, you're not trying to hurt anyone. That is the first rule." Paula patted my hand. "Are you going to tell Jeffrey about the gifts you bought for his kids?"

"Not yet. I'll hold onto them for a while and see what happens. Maybe Christmas?"

"Will you see Louis today?"

"No doubt. After all, he is the star of the film" I entered the house with Paula.

"Will you see Scott anytime soon?"

"He hasn't called me lately. I'm confused after seeing Jeff, especially since Cindy might not be here very long. I guess that's a terrible thing to say, right?"

"No, it isn't. Don't be so hard on yourself. After all, Cindy made you promise to help Jeff raise the children. I'll bet you haven't told him that yet, have you?"

"No," I said, picking up my overnight satchel. "I'm the one who made the promise. And, when it comes right down to it … that's all that really matters."

It felt really good to get better acquainted with the rest of the cast. I was impressed by the quality of all the actors. It was also good to get the director's take on how we were going to start with the scenes in Colorado. Indoor sets were being built on the soundstages at Colossal. I suspected trouble with Retrograde Mercury. There were constant delays and postponements during the entire month of July.

During the meeting and afterwards, Louis appeared distant. I wasn't sure what to make of him, thinking perhaps he had reignited the flame with his old love in Paris or the Italian temptress, Sophia Basso, as the gossip columnists had reported. I wondered if he was trying to appear detached in front of the others to dispel any rumors about our personal relationship.

Then, right after the meeting, Louis walked over to me. "I'm flying back to Paris on Friday to bury my father," he said as tears filled his eyes. "He passed away early this morning. I was unable to sleep last night between calls to my family and getting ready for the meeting."

"I'm so sorry, Louis," I said, relieved to learn his mood had nothing to do with me.

"Eighty-seven is a long life. And my father had a good life. He was a good man. I did whatever I could to see that he had everything to make his life comfortable. I don't expect to live as long," he said in a weary tone.

"Did you just arrive from Paris this morning?"

"No, at noon yesterday. I tried to call you, but you didn't answer."

"I was at Paula's at the beach for the weekend. The air quality in the city was awful. Beau is flying Paula and her children to Texas for two weeks at his ranch."

"Ah, romance has bloomed with the cowboy, in accordance with your plan. You are indeed a matchmaker!"

"So far so good. She's already spent a week in Texas. Now, she's taking the children. I just got home this morning, changed and headed here for the meeting."

"You say it's a wonderful place for Paula and her children, this Texas ranch. Beau seems like a good man. After all, he is part French, oui?" Louis smiled.

"So you are flying back to Paris today?"

"Not today. I have costume fittings. I leave on Wednesday. Kindly forgive me, Dana, but I need time alone. Next week, I fly to Colorado. I would like to spend time with you, however." He raised my hand to his lips and kissed both my cheeks before he turned to hurry toward a waiting limo.

I was saddened by the death of his father. My father was nowhere near 87, but the thought of losing him gave me plenty to think about.

# Chapter 34

That was my only time with Louis that week. Suddenly, it seemed that too many people around me were either ill or dying. Only that morning, Florence had told me about a neighbor rushed to the hospital who had died in the ambulance on the way. Gus was 67. Recently, Florence also had a friend diagnosed with leukemia. I went home and sat out in the sun to dispel my growing sense of darkness, with Cindy Waters on my mind.

I resisted calling my father, as a sense of dread held me in check. Part of me wanted Cindy to miraculously recover, while another part wanted her to let go and move on. She was on high doses of morphine. I prayed for her release from her pain and suffering, and not because I wanted Jeffrey, though my feelings for him were strong. And not because I wanted to be the mother of his children. I wondered if I even qualified for that role in life. I simply wanted Cindy in a place where she might be whole again, if only in spirit.

Back in 1964, Paula and I would often drive to the San Fernando Valley to see a spirit medium in Tarzana. He said that people are whole again in their spirit bodies after they leave the physical body to return to the elements. That sounded right to me.

When I was eight-years-old, a cousin the same age died from polio. On a Saturday morning three months later, she appeared in my bedroom. Carol was walking again and she looked radiant. She hadn't walked since she was five. She had spent three years in an iron lung. My tears were of joy when I saw her skipping around my bedroom. She looked happy right before she disappeared. From that experience, I figured everything would be fine when I died. We go to another place, a beautiful place filled with light, to join all our loved ones that passed on before.

It was near the time of her divorce from Dan that Paula and I heard about the Reverend Plume. He was a trance medium and healer who held weekly services in a strip mall in Tarzana. Next to his storefront "church" was a small pizzeria where we sometimes grabbed a bite before the services. It was a sad-looking, dirty, rundown strip mall with many of the storefronts already boarded over.

Jeanne, my astrologer, told us about the gentle, white haired English gentleman who channeled different disembodied spirits. I'd never been to a séance and was interested having in the full experience after seeing my dearly departed cousin as a child. There was no charge. They just passed around a plate for donations. At the time, I was game for anything that involved the supernatural. Paula was having kidney-bladder issues, so we went in search of an extraordinary experience with the hope of a possible healing for her.

There was an altar up front with a large, faded print of Jesus. On another wall were pictures of monks in orange robes, with the snow-capped Himalaya Mountains behind them. These men were called spiritual Masters, members of the White Brotherhood associated with Madam Blavatsky and the Theosophical Society. These were mystical, far-out Christians, with an aspect of Eastern religion added for good measure.

There was an old organ on one side of the room. The Reverend Plume was a small, wiry man with white hair and soft blue eyes. From the energy he projected, you felt as though he loved everyone there. Mrs. Plume, Margaret, had her white hair pinned up in braids, with a cheerful, rosy pink face to go with her soulful blue eyes. On the plump side, she played the organ with Christian enthusiasm in her renderings of *Rock of Ages* and *Amazing Grace*.

Margaret Plume, half-Scot half-English, was raised a Presbyterian before she fell in love with Reginald Plume, a member of the Spiritualists Church of England when they met. Her soul mate, Reginald, gave her a message from her dead grandmother on their first date. That had to get her attention. He provided her with her granny's name and birthday as well as the name of her grandfather. Naturally, her deceased grandmother approved of the young minister who regularly spoke to disembodied spirits. At least that was what he told her that first evening out and about in London. Talk about a line! They ended up with six children, only half of them mediumistic, but all the children were devoted to their loving parents.

Besides allowing other entities (as he called them) to use his body to communicate with those assembled, the reverend could see and talk to spirits himself. He described departed relatives in great detail, sometimes revealing the way they had died. He said that this was because his third eye was open, the eye in the middle of our forehead. He claimed many other people have the same abilities, sometimes without knowing it. He said that one day everyone will see beyond the veil, with communication free between this world and the next.

Far out, I thought. I had lots of questions for him, especially regarding Grandma Rose, my maternal grandmother. I looked a lot like her. But Rose took her own sweet time to show up at the strip mall.

The Reverend said, "Relatives who show up are not always the ones you want to see, but those you need to see to make things right."

At that time, Paula and I were playing with an Ouija board down at the beach. We thought we communicated with her dead mother who was a riveter in a defense plant during World War II. Her mother, Ann, never wanted Michele to sleep in a friend's top bunk from a fear that she might fall and get hurt. For that reason, Paula kept her daughter home from that sleepover, which didn't please Michele one bit. And yet, Michele never fell out of that top bunk.

During another visit, Geoffrey the fishmonger came through to talk to the group. Talk about a trip!

"I was trying to get through to you ladies the other night when you were mucking around with the Ouija board," Geoffrey said in his Cockney accent, "But you wouldn't let me talk to ye."

We were 'mucking around with the Ouija board,' so we both paid closer attention.

"Ye had a whole roomful of spirits, ye did. When people use those silly boards, a whole lot of folks on the other side gather to try to get a message to a loved one in your dimension. It is best not to mess with it unless you want to be a medium and help others by passing on the information."

That was a revelation!

"And keep it away from Michele," he said to Paula. "You're a bit psychic you are, with your art and all. Have a couple master painters hanging around from time to time. The masters are pleased with your progress, Renoir especially. He's one of your favorites, is he not?"

Renoir was Paula's absolute favorite impressionist painter. Her work was reminiscent of his.

"And your daughter is very psychic. Michele could talk to your dead parents for you, if you let her. She has seen them more than once."

Stunned, Paula and I glanced at each other. When she was small, Michele used to talk to the old pictures of her grandparents on the wall. There were Renoir prints on Paula's studio walls. The fact that he was helping her with her painting was exciting to the both of us!

It seemed that Geoffrey had a job on the Other Side. He was assigned to telling those who didn't know they were dead that they had died. Years ago, he lived in a boarding house in East London. One day he went to his favorite pub for a pint and the bartender he'd known for 30 years fully ignored him. The bloke acted as though Geoffrey didn't even exist. That was after shouting at him. Upset, Geoffrey went to another pub and received the same rude treatment. All the bartenders acted as though he wasn't even there.

Finally, a priest stopped him on the street and told him that he was dead. No one could see him anymore. The priest was also dead, Geoffrey explained to the group.

At first, Geoffrey balked. Then, the priest took him to the boarding house to show him his body was still in the rocking chair. No one had realized he'd died of a massive stroke. The priest showed Geoffrey around, and after a while, he was also assigned to helping people learn that they had "crossed over to the other side."

"Your grandmother didn't like being dead at all," he said to me. "Gave us an awful time. Called me a liar. Rough, that one. She screamed at me bloody murder!"

I could see Grandma Rose doing that. She was bossy.

"She is fine now, so don't you worry. She sends you her love and is right proud of your accomplishments with your acting. You have much success still ahead of you."

Then he turned to Paula, "And your mother, Ann, is such a joy. Didn't know she was dead at first, either. Lots of folks are surprised to find themselves on this side of the veil, only to discover they are still themselves, nothing more, with as much to learn as ever. Quite a shock to the suicides, those stuck in the twilight, purgatory for the Catholics. Suicides are always surprised or shocked. It sets them back a touch, depending on the reason for killing themselves."

When the reverend did his healing work, he took on the spirit of a 2,000-year-old Chinese doctor. The old gent still healed folks on this plane from various illnesses and diseases. Watching him take on the entity was strange. His face changed, his eyes became Oriental, for want of a better word.

Paula sat in a chair. Then, Dr. Hu, occupying the reverend's body, looked up and down her body while providing a verbal rundown of her pregnancies and illnesses experienced over her 27 years. Paula suffered from strictured ureters and was forced to endure painful treatments where the doctor ran metal wires through her bladder and up through her ureters to her kidneys to break up the scar tissue.

Two women were instructed to place their hands and arms on the front and back of Paula's body. After about 15 minutes, Dr. Hu said, "You should have come to me a long time ago and you could have avoided these painful treatments. Go back to your doctor. You no longer need these treatments. You are healed."

We were both big spenders on that night. We each put in five dollars. But later, after she saw her urologist, to her utter amazement, her urinary track was normal. The doctor said that Paula no longer needed the treatments and she never had another.

We made about a dozen trips to see the Reverend Plume at his Spiritualist church in the dilapidated strip mall during the summer of 1964. We received messages from the departed that convinced us that his work was genuine. Several people were cured of ailments where a death sentence was issued by the medical community. But the reverend said, "People are not always healed, should it be their time to leave this plane of existence, they will leave for a certainty."

Late that afternoon in 1967, I drove all the way to Tarzana in search of that old strip mall. All the buildings were torn down. A self-service gas station and convenience store now stood where the shopping center once stood. I bought coffee and filled my car with gas.

After getting home, I searched the telephone book, but found no Reverend Plume. I even called Jeanne to see if she knew where he might be, or if there was anyone else like him anywhere at all.

There was apparently no other spiritualist healer to be found anywhere near Indianapolis or in the states of Indiana or California that I could find. Cindy's life was in God's hands—no doubt the greatest healer of all.

# Chapter 35

That Saturday, my father called. Cindy was about the same. Some days she knew who people were, other times her consciousness slipped off somewhere else. He visited her once a week. Sometimes Martha went with him, either to see Cindy or another friend in hospice. Daddy had run into Jeff and the kids during the past week.

"Terry and Angela say hello," Daddy said. "There daddy was taking them shopping for school clothes. Jeff looks pretty haggard, Dana. Martha invited him and the kids to Sunday dinner, but it seems that his and Cindy's parents alternate Sunday dinners. He's taking the kids camping before school starts, somewhere near Michigan City to hike the Lakeland Trail, I imagine."

"They can use some fun."

"Jeff said to say to say 'hello' to you, daughter. There's not much more a good man can do when his wife is dying."

"I know, Daddy." Suddenly, a tangible heaviness settled over me.

"So you're leaving for Colorado on Monday. Mighty beautiful country, hear tell. Just about everywhere in the Rockies. I watched one of those travel logs on Public Television about the Grand Canyon last night. Mighty beautiful country."

"We won't be going to the Grand Canyon."

"Well, that's a damn shame. You should go river rafting. Terry and Angela might like doing something like that with Jeff."

I reserved comment.

"Except, it looked pretty dangerous to me. I'd never get Martha into one of those rafts ... not on your life!"

"You'd probably never get me into one, either, Daddy. I'm not the out-doors type. You know that."

"I know. Five star hotels, the lap of luxury, that's my girl. You got that from your mother who found her rich prince charming at that goddamn spa in Miami. Goddamn son-of-a-bitch! Oh, well, that's ancient history." He chuckled low in his throat.

"You stay away from the Grizzly bears and mountain lions. I don't want any wild beast eating you. And don't forget to take along your camera and remember to take some pictures, so your family can see where you've been and what you've been doing. Get double snapshots and send me some, okay, sweet patootie?"

"Okay, Daddy. I just got a new camera." He hadn't called me 'sweet patootie' for years. It made me laugh.

"I'll give your best to Jeff and the kids. You take care and keep Cindy in your prayers."

"I will."

I'll keep Jeff, Terry and Angie in my prayers too, I thought, hanging up the telephone. Then I walked out into the backyard with Frisky. Like it or not, Frisky was going to Colorado. I hoped he didn't get eaten by a bear or mountain lion, either.

* * *

Eric invited me to dinner at the Luau that Saturday. He was excited about some breakthrough in genetic engineering at MIT. He couldn't stop talking about it, though I had trouble understanding what he was talking about.

Let's face it. It had been fairly quiet for weeks. Louis was in Paris, and I was starting to feel like a wallflower. Scott had dropped out of sight since our encounter at Don the Beachcombers. Me with Louis, Scott with Miss Sweden of 1965. He could have already started shooting *Speak Softly, My Love*, but I wasn't sure.

That afternoon, Paula called from down in Texas.

"We arrived safely and we're having a great time," she said. I could hear Michele chattering in the background. "Here's my daughter. She wants to talk to you."

"My pony's name is Tootsie. And she is a tootsie, too! She loves sugar cubes and carrots. Beau says she's my pony now, except I have to leave her here. I can't take her home with me. But that's okay. I love the ranch. This house is like being in a huge, beautiful palace."

"I guess Beau expects you to come back, huh?"

Michele giggled. "Of course, he does! Christopher wants to talk to you."

"I got to feed Bambi," Chris said. "The deer likes to cuddle and follows me around. My pony's name is Harry. He's mostly black and he is hairy. But I guess all ponies are hairy."

"Harry and Tootsie sound like a pony couple to me."

"They're brother and sister, the same as me and Michele."

"I'm glad you're having a good time."

"We're going to the Alamo. Lots of famous people died there. Cowboys, Indians and Mexicans. Mom says the place must be haunted."

"That is possible."

"You're invited for Thanksgiving!" Michele was on the phone again. "We're all invited. Isn't that neat? Thanksgiving dinner on a Texas ranch? Beau has a ton of bedrooms and a game room with everything ... and a gym with all this equipment, too."

"I just might accept the invitation, if I can get away from the film. But shouldn't the invitation be extended by Mr. Beau Kandell?"

"He doesn't mind if I ask you. He told me to," she said in an adult tone.

"I see."

"Tomorrow we're having lunch on the River Walk in San Antonio where a river flows through the middle of the city. I'll buy postcards and send you one, okay?"

"Okay, Michele." I was pleased by her genuine excitement.

"Today we went water skiing. It's good that we already learned up at Lake Arrowhead. Beau's boat is really fast." She paused. "Here's Mom!"

"Well, as you can see, Beau has completely won over my two," Paula said. "They're on their way to jump back into the pool. Beau makes sure there's always a lifeguard. The chef made us a fabulous breakfast before we went water skiing. I think I could get used to this life style. I'm feeling pampered. The cowhands are great with the kids. Hank is teaching Chris how to lasso a steer. I think he needs to be a bit older and bigger to do it, but he's giving it his best shot."

Hooray, I thought, but what I said was, "You may have to stay longer."

Paula laughed. "I think not, my dear. But I will keep you posted. Have fun in Aspen and send us a postcard, too, okay?"

"I will ... I promise."

"And you are coming to Texas for Thanksgiving, right? It's the least you can do after instigating all of this."

"Sounds like a plan to me. Give my best to Davy Crocket and Jim Bowie, and don't forget to take your sketchbook."

The food at the Luau was excellent. I slowly sipped my Mai Tai and enjoyed the appetizers before the Lemon Chicken, Peach Blossom Duck and Beef Broccoli with tomatoes. Eric was attentive. I enjoyed gazing into his startling blue eyes in the pleasant tropical setting. He was one of the most gorgeous male biological specimens on the planet, and so smart it was scary with his two Masters Degrees and Ph.D. in biochemistry. But somehow, I couldn't see myself spending the rest of my life with him. It didn't feel like it was part of my plan.

I didn't object later, however, when he invited himself into my bedroom. I was hungry to be touched, held, kissed and make love. Eric qualified in that respect for another master's degree, and he'd brought along the Kama Sutra in living color!

In days, Louis would be fulfilling my erotic fantasies. But on that night, Eric was ready, willing and fully able. Who was I to deny either of us the pleasure of emulating the pictures in that graphic book? Neither of us was committed to anyone. And the man I thought I might want to be with for the rest of my life was still married to my dying friend.

First, we looked at the pictures. Then, we tried a few positions. The kisses got longer, deeper and wetter. My new pink satin sheets were ready for amorous antics. Eric's hard male body felt good against my soft, yielding flesh, to my touch, to my taste. I loved the way he kissed me everywhere. The way his able hands moved over my warm, willing flesh, finding just the right spots to arouse me to the heights and cause streams of pleasure to run through me. Lovely! It was even more delicious than the Cantonese food.

His tenderness and control were admirable, except maybe for our romp on the bathroom floor at the beach when we were like a couple of wild animals in heat. That Saturday night, the lovemaking was lingering, tender, producing pleasurable sensations just about everywhere. And during the throes of passion, I had to admit that there was something wonderful about Dr. Eric Whitley. He was decent, honorable, and brilliant, and yet, I was not in love with him. I was in lust, not in love. Perhaps I could learn to love him. But I didn't want to try. That was the bottom line.

Right after making love, Eric caught me completely off guard when he asked, "Will you marry me, Dana Scofield?"

I was speechless. Instantly, my mind started to race. "I don't see you down on one knee," I teased.

Eric slid off the bed to get down on both knees.

Reaching out, I grabbed his hand, shaking my head. I was trying to stop him as his beautiful eyes searched mine. I was really beginning to feel foolish.

"Don't be silly." I finally said, doing my best to be kind. "I hardly know you, Eric. Why would you ask me to marry you?"

At first, he looked startled. After that, embarrassed. After all, he had just provided me with an excellent orgasm. But that didn't mean I wanted to marry him.

"I want to marry you," he said, sitting on the side of my bed. "I know it hasn't been long, but I love you, Dana. I fell in love with you the first time I saw you that Sunday on the deck. You are beautiful, intelligent, talented and everything else I've ever wanted in a woman. You have a marvelous sense of humor and you're fantastic in bed. You have to admit we're sexually compatible. You have all the qualities I've ever wanted in a wife. I never thought about getting married until I met you."

Wow! My mind had flinched at the word "wife." I could never be Eric's wife. I didn't want to hurt him. I enjoyed his company. Suddenly, it seemed impossible for me not to hurt his feelings.

"I'm not ready to get married. I don't know if I even want to be married." That wasn't exactly the whole truth and nothing but the truth, but I hoped my words helped him to feel better.

"I can wait," he said, and that remark nearly broke my heart. "I'm sorry if I'm in too much of a hurry ... if I'm taking things too fast." He paused, smiling his handsome smile. "A commitment then, a promise not to see anyone else ... that it will just be you and me. Then later, we can talk about marriage."

Those beautiful blue eyes searched my startled green eyes so tenderly in the dim candlelight of my room, adoration on his gorgeous face. It was a look I had often seen on men, even those never kissed; and on the many faces of the love-starved, sex-hungry men who had made me the love goddess of their countless wet dreams.

The idea of Eric proposing had circled through my head all evening, with me wondering what I'd say if he did ask me. Was I foolish not to marry the beautiful, brilliant, sexy Eric, who could well one day receive the Nobel Prize? He deserved a woman who was crazy about him. Perhaps I was crazy not to be crazy about him. He had qualities that any woman would want in a man, but that woman wasn't me.

"I'm sorry, Eric. I don't love you. So how can I make a commitment?"

The initial look on his face was one of disbelief. He had to think I was mad to turn him down. The sex was fantastic. And he was such a great catch!

"I see," he finally said in a dismal tone. "I suppose you're in love with the French actor." Hints of hostility had crept in. "I read about you in a movie magazine in Boston."

The Nobel Prize winner of MIT reads movie magazines? What a revelation!

"You can't believe what you read in movie magazines, Eric. Louis Lamprais and I are making a film together. Publicists plant all kinds of garbage in newspapers and magazines to whet the appetites of the fans and future audience. Gossip makes money. Studios love that."

He nodded. The pensive expression turned into a scowl as he stood. He dressed in mechanical motion, barely glancing at me while he put on his socks and shoes. Was he in shock?

All at once, I felt naked. I put on my silk robe and lit a cigarette, blowing smoke into the room. I'd promised myself not to smoke in my newly appointed bedroom. At that moment, I was breaking my promise!

Fully reassembled, he actually tied his tie and said, "You know you shouldn't smoke. It's bad for your health."

"I know," I said, puffing and filling the room with disgusting smoke.

Eric had just provided me with an excellent reason not to marry him. Then, I coughed and he gave me a supercilious look that made me want to blow smoke into his bloody, handsome face.

"It's been good to know you," he said in a snotty tone. "I hope we can remain friends."

"Of course," I said, filling the room with smoke. He had pissed me off. "Thanks for dinner," I said in my snotty tone.

He didn't answer. Instead, he just looked sad. Then, he opened the door and disappeared into the darkness of night.

Luckily, it wasn't too late for me to catch a movie on TV.

I poured a double Courvoisier and watched *Casablanca* in bed, fondly remembering my two wonderful years with Jeffrey Waters.

Right before falling asleep, I said aloud, "We'll always have Indianapolis!"

# Chapter 36

To me, the entire State of Colorado was beautiful, especially near Aspen where the picture was being shot. Mountains were among my favorite things: Rugged, towering mountains that combined the masculine and feminine principles of metaphysics. Many of the mountaintops in the Rockies reminded me of ancient citadels guarded by threatening warriors of a giant stature from another era, or from another dimension in time and space. Did an abominable snowman or woman prowl near the craggy peaks to make a home in a comfortable cave in the snowy heights, far from the prying eyes of mortals?

In Aspen, picturesque postcards were dutifully purchased and written to all my near and dear ones, even Helen in Miami, though I doubted she would be home to receive anything from her wayward daughter. Another postcard was written to Paula. With separate cards for each of my young favorites: An impressive grizzly for Christopher. A soaring bald eagle for Michele. Angela was going to receive a mother deer with her fawn. Terry a silly moose that looked like it wanted to ask you a question. The card with the high waterfall was for Jeffrey. Luckily, I remembered to bring along his business card with his home address, which was transferred into my travel address book on the plane.

I didn't send a postcard to Eric, poor man. Or to Scott, who was fairly scarce by then. Louis was at my beck and call whenever I wanted the pleasure of his company. His amorous overtures reminded me of my basic bodily needs. I was a liberated female, with him satisfying my every need with savoir faire. His suite was right across the hall from mine at the Hotel Jerome in quaint, bustling downtown Aspen.

Nearly everyone in the cast and crew was fun to be around. We held group lunches when the caterers had a problem, along with many delightful dinners in town with interesting stories shared around the table. In the beginning, there was night shooting, dinner served in huge tents with folding tables and chairs. Kerosene lamps flickered to provide the real feel of the mid-1800s. It was the time of the mining and refining of a migrating humanity, with new trails being blazed and brand new communities established in what was once known as a raw and glorious wilderness in the West.

Some scenes filmed in downtown Aspen involved horses and carriages. Stagecoaches filled the streets, with costumed actors and extras providing entertainment for the locals and the tourists. It appeared that vacationers flocked to Aspen every season of the year. Some of the old buildings were reminiscent of the years of our story.

All of those involved in creating our epic were housed in Aspen, Snow Mass and Buttermilk. Several wanted to stay for the winter to snow ski, since December in Aspen guaranteed snow. The Sierra Nevada Mountains in California were also under consideration and closer to the studio, with no decision made early on.

Business in the local bars and restaurants was booming because of our picture. A favorite hangout for the cast: The Owl's Nest, a quaint bar with sawdust on the old pine floors and owls of every size, color and description in residence, some stuffed. The owner's brother was the local taxidermist. In the evening, live owls entertained the customers, some behind a glass enclosure where the birds of prey could fly and perch on the branches of real trees and hoot as often as they pleased. Some nested in the hollowed out trees, compliments of the local woodpeckers, chief contractors of the wild in fashioning suburban housing inhabited mainly by owls. The outdoor owls were seldom seen during the day, their cute faces and soulful eyes only glimpsed occasionally. Sometimes a disinterested bird peered out at a human joying a beer whose primary objective was to observe the owl's curious antics.

At night, there was some real hooting going on. Live mice or rats, even a snake or two, were released in the enclosure so the owls might hunt. The owner did feed his fine feathered friends specially prepared pellets, which was more to my liking. I was too squeamish to watch a kill. As a child, I had a pet mouse that died of sunstroke when my mother aired it in direct sunlight on a hot Indiana day. Little Herbert was buried in the backyard under the oak tree. My friends and I read over his small grave from the Bible.

In the Owl's Nest, near the bar were two live, wise-looking owls. Bachelor Flammulated Owls were the primary residents in that part of Colorado. These two seemed to be having as much trouble finding a mate as some of the males that frequented the bar. The larger, older male, in his hollowed out log attached to the bar, was named Hooter. He never gave up on attracting a mate, for each night he was known to hoot with regularity, which increased the sale of drinks. The purpose of male owl hooting was always to attract a mate. Their human counterparts had the same objective, at least temporarily, it seemed. The bar's owner was into falconry, breeding and training birds of prey. He also taught humans how to hunt with Peregrine falcons. A keen-eyed beauty perched near the bar with a sign that read: *Do not feed. Beware the bite of Fredrick the Falcon.*

Louis, Geoffrey and I hiked some of the trails. Others in the group joined us at times. I lost five pounds from just being at that elevation, 10 pounds during the shoot, while denying myself nothing in terms of calories. That was a plus. Some of the restaurants were excellent. Our caterers did a fine job. Everyone enjoyed working in beautiful, charming Aspen.

That Friday, I was supposed to have dinner with Louis. Earlier than planned, I knocked on his door with the thought of spending time with him in the Jacuzzi or swimming in the indoor pool. You can perhaps imagine my surprise when Gloria, one of the makeup artists, opened the door in nothing but a hotel towel, her face flushed. She was a pretty, platinum blonde, age 40, with blue eyes and a remarkable figure that included a round behind and breasts the size of large grapefruits.

"We're busy," she said, looking into my eyes with a silly smirk on her face. "You can't have him until I'm finished," she added, closing the door in my startled face.

I hadn't missed the look of triumph on her pretty though mature face. Perhaps she thought she was stealing Pierre Pomeroy from Victoria Rutherford. It seemed to me that Louis had added another notch to his bedpost. No wonder his nickname was Lucky Louis!

After recovering an aspect of my dignity, I called Keith, our director, and suggested we have dinner together that evening. "I need to discuss the scenes we're doing on Monday," I said.

"I thought you were having dinner with Louis," he replied.

"Not tonight," I said, concealing my fury. "There has been a change of plans."

"Sure. I'll meet you in the bar at seven."

"How about 6:30?"

Louis and I were scheduled for seven. I would be unavailable, if he was stupid enough to knock on my door. How could Gloria keep a secret concerning her conquest of Mr. International Super Star? Suspecting there were other women in Louis's life was one thing, having one flaunted in my face was something else.

"6:30. I'll meet you in the bar."

"Great!"

Unexpectedly, another summer lover had become a thing of the past, but not soon enough to suit me on that day. After all, I still had BOB! And plenty of batteries.

\* \* \*

The ringing of the telephone woke me at 4:00 a.m. Martha said my father had suffered "a minor heart attack." No heart attack was minor where my father was concerned. He was in ICU at Community Hospital in Indianapolis.

"Your father wants you to come home immediately," Martha said.

Daddy could never think of Beverly Hills as my home.

I called the second assistant. I didn't want to wake Keith that early on a Saturday morning. It had been a demanding week and he had worked hard. The group had planned to meet for breakfast at the Rainbow Cafe before hiking up to Difficult Lake and Snow Mass Creek. There was an excellent pizza parlor out on the highway. Tony's Place had an incredible view from every window for dinner. That evening, the new release of *Bonnie & Clyde* was being shown to the cast and crew. Keith had enough clout to get a print sent to Colorado. Everyone was eager to see the new film. But my plans had suddenly changed.

Clothing and cosmetics were tossed into my small suitcase. Then a driver took me to the Aspen Airport where I boarded the first commuter flight for Denver. By 10:30 a.m. I was on my way to Indianapolis via Chicago. My roundtrip ticket was supposed to bring me back to Aspen on the following Tuesday. They would shoot around me. Keith would be called as soon as I learned of my father's condition. Fabio, this cute Italian makeup artist, took Frisky for me. Frisky loved Fabio nearly as much as he did me.

Worrying about my father, I swallowed a tranquillizer and chain smoked in first class. At O'Hare in Chicago, I tried to call Martha. No answer. I thought of Jeff and wondered if my postcards mailed 10 days earlier had arrived. Calling Jeff didn't feel right to me. Martha was crying on the telephone. I cried on the airplane.

The long weekend was coming up: Labor Day. I thought of flying home to see Paula and sleep in my own bed for a few days. Michele and Christopher were ready to return to school. I had souvenirs for everyone. Before the bleached blonde in the towel, Louis had spoken of a romantic getaway for the two of us over the weekend. Now, he could take Gloria. They deserved each other. With minimum effort, she might be able to make him look young indefinitely. I suspected he was already being photographed through special lenses.

That day, I was relieved I didn't have to face Louis. I seriously doubted he was caught 'in the act' for the first or last time. The little shit! Praise the Lord I had not fallen in love with him or there might have been a double homicide at the Hotel Jerome with both of them in bloody towels. Not a bad plot for a movie!

"How tacky!" Paula said when I called her from Chicago. "Let me know as soon as you know about George. I'm really sorry, Dana. I'll send flowers to the hospital."

"I'd been thinking about coming home for the long weekend, but I might stay longer in Indianapolis, if Daddy wants me there."

"I can't imagine that he won't want you there. Call me as soon as you know."

The flight to Indianapolis was bumpy. I had a martini, but the alcohol did little to help my state of mind. I slept for an hour. No baggage was checked. I hailed a cab to take me directly to the hospital.

Daddy was out of ICU. He looked nearly normal as I entered his room, except for all the monitors with blinking lights and squiggly lines, humming. Martha was holding his hand and whispering. There was tenderness in my father's eyes, something always there for Martha. It warmed my heart to know how much they loved each other. I was never jealous of her. After my parents divorced when I was 16, my father remarried two years later. He was not a man to be alone. Daddy enjoyed being married.

My father's face lit up the moment he saw me.

A nurse entered the room behind me, carrying a huge vase of summer flowers she placed on a stand. I kissed my father and looked into his eyes.

"You don't look so bad," I said, as tears coursed down my cheeks.

Grasping my hand, he smiled and said, "It was a blockage. It didn't kill me." He squeezed my hand. "It looks like you're going to be stuck with your old man for a while yet, sweet patootie."

"These flowers are from Paula Marlow, Dana's good friend in California, and her children, Michele and Christopher. I remember her darling children. I'll bet they've grown a lot since we last saw them," Martha said.

"Michele is 10. Christopher will be six in September. They are growing up too fast to suit me."

"Children do," she said, turning to my father, "Paula wants you to get well as soon as possible, George, and so do I."

"Me, too!" I kissed his forehead and gazed into eyes the same color as mine.

"So how is the movie going?" he inquired. "It must be beautiful in Aspen this time of year."

"It's amazing. The movie is going fine. They're going to have to get along without Victoria for a few days. They can shoot around me."

Suddenly, my father's face looked drained and he narrowed his eyes. "I guess you don't know about Cindy," he said, turning to Martha with a long, sad face.

The two of them exchanged solemn glances before both of them turned to me.

"What is it?" I asked, my solar plexus tightening.

"She passed away yesterday," Daddy said. "I'd just gone to see her on Wednesday afternoon and she wasn't looking so good. She lapsed into a coma that night and passed on Friday morning. It's for the best, Dana. She was in terrible shape toward the end."

I sank into a chair and suddenly felt weak trying to assimilate the bad news. My childhood friend was dead at the age of 32. Good grief!

"The funeral is Tuesday at the Methodist Church," Martha said. "Jeff called and left a message on that answering machine you gave us. It works ... sometimes."

"When you remember to turn it on," Daddy said. "I hope you can stay for the funeral. Jeff and the kids would like to have you here. And I'd like you to stick around for a while. The doc says I can get out of here maybe Monday, if I'm a good boy and all." He chuckled.

"We both want to go to the funeral," Martha said. "Such a shame to lose a child before the parents. Both her parents are devastated. My heart goes out to them, Dana. It really does."

All at once, I felt numb. "It must be terrible for everyone. I'll stay, Daddy. I'll see that you get home and settled, and I'll be here for Cindy's funeral."

Under the circumstances, what else could I do?

# Chapter 37

That Sunday, we prepared barbeque-style chicken and brought it to the hospital for Daddy. We had checked it out with his doctor first. It was baked without the skin. Martha made her famous coleslaw with honey, German potato salad, and flaky biscuits. It was a favorite meal of my father's. We were having a picnic at Community Hospital. Judging from his appetite, my father was staging a rapid recovery.

"No mashed potatoes with rich gravy, George," Martha said. "It's against your doctor's orders."

"This potato salad is delicious. It's a whole lot better than hospital food. Bland, bland and more bland. I'm sick of Jell-O. Any flavor. And tapioca pudding."

"Are chocolate chip cookies all right?" I asked, opening a tin of freshly baked cookies. "With walnuts?"

"That's more like it!" Daddy said, and he took two. "I can't wait to get home to Martha's cooking. The doc says I need to walk more, maybe jog. I've never been much of a jogger. Guess I need to play more tennis. I've been slacking off lately. I need to find someone new to get in a good work-out. Stewart died last year … heart attack. He was 64."

Martha and I exchanged anxious glances.

My father pensively studied his second cookie before he ate it. "Yum," he said, "I'll have another."

"Less fried foods, George," Martha said.

"I need to get my cholesterol down. The bad kind. The doc says my blood pressure is okay, but I sure as hell don't want to have open heart surgery and have my chest cracked open. No thank you!" He glanced at the flowers. "In here, it looks like I've already died and gone to heaven."

We all laughed.

"We don't need to buy any flowers for a while, George," Martha said. "Although the garden looks good for the end of the season. The Harris boy is mowing. I let him use your John Deere."

Daddy looked alarmed. "Does he have his driver's license?"

"Yes, George. Jerry is 17. Calm down."

"Well, I don't want him to wreck my power mower. It was damn expensive."

"He's not going to wreck it, George. Have another cookie," she said, holding out the tin to him and he took two more.

"Am I intruding?" a male voice asked from the doorway.

Jeffrey Waters was wearing a dark blue suit and a blue and red paisley tie. He looked like he'd just been to church. All at once, my stomach was aflutter. I wasn't sure what to say. I just stared at him and he stared back. Then, he walked over to my dad and patted his arm in a gentle display of affection.

"How are you doing, George? Dr. Patterson says you've had a mild heart attack. I hope it wasn't too serious. But maybe not, if you're eating chocolate chip cookies." He grinned.

"It didn't kill me. I guess I was lucky. But the young doc says I need to change my ways. Not so much butter. Gol dang!" He looked at the remains of the cookie in his hand and finished it off. "Not so much ice cream, maybe. Damn! I sure do like ice cream, especially in the summer."

Everyone laughed.

"I like ice cream, too, George," Jeff said. "That ice milk just doesn't cut it, does it?"

Daddy made a face and shook his head. "Not at all. And I'm losing my appetite for Jell-O. It just doesn't satisfy me anymore. If you know what I mean?"

"I do, George." Jeff smiled before his expression turned somber. "Will they be letting you out of this place anytime soon?"

"Tomorrow," Martha said. "Monday afternoon."

"Daddy wants to leave before lunch," I said, holding out the basket of baked chicken to Jeff. "Would you care for a drumstick?"

"Why, thank you," he said, helping himself, as I handed him a paper plate and napkin. "I haven't eaten yet today. I must look hungry. Did you cook this, Martha?"

"I did. No skin," she said, dishing out some coleslaw and potato salad and handing him a fork. "You eat something, Jeffrey. You've lost way too much weight lately to suit me."

"Yes, ma'am," he said, eating coleslaw and potato salad, chewing and swallowing too fast. "It tastes really good, Martha. Thank you, kindly."

His expression was serious, as though he thought we might need to be told about Cindy. We were watching him eat as he started to act self conscious, and then, he suddenly turned to me.

"I thought you were making a movie in Colorado. That's what you said when you were here last month."

"I was until early yesterday when Martha called about Daddy and his heart attack. Air travel is a blessing in the event of an emergency."

Jeffrey took another bite of potato salad and chicken, thoughtfully chewing as he watched me, perhaps unaware of what he was doing. He pensively turned to Martha. "This is really good, Martha," he said before turning back to me again.

"Will you be leaving right away?" he solemnly asked.

"I'll be here all week. I called my director to let him know I'll be staying in Indianapolis longer than planned because of the loss of a dear friend."

Suddenly, everyone was silent.

All eyes were on Jeff.

He sighed and slumped, as though he had been carrying the weight of the world. Then he looked at me again like he wasn't really seeing me.

"I'll be here for Cindy's funeral," I said. "I'm really sorry for your loss, Jeff."

Slowly, he nodded, staring off into space.

Tears filled my eyes, as a deep sadness filled his face. There was a trembling inside me that made sit down for fear that I might faint with the plate in my hands. I was overwhelmed by the events of the past three days.

Jeffrey's face and body language changed. He stood taller and handed his empty plate to Martha. His emotions appeared to have gone from deep pain to relief in just minutes.

"Thank you, Dana," Jeff said. "It seems to me that we all need you here right now. My children will be pleased to know that you'll be with them on what has to be the saddest day of their young lives. I wasn't sure whether you were home until I came here today. I figured you might be. I'm really grateful that you are here."

His eyes locked onto mine with a noticeable depth of emotion. It was something I'd never before experienced with Jeffrey Waters. But then, we never had to deal with real tragedy before that time.

"I'm glad I'm here, too," I said, as the words caught in my throat. "I just learned about Cindy yesterday."

"I guess there wasn't much time with your father's emergency. I just learned about your condition at church today, George. I thought the least I could do was drop in and check on you." Tears spilled from his eyes. "You were awfully good to Cindy, George, visiting her, bringing her flowers from your garden, reading her the news." He reached into his pocket for a handkerchief and blew his nose. "My entire family is sincerely grateful to you. Your kindness is appreciated far more than you will ever know."

"It was my pleasure," Daddy said, fighting back his tears. "Cindy was a lovely girl and a good friend to Dana. I'm sorry there wasn't more I could do. I'm sorry Cindy got cancer and died so young."

"We're all sorry about that," he said. "Thanks for lunch," Jeff said to Martha. "I guess I'll be seeing you all on Tuesday."

Martha and Daddy nodded.

"Yes," I softly said.

He looked at each of us in turn, perhaps to acknowledge our solemn promise to attend his wife's funeral. Then he turned and was out the door.

I took a very deep breath and found enough strength to stand. I was extremely grateful that the moment had passed.

# Chapter 38

Bringing Daddy home from the hospital was the easier part of the deal. He was happy to be back in his own home. His own bed. And have his own bathroom again. He was glad to be rid of the orderlies and nurses that disturbed his rest. That made him take pills and got on his nerves in general. The master bedroom was upstairs, however, and the doctor wanted him to take it easy with the stairs for a while. That meant Martha and I got our fair share of exercise running up and down the stairs to do the bidding of King George. He really seemed to enjoy that part.

Then, the strangest thing happened.

Scott Wellington called me from California. He said he'd tried to reach me in Aspen, only to discover that I was Indiana for a crisis with my father. George and Martha had visited me in California the first year that Scott and I were an item. Scott spent time with my parents and took us to Disneyland at his expense. He also covered the cost of dinner at several expensive restaurants. One dinner at the Chart House also included Paula and her two kids. Scott's generosity was a pleasant surprise. But then, Daddy was a Leo. Most Leos are generous. The two men had argued over checks with the younger lion claiming leadership of the pride.

"So how is your father?" Scott inquired in a tone of concern. "Is he all right?"

"He had a mild heart attack. He's home now recovering and acting like King of the Manor with his 'bring me this, bring me that' routine. But he is my father."

"I'm really sorry, Dana. George is not that old, is he?"

"He turned 62 this month. I'm not sure how old you have to be to have a heart attack. Charlie Furman at Stromberg died from one last year at 43."

"I remember." There was a significant pause. "As I recall, your father's birthday is the day after mine. You've never forgotten my birthday before," he sounded like a hurt child. "You never even wished me a happy birthday, Dana."

"Happy birthday," I said. "How does it feel to be 40?"

"Old. On my birthday I was in Albuquerque scouting locations. We celebrated at a Mexican restaurant with too many margaritas. I was surprised you didn't even leave a message on my answering service or send me a card."

"I forgot," I said in a my further effort to punish him. Ignoring Scott really pissed him off. He would rather be hated than ignored. My decision was not to call him.

"I find that very hard to believe when my birthday is the day before your father's?" he said in his typical dramatic tone.

"For his birthday, I sent Daddy and Martha to the country club in a limo for dinner and bought him that new tennis racket. He needs to use it, however. Carefully, at first. A heart attack can be very debilitating."

"I would imagine. Where were you on August 7th?" he sounded testy.

"I think I was at Paula's in the Colony. It was right before she took her kids to Texas. Paula has a new man in her life, Beau Kandell. We filmed on his ranch near Fort Worth. Remember? In my opinion, he's perfect for her, and so far so good."

"So you played cupid!"

"I would very much like to see my dearest friend with a man who makes her happy."

"So how are you and your Frenchman doing, the famous Louis Lamprais?"

"We're not."

There was a brief pause. "What happened?"

"I don't care to discuss it."

"So you're no longer seeing him, romantically?"

"No. But we are working together. That means we're still friends."

"Then that must mean you'll see me again?"

I waited for a moment before I said, "I'll think about it," and reached for my cigarettes without lighting one the moment I remembered Daddy. "I won't be back in town anytime soon. A friend of mine here just died. I'm staying on for her funeral. Plus, Daddy wants the pleasure of my company for a while yet."

"I understand. I'm sorry about your friend. How old was she?"

"My age. Her ovarian cancer spread everywhere."

"How awful! At 16, I lost a friend in a nasty automobile accident," he said. "When do you think you will be in town? I finish in New Mexico in two more weeks. The rest is interiors to be shot in town."

"I have at least another month in Colorado. We're doing the autumn foliage. The aspens are starting to turn. It's quite beautiful."

"May I call you in Aspen?" He waited. "Where are you staying?"

"The Hotel Jerome. We have a fun group on this film. I've also been doing some hiking."

"If it's all right, I'll call you," he sounded unsure of himself, so unlike him.

Suddenly, everything in my life was taking a turn that made me feel uncertain about just about everything, as I replied, "It's all right if you call me, Scott. Thanks for asking about Daddy. I just hope I don't gain any weight with Martha's cooking. Those corsets are murder. I'm awfully glad us ladies don't have to wear them anymore."

"I'll bet you are. You have a great body, with or without a corset."

Now, he was sounding like Scott again, with the remark ignored as I said, "I need to go, Scott. I have to say good-bye for now."

As soon as our conversation ended, the wheels and cogs in my mind began to spin. As strange as it seemed, the sound of Scott's voice had lost its hold on me. No more butterflies. No more creaming in my jeans. That amazed me.

Eric was finished, the handsome biochemist with the bright blue eyes. Louis, the charming, over-sexed, two-timing French actor of international fame was finis, although I would be happy to be his leading lady in any number of motion pictures, present or future. My suspicion: *View From the Mountain* would be our one and only major motion picture extravaganza.

After preparing a leafy green salad in the kitchen, I took multiple laps in the pool. Daddy was well on the road to recovery. The doctor said he might avoid further trouble by strictly following orders, since except for this one episode, he had the body of a much younger man. That pleased me. My tears of gratitude mixed with the water in the pool. My father was likely to be around for many more years. That was good news.

Floating on my back, I sent out white light to Cindy on the Other Side. Now she was finally free of her pain and suffering, and hopefully, she had her wits about her again. My heart went out to Angela and Terry for losing their mother. Everyone seemed much too young to experience such a trag-edy. It seemed unfair. My hope was that my father's genes for good health were passed on to me. That was something a certain biologist had explained to me in greater detail than I ever planned to hear. Nonetheless, I planned to have no minor heart attack at age 62. And yet, neither did I want to live forever. That was a dreadful thought.

On the premise of having inherited more than my father' green eyes, I seemed guaranteed another 30 years of worry-free health. If only I could find true happiness with a man who was faithful and loved and adored me—a man with whom I could raise a family.

All at once, on that afternoon, those things seemed incredibly impor-tant to me, perhaps for the very first time in my life.

# Chapter 39

The funeral was a simple affair, not much over an hour and half in time. Perhaps it was a typical Midwestern funeral. I had no idea. I was asked to say a few words in memory of my long time friend. Perhaps I was the token hometown celebrity of questionable stature, in my opinion.

Almost everyone was dressed in dark colors: Navy blue, dark brown, mostly black, except for Angela. She wore her emerald green velvet Christmas dress: Her mother's favorite. Most of the extended family was in town, including Cindy's old friends from elementary and high school. Many I hadn't seen in what seemed like forever. It was fun seeing some of them, even though it could have been under more pleasant circumstances. There were a few I recognized. Everyone seemed to know who I was. Of those I remembered, some were shy or acted distant. I tried my best to let them know I was just another old friend wishing Cindy well on her journey to the heavens.

I wept during the service. At least we thought to bring along tissue. There was a whole lot of sniffling in that church. We joined the procession to the cemetery for the interment. My family had sent a large wreath of yellow and white roses positioned near the casket, along with all the other wreaths and bouquets. Many were placed next to her open grave. The experience was surreal. It wasn't a movie. It was honest-to-goodness life.

We dropped by the house afterwards. Neighbors and friends had brought casseroles. There was ham and chicken, roast beef, salads, gobs of desserts, and everything to drink. Food seemed to help people in such situations. Perhaps it helped to fill up the empty space created by the loss.

Jeff and Cindy's three-bedroom, two-story, wooden framed house was average in size and decorated with simplicity. Cindy liked early American, along with some antiques. Apparently, Cindy loved estate auctions. The family pictures covered several generations. The color scheme was blue and gray, off-white with a touch of red, and reminded me of my downstairs, which was hardly done simply.

Out of the corner of my eye, I was keeping track of Jeff, and usually caught him watching me. He was being Mr. Cool, though. I doubted that anyone else there was aware of his eyes following me around. But every time I looked for him, he was looking at me. It was synchronistic and utterly strange.

All the friends and cousins of the children were outside playing in the huge backyard with its magnificent maple tree. There were swings and a play house. Some adults took their food out to the tables on the patio. It was a beautiful, late August day. Two more days and it would be September.

The children would return to school soon. Studying might help Terry and Angela think of something other than the loss of their mother. But it might not be that easy. It would be the first year she was not around to help out with their homework. The first year of loss was always the hardest for me, even when it involved my mother running off with another man, perhaps not nearly as difficult or permanent. Death had to be hard on children, especially the loss of a parent. Gratefully, their grandparents were still around to give Terry and Angela love and support.

Cindy's folks were in their 60s, the same as mine. Her two brothers were younger and very much alive. Robert was married with two children, a daughter aged five and son three. He was a teenager the last I saw him. By then, he was 30, and his pretty girl-next-door wife was 26. They had two adorable kids. Cindy's brother Tad was 27 and single. But his girlfriend attended the funeral. Family gossip had him marrying her soon. Carolyn was in nursing school; Tad serving his medical residency in pediatrics. The Hanson's now had a doctor in the family to help care for the next generation. I liked that idea.

Standing alone in the dining room, I was silently observing the group in the house when Jeffrey walked up to me. Across the room, Kathy Webber from high school was talking to his mother. Kathy had really packed on some pounds, like 30. I had never seen her that heavy.

"Kathy is married, isn't she? The girl talking to your mother?" I asked Jeff.

"Recently divorced. I was her attorney." His smile was sheepish. "She's been hovering lately, calling me with these ridiculous questions." He was amused.

"Still after you, huh?"

His smile softened and he steadily looked into my eyes. Then he shrugged and gave me one of his 'what can I do' looks. The way he was looking at me was giving me butterflies and making me feel all gooey inside.

"How about pizza on Thursday? You can't just sit in the house yakking with George and Martha, day and night. You'll get lockjaw." The expression on his face increased the number of butterflies in my stomach.

"With the kids?" I responded, trying to break the spell and nervously glancing around to see who might be watching us, or listening. Kathy Webber seemed to scrutinize our every move. She'd always gotten on my nerves with the way she followed Jeff around and tried to get his attention in high school. Notwithstanding, I felt a touch uncomfortable with the way he was following my every move on that day. Cindy had only been buried for a few hours.

Jeff smiled and said. "Angie and Terry love pizza," in a chastising tone. "They're the ones who asked me to please invite you for pizza again. They like having dinner with a movie star," he added, and then, he winked and grinned. "Is it a date?"

"It's a date."

Daddy and Martha were observing our exchange with approval all over their faces. At that moment, I wondered if my father had arranged his heart attack just to get me back to Indianapolis.

# Chapter 40

The three members of the Waters' family picked me up at six o'clock sharp that Thursday. Terry and Angela were in the backseat as Jeffrey opened my car door. We were all dressed casually. I had on jeans and my pink T-shirt with sandals, my hair pulled up in a ponytail to keep it off my neck in the suffocating heat. Jeff wore a blue knit shirt that matched his eyes. He always looked good in blue and he did on that evening, as usual.

On the way to the restaurant, I complained about trying to keep my father off his feet and resting, something proving nearly impossible. Daddy kept calling editors about books ready to be released. He was driving us crazy, including the editors who were running back and forth, up and down the stairs, with the telephone constantly ringing. I needed a break from the house on Pimmit Drive to escape from my rapidly recovering father.

"There's just no way to keep him down," I said. "The man had a heart attack and he will not rest. It's maddening."

"I'll pay George a visit next week to see if there's anything I can do or get for him," Jeff said. "He was a true gem with Cindy. He saw her every week, sometimes twice."

"I know. He read her the newspaper to keep her up on the news." I cast a doubtful sideways glance at Jeff. "That's Daddy, keeping everyone up on the news. He was reading aloud to himself."

"Mother liked for him to come and visit," Terry said.

"Not that many people came to see her," Angela said in a sad tone. "Maybe they were afraid of catching her cancer."

"No one catches cancer," Jeffrey said in an irritated tone. "It's just that some people have a hard time dealing with other people's illness. It brings their own mortality into too close a scrutiny."

"But Dana came to see her," Angela said, "Twice. Right, Dana?"

"Yes. Twice, when I was here before."

"And Dana came all the way from California," she said. "She wasn't afraid of catching cancer or of her ... mortality?"

We all got out of the car at once, with disapproval on Jeff's face as I opened my own door. He made a point to open the door to the restaurant. We all sat in a large booth and ordered salads and two large pizzas with different toppings. Jeff wanted enough to take home.

"Make sure some of the pizza doesn't have mushrooms, please," I said to the waiter. "At least half of the double cheese, okay?"

"You remembered," Angie shyly said. "Thanks," and she blushed, smiling at her father.

Angie made a point to sit next to me, with Terry on my other side, farthest from his father. Jeffrey was forced to yield to a younger generation, which I thought may have annoyed him a tad.

"It wasn't long after you were here that our mother didn't know us most of the time," Terry said. "Sometimes she remembered, but not often. It was really hard to deal with her not knowing that I was her son." Tears filled his eyes.

"I'll bet it was. It must have been very hard for everyone. Your mother was very young to have this terrible disease claim her life."

"She was your age," Terry said, his teary blue eyes looking much like his father's.

"Yes, my age."

The waiter served our salads. Before long, pizza was on two pedestals with everyone reaching and dividing up the pies. No mushrooms for Angie. The pizza was delicious, thin crust with a tasty sauce, pepperoni, sausage, some mushrooms, and lots of cheese. I briefly thought of the corset I would soon be wearing. Indianapolis was not a mile up where added calories were easy to burn off. It made me wonder why the Midwest was so flat.

The children asked questions about the film, about the actors, and about Colorado. How many wild animals had I seen up close? Did I like to hike? Was I afraid of grizzly bears or mountain lions? Had I seen a buffalo? In what seemed like minutes, they were begging their father to take them to Aspen to see the Owl's Nest so they could watch the birds of prey hunt mice and snakes. They enjoyed their postcards, which were proudly displayed in their rooms. They wanted my address in Beverly Hills, so they could send me a postcard or a letter.

"Could I please have an autographed picture of you?" Terry begged.

"Me too," Angela said. "Something glamorous to make my friends jealous signed Love Dana ... or at least, affectionately?" There was pleading in her hazel eyes. The tone of her voice and her actions reminded me so much of Michele.

"Angie!" Jeffrey said in some heat, casting her a fatherly scowl.

"I'll be happy to sign pictures for each of you when I get home, but that won't be for a while. I'm flying back to Colorado. I won't be in California for at least another month."

"I brought my camera tonight," Terry said.

Soon, the waiter was snapping a picture of the group, then one of me with Angie, me with Terry, but none of me and Jeff. I wondered if I still had the volumes of pictures from all sorts of events, including the Indiana State Fair from half a lifetime ago. Those old boxes in the attic were going to be searched when I got home.

"This way, I'll have a picture of all of us together so the kids at school will believe I really know you," Terry said. "Some of the scouts think I'm making it all up."

"Well, I hope you send me some pictures," I said to Jeff. "Will you see that I receive copies, please?"

"Sure," Jeff said, pouring more Chianti into our wine glasses.

"Dad says he might bring us to California in the spring to go to Disneyland," Terry said, with the twinkle in Jeff's eyes immediately observed, "And then we could visit you in Beverly Hills, perhaps?" he tentatively added, with a coy look on his handsome, young face. His eyes went from me to his father to make sure he had said the right thing.

"You did invite us. You remember that, don't you?" Terry added.

"Terry!" Jeff exclaimed.

"Yes, I remember," I said, "And I have enough room for all of you to stay with me as long as you like." I had a bite of pizza and chewed, looking directly ahead to avoid Jeff's gaze.

"For as long as we like?" Jeff said, studying me with a look on his face well remembered from long ago, an expression that appeared more than just friendly.

"You will go to Disneyland with us, won't you?" Angela inquired.

"Of course. If I don't have to work on those days."

The children looked at each other and scowled. Then they looked at their father and scowled again.

"Perhaps you can arrange your schedule the way Dad does," Terry said. "And get the studio to work around you like you did this week because of your father's heart attack."

"Miracles do happen," I said, forced to laugh.

And we all finished our dinner.

Jeff walked me to the door the way he did back in the old days. But this time, his children were waiting in the car. Angela got out of the backseat to sit in front and waved at me. Prying eyes were glued to us.

"There's a picnic on Monday," Jeff said, glancing at the swing on the porch where we used to neck as teenagers, sometimes more than neck. Most serious action had taken place in the backseat of his car or the apartment of a college friend. That was real comfort with a bathroom near and a bed for making love. We always promised to change the sheets, but rarely did. Ah, the folly of youth.

"I'm sorry. I'm flying back to Aspen on Sunday to avoid the holiday crunch. I couldn't get on the commuter on Monday. At least that way, I'll have a day of rest before going back to work."

Again, he glanced at the swing before turning to me. "How about the Indiana State Fair on Saturday afternoon? I promised the kids. It's the closing weekend." His smile faded as he watched me with a touch of longing on his face, the same longing I was feeling deep inside.

"The Indiana State Fair?" The scene of our first date and other dates every year we were a couple.

"Maybe we can ride the Ferris wheel," he said, smiling his wonderful smile that made chills run up and down my spine.

"Maybe," I said, suddenly feeling half my age.

And it was a date.

# Chapter 41

After the ride in the Tilt-a-Whirl, I was ready to throw up. Sheer stupidity on my part to let Terry talk me into that one. No roller coaster. Angela and I sat on a bench watching the boys' race through the air with the rest of the lunatics. Everyone screaming at the top of their lungs, arms up in the air. Not even Jeff could talk me into that one, not at 16 or 32. Thank you very much! They sulked off to the cars of fright without the girls.

"That was fun!" Terry bragged, his face ashen.

"Yeah," Jeff quickly added, after only the slightest hesitation.

We walked over to see the livestock and browsed through booths and various demonstrations. We went through the fun house and the house of mirrors. We threw baseballs and darts. We won stuffed animals: A blue teddy bear. A purple elephant. There were bumper cars. The carousel. And finally the Ferris wheel, except, I sat with Terry and Jeff sat with Angela, not the way I remembered things back in high school.

Perhaps we were both disappointed. As a parent, Jeff had made the right choice, hadn't he? Nothing ever happens exactly the same way twice. Sometimes, after ordering the same food in the same restaurant, it tastes different. That's a fact of life.

We ate hotdogs. Pizza. Popcorn with butter. Cotton candy. For a few hours, I forgot about corsets in Colorado. We walked all over the fairgrounds, although I'd consumed at least a year's worth of junk food in one day. I vowed to ignore the bathroom scales. The one at the house was probably too old to be trusted, anyway.

On the way home, I learned that the children were spending the night with his parent's. They were going to church with their grandparents the next morning. Jeff would meet them at church and Sunday dinner. It was something planned for every other Sunday. Next week, it was the Hanson's turn with the children.

I stayed in the car while Jeff walked his two into the house. It was a big, old, friendly house where years of good times were shared with his family on holidays. Suddenly, I felt awkward about even being there. I wondered what his parents thought, probably that his old girlfriend was ready to leap back into his arms after dumping him his first year of college. Leaping back into Jeff's arms was what Daddy and Martha had encouraged me to do since the day of Cindy's funeral.

"He's such a fine man," Daddy had said, "A stable man with a promising future. He'll likely be elected to the House of Representatives and might end up as a Senator."

"Jeffrey Waters is a catch," Martha insisted.

"That wouldn't surprise me about Jeff and politics," I told them.

"You can't really do better than Jeffrey Waters, considering all those other fellows you've been dating," Martha said. "Getting their names in gossip columns and marrying one woman after another. Spreading their seed to kingdom come. Whatever is the matter with those men?"

"I hope you don't end up like your mother," Daddy groaned.

Martha narrowed her eyes and hissed, "George!" But she knew better than to push my father too far, especially after reminding her how my mother left her wedding rings on the kitchen counter with a note saying it was mine when I grew up.

Poor Daddy. Poor me.

"I hope I don't end up like her, either," I said, cringing at the thought.

Terry and Angela had both given me kisses and hugs after getting out of the car. Terry also reminded me of the 8 x 10 glossies to be signed and sent to each of them. Angie made me promise about Disneyland again, even though it was far away from Beverly Hills. They were pleased about my swimming pool and were looking forward to meeting Paula, Michele and Christopher, and to spending time at the beach.

Time with the children would be special for me. Being with their father had made me feel like a schoolgirl again, perhaps much the same as on my first date with the student body president so many years ago. I was the envy of every girl in high school, in my mind.

# Chapter 42

On the way back to my parent's house, we were both quiet for the whole two miles. I waited for Jeff to open my car door and draped my arm through his as he walked me to the porch. Once we were there, he nodded toward the swing where we had sat together so many times long ago. Considering all the sex we had in those two years, it was a miracle that I wasn't Terry's mother.

"You feel like talking?" he said in a soft tone.

Glancing at the swing, I hesitated briefly, remembering the years of little talk and plenty of action. Momentarily, I was afraid to even look at him. With mixed emotions, I walked over to the swing and sat, my heart starting to pound. Still fearful of looking at him, I waited for him to sit.

All was quiet inside the big house on Pimmit Drive. One lamp was on in the living room, the same as back in the old days when the teenage daughter was out with the promising Waters' boy. Daddy and Martha had retired or might have been watching TV in their bedroom.

Silently, Jeff sat. Then, he started to rock the swing back and forth, pushing off with his feet. My instant reaction was similar to the tilt-a-whirl. My heart raced faster as I toyed with the charms on my gold necklace.

"I've never found another Ferris wheel like that one," he said. "You have some collection. Do people still give you charms on special occasions?"

"Not for years now," I said, turning the Ferris wheel around. "It still turns around and around."

He looked at me and nodded before he turned to look across the street.

The neighbors on the other side were watering their lawn at that late hour. The lightning bugs were gathering in large numbers, flashing and flitting around the edge of the yard near the moistened plants, darting in and out of the intermittent spray. Fireflies always came out in the evening after it rained. I hadn't seen any for a while. They didn't seem to exist in California or even Colorado.

"Fairy lights," Jeffrey said. "Isn't that what you always called them?"

He was watching me watch the lightning bugs fluttering about, blinking off and on, as though they were signaling each other. It seemed to me that they were dancing with all their lights blinking together in the late evening watery mist.

"Fairy lights," I finally said. "What else could they be?"

"I used to catch them and put them in a glass jar to keep in my room. Sometimes I pinched off their tails as a ring for my sister. She couldn't stand to do that," he said, turning to me with his wonderful eyes and a wistful expression on his handsome face.

"You're not supposed to kill fairies. Mother Nature doesn't like it."

"You said that way back," he said, chuckling. "Maybe Mother Nature punished me. By 17, I'd stopped killing them for my sister. I remember doing it once for you, and you nearly tore my head off screaming about fairies and Mother Nature. That cured me good."

"I did some good then. Who knows how many fairies I may have saved?"

"You saved them all thenceforth from the cruelty of one Jeffrey Waters."

I turned to him and smiled. I guess I shouldn't have been surprised when he took my right hand into both of his. He was watching me with fondness in eyes a different shade of blue than Scott's or Eric's, not nearly as startling, but just as appealing.

I swallowed with difficulty and glanced away, suddenly feeling inexperienced with boys. Maybe it was because I was sitting on my folks' porch at the house I grew up in, or because I was on the very same swing with Jeff on a dark, moonless night. Perhaps briefly, I was transported back to another decade in time. The circumstances made me catch my breath, because the way Jeff was looking at me made me come unglued. I didn't know how to act or what to say to him.

Something serious was happening. Something more serious than anything I'd experienced up until then. My hand felt wonderful in his. I don't know how to explain how happy he made me feel. How happy it felt just to be there with him on that early September evening with only lightning bugs and sprinklers for our entertainment.

"My father always said I should have married you," he said in a soft voice. "I always thought he was in love with you too."

Suddenly overcome with emotion, I managed, "Did you tell him that you tried to marry me ... that you asked me once?"

"Both my parents waited up for me after your prom to see if you had accepted my proposal." Now, he turned to me, and at that moment, I could swear my heart skipped a beat.

"My parents were crazy about you, Dana. The ring was my grandmother's resized diamond engagement ring and happens to be one of our family treasures. Your hands are smaller than hers, so I had it resized for you."

"I see." It was difficult for me to even breathe. "It was a beautiful ring set in platinum, wasn't it? Is that the ring you gave to Cindy?"

He shook his head and glanced away. "Cindy didn't want an antique engagement ring. My mother still wears it, sometimes. Her hands are about the same size as yours."

"That's because we're little people," was my lame attempt at levity.

"Mom is five-foot-three."

"She's got me by a half inch. I'm only five-two and a half."

"I've always questioned that additional half inch. Do you think you've grown since you were 18? You never even came up to my chin in your bare feet."

I simply shook my head.

He was watching me closely, with my hand still in his, with seemingly no plan on his part to let go. I had no plan to take my hand away from him, either.

"Are you really serious about us coming to stay with you in the spring?" Jeff was studying me and holding my eyes with his. "That you want all of us to stay with you in your home?"

"Absolutely! And your children aren't likely to let you to forget about it, either, Mr. Waters."

He laughed. "That's for damn sure!" He glanced away. "My two really seem to like you. They've latched onto you good and tight. I hope it doesn't put your off any."

"It doesn't. And actually, we could all get together long before next spring."

"We could?" He turned to me with surprise on his face.

Of course, Jeffrey had no knowledge of my conversation with Paula the day before on the telephone, or about the sneaky conspiracy going on between us California girls.

"Will you be coming home for Christmas?"

"Maybe," I said, pausing before I added, "Have you ever been to Texas?"

"No," he said, and again he looked at me in surprise. "Texas?"

"How about you bring your kids to the ranch of a friend of mine near Fort Worth, Texas for Thanksgiving? Say for four days? His name is Beau Kandell. You can fly into Dallas-Fort Worth and his place is not that far from the airport. I can help you out with the airfares, since I'm the one inviting all of you."

"Now, wait just a minute!" He appeared stunned. "You mean to tell me that you're inviting me and my children to a Texas ranch for the Thanksgiving holiday?" He let go of my hand and straightened up, suddenly stopping the swing with a lurch. "Me and my children?" He frowned and pursed his lips. "Are you sure that it's all right for you to even invite us? Is this something you've already discussed with this rancher friend of yours?"

"It's something I've already discussed with my friend, Paula, who is dating the rancher. She will be there for Thanksgiving with her two children, Michele and Christopher. It would be lots of fun. Beau's ranch is fantastic. He owns oil wells. Plus, he has horses and cows and chickens. I was in a Western film shot on his property. I introduced Beau to Paula. The film won't be out until next year. It was my first Western movie."

"I see," Jeff said, obviously taken aback by my unexpected invitation.

"Paula is my best friend, Jeff, the artist who lies in Malibu. Her kids are great. They've already been to the ranch and they love it. Beau gave each of them a pony, and Paula has her own horse now. I guess he has about 20 horses. Terry may not mind being the oldest, although Michele might object if he tries to boss her around. She has a mind of her own, not unlike Angela, I might add."

"Sort of like someone else we know?" he said, meaning me, of course.

"Beau has a huge herd of cattle," I went on, nodding, surprised to find him nodding with me. "He has milk cows and goats. He makes his own cheese and butter. He has chickens and a pet deer. There's a big swimming pool besides the lake. He has boats and his own small airplane. The house has tons of bedrooms, so that is not a problem. It is a really, really huge house."

"Is that right?"

"Beau is a genuine Texas cowboy. Tell me your kids wouldn't like to go to a Texas ranch."

All of a sudden, he seemed to be warming to the idea. After all, I had promised Cindy to take care of him and the children, even though he didn't know about that yet. But he seemed to be thinking things over pretty good.

"Please say that you'll at least think about it! You'll have your own suite with your kids, two bedrooms joined with a big bathroom with a whirlpool tub for bubbles. Paula said the suite has a nice view of the lake. Imagine, deep in the heart of Texas with a gourmet chef and all these men to teach your kids how to ride a horse. It'll be wonderful, Jeff."

"Well, I'm not exactly sure how the grandparents might feel about the kids being away on their first Thanksgiving without their mother."

"Talk to them. It will be perfect! There will be new people with them out of their old environment, but they will still have you with them, their dad. They will make new friends, and so will you. They've never been to Texas before, have they?"

"Neither have I."

"It will be fun. Honest."

"And you don't happen to  have some other man, without children, you'd like to invite?" He narrowed his beautiful eyes and studied me. "No marriage proposals lately?"

"As a matter of fact, I turned down two marriage proposals in the past two months!"

"Still a hard sell, huh?"

"Another man wants me to have his child," I threw that in for good measure.

"Without marrying you?" Jeff responded with his Midwestern morality surfacing, which pleased me no end. A man with morals suddenly held far more appeal to me than all the rest. Was that ever a revelation!

"He's not good at marriage. He's a famous actor. But he has produced some beautiful children all over the world."

"And he's someone you're dating?" He was taken aback.

"Not lately."

"Well, I guess you still have men falling at your feet?" Was it bitterness or jealousy in his tone, or a little of both?

"It's the acting thing, Jeff. Men fall in love with who I am on the screen rather than who I really am."

"Well, you are even more beautiful than you were, and that's saying something. You seem to be aging rather nicely." He had a wicked look on his face with that remark.

"I don't know whether to hit you or say thank you."

He laughed and started rocking the swing back and forth again.

"You never told me I was beautiful when we were young."

"You didn't need to be told. You won beauty contests and had my undying love. You knew that." He took my hand again. "Dana Scofield, you broke my heart."

"I suppose I was a selfish, self-centered twit," I said, smiling at his facial response. "I needed to do my thing. I had to go to Hollywood and be an actress. It was my big dream. Surely you knew that much!"

"To be a movie star." The expression on his handsome face softened as he held my hand like he was a schoolboy. "It seems to me that you've already fulfilled many of your dreams."

I sighed. "I'm not through with my acting career, if that's what you mean. You need to know that I love acting. I crave fame and make a great deal of money doing what I like to do and seem to do rather well."

"You're a fine actress. I never miss one of your films."

"Thank you."

I loved the way he started to play with my fingers. The sense of intimacy between us was always seductive and ran deep. It amazed me that I could still feel the same about him after so many years.

"Maybe I should marry you for your money. Then, you could support me in politics. Flash that beautiful smile and win me some votes. My mother says the ring is still mine."

Those words took my breath away. But I merely watched him as he raised my hand to his lips and kissed each finger, and then, the palm and the back. And he wasn't even French. He watched me with an amused glint in his beautiful eyes, perhaps wondering just how far to push me. He had already pushed me to the place where I was well aware that there was still a whole lot of unfinished business between these two Hoosiers. Maybe Cindy was right. Maybe he never stopped loving me.

"I don't think I've ever stopped loving you," he said out loud.

Was the man reading my mind? My heart started to race. I felt like it was beating in my throat. Could I say it? Could I actually tell Jeffrey Waters the whole truth and nothing but the truth, so help me God?

"I've never stopped loving you, either. I'm amazed I'm still in love with you after all these years."

It was one of those moments you can never forget, a moment in which your life miraculously and suddenly changes forever. We stared at each other for the longest moment, looking deeply into each other's eyes, with only fairy lights and the faint swooshing of a sprinkler still watering the lawn across the street.

"You are coming to Texas?" I said in a whisper, leaning back to look into his eyes.

"I guess I might as well. I've only met the cowboys at the state fair, and I don't imagine any of them have any oil wells, or they would hardly spend their lives getting bucked on those crazy bulls."

"Beau used to ride Brahman bulls."

Jeff looked surprised. "Is that right?"

"His back has been bothering him lately, so he's given it up. Beau is 36."

"Is that a fact?" He laughed. "I guess I have to meet this man. Maybe he could help me finance my campaign. But probably not, since he lives in Texas."

"Are you planning to run for office?"

"Congress. Maybe next year. I'm planning the strategy and have some good people on my team who think I might be able to win."

"You always were a winner, Jeffrey."

That night in my bed, my mind was filled with thoughts of Jeffrey Waters, especially of the way he held me in his arms for the longest time. He was primed for action, but not pushing his luck. I knew he needed time. But we both really needed the holding.

The kiss was long and wet and deep. Delicious. Things had heated up the way they always did all those years ago. Yet, this time, Jeffrey backed off in something of a bother, breathing hard. The same as me, if the truth be told.

"I don't want to start anything I can't finish. I need time, Dana. But you'd better watch it down in Texas. You may not be able to get away from me this time."

"I may not want to."

Our laughter was nervous, but the moment was precious beyond belief.

Each of us understood exactly what was meant late on that early September night.

I still hadn't told Jeff about my promise to Cindy. And yet, I had to wonder if she might not be helping us to get back together again from where she was over on the Other Side.

That fact seemed more than likely to me during that marvelous, magical and magnificent Summer of Love.

### THE END

# About the Author

Patricia McLaine is the author of *The Wheel of Destiny – The Tarot Reveals Your Master Plan, The Recycling of Rosalie* (novel) and *Cosmic Conspiracy – Psychic to the Rich and Famous* (memoir), and *Bittersweet Summer – Paula's Story*, the companion novel to this book. She is an international psychic with worldwide clientele and has been featured in newspaper and magazine articles in the U.S. and U.K. as well as appearing on numerous radio and television shows in the U.S., U.K. and Hong Kong, China. Her Blog Talk Radio Show is Exploring the Paranormal with Pattie. Her website: www. patriciamclaine.com .

Patricia resides in Alexandria, Virginia.

Also connect with the author online at:
http://www.facebook.com/pattiemclaine

http://twitter.com/#!/psychicpattie

http://www.linkedin.com/pub/pattie-mclaine/10/345/898

http://www.pattie-mclaineblog.blogspot.com/

http://www.pattie-tarotblog.blogspot.com/

http://www.blogtalkradio.com/pattiemclaine

www.ingramcontent.com/pod-product-compliance
Lightning Source LLC
Chambersburg PA
CBHW062135170626
46813CB00002B/706